C0 2 71 65468 E9

disunited states

By the same author:

Coup, Book Guild Publishing, 2011

disunited states

Hedley Harrison

Book Guild Publishing
Sussex, England

Durham County Council Libraries, Learning and Culture	
C0 2 71 65468 E9	
Askews & Holts	
AF	

First published in Great Britain in 2013 by
The Book Guild Ltd
Pavilion View
19 New Road
Brighton, BN1 1UF

Copyright © Hedley Harrison 2013

The right of Hedley Harrison to be identified as the author of this work has been asserted by him in accordance with the Copyright, Designs and Patents Act 1988.

All rights reserved. No part of this publication may be reproduced, transmitted, or stored in a retrieval system, in any form or by any means, without permission in writing from the publisher, nor be otherwise circulated in any form of binding or cover other than that in which it is published and without a similar condition being imposed on the subsequent purchaser.

All characters and organisations in this publication are fictitious and any resemblance to real people, alive or dead, and to real organisations is purely coincidental.

Typesetting in Baskerville by
Keyboard Services, Luton, Bedfordshire

Printed in Great Britain by
CPI Antony Rowe

A catalogue record for this book is available from
The British Library

ISBN 978 1 84624 838 2

'A written constitution is only as good as the people who administer it'

1

1990

Nobody told Yuri Kirovsky that he'd been fired. The money just stopped coming in 1990 and one Colonel General of the former Soviet Union was adrift in Western Europe with no obvious means of support. But then KGB officers were supposed to be resourceful and self-reliant, and Kirovsky was certainly that. And when by 1994 his termination was finally formally acknowledged he was well into a new life.

'I wouldn't underestimate old Yuri.'

The old Russian hands from the European intelligence community had steadily been paid off and had largely retreated into various forms of comfortable retirement and anonymity, making way towards the end of the millennium for the fighters against Islamic terrorism and international people trafficking. However, those who came to hear of his predicament were confident that Yuri Ilyich Kirovsky would survive and thrive.

The predictions about Kirovsky were being shared between two old comrades, neither amongst those put totally out to grass, as they drank themselves into nostalgic but cautious oblivion in the bar of the Hamburg Intercontinental Hotel. The austere but disabled Brit and the amiable Yank, friends despite the periodic differences between their two countries, or at least between their two intelligence services, knew their old opponent only too well.

'He'll show up. If he ain't what you Brits call a bad penny, I guess I don't know what is.'

The truth was acknowledged by a raised glass. The tales of Kirovsky and his villainies flowed with the whisky. And they got better and better as it took effect until in the end 'old Yuri' turned into a hero. But he certainly wasn't that. He was a villain and when he turned up again, as they fondly believed he would, he would still be a villain.

2

2026

John Harcourt was also in Intelligence, or rather he had been. Now, at the age of sixty-seven and enjoying the pleasures of an almost non-existent British winter, he was happy to have escaped, as he believed, from the clutches of the most demanding profession in the world.

In his more honest moments he doubted that he had been very good as a spy. But since he had been freelancing for British Intelligence for the whole of his career in an arrangement that had made him very rich, he was at least grateful. Nonetheless, when he did the reckoning he was far from satisfied that his fellow citizens got the best of the deal.

'So what did I achieve?'

It was a question that John had asked himself more than once in retirement. The director, at his leaving party, in the sort of eulogy that John found it hard to recognise himself in, claimed that achievement to be an intricate and all-embracing financial monitoring system that contributed massively to the control of international terrorism in the 2010s and to the final defeat of the more extreme forms of Islamic terror towards the end of that decade.

John wasn't so sure. In some of his earlier exploits he could put his hand on an action or describe a situation, a successful operation that was real. Success lost in the depths of online, international, financial manipulation was very hard to identify, to judge the benefits of or to be proud of. And with relations between the US and Europe now in such a sorry state, John sensed that the sort of computer skills that were going to be required in the future would be much more sophisticated than he had been capable of.

'Ross Metcalfe!'

It was a name that resided very close to the surface in his mind. And it had always been there, even if it was twenty-two years since he had known the young computer wizard. Ross would be capable of meeting the computer intelligence demands of the current day.

He had thought about Ross often over the years but rekindling the passion of their encounter in 2004 had always seemed so daunting. He knew that his inaction said something about the depth of his feelings but it was also about the depth of hurt inflicted on her all those years ago at Gatwick Airport. There had always been some urgent task in some other part of the world that required his attention. And she was as dedicated to her work as he was to his. The relationship had been intense while it lasted but time was a great destroyer of passion.

There had been no other woman in his life. His marriage had collapsed before he had even met Ross Metcalfe and his ex-wife was an indistinct memory.

* * *

'Premonition? Do we have premonitions in our business, John?'

'Well, we sure as hell have something very like them or why was I thinking about Ross again only the other day?'

'Come on, John, I didn't ask you here to talk about vague forays into your past. I'm going to stick to playing director and leave you to deal with your own ghosts.'

'Okay, so you want me to go to Scotland and talk to Ross Metcalfe. About what?'

'You'll probably have noticed that the US is getting belligerent at the moment and most of their bile is being directed at Europe. You may be one of those people who think that the US is now so locked into analysing what it sees in its own navel and is so disinclined to bother about what goes on outside of its borders that it has no impact on the rest of the world. But in the last couple of years there has been such an upsurge in the religious right's Neoconservative activities that Europe simply can't ignore what's happening any more. The fanatics aren't exactly taking over yet; more the political extremist hard-core are manipulating them more obviously and more dangerously.'

'Neoconservatives with fascist overtones?'

'Or Neoconservatives with missiles perhaps?'

'What?'

'No, no, John, we don't know there's any connection for real. That's just me being provocative. It's the way they talk and the way they see the rest of the world now; nuking their enemies with missiles would fit into their sort of doom scenario very well. All we know is that there's likely to be another move to the right developing, but when it comes it will be through the established processes, using the constitution, which makes it much harder to combat.'

'Okay, yes, I'll buy all of that. But what do you want me to talk to Ross about? She's no politico. That's not what she does. She might be able to do anything with anybody's computer, but politics used to bore the pants off her.'

'I haven't heard that expression in a while, John. Never mind. The modern-day politicos in the European intelligence community are into scenario planning and old missiles are just a part of that. What started them on it God only knows. We haven't seen anything that points to that, but they're off working themselves into a discreet frenzy. The US has some unaccounted leftover ICBMs, over and above whatever the old US-Russian treaties said. We know that from past intrusions into their defence systems. You'll remember Kirovsky and Intercontinental Veterans Anonymous, yes?'

'Jesus Christ! What are you saying? No, no, the technology is far too old.'

'You know that for a fact do you, John? Or maybe Ms Metcalfe will know better. Go and see her, that's all I ask.'

'For the present?'

'Yes, for the present, John. We have to follow our noses on this.'

3

2004

'Two dead prostitutes? Why should we be interested in two dead prostitutes for God's sake?'

John Harcourt had been incredulous when the duty officer had drawn his attention to the reports by the Amsterdam and then the Hamburg Police. The reports had certainly been mystifying, but it was the similarities that had struck the woman and had equally forcibly struck him.

'You say they both were wearing underpants that were only available from the shop reserved for high-ranking Soviet officials? 2004; that makes them at least thirty years old!'

'That's what the reports say.'

She didn't mention that it was only the pants that were old; it was a detail that didn't seem important.

'And as far as I can tell, both lots of politzei worked it out independently. Our continental chums are certainly on the ball. I wonder how long it would have taken our dear old British Bobbies to suss this lot out?'

He ignored the duty officer's comments about their police colleagues. He was also more than a little sceptical about many facets of the British character, and as a whole-hearted European he had put his faith in closer relations with the continental nations to cure many of his country's social ills, but he was not about to join in any talking down of Britain.

Intrigued, John had headed off to the records section and to the comforting presence of its head as soon as the duty officer had reported the curious sequence of entries on the central computer information board.

'So what do we know about things Russian these days?'

'Dandy' Thomas (very few people outside of personnel knew his real name) was a source of unlimited support, sympathy and expensive malt whisky to most of the middling echelons of the London-based intelligence service. With a mind that refused to succumb to the realities of a developing European dream and a memory that many a CIA or KGB man would have killed for, he, so John thought, was bound to know somebody who could make sense of the allusions that he had seen in these Dutch and German reports. And of course he did. That was how Harcourt became aware of the old Russian's hands, so called, and in particular an interesting character called the Colonel.

John's director's reaction was sceptical verging on disbelief, but valuing John's judgement he heard him out.

'Get up to Scotland, John, and talk to this Colonel.'

The instruction was clear enough, even if it was given with obvious signs of reluctance.

John's boss was one of the new breed of intelligence managers, desk-bound and a slave to both his computer and to his departmental accountant. With the Labour Government in the early years of the century determined to keep intelligence spending to a minimum, John's request to initiate an investigation was not something that the director was very keen to expend either time or money on.

'You've got a week. If you think there's something in this weird trail of yours, you'd better be able to tell me what it is within a week or it's dead and forgotten.'

The conversation was in the director's office; John wondered vaguely whether he actually saw the magnificent view along the Thames that he had. He rather doubted it but having been given his instructions he didn't hang around; which was how he got to be sitting in the departure lounge at Heathrow Airport waiting for his flight to Aberdeen to be called.

Relaxed and with time on his hands, his mind began to wander.

Being a European was his second choice in a sense. He had been a great admirer of America and all things American for many years and had only become a pro-European after what he saw as the decline in the ethos of US society.

'... flight to Aberdeen has been delayed. Please await further announcements.'

The canned airline voice penetrated his consciousness; he reached for a discarded copy of *The Washington Echo*. With unexpected time available he gave the newspaper his concentrated attention, but what he was reading didn't do much to encourage him. The war on terror seemed to dominate everything, yet he could see no way through to a conclusion or a will amongst the American ruling elite to recognise the mire that they were sleep-walking into. It wasn't always so. America always seemed so focused in the Cold War days; it knew where it was going and why, or so Harcourt thought. But then his vision was more than a little rose-tinted. He'd gone to the US fresh from Cambridge, brim full of self-confidence and wondering why he'd taken a classical degree when all he needed in life was a good head for figures and a mental nimbleness that he found came quite naturally to him.

'Commodity trading, that's the thing.'

John never ever quite understood how his tutor had got to know so much about such things. But as unworldly as he appeared to be, having been rooted in the university for as long as anybody could remember, he was totally confident in his predictions of John's success.

And successful he was, first as an oil trader with an international oil major and then on his own. At least he was successful on his own until the late 1990s, but his finances weren't always substantial enough to withstand the periods of instability in the oil markets that flowed from every upheaval in the Middle East. And he found the lack of challenging diversity increasingly burdensome; so with both this lack of interest and lack of reward he quit the field. He was happy enough to live off his bank balance and the proceeds of a rather unlikely consultancy with the CIA for a while and until his home intelligence service finally recruited him in 2001.

'... flight to Aberdeen is now boarding.'

He gathered his belongings.

The CIA had taken to John as soon as they had become aware of him. And they had become aware of him because he had obligingly bankrupted one of their prime suspects in a drug money laundering operation. The gentleman in question, of uncertain South American origin, had angered John by some dubious dealings that had been unnecessarily and deliberately harmful to a friend of his. The upshot was unfortunate for the drug dealer, as the money was not his to lose, but fortunate for John Harcourt, as the CIA, who had been watching the whole episode, was highly impressed with both his forcefulness and his skills. And what was known to the CIA also become known in London. At the right moment he was recruited, set up in business as a trader to give him cover and freedom of movement, and for his pains he was now off to Scotland on a cold January afternoon, with snow promised and a frost of Arctic severity, to chase what his director chose to call ancient Soviet rainbows.

4

2026

John Harcourt's trip to London from his retreat in West Bexington in Dorset gave him plenty of time to think. The train journey was fast enough but as always the initial hanging around for the Dial-a-Bus took much longer than he expected. Since route and congestion charging had effectively removed any benefit of running a car, he had had to rely increasingly on public transport and in the way of these things, demand exceeded supply for every new venture that emerged. Still, with climate change accelerating despite the US's conversion to the need for action in the last decade, everybody had to do their bit and John was ready enough to do his. So it was Dial-a-Bus to Dorchester Station.

As the outer counties and then the Home Counties and the London landscape flashed past his unseeing eyes John Harcourt detected a small but gratifying surge of excitement at being back in harness, albeit unofficially and on expenses only. But then, as he knew, such informal arrangements were the way of the intelligence service when something out of the ordinary needed to be done.

His sense of rejuvenation told him that all his self-delusions about his satisfaction at being retired were just that, self-delusions. When he had turned sixty-five he had felt himself to be past his prime whatever warm words others offered him and that early retirement was his best option. Slaving away even in a comfortable office until he was sixty-eight held no appeal for him; however, he had soon found that the quiet life was harder to become reconciled to than he had imagined. So, as soon as it was apparent that the director wanted him to do one more job his spirits lightened. He was wanted again and that, even now at sixty-seven and with his eclectic mix of life's experiences, gave him a great feeling.

'Ross Metcalfe, how extraordinary that I was thinking about her again only the day before I was summoned.'

The young woman opposite him on the train looked at him quizzically and he began to wonder whether he had spoken out loud. He hadn't but he had an expectancy about him that had alerted the young woman and put her on her guard. You never knew who you were travelling with these days.

Through a neutral smile he appraised her and set her image against his memories of Ross. The comparison didn't last. The woman opposite him was an eco-fashionista, a devotee of only natural fabrics and styles that were supposed to be un-polluting to the eye. John winced as the concept passed quickly through his mind. To him it was simply wool, cotton and leather produced organically and fashioned by hand with a minimum of energy consumption. Ross was practical in everything she did and wore, but was never prone to fads however commendable they might be.

Never one to waste his time on speculation, John made no effort to think about what Ross might be like now. He would know in a couple of days.

'The last time I went to Scotland to see Ross and the Colonel I was chasing Russian rainbows. What am I chasing now? Not Russian rainbows or nightmares. More American nightmares and leftover business I guess.'

5

2004

John Harcourt liked aeroplane journeys. He liked the ceaseless activity and he liked the comfort of the sameness of it all; wherever you were and whoever the aircraft was operated by, the routines and the rituals were reliable and unchanging.

'Would you care for a meal, sir?'

'No thank you.'

His appreciation of aeroplane journeys didn't quite stretch to the low-cost carriers and since his resources did stretch to full-fare carriers, the offer of a British Airways meal came with the territory. Not that he ever ate on the plane if he had a chance for a meal at his hotel. And tonight he was headed for a country house hotel recommended by a shooting and fishing friend who regularly indulged in slaughter in the surroundings of Royal Deeside and other areas adjacent to Aberdeen. Geographically it was not a good choice for his overnight stop, but he had yet to realise that.

The flight was full. His neighbour was statuesque and powerfully built, but definitely limited in conversational ability. After a discouraging grunt at the only remark that he addressed to her, she showed a far greater interest in a body-building magazine than in John or her other travelling companion. So with no distractions he allowed his mind to regurgitate the information about the deaths of the two prostitutes and the other events that seemed to be related to them. It was another vain attempt to understand what they meant. He'd told the director that it was a trail. He was convinced that it was. But trails go somewhere; in this case he had no idea where it led.

The body of the first prostitute had been disturbed by an early morning Amsterdam Waterbus trundling along the Herengracht. The only passengers, a hardy German couple, noticed it as it floated into the vessel's wake as the waterbus emerged from under the bridge where the Raadhuisstraat crossed. The Dutch Police were immediately mystified. Everything about the body was wrong.

It didn't take them long to identify the young woman. But instead of the all-leather outfit that she had last been seen wearing, she was dressed in a tracksuit of a make available almost anywhere in Europe, a cult Marks and Spencer T-shirt – unusual but not exceptional – cheap trainers, a pair of flashy boxing shorts and the now infamous but ancient Russian panties underneath.

I guess, he thought, if the pathologist hadn't been a woman, we might have missed the Russian gear. But it was the first thing that had attracted the woman's attention.

The girl – she had been barely eighteen – had died of a heart attack. She had been severely beaten up but she had been dead for many hours before her re-clothed body had been dumped where, as the police immediately recognised, she would inevitably be found.

The Hamburg story was the same, occurring a week later. The prostitute – in this case she was much older – looked to have been killed in a car accident, but she was wearing the same clothes, right down to the flashy boxing shorts and the neat Russian underpants. They were noticed this time because they didn't fit too well.

The pre-landing gibberish had completely invaded John's thoughts, so he collected himself and waited for the aircraft to land. The ordered chaos of a couple of hundred people trying to squeeze out of the now motionless metal tube amused him but he rarely allowed himself to become a part of it. As a consequence he was usually left at the end of the taxi queue.

'What was underneath in Amsterdam will appear in Hamburg.' That was the first message. 'What was underneath in Amsterdam and Hamburg will next appear in London.' That was the second.

John repeated the two entries from *The Times* as he waited for his transport. The readers, the security service operatives who scrutinised virtually every publication on earth, online and off, had picked up the messages and entered them into the intelligence database. The duty officer passed the information to John just as he left for the airport on his way to Aberdeen.

'Where to?'

Away with his thoughts, at first he hadn't noticed the taxi finally arrive. He gave the name of the hotel. The driver sped off with rather less regard for the treacherous conditions than John himself might have shown, but despite a number of unplanned and uncontrolled detours to rather less-well-used parts of the carriageway, they arrived safely enough. John was not, however, able to re-establish his previous rather detached frame of mind.

The hotel was old, intimate and rather splendid. It also struck John as being rather further out of town than he would have preferred and definitely not in the direction he believed he needed to go the next day.

'New Pitsligo, sir? You're a bit of a way off for that. Hour and a half in this weather at least.'

The hotel owner himself provided the information. He was solicitous of John; his friend, a very good customer of the hotel, had been on the telephone. He was made welcome even if the geographic information was discouraging.

The dinner was first rate and John indulged himself. He enjoyed his food. He had a wide circle of friends, both male and female, which initially included his ex-wife. However, the promiscuity that had led to the breakdown of the marriage intruded as his former partner introduced a stream of unsuitable companions to his friends' social gatherings until the invitations dried up. After that he rarely saw her. It was easy enough to avoid her with his occupation, although it took him some time to get over his initial guilt at the failure of the marriage. He questioned himself many times on whether his job and lifestyle, which was inherently neglectful, was the root cause of the rupture. But he would never know whether the stream of lovers that she took, and continued to take, and her heavy drinking, were because of his frequent absences or would have happened anyway.

Even outside his circle of friends he was rated as excellent company and was much sought after both by hostesses and by optimistic young women who saw him as a worthwhile catch. However, he told himself that he wasn't ready for another close relationship.

So, having extended his range of culinary experiences from the hotel menu, he retreated to his bedroom, sampled the array of Speyside Whisky miniatures left for his further indulgence and wound his brain back into some sort of reasonable functionality.

'Well now!'

Having hooked up his computer to the hotel's network he was revisiting the duty officer's reports to him.

'The messages in *The Times* were placed by a Paris-based fruit import/export company with business connections in Bulgaria? The whole thing gets more obscure by the minute.'

The report on the messages was brief and the duty officer gave it as her opinion that it had been far too easy to trace their origins.

'Wanted to be found,' she suggested in a footnote.

'Okay, but why?'

But it was the second report that really got his mind into top gear.

There were two identical incidents again. German Customs had been tipped off about some drug courier runs into London, from Munich in each case. Alerted, British Customs detained and searched the two couriers. There were no drugs, even after full screening and internal inspection. The two women proclaimed their innocence throughout, with some justice, and were eventually allowed to go. But it was the details of the report that fascinated John. In each case, after describing the sequence of events, the Heathrow Customs officers carefully noted the contents of the minimal luggage being carried and item-by-item, because they had been strip-searched, what clothes the two women were wearing.

'I don't even need to guess,' said John aloud as he worked through the list.

The tracksuits were the same: the Marks and Spencer T-shirts, the trainers, the flashy boxing shorts and the underwear. However, the duty officer had had to ask for verification from the German Police about the underpants, as neither the British Police nor customs could identify them.

They were Russian and they were old.

'What was underneath has surely turned up in London.'

John felt inordinately pleased by this new development; it somehow justified his being there. As he headed for bed he wondered what this mysterious Colonel was going to make of all of this.

* * *

The police in Detroit didn't check the undergarments of the man whose body they had had to fish out of a partly frozen, backyard swimming pool. They didn't get the chance.

The shooting had hardly been reported when a posse of CIA agents appeared and demanded the body.

'Let 'em have it.'

The police captain was angry at being steamrollered by his boss. The police chief was no less pleased to be ordered about by Washington, but he had been given a very clear message that he had no choice.

'Must be one of them,' remarked a patrolman as the body was driven away. In the way of the CIA they neither confirmed nor denied this assertion at any time.

The death was reported in the local paper, but it was so sanitised that even the policeman who had discovered the body didn't relate the unfortunate government servant, killed whilst on leave from his overseas posting, to his grisly find. But those in the intelligence world who still monitored such things would have recognised the code: government servant equals secret agent. They might also have recognised the mode of death as an execution, or compared it with a similar incident some months earlier.

The death was lamented, not just by the poor man's family, or his CIA colleagues, but even by those in the former KGB who knew him and who had worked with him. But his death was not lamented by the ex-KGB man who knew him best. You didn't ordinarily get to being a colonel general in the KGB if you could still manage such human feelings.

6

2004

John Harcourt was up early. He always was, irrespective of what time he'd made it to his bed. He was also hungry. His stomach, having long since forgotten the joys of the previous evening, was ready for restocking.

There had been snow overnight, not much, but enough to focus his attention clearly on the journey ahead. The hotel owner reiterated his view that he was faced with an hour and a half's hike across country and he was heading into more bad weather. The foolishness of having depended on his sporting friend really began to hit home.

'Breakfast! First things first!' And so he was directed back to the dining room.

Between the time of his awaking and his return to the table he had channel-hopped the TV in his room, seeking to update himself on the affairs of the world at large, and of Europe and America in particular. His concentration had been interrupted only with the arrival of the chambermaid and a tray loaded with tea and oatcakes.

'Good morning to you, sir.'

John hated the false early morning cheeriness of hotel staff, but the novelty of a chambermaid, an institution he thought had been long dead, killed his irritation. She was full of the weather, that's how he'd known it had snowed, and of overnight local dramas, not the least of which was the seemingly lamentable performance of Aberdeen Football Club against its old rivals Dundee United.

'They were rubbish, terrible. They didn't deserve to win!'

The forthright but affectionate comment faded as the chambermaid herself faded from the room.

'What else?' he muttered, moving from the TV to check his electronic mailbox.

The duty officer had chased down the import/export company that had been leaving cryptic messages in *The Times* but had come up against some rather angry French officials. The company was well enough known to the regulatory authorities in Paris, but only because it hadn't yet been persuaded to share the names of its directors with them. It had offices in a rather bizarre range of European cities and as the duty officer was at pains to point out, in Detroit in the USA. Her theory that the sender of the messages wanted to be identified took a bit of a knock when the obvious transparency of the company was matched by the total obscurity of the people running it.

There was nothing more of interest to John in his mailbox beyond confirmation of his travel arrangements. Since his hunger was also getting the better of him, it was then that he checked for his hire-car in reception and set out to do yet further damage to his cholesterol count by consuming the full breakfast menu.

The journey to the Colonel's Buchan farmhouse turned out to be every bit as tortuous as the hotel owner had predicted. The hire-car's satellite navigation system effectively gave up at the first demand on its skills. The screen was filled with a complete list of the routes available to him, but all of them were 'not advised in the conditions'. The police were more helpful, but still made every effort to dissuade him from the trip.

'Nothing for it,' he told himself as he set off.

At various times during his slow and decidedly erratic

progress he attempted to contact the Colonel and report his whereabouts. It was a courtesy that seemed appropriate. However, neither the mobile phone in the car nor his own were up to the job in the weather conditions.

'He isn't going anywhere,' he said to himself after his final attempt.

Indeed he wasn't and although he was expecting John, the Colonel was entirely unconcerned about his guest's passage towards him. Making the trip to see him was something that was beyond his control and therefore something that he didn't attempt to engage his thought processes with. He was aware of the weather and knew something of the man heading out to talk to him; that was sufficient knowledge to give him confidence that the meeting would take place and for him to devote his morning to other things and await the eventual arrival. The knock on the door would be time enough to bring his mind to bear on Mr Harcourt.

Had he been less occupied with the business of getting himself to that door, John himself might have pondered the mystery man that he was scheduled to meet. 'Dandy' Thomas spoke of him in hushed tones, but beyond the fact that he was in awe of him, he had learnt nothing. That the Colonel had retired from the intelligence service he did know; that he was supposed to be the greatest living expert on the old Soviet Union intelligence services, he had been told; that he could elucidate John's famous trail, he had been assured of by Dandy, but that was it.

'Ah, New Pitsligo!'

By dint of following a snowplough for the last few miles he had successfully made it to the village of the Colonel's address with rather less hassle than the earlier parts of the journey. The place was not a bustling metropolis. In fact, locating a living person to consult with proved difficult and he was about to try a random knock on a door when the solution to all such problems in the country hove into view: the post van.

Five minutes later he pulled up at the Colonel's front door.

The farmhouse was typical of that part of North East Scotland. Like many, it had been modernised, but it had also been joined to the steading building behind it. Consequently, it was an unobtrusive but substantial dwelling.

He could at first hear no sound as he rang the doorbell, even as he crouched close to the door to avoid the biting wind that was whipping around the building. Then came sounds of activity inside and other doors being opened. After that came the first of the many surprises that he was to be exposed to during his relationship with the Colonel.

'John Harcourt?'

He acknowledged that that was who he was.

'Do come in.'

He did as he was bid.

'I'm Ross Metcalfe. I'm the Colonel's partner.'

Whatever he might have been expecting of the Colonel, he was not expecting a partner, nor was he expecting such a young woman as this.

7

2026

To suggest that John was plagued by any sense of déjà-vu was to misunderstand his character. If anything, he was a here and now man and dealt as far as he could with the present. At least his conscious brain did. However, somewhere buried and ready to surface there were certainly thoughts about Ross Metcalfe. And sometimes they did surface unasked. But as she was now in the here and now for him, the past slotted into the timeline of his mind and would emerge when triggered by some current event. The trigger, he knew, would be the meeting and he would deal with that when it happened.

His briefing from the Director of Intelligence Services had been sparse to say the least. The two threads that did run through his comments were couched in cautious terms but were clearly causes of sufficient concern to prompt John's own recall to service. Worsening relations between the US and the European Federation was one theme; the other was rather less tangible, but nonetheless pertinent: the status of the US's ability to wage war against a power of equal capability and determination. In the last twenty to twenty-five years the US military strength had been pitted against an entirely different type of opposition. Something was known of the successes and failures of the various Star Wars initiatives. However, what little was known about the US's current conventional offensive capabilities suggested limited effectiveness, underfunding and friction with the political establishment. The collapse of NATO towards the end of the second decade had meant the suspension of open military and security cooperation and increasing US military isolation.

What contribution Ross Metcalfe and her organisation could make to rectifying this lack of knowledge was the justification for John's airfare to Scotland. What she contributed beyond routine feedback to London was yet to be debated.

The flight to Aberdeen was full. Since the number of airline flights was now heavily regulated and tickets had to be bought partly in carbon credits, people only flew in exceptional circumstances and planes only departed when full within a very broad time window. And since the train companies ran frequent traveller reward schemes paid out in carbon credits, the train was now the dominating feature of long-distance travel. That John was flying at all spoke volumes of the perceived importance of his mission and the high regard for Ross Metcalfe and her skills.

The Colonel had died in 2015 at the age of eighty-four; he had written to Ross on the occasion. The exchange of letters was friendly and sensitive to the pain that the old man's death had caused Ross, but at the time John had been in Tehran negotiating an oil deal with the newly formed Democratic Republic of Iran. Peace in various parts of the Middle East had become a reality but he couldn't be spared to go to a funeral in Northern Scotland.

Having driven more cars than he cared to remember, John knew that his all-time least favourite was the sort of hydrogen-powered car that he picked up when he had finally disembarked from the plane in Aberdeen. The flight had been uneventful and free from the endless and unsought attentions that the low-cost airlines of the past had seemed to think passengers needed. Pared to the bone, the flight provided nothing beyond a seat and a TV screen powered by wing-mounted turbine generators.

'Haven't missed flying,' John muttered as he confronted the bored and surly car hire receptionist.

With no carbon credits to pay for the car, he (or at least the intelligence service) paid premium rates and left the airport with a sense of dissatisfaction.

It was April. The hotel room was cold since the director's administration service had obviously thought that heating premium payments weren't justified. But the TV, powered by in-house generation, was available and switched on when John got to his room.

The first thing that came to his attention, as if to reinforce his mission, was the growing row between Spanish fishermen and the American Coastguard. The interview in progress was being relayed by CNN: not the favourite station of the US Administration any more, but still a largely unbiased commentator on the American political scene. The position of the US Secretary for Agriculture and Fisheries was absolutely and totally clear. What had begun as a minor game of cat and mouse on the edge of international waters had become a big issue at government level, and the Americans were not going to stand for the sort of intrusion that the Spanish had supposedly been guilty of. And the Europeans had better believe that!

The impassioned tones of the worthy minister amused rather than angered the European Federation Commissioners when they were briefed on the speech, but they recognised the gravity of the situation sufficiently to send a couple of warships scurrying to the area.

With his past knowledge of the Americans, John was rather bemused by their curious behaviour. As he poured himself a dram of the hotel single malt whisky he pondered the disproportionate nature of the US response.

'What the hell's the matter with them?' he demanded of the room at large.

Like the Federation Commissioners and the Regional Governments, John could not see the fishing dispute as seriously important. Only a few boatloads of fish were at stake. A little bit of token huffing and puffing and the situation would have faded away.

'It's as if they want a confrontation. But why the hell should they? What's in it for them?'

These were the sort of questions that he knew would be being asked by the bright young things who worked for the intelligence service and the conclusions to which these fertile minds had come would no doubt be relayed to him if they were thought to be relevant to his task.

'It's all about bread and circuses; it has to be. Their military are too rundown for a fight with Europe. And in any case, their government could never get its act together long enough to make the necessary decisions. They're just trying to distract the populace. It's a ploy as old as time.'

The theory hadn't taken long to emerge. And when it was passed onto him John's instinct was to agree with it. And it fitted the prevailing opinion within the inner intelligence circles and the related government departments. A combination of weak government and an ineffective president coupled with an aggressive Congress had undermined the integrity of the American public service, and powerful state-based coalitions had begun to subvert federal authority. Many major institutions like the SIE (the Secret Intelligence Executive), the successor to the CIA, had become very powerful, introverted and self-seeking. They had agendas of their own which were not necessarily in the best interests of the American people, and they often cloaked them in a form of extreme nationalism or religious fanaticism that increasingly focused on Europe as not just a competitor, but also as an enemy.

John just hoped that the rather patronising assessment of the US military capability was accurate.

8

2026

'Say no to confrontation!'

The scruffy knot of protesters at the front of the crowd stood out. Chanting their message in ragged unison, they waved their placards of intransigence with only token enthusiasm. Nobody took any notice of them. The Socialist Front had developed the inappropriate and inopportune protest almost to the level of an art form, and there was a view going about in demonstrating circles that without them there opposing the mainstream at any particular event, it couldn't really be said to have made its mark. On this occasion, swimming against the tide was clearly impossible and these protestors knew it.

As John Harcourt was admitted once again into the warmth and comfort of the converted Buchan farmhouse, and the renewed acquaintance of Ross Metcalfe at the other end of Britain, the crowd outside the American Embassy in London undoubtedly did not want to say 'no' to confrontation.

Inside the embassy building there was concern, even apprehension; the sophisticated anti-terrorist defences weren't intended as a protection against a seething mob of people arriving in their hundreds on their feet. With a staff reduced to only a fraction of its former size, the few that had arrived for work on the mild April morning would have preferred to be somewhere else.

'Okay guys, you gotta keep cool!'

The speaker, the head of embassy security, was everything that old Hollywood myths would have the world believe a US Marine Corps colonel should not be: thoughtful, cultured, black and female. But Dotty Wedgewood was all of these and more; she was tough, decisive, uncompromising and scrupulously fair, and the picket of anxious marines in front of her knew exactly where they stood with her.

'Keep out of sight; I only want the normal guards visible out front. And nobody loads their weapon until I say. Understood?'

As always with her, they understood.

'Don't agree with that, Colonel. They should be loaded and ready,' said a quiet but harsh voice behind her.

'I say not, sir, and it's my responsibility.'

But Dotty was used to brushes like this with Melvin Fitzallan, the ambassador. He was prone to creeping up on her at critical moments, and he was always trying to undermine her, but in front of her own troops he knew that she wouldn't yield to his view. Manipulative and selfish, the ambassador had no power over Lieutenant Colonel Wedgewood, and that was something that rankled with him. Everybody else in the building he could intimidate or dominate, but security was beyond his reach.

'On your head be it, Colonel. On your head be it!'

'It sure as hell will be!'

The nearest marine to her could have sworn that he had heard a female voice say 'Piss off', but as his commander smiled sweetly at her minute army of eight, it was the roars of the crowd penetrating the building that began to take everyone's attention.

'Okay, let's get to it!'

The marines dispersed to their posts. The colonel moved into the foyer and looked out onto the burgeoning crowd. Fitzallan had taken himself off as silently as he had arrived.

The area in front of the embassy was all people. Roads,

pavements, grass, trees, statues, everything was covered with people. And not a single one of them was silent. The roars and howls, and the blasts of electronic noise were shattering; it was as if the crowd was trying to batter the embassy into submission to its will with decibels.

'So, what are they protesting about this time?' demanded Fitzallan.

Back in his own quarters at the rear of the building, the barrage of sound was no longer as noisily audible. Irritated again at failing to make a dent in the colonel's composure, he was preparing to take his anger out on his personal assistant. She was unperturbed. Well used to the ambassador's uncertain temper, she had never been known to react to his pointless bullying.

He didn't really care what they were shouting about; over the last few weeks he had become well used to being abused, heckled and even pelted with a variety of unsavoury objects on his trips around Europe. The pretext for any demonstration no longer had any impact on him. He just yearned for his country to find its backbone as of old, and to respond in a way that the miserable Europeans would remember. Had he the power, he would have shown them.

With the UN long since departed from America for its new headquarters in Munich, the US had increasingly ignored the international community. With Congress having refused to fund the UN and its agencies, despite the president's pleas, the Neoconservatives and the SIE felt no obligation to anything outside US borders. With an almost panic-stricken withdrawal of European and Asian investment and with cultural contacts now almost non-existent, the likes of the ambassador almost had the isolation that they sought. The final straw was the closing of the border with Canada, except to genuine refugees, and the reversal of the human traffic back to Mexico. Again, despite the president's pleas,

Congress chose to ignore the impact of all of this on the US economy, which was disastrous.

'They're demanding that we respect international law and let their fishing fleets go wherever they please.'

The crowd were demanding rather more than that, but messages like 'Shitty Yanks go home', and other less complimentary variations on that particular theme were hardly likely to improve the ambassador's frame of mind, so the PA thought it better not to bother him with them.

The grunt that followed her answer she knew to be dismissal and she took immediate advantage of the opportunity to escape. The ambassador was at his desk and delving into the mass of paper that covered it; he would soon be oblivious to her. In any case there was much too much going on outside for a healthy young woman to be cooped up with an ill-tempered and ill-mannered, middle-aged man who never smiled and whose main instincts in any situation were contemptuous, cruel, self-seeking and destructive. How her father had ever got to be a friend of Melvin Fitzallan she had long ceased to imagine, nor why she accepted his offer of this job. She had surely regretted it. She was certainly seeing a lot of Europe, but hardly in the most congenial of circumstances.

When the European Federation was formed, the US Government, for reasons that defied logic, lacked conviction or imagination and ignored current technology, had decided that it wouldn't conform and set up a single embassy in Brussels. So it still maintained its facilities in the old countries, although not the huge staffs, and had appointed Consuls-General when the Federation flatly refused to continue to receive a myriad of ambassadors. The US Ambassador to the Federation therefore lacked a permanent home and commuted around the component countries according to the needs of the political situation or the fancies of the incumbent. His staff did see a lot of Europe, but like his

PA they found their existence extraordinarily and unnecessarily stressful.

Fitzallan was a bully and a man of a devious but ambitious mind. He had aspirations for higher things and sympathy for those who believed that strong action was necessary to stop the rot in America and to re-establish the country in its former pre-eminence. The rot in his mind was the factionalisation, the nationalism in individual states, the rundown of the military in the face of no perceived external threats and the complete dominance of Congress over a succession of weak presidents of both political persuasions. The fact that his Neoconservative friends were actively encouraging the rot passed him by.

'Strong, autocratic rule is what we need,' he was fond of saying amongst his cronies in moments of excitement or intoxication. He was also prone to admiring dictatorships if not dictators.

Since many of these cronies held high rank in the SIE, his message was taken to heart by people who thought they had a right and a duty to influence things in their country. So, he had started to preach a philosophy that had taken root very firmly in the SIE and elsewhere.

Two floors up and overlooking the growing action, the ambassador's PA watched from the offices of a friend in the SIE (not that she knew he was in the intelligence service).

'Wonder what happened to Rick.'

'Rick?'

'New guy; just arrived from the States.'

She rightly assumed that Rick shared the office, although her interest was only passing. Things were happening outside and her attention had soon been grabbed.

The seething mass of people was surging forward. The police lined up in front of the crowd began to show signs of tension, the horses moving restlessly. Suddenly the pressure of bodies overturned the first row of barriers and a disordered horde, including the hapless band of Socialist Front supporters was forced into the police lines. Cries of pain and angry shouts punctuated the general noise of the crowd; injuries were occurring and patience was fading. The troublemakers at the back became active and missile showers began to land on police and protesters alike. Pressed against the anti-car-bomb emplacements the police had nowhere to go and a movement to clear the area started. Gathered by Internet and mobile phone communications, the crowd was being dispersed by good old-fashioned police crowd-control tactics.

It was a movement that overwhelmed the limited traffic of people in the streets and byways of an area surrounding the embassy. And as it overwhelmed and passed by a party of two just emerging from an upmarket coffee shop, it left a cameo of one man lying dead and of another heading off in pursuit of one of the departing groups. It was a short chase, almost instantly given up as hopeless.

Rick Blackford returned to crouch over his dead companion, checking what he already knew. Shot through the heart at close range, his survival chances had been nil. The obvious deadness of the man at least held the crowd back.

Now what? thought Rick.

Only too aware that to ask around for help in an agitated American voice might not be the best thing to do, he reached into his pocket. A telephone call seemed to make the most sense but the call was never made.

'So what happened here?'

The policewoman challenged Rick as her colleague followed him in checking the obvious fact that the man was dead.

'He got shot.'

'American?'

A small gaggle of people gathered. The police weren't

hostile but some of the congregating mob were. The policeman joined his partner and moved to protect Rick from what for the moment was only verbal abuse. They didn't want any violence.

'He American too?' the policeman asked.

He had retrieved the dead man's wallet. The answers to his questions were all in it.

'Diplomat,' he said to the policewoman. 'That's all we need!'

'Second Secretary,' added Rick when he realised that the policeman had his compatriot's papers in his hand.

The police officers exchanged questioning looks and then included Rick in their query.

'We were holed up in a coffee shop.' He gestured up the street. 'It seemed quiet so we were headed for the embassy back door. Suddenly the mob was everywhere.'

The police back-up teams arrived. Rick was ferried away. He was relieved. Despite the police continually moving them on, the sound of Rick's accent kept prompting reactions from the more persistent of the onlookers. He certainly felt more comfortable once he was out of the area.

He had only been in Britain for a month. He hadn't been exposed to too much friendliness, but he soon realised that neither had anybody else who didn't talk with one of the recognisable British accents. It was only on that day that he had detected a feeling around that was undoubtedly anti-American.

The police didn't keep him long; there wasn't a lot to tell. An hour and a half after leaving the coffee shop he was sitting in the head of embassy security's office feeling the first impact of shock. It was not a comfortable meeting. It felt almost as bad as being in the mob that he'd just left; a mob that had now worked up quite a head of anti-American steam.

Apart from Dotty Wedgewood, there was his section leader and a rather unpleasant man in his forties who Rick supposed, like himself and his superior, was from the SIE. The dead man barely rated a mention in the conversation. Most of the attention was focused on the killer and how much Rick had managed to see of him.

'Okay, tell it to us again, slowly. You came out of the coffee shop?'

The Colonel restarted the conversation after Rick had told it all once, or rather he had told almost all of it once. He shared the facts as he saw them but he didn't share his suspicions or speculations.

'Yep, it was actually quite quiet where we were. The noise from the crowd in the background was horrendous. It was only a couple of hundred metres to the back door here. There were people about, on the sidewalk, in the street. They were going all ways, up the street, down it. Not many. There were groups stood about but none particularly near to us. Then the mob burst out; on the run. The people in the street panicked in all directions.'

What he didn't report, because he couldn't be sure of it, was a shadowy figure who had moved down the street past them and into the approaching mob, seemingly then to be swept back up the street again by it. Could it have been the killer?

He gave the details of the shooting. He'd been pushed to the ground and separated from the second secretary. He'd heard the shot and seen an arm and a gun before it was swallowed up again amongst the surprised demonstrators milling about them. However, he'd seen more, although again he didn't share the information. He'd observed enough of the actions of the killer to conclude that they were controlled and calculated. He was convinced that he had witnessed an execution: well planned and expertly carried out. However, knowing himself to be in shock and fresh from his SIE training, he decided to hold back his suspicions until he could think them out more clearly. Facts and only facts lead to conclusions he had been taught time and time again at training school and here was his first chance to practise the dictum.

There was then a string of questions for him. How well had he seen the killer? Could he describe him? It was a 'him' presumably? Would he recognise him again? It was only later that Rick realised that the SIE people seemed to be in no way surprised or unhappy that his answers were so vague and unhelpful. As he later imagined it was as if they, or rather the surly stranger, didn't really want to know who the killer was, but wanted to be sure nobody else found out either.

As the questioning went on, he knew that there was something else eating away at his brain but he couldn't bring it to the fore.

'Okay?' asked Dotty Wedgewood of the others present. 'Heard enough?'

The atmosphere in the office suddenly became intimidating as the unnamed SIE man stood up and moved to stand over Rick.

'The fact is,' he said with heavy emphasis, 'you didn't see anything. The mob attacked you because you were American, you were knocked down and you didn't see what happened to Spencer.'

He gave the second secretary's name in a low voice as if he didn't want anybody to know who he was.

'But–'

Rick's supervisor gave him a hard frowning look.

'Okay, I didn't see what happened to him!'

'That's good. You're in shock. When your mind clears you'll see you were imagining a lot of this.'

The man's efforts to appear benign after being so threatening were ludicrous, but Rick was no longer sensitive to such things. He just wanted to escape, which he did, but his escape didn't last for long.

Back in his office his colleague was sympathetic; equally, he was curious.

'What did Jordan want?'

Rick had slumped at his desk, taken a few deep breaths and then made a couple of trips along the corridor to get himself settled. Finally back at his desk again, he wasn't exactly ready for another inquisition but he knew that his office-mate's interest was inevitable. The coffee collected during his second trip was helpful.

'Jordan? Who the hell's Jordan? Oh, that was Jordan?' He eventually caught up to where his questioner was at. The stranger at the debriefing was Alex Jordan. He was the head of the SIE's Internal Investigation Department. If that was the case he was going to be cautious. His knowledge of SIE politics was not great but it was sufficient for him to know that a brush with this man was not a guarantee of career advancement.

'Oh, he just wanted to know what I could tell him about the killer; any description or anything. Bit late; he was long gone.'

'Spencer was one of us you know. When somebody hits one of us Jordan is bound to want to know everything he can.'

Rick was surprised by this information. He had heard that the SIE placed people in other government departments, but he wasn't sure he had ever quite believed it.

'I didn't know that, Joe. But why would Internal Investigations be interested?'

'Spencer never did quite fit. Something to do with a buddy of his found dead in Detroit. It was a good few years ago. But Jordan was here to see him for some reason and suddenly he's dead before he could. Does that sound suspicious to you, Rick?'

Being but lowly servants of the SIE, what Joe and Rick shouldn't have known was that the dead man in Detroit was a long-standing KGB double agent. Rick however knew more about ex-KGB double agents than he would have admitted to his colleague. The man had been cast adrift after the demise of the KGB, but seemingly had not been inactive nor had he been out of touch with his old master. It was twenty-two years ago but intelligence services have long memories. Spencer, the Detroit man's friend, had never been trusted after his death. There were sufficient suspicions of score-settling in the new SIE to attract Mr Jordan's attention, especially as he knew the true story of how the Detroit man met his end.

Joe would have liked to ask Rick more but a marine appeared at the office door.

'Mr Blackford, sir. The ambassador wants to see you.'

Melvin Fitzallan had found out about the death of his subordinate as soon as Colonel Wedgewood could get a message to him. With the demonstrations outside he had cancelled most of his day so he had time to take an interest in what was going on inside the embassy and that meant basically to interfere with what security were doing. The mysterious Mr Jordan had left the embassy as informally as he had entered it and the ambassador never even knew that he had been there. So the only person he could interrogate was the unfortunate Rick Blackford.

'The guy's in shock, sir, and he didn't see anything. Believe me, you're wasting your time.'

The colonel's resistance only encouraged him. Rick was sent for.

Rick had never been to the Ambassadorial Suite before and as the marine guided him through the unfamiliar corridors, he wondered nervously why he had been called now. He also wondered whether the ambassador knew anything about him. He didn't suppose so, but the shocks sustained by his mental processes were making him paranoid and he was not in an ideal frame of mind to be confronted by a man as insensitive as Fitzallan, who had been joined by another man that Rick didn't recognise.

'Blackford, sit down. Coffee?'

Fitzallan certainly wasn't going to make the conversation easy for his visitor, nor it soon transpired was he going to introduce the other man in the room.

'You saw Spencer killed. I guess you know he was a Russian mole.'

This was immediately too much for Rick. He heard the words that the ambassador had used but it's doubtful whether in his existing frame of mind he fully understood what they meant. He shook his head; it was the only gesture he seemed capable of. But there was more.

'You know the SIE killed him!'

Deep down in his brain Rick did know that but it was the ambassador's statement that clicked all the evidence into place. Everything about the killing as he had observed it was textbook stuff, SIE training manual mark three, and he'd just been through it on his own training course. He was stunned, and his surprise and devastation showed.

'Back off, Mel. The guy can't cope with this.'

Rick almost didn't hear what was said. Then the lank lounging figure of Fitzallan's other visitor took on some substance as he stepped up beside the ambassador and urged him to let Rick be. Had he been more his normal self, Rick would have recognised the man as a senator from his own home state, but he was now beyond absorbing any more images. His mind was beginning to seize up inside his head. All he sensed was a fear that he couldn't understand; an indefinable menace from the cold and unpleasant man that sat opposite him.

But the ambassador didn't let up.

'Only the three of us in this room know that Spencer was killed by an SIE death squad... As all traitors will be.

You'd better see that nothing gets out about this, or you'll be next on their list.'

It was such a melodramatic and pointlessly unnecessary statement that the senator actually laughed. He was no more interested in Rick and his wellbeing than Fitzallan was; he was just concerned about the practicalities of trying to terrify an already traumatised man into silence, especially since it was inevitable that rather more than just the three of them already knew about Spencer's assassination by his SIE masters and leakage was bound to occur. Killing Rick Blackford if word got out would just be another unnecessary death.

9

2004

Ross Metcalfe was not dressed for the icy weather that confronted her when she opened the farmhouse door to John Harcourt. She held the door part-open protectively.

'Do come in.'

Two split-second photo scans took place. Ross's china blue eyes scanned John as she spoke, the faint accent of the upper-class Scottish south impinging on him briefly. Expecting him, as surely as he was not expecting her, she registered the tall but muffled figure favourably. They were in contrast in colouring she noted, and she sensed strength even as he materialised through the widening aperture of the door. As John's hazel eyes then scanned her, her face moved into welcome mode.

'Come in, please.'

She repeated the invitation with a tinge of urgency as the blast of cold air that accompanied John Harcourt surged passed her. Equally anxious to be out the Arctic conditions, he slid into the hallway of the Colonel's home with an economy of movement, but lack of hurry that immediately impressed the young woman standing waiting for him to remove his coat.

'Thank you.'

The coat disappeared into a cupboard before John was aware of it and she was gesturing him towards a door at the end of the hall. There was no fuss or subservience about her; taking his coat was a piece of courtesy that she extended to him as he might have to her; leading him into the Colonel's sanctum was the same. Ross Metcalfe had the appearance of very confident young woman and saw herself the equal of any man, intelligence service or not.

'Good to see you.'

The Colonel propelled his wheelchair a yard or so towards his guest and held out his hand. The handshake was firm and positive. Both men drew confidence from it.

'Have a seat.'

The invitation was offered over the shoulder as the older man manoeuvred himself to a tray of drinks. The Colonel was of almost identical build to John Harcourt – 6 feet, 12 stone – and not for the first time Ross Metcalfe wondered at how he, wheelchair-bound as he was, kept himself as tight and spare as someone who she guessed not too accurately was about half his seventy-three years. John was forty-five years old. Ross herself, at 5 feet 7 inches was no dwarf and carried her thirty years well enough to also confuse John into underestimation.

His hair's darker in the light, she thought.

Her own natural blonde hair was the envy of the local lasses, many of whom tended from the brown to auburn.

'Whisky?'

'That'd be great.'

John sipped the generous helping with appreciation. As with everything he had seen so far, including Ms Metcalfe, the whisky was of high quality.

The Colonel made no effort to supply Ross with a drink; he just served himself and John. It was the first manifestation of the relationship between the two of them. John sensed an equality that he found surprising in the face of the obvious age difference.

'She's my eyes and ears, and sometimes even my arms

and legs,' the Colonel remarked as if reading the thoughts beginning to form in John's mind.

Ross had sat herself opposite Harcourt on an elegant, antique chaise longue, stretching her long, booted legs out in front of her and settling herself comfortably to listen. She pulled ineffectually at her brief skirt, but it was an unconscious gesture at adjustment as there was no way that the garment could have been made to cover her legs to her knees, let alone any further down. Harcourt noticed that there was no allure or other sexual message in her movements, despite her being fully aware that he was watching her.

The Colonel was watching her too but John could find no clue as to what he was thinking or feeling from his expression. At no time during the subsequent passages between the three of them did John get any impression other than one of mutual acceptance as common participants in the affair in hand.

'Ross's the computer expert. That stuff's way beyond me. She listens to everything and sees everything, but don't ask me how. Computer surveillance she calls it, hooked up to God knows who and what around the world.'

The two of them smiled companionably at this description of her role, Ross showing no modesty and the Colonel a certain pride.

'Probably illegal; don't want to know. Anyway, let's have a brief chat about how all this arose then we'll have some lunch, and then we'll see what we can do to help.'

'All this', John assumed, was the trail that he had come to discuss.

The next half hour was surprisingly demanding for him. The Colonel's knowledge of the workings of the European intelligence services was considerable and his probing sharp and well-informed. John responded carefully and the less-than-full answers that he gave on some occasions were met with appreciative grunts from the Colonel. It was sparring, but it was also a trust- and confidence-building exercise. By the time a raw-boned lady with an accent that was way beyond John's comprehension came into the room to announce what was obviously lunch, the trust and confidence was substantially built.

John had noted the faint clicks as they spoke and as the voice-activated recorder went into action. He was not surprised that their conversation was being recorded; it in no way undermined this emerging trust and confidence.

The tape recorder was amongst a mass of electronic equipment sat on the shelves that covered the walls of the room on two sides. The shelves were otherwise jammed with a vast array of books that John would dearly have liked to have browsed through. The bay window was filled with a table that John put down as Regency and which the Colonel clearly used as a desk. There was a log fire in a huge grate: a rare treat for a big city dweller like John.

The room was a curious mix of modern and antique, and John found it very hard to fix the Colonel's character from it. It seemed to signal the exclusiveness of the military class to which the old man clearly belonged, but the electronic gadgetry was almost a parody of that. I'm an old-fashioned spy caught in the modern world, it seemed to be saying, but as John was to discover, the Colonel was anything but old-fashioned.

'He's always called the Colonel,' Dandy had confided to John earlier, 'but he's really a lieutenant general.'

His early life was archetypal: military landowning family; following the Guards and Sandhurst (at a record young age) he was thrust into the real world of soldiering at the tail end of the Suez campaign in 1956. He switched to Military Intelligence in Berlin in the 1960s and worked his way up, keeping his military rank. Apart from a short and unexplained foray to the Falklands in 1982 and 1983, his service was all in Europe. Keeping track of senior KGB officers was his speciality.

'So why's he called the Colonel?' John inevitably asked Dandy.

'Only rumour, of course, but as a very young lieutenant he's supposed to have imitated a colonel to get a date with the daughter of some stuffy old major.'

The major had been outraged but his own colonel had taken his high-spirited lieutenant's escapade in good humour. However, he had packed him off to British Honduras, as it then was, for form's sake and then allowed him to resume his upwards path. The nickname stuck and the Colonel married the young woman, much to the major's disgust. It was a happy if unfruitful marriage. The Colonel had been a widower since 1997.

Lunch was plain, wholesome and quickly over. The table conversation was revealing but unrelated to the business in hand. Ross Metcalfe disappeared for a few moments before they started to eat.

'Aberdeen Airport's closed; heavy snow. I've booked you a flight for tomorrow morning and called your office.'

'Ah, okay. Thanks. Is there a local hotel?'

'Better stay here,' said the Colonel.

'That's very kind... If it's no trouble?'

Ross's expression was one of genuine pleasure. She at least was happy with the turn of events. The social life around the Colonel was not the most exciting; an interesting male of her own sort of age around the place, albeit briefly, was a rarity to be relished.

'Delighted.'

And she clearly was. So too was the Colonel. He was well aware of the limitations of the company that he provided and any chance that Ross had to spend time with somebody younger and more active was welcome.

'Okay, let's get down to it.'

They were back in the Colonel's study. The atmosphere was relaxed and there was a sense of anticipation in Ross that John hadn't noticed before lunch. He wondered why.

'It started with two dead prostitutes – sad but not exceptional. Then two advertisements in *The Times* and two live girls at Heathrow.'

At the Colonel's request John began to repeat the sequence of events starting from when the duty officer at the intelligence service HQ picked up the Amsterdam and Hamburg Police reports. He was only interrupted by the Colonel to reconfirm details of fact; the older man offered no comments or opinions throughout the whole of John's narrative. Ross Metcalfe said nothing. She kept John within her gaze but gave no clues about what she might be thinking. In true intelligence service style the Colonel was checking John's story against what he had been told before lunch. It was soon apparent that he was satisfied with the coherence of the information he was being given.

'So both of these prostitutes were long dead before they were tossed into the water? And their deaths are presumably nothing to do with what's going on here? Calling cards – the means of getting attention?'

John nodded. The Colonel made a face; the deaths were a rather unpleasant way of attracting the notice of the authorities.

'Yes. Whoever's doing this wanted the bodies to be found and their clothing to be identified. Particularly the underwear it would seem.'

'Thirty years old, you say? GUMs, no...' The Colonel pondered before he came up with another Moscow department store. 'High quality, silk knickers, for the use of wives of senior party officials.'

'So it seems.'

'Could be any number of ex-Soviet officials around who used those shops.'

John gave more details of the messages in *The Times* and what the duty officer had found out about their origins.

'She reckoned that it was far too easy to work back to the import/export business and its links with Bulgaria.'

'Bulgaria, you say. A lot of old Soviet officials headed for Bulgaria as things began to crack up. It was a kind of halfway house to the West. Used to be Yugoslavia, but when that lot fell apart they needed another bolt hole.'

'Somewhere safe if things didn't work out in the West, eh sir?'

John was beginning to understand where the Colonel's mind was going. This was about somebody who had wanted to leave the old Soviet Union or more likely had already left it.

'Amsterdam, Hamburg, leading to London. So who wants to come to Britain?'

'And why?'

'Yes,' said the Colonel, 'and why?'

The rest of the details didn't take long to retell. The two young women picked up at Heathrow were not prostitutes; they were students – a day's work, €1,000 and keep the clothing. That was all that the police and customs could find out, bar the fact that they were recruited by a young woman, thought to be French, and an older man who never spoke throughout the whole time that the arrangements were being made. One of the girls, however, gave it as her opinion that the man was not French but Eastern European. 'Bullet-headed Slav,' she called him.

'Bullet-headed Slav,' repeated the Colonel.

'That's it?' said Ross, her only contribution to the debate for nearly an hour.

She was breaking a rather lengthy silence during which John and the Colonel were both reviewing the information imparted; John, to be sure he had given it all, and the

Colonel to be sure that he had ordered it in his mind before he began to try and analyse it.

'Let's break,' said Ross.

She knew how her partner worked. The Colonel would now cogitate. He was a man of sharp and incisive thought processes but he liked to take things steadily and in an ordered fashion. Ross discounted his assertions that his powers were fading with age; arthritis might have been claiming his body, but it certainly wasn't claiming his mind. Somewhere in what John Harcourt had presented to him was a pattern or common theme or something that would eventually trigger understanding in his brain.

'I need to pick up some data,' Ross continued, 'let's go.'

It was almost a command, and she marched out of the study, sweeping John along with her. The Colonel nodded; there was a faint smile edging into his lips that surprised Ross but she didn't stop to question its origins.

John scurried after Ross as she headed along the glass-sided corridor that linked the old farmhouse to the converted steading. This new part of the building was much larger than he had expected. As she turned along another corridor he was all too aware of the slender figure striding out in front of him, long legged with a fitted, sleeveless, A-line mini-dress that shimmered slightly in the artificial light. It crossed his mind that his rather elderly and nondescript suit must have made him seem rather staid and boring to her. But he hardly needed to worry; Ross had already got past the trappings to the man underneath and she found his open friendliness attractive.

'Welcome to my sanctum,' she said as he caught up with her, emphasising the ownership.

It was a room full of computers and other electronic wizardry. At least four monitor screens flickered various patterns as they went about their hidden and mysterious business. At least it was mysterious to John; he wasn't a computer ignoramus, but he knew his limitations and he was absolutely sure that what was going on in this room would be well beyond him.

Ross immediately set to work at one of the keyboards and clattered away until a printer started to disgorge a stream of paper. John watched; it was all he could do. Then a light flashed and an electronic bleeping sound intruded.

'That's the Colonel,' said Ross. 'He's solved your problem.'

Ross chuckled at John's surprise. It was a piece of the gadgetry that the Colonel so loved; it allowed him to contact Ross anywhere in the house.

They made their way back, walking side by side, and although that denied John the chance to enjoy the sight of her boldly moving figure again, it signalled a relaxation of her otherwise rigid self-control and augured well for the evening that they were about to spend together.

When they re-entered the Colonel's study, to their mutual amazement, they found that he was laughing and had been doing so for some time.

'Yuri Kirovsky,' he said. 'It has to be. Yuri Kirovsky!'

'So, who the hell's Yuri Kirovsky then?' demanded John, somewhat nonplussed by the Colonel's almost uncontrolled laughter.

Ross said nothing. She knew they would be enlightened and found John's harsh tone disconcerting.

'Yuri Ilyich Kirovsky; Colonel General of the Soviet Union; retired without pension sometime around May 1994 officially, but he quit the service sometime before that. He was one-time head of the KGB Western European operations. Inexplicably for someone like him, he was booted out for freelancing in the US when the USSR began to fall apart. Why they didn't eliminate him God knows. Be about my age.'

The Colonel paused both to allow John to digest the information and also to enjoy whatever the joke was.

'Okay, so some ex-KGB general is laying a trail. Why?'

It never occurred to John to doubt the Colonel's identification. His reputation as defined by Dandy Thomas was too powerful for that.

'Ah, I guess that's what he wants us to find out. In the way of these things he'll either want something from us, or much more likely in his case, have something to sell to us. The rumours on the street are that he's been making a fat living since the Russians threw him out by dealing in saleable information, legitimate or otherwise.'

'But how can you be so sure?' Ross asked. She was not as trusting as their visitor and she had her curiosity rather less well under control. And she couldn't see why the distasteful antics of this Russian were so amusing to the Colonel, who had one more chuckle and then picked up some scrawled notes from his lap.

'Obviously this has to be some highly placed Russian from way back. It has to be somebody with resources; there's evidence that Kirovsky has kept his networks together both in Europe and more importantly in America. And it has to be somebody who knows a hell of a lot about how the Western European police and intelligence systems work. He'd have to have known that all of the pieces of the trail would have been pulled together and how that would have been done. That says it has to be somebody very special from the KGB. And ... And it has to be somebody who understands the way our minds work. Someone who would know that the likes of me would get involved and who would know that such a whimsical yet sick approach would rivet our attention. There aren't many Russians like that.'

'But there must be several options,' persisted Ross.

'Two,' replied the Colonel. 'Kirovsky or a man called Vladinsky.'

'Picked out of a gutter in Munich last March,' said John.

'Exactly so. That leaves Kirovsky who is known to be active on both sides of the Atlantic, and who has the flair, the panache, the sense of the ridiculous, or whatever you'd like to call it, to do something like this.'

'But this is absurd. Why go to all this trouble? Why so tortuous? There have to be easier ways to make contact ... And who's he trying to contact anyway?' Ross still had a raft of questions demanding answers.

'Ross, this guy's spent his entire adult life submerged in an unreal world of subterfuge and counter-subterfuge. It's the only world he knows and no doubt feels comfortable in. This might seem complicated to you but to old Yuri it's kids' stuff. But I don't think that's your answer,' the Colonel continued. 'As I remember the old rogue he'll know what's real all right, and he'll know exactly how this little game is likely to go. I think this is about signature; something that will uniquely identify Kirovsky to people like me and something that will make us take him seriously. I can imagine why. After all the deception over the years, and his absence from view for the last decade or so, I reckon he's trying to re-establish his bona fides because, like I said, he's got something serious to sell and he wants something for it from us. He knows an open and direct approach would be distrusted, so he goes for the complex, the convoluted. And he succeeded didn't he. And,' he continued as an afterthought, 'I reckon it really is me he's trying to communicate with. This is like a trick one of his chums in Japan tried many years ago, and he'd know I'm about the only person on our side left who'd remember it.'

The Colonel held his hands up to call a halt to the discussion. As far as he was concerned they'd identified what the trail was about and who was laying it. They'd have to follow it to find out why; that was the next question. But what they should do he wasn't prepared to discuss until he'd given the next steps more thought. He said as much. He also added as yet another afterthought that he was sure that Kirovsky hadn't killed the prostitutes. That would have been a pointless killing and Kirovsky never killed pointlessly. And that was that for the day.

Ross and John spent a pleasant but carefully controlled evening together and then after an all too short night's sleep, prepared to renew their acquaintance over breakfast. They had both decided that the other was worth knowing better but were less than clear how they might further that aim. Of Yuri Kirovsky they thought nothing but that was not to say that he wasn't in other people's thoughts.

* * *

'So what do we do about ex-Comrade Kirovsky, then?'

The four, hard-faced, elderly men seated around the battered table exchanged glances before any of them ventured a response to the rather younger military man seated at its head.

Yuri Kirovsky was no friend of any of them, but he at least had their respect, and the vengeance that they had come together to plot would require long and careful planning. The young general, however, was not noted for his patience; his political ambitions were too potent for that, and in the emerging pseudo-democratic society of Russia in 2004 quick solutions were his priority.

'General,' said one of them, Stalinsky, the oldest, 'Kirovsky is a cunning old fox. And in the West he has more freedom than he ever had before.'

'Hear me,' said the general. 'I want Kirovsky dead and forgotten, and I want it within a month. If you want your KGB records dead and forgotten also, and your fat KGB pensions intact, we'd better see to it that it happens. Understand?'

They understood. They had good memories. Their experience reached back to too many KGB director generals, too many Communist general secretaries and too many maverick generals for them not to. And the present regime at heart wasn't so very different in their eyes.

'All I want is proof that it's been done.'

It was certainly a short meeting. Arrangements were made to meet again and they dragged their old bones away from the general's office. They had waited a long time for such a chance as this and there was anticipation, even relish. Comrade Kirovsky would not reap the benefit of his ill-gotten gains for much longer. At least that was what they told themselves; envy was a powerful motivator, especially if the grievances have festered unchecked for as many years as theirs had.

* * *

'Good morning!'

Ross was in a great mood. The Colonel breakfasted in his own room as he took time to get going in the morning, so company was rare for her. Very few people stayed overnight with them.

John was slower and hated too much exuberance in the early morning. Ross sensed this and was careful to be friendly but subdued. She, as always, had been doing some early morning data trawling or rather she was catching up on what her computers had been doing.

'Interesting little snippet. A KGB double agent no less, supposedly retired by his Moscow masters, but still very active apparently, was found frozen into some poor soul's swimming pool in Detroit a few days ago.'

'Active doing what?'

John didn't doubt that Ross would know. Even in the short time he had been at the farmhouse he had been impressed by the reach of her electronic intelligence gathering.

'Information peddling was his business, apparently. He was some sort of specialist in industrial espionage and the like. The CIA is in a bit of a panic.'

'Why?'

Ross was surprised again by the sharpness, harshness, almost violence of John's tone. It was something she had noticed in him the previous day.

'Just telling you what I know,' she said quietly.

'I'm sorry. I get carried away when something intrigues me.'

He was contrite. It was a bad habit. Unlike the Colonel he thought very quickly, and as a problem was presented to him he was inclined to demand information to feed his high-speed, analytical processes.

'It seems that they've picked up one or two others of his ilk. But worse still, they appear to have evidence that there were even more ex-KGB types still around that they were unaware of. They have a name, Spencer, but nothing else. There are seven hundred and sixty-one Spencers in Federal Service alone and thousands more around the country, so the name isn't too much use to them on its own. Except that whichever Spencer it is, they know he's young, certainly working with both sides, and was certainly recruited post the KGB, so whatever's going on is thriving despite the Cold War having long ended.'

If Ross thought that they had identified a link with Kirovsky she gave no indication of it. Deep in John's brain the tentative link formed itself unasked.

'The CIA lost their way several years ago; 9/11 probably proved that. It doesn't surprise me that they don't really know what's going on. Do they have anything at all on this Spencer?'

John Harcourt was confident that Ross would know more than she was telling him.

'Not a lot. Their best guess is that he's a diplomat. He's very bright and they're worried that it could be years before they can bring him to book with all the distractions they've got and the pressures on their resources.'

'What's new?' said John. 'D'you suppose he could be one of Kirovsky's men?'

The hidden thought popped out.

'That's jumping ahead a bit wouldn't you say?'

It was, but John and certainly the Colonel, knew that if what was beginning to emerge about this Kirovsky was even half true, almost anything was possible.

Further conversation was suspended by the arrival of the Colonel. It was somewhat before his usual hour of emergence but he was mindful of his duties as host. John was quick to notice the concern in Ross's eyes. The effort that he was making really meant something to her.

'Need to give some thought to a game plan,' the Colonel said as he got started on his second cup of coffee. 'Probably be worth a pot-boiling response but we shouldn't rush things. Guy like Kirovsky could easily be frightened off, even if he's sitting comfortably and safely where he is. And I'm sure he will be. Paris, the rumours have it. We have to know what he really wants and he isn't going to be rushing to tell us, that you can also be sure of. He'll check and double check, play games. There's a whole gamut of ploys for him to use before he'll be sure.'

'Yeah, okay.'

John wasn't quite so happy with this. His director had given him a week; at this rate that would be gone before they'd even decided how to react, let alone started doing anything.

The Colonel's apparent mind-reading capability was prominent again.

'I just spoke to your director in London.' There was a faint tinge of disapproval in the way he pronounced 'your director'. 'He's freed you up for as long as it takes. Seems there's been some sudden activity amongst the cousins and resurrecting elderly KGB links has become the vogue. Not sure what's going on yet, but I've no doubt that Ross will be able to brief me within the hour.'

'Within the minute if John didn't have a plane to catch.'

10

2026

The United Nations General Assembly didn't traditionally meet in April, but since its removal from New York to Munich in 2020 it had started a twice-yearly regime of plenary meetings to try and overcome the sense of disempowerment and irrelevance that had long since developed amongst many of the smaller and less committed nations. The non-attendance of the US at the sessions was noted but since it also meant the absence of its negative attitudes no one was too bothered.

The second decade of the twenty-first century had proved to be one of the most intense periods of international activity in the memory of most historians. The UN Security Council had continued to evolve almost despite the rivalries of the so-called great powers rather than because of them. It now had seven Permanent Members with a veto: the US, Russia, the EU, China, Brazil, India and Nigeria, plus two without: Japan and a second EU seat. The non-attendance of the US also meant that its ability to obstruct the UN's decisions was curtailed.

The establishment of the European Federation and the haggling over preserving the old British and French seats and vetoes had taken years but had finally resulted in the compromise that allowed Brazil, India and Nigeria, whose economic power could no longer be ignored, to take permanent seats. Both China's and Russia's internal democracy struggles had reduced their clout and modified their burgeoning economic capabilities; that had also encouraged the US and Europe to concentrate more on what divided them than on what united them.

The issues between the US and Europe were initially financial and commercial. It had been many years since the dollar had lost its primacy as the leading currency of the world. The basket of currencies comprising the yen, euro and rupee now determined world exchange rates. The withdrawal of European and Asian capital from America and the repatriation of a major portion of its investment in Europe had sent the US economy tumbling down the pecking order. After years of depending on imports the processes of readjustment were proving very painful and the level of discontent amongst the less well off in the United States was escalating.

Try as he might, the US President, like his immediate predecessor, could not persuade the Neoconservative majority in Congress and their religious right-wing mentors that they were building up trouble for themselves. The ever-present gap between rich and poor was now being reinforced by political doctrine and a form of class distinction entirely unknown in US history.

John Stuart, the UN Secretary General was a lanky, straight talking, occasionally pugnacious Australian who came to the UN with only one aim. His mission as he saw it was to create a world of stability and peace.

It wasn't going to be an easy task because bubbling below the surface was the fundamental split between the Neoconservative right that was driving thinking in the US and mainstream European thinking on the role of the state in social engineering.

For the rest of the world the growing confrontation between the US and Europe started out as great spectator sport but soon deteriorated into something far more sinister and disturbing.

In 2024, a Democrat President had been elected in the US. With the perennial ingratitude and inconsistency of the American electorate voters rejected the Republican incumbent accusing him of having fatally weakened the US as a world power. The electorate, however, with memories of previous Democrat incumbents, again hedged its bets and voted in a Republican majority in Congress, thereby neutralising the president and causing an increasing shift in power into the States at the expense of the Federal Administration.

With the success of the right wing Republicans, the bulk of the House of Representatives and the Senate majority were Neoconservatives.

Although it was going to strongly influence the work he was about to undertake, none of this was in John Harcourt's mind as he made his way to the Aberdeen hotel dining room for breakfast. Whatever his feelings about his impending meeting with Ross Metcalfe were, for better or worse he was back in harness and he had to meet with her, consult with her, and not let their past history interfere. His instinct was that it wasn't going to be easy. Restraint at the first meeting was the intention for both of them.

'John!'

Ross was aware that she had opened the door of the farmhouse too quickly and that she had come forward to greet her old lover too eagerly but she really didn't care. They were old friends, old colleagues and had shared a bed enough times to be able to treat each other just as they wished.

'Ross!'

She was as comfortable in his arms as she had always been. The embrace had been instant, instinctive and un-inhibited. They clasped each other tightly and breath-defyingly for several moments before coming up for air. Good intentions on both sides disappeared unnoticed. John's instinct on the difficulties of getting back to working together was immediately proving wrong.

'How are you?'

They both laughed at the question in unison, but neither of them answered. The first moment had passed and whatever anxieties their hidden minds had had, they had proved groundless. As Ross backed into the hall and John followed her into the bowels of the farmhouse, familiarity was automatic. They immediately shrugged off twenty-two years. No baggage from those years was in evidence. It was a surprise to both of them.

They knew that in quiet moments when their business was done or suspended, the past would have to be dealt with; equally, they both felt instinctively that it wasn't going to be a major problem for them. Ross in particular knew that the feelings that held her back in 2004 had been dramatically changed during the years of separation. The pain of that fateful day at Gatwick would never completely go away but as she felt John's contact with her both physically and emotionally she at least felt that closure had started. She knew that there would be doubts over time but as always she would address these when she came to them.

As they spent time together, the surprise at the ease of their first meeting turned to wonder for John as he slowly began to understand the extent of Ross's hurt in 2004 and the immense expenditure of emotional energy that she had made in dealing with this hurt. If it hadn't completely gone away it was never going to come between them again.

'Let's go into the Colonel's study.'

John's raised eyebrow produced an almost girlish giggle.

'Not everything has changed,' she said simply, 'and I never really saw the point of trying to call it anything else.'

Not a lot had changed at all. The room was furnished with more modern armchairs but the chaise longue remained a prominent feature, as did the Colonel's antique desk. The electronic gadgetry had been updated and a plasma screen television had replaced the reproduction Gainsborough over the fireplace that John only remembered now by its absence. Somewhat to John's surprise there was no evidence of a computer in the room.

'Oh, I still have my den at the back,' Ross said, instantly reading John's thoughts. 'We'll go there later.'

The helping of whisky was as generous as the Colonel might have offered. The careful positioning of herself on the chaise longue opposite John was practical and uncontrived but both of them were aware that it was a conscious gesture.

Before seating herself, Ross had cleared away some loose electronic gadgetry from the seat.

'There was a BBC podcast,' she remarked, using her activity before John had arrived as a link to open the discussions. 'There was a bit of a riot outside the US London Embassy. It was about fishing rights or something. Plenty of noise, a bit of shooting, police charges, the usual stuff, but...'

Ross tugged at her skirt, a gesture John remembered fondly; although this time the fine, Indian, worsted plaid was more than adequate to cover her knees and her legs down to the calf. She shuffled her legs across each other and flexed her ankles in her comfortable-looking Granny boots. Something in John's lower regions surged briefly.

'But?' he said hurriedly.

'When the dust settled the police found the body of a middle-aged American diplomat who they claim had been executed under cover of the riot.'

'What?'

Ross remembered the sharpness of John's tone when confronted with the unexpected. But she was surprised to find now that, although the underlying images of the violence of John's reaction to the events in 2004 at Gatwick returned momentarily, almost as a reflex, a sense of detachment accompanied them as if she weren't involved. It was closure in practice she told herself.

All he had expressed was surprise at an unexpected death, she told herself. So he still reacts quickly?

The man sitting opposite her, busy with his own thoughts, didn't seem to notice the pause or the mixture of expressions that flashed across Ross's face.

'Apparently he was an SIE mole in the State Department. And...'

Another abortive tug at the skirt and a half turn to profile as she took a drink distracted John to her tight and still well-honed figure.

She still uses the gym, he thought. Concentrate!

'And?'

'And,' she said, 'the dead man was called Spencer. My archive matching tool threw up a Spencer who it turns out was one of our old friend Yuri Kirovsky's doubles recruited after the demise of the KGB and buried deep in the US establishment as a source for tradable information. There's a link with the past.'

'Indeed,' said John thoughtfully.

Not sure how to interpret John's non-committal response Ross instead outlined her thoughts on the arrangements for the day.

'Okay, we'll have some lunch. You can meet some of my people and hopefully by then we'll be ready to talk about why you're here.'

'Sounds good to me.'

'Then we'll have some dinner...' She left the sentence hanging.

'Now that sounds even better still to me.'

Since he had a walk-on flight ticket, John had no concerns about when or what time he had to leave and so had enough freedom to stay as long as the job, not to mention his own preferences, required it.

'So, Spencer?' said John. He sensed that Spencer's death was important although he wasn't clear in his mind why yet.

Ross continued her briefing.

'The SIE traffic was a bit hectic earlier in the week when they realised that Spencer would be in London at the same time as the demonstration. It was a text-book hit: obvious to the police in London and your lot. The SIE tried to feed a suspect to the police but they didn't buy that.' That was all Ross thought appropriate to say about the incident. It was only peripheral to what she believed that John and the British Regional Intelligence Service were interested in and what she expected to be asked to do for them. But it was another piece in the jigsaw.

The ease with which they had resumed their business relationship didn't immediately strike John. Ross had so readily resumed reporting the information that her computer systems were providing that it was only later that he realised that twenty-two years on her skills were even greater than before.

John knew that no computer system had ever been entirely proof against Ross's skills and time had not changed that. That the SIE systems were no safer from her than the old CIA ones had been didn't surprise him. This skill was of course what John had been counting on. As had his director, who had done enough homework to be aware that both John's and Ross's contacts with the old Kirovsky organisation had been deep enough for them to have a good insight into the state of its current undercover activities in the US. That Intercontinental Veterans Anonymous still existed and was active was taken as a fact by both the director and John.

The information that Ross gave him proved that her help on his project was going to be as invaluable as ever and confirmed that the organisation that Kirovsky had set up all those years ago really was still largely intact and still absorbing a significant amount of resources from various US agencies to combat and attempt to neutralise it. That there was an immediate link to action in the present, the death of Spencer, albeit a rather negative one, was enough for John to know that his chances of understanding what was going on in the US intelligence services and with the Neoconservatives were better than he had been expecting.

* * *

'This is Alanda Ngozie.'

John almost gasped. He had never seen such a beautiful girl. Even the famed Somali models didn't match her finely drawn and exquisitely chiselled features.

The farmhouse had been extended beyond the old converted steading and now included a single-storey office block housing the five members of Ross's staff. John already knew that she had carried on with, and had expanded, the Colonel's business and that she had contracts with a much wider range of both governmental and commercial organisations than the Colonel had chosen to deal with.

With the exception of a representative who worked in Brussels the entire organisation was female. By 2026, as John was well aware, the cream of the production from the education system was evenly balanced between male and female, a change from the earlier years of the previous decade when the female element of European society seemed to be outperforming the male at every turn. However, Ross had found from experience that women had a multi-skilling capability that fitted her needs better than the single-mindedness of the best male computer brains.

'Alanda specialises in implantation and mimicking.'

Neither Ross nor the grinning young Nigerian thought to explain what these terms meant and John was sufficiently intimidated not to ask. In any case, he was only interested in outcomes not the processes of achieving them.

The rest of the team weren't as personable as Alanda but they represented a formidable concentration of brain power that impressed and also rather frightened John.

Back in the Colonel's study, Ross sat at the magnificent Regency desk and turned sideways to John to study him as he toured the room rather restlessly before himself sitting on the chaise longue.

Doesn't seem anything like sixty-seven, she thought as she watched his slightly tense movement around the room. Not a lot of hair, and grey with it, but he still looks pretty tough. And he dresses better. But then he always was better at casual clothes.

A vision of John with no clothes leapt into her mind and out again before she could even grin. Pays a bit more for his gear, I'd say; wears it now rather than having it on his body.

Back to business!

'The email I got from your director said that he'd called you back to the colours because you were one of the few people left with any sort of detailed knowledge of the US intelligence services and how they had mutated since the formation of the SIE. But he also said that with the way things were going with the US, even your great knowledge wasn't going to be enough and his lot needed to be able to access more up-to-date and on-going information, on the more obvious operations, but also on the factions and infighting that was going on within the SIE.'

Ross gave a little pant and a grin to acknowledge the length of her speech and the mischievous paraphrasing on some of the director's words.

'That's about it, I guess.'

'But?'

'But, Ross, as always, life isn't as simple as it seems. There's a huge amount of concern about the Neoconservatives and their influence within the corridors of power. So, it's not just what the SIE is doing, or the politicians in and around US Government, it's also about what the religious right at the extremes is doing, thinking, planning, etc.'

'Jesus,' said Ross with a sudden explosion of giggles worthy of her persona of twenty-two years ago, 'Kirovsky fighting the God people. How he would have loved that!'

John's smile was more restrained, almost fastidious. His vision was more of the Colonel who would have found the modern day intelligence work a mite dirty by his standards.

'Okay, let's talk details and then I'll get back to you with a proposal of what I think I'll be able to do. Your director has asked that this have the highest security level and he also reminded me of the subsidy I get from Treasury funds and the obligations that that carries.'

'Cheeky sod! That's him all over.'

'I'll get Alanda in.'

By the time they'd finished John was feeling his sixty-seven years.

'I booked a table at the Power Station; it's a bistro in Peterhead.' Ross assumed that John would be happy to eat out. She knew he enjoyed his food as did she and the catering arrangements at the farmhouse had changed considerably from the home-cooking days of the Colonel. The Power Station was an organic restaurant which took environmental credits as well as carbon ones and since the farmhouse, despite its considerable energy usage, was totally self-contained on wind-powered generation and was a gold-star, totally recycling site, Ross always had a ready supply of credits.

John, almost out of habit, settled for fish followed by a steak. Ross opted for fish and fish.

'You should try the Fifeshire Red with your steak,' Ross said with a knowing grin.

Climate change had some benefits according to Ross's view of the world and the wine now beginning to be produced in Scotland was one of them. Whilst no connoisseur, John liked his wine and the red was a success.

Since neither were particularly good at small talk and saw very little point in it, Ross took the lead as the waitress finished serving the main courses.

'So how's it been, John? The Colonel and I followed your career from afar and vicariously through the data-trawling programmes. I'm amazed you look so well considering the pace you seem to have been living at.'

If she hadn't known, Ross would not have put John at his current age any more than he would have fixed her at fifty-two. And she thought he had rather more gravitas than he would have been prepared to admit to. And she had to admit to herself as they had worked through the day, that his tendency to overreact to anything unforeseen was largely under control. Except that Ross did still sometimes detect the trait.

'So what happened to the business when you retired?'

John's business had been his cover for decades. His legitimate financial activities had made him very wealthy and after having paid back his original stake he continued to pay a useful dividend to the Treasury. The arrangement was one of Whitehall's best kept secrets.

'I formed it into a trust for the people who work there. I got a long-term contract from HMG so it should survive for as long as they want it to.'

'You're a good man, John.'

A softness crept into Ross's voice that John noticed immediately. Any remaining tension in their renewed friendship melted away. They both felt it. There was now a comfortable, calm and undemanding feeling about the evening and about their relationship that pleased them both. And there was understanding, sensitivity and recognition that the white hot passions of the past weren't going to be rekindled, but the closeness, support and affection most certainly were going to be re-established.

The meal, like the red wine, was a success. The return to the farmhouse, the nightcaps and reminiscences, and the quiet disposal of any baggage of their previous parting were all worked off with amiability and humour. Ross was glad that they had got it all out into the open. John was sad to find that his worst fears about why their relationship had foundered were true, but it was twenty-two years ago and although it was hard to accept the hurt that he had caused had produced such a rupture, it was equally hard to accept that it had been so easily reconciled. But it had. Deep down in his brain this made John feel both foolish and remorseful.

'The past's the past,' Ross said; it was in neither of their natures to dwell on it.

'Yes, but I fear that what we are being asked to get into is very much about stirring up the past. The legacy or whatever we want to call it of past Russian machinations is still of use to us, even if it turns out to be more a Pandora's box, and it's our job to make this past work for us.'

'That's for another day, John. Tomorrow we'll pull together all we've got and what Alanda will have picked up since we talked. Then we'll have a better idea of the shape of the organisation that dear old Yuri left and what it means for us now rather than in 2004. And you'll be in time for the mid-afternoon flight to London.'

11

2004

'Good to see you back, John!'

John was instantly on alert. He'd only been away a couple of days and the director had already exceeded his annual average of conversations with him. And it was only the third week in January. Something had clearly changed since they had last spoken and the brief conversation with the director that the Colonel had reported didn't tell him much.

'How'd the trip go?'

'It went very well. The Colonel reckons it's some geriatric ex-KGB general. Yuri Kirovsky. Apparently, he was freelancing on the Soviets before the KGB collapsed and they cut him off.'

The director had by now done some homework on the ways of the old KGB so he had immediately picked up on the astonishing fact that the Russians had seemingly just fired Kirovsky, let him go and no questions asked. For someone as intimately knowledgeable about their internal affairs as the old general was, such a mild response was deeply suspicious. He said as much.

'Colonel's view is Kirovsky had been preparing his exit for years and was virtually fireproof before he faded into obscurity.'

It wasn't a point that had been discussed at any great length and John was reporting his surmise of what the Colonel had thought. He'd noticed that the old man rarely speculated and had already said that the past didn't matter unless it informed the future. In this case it did inform, but not on why the old Soviets had simply let Kirovsky out of their control without taking any action. But then, the Colonel was really only interested in what the Russian wanted now, and what he was likely to do next.

The director didn't want to let the point go. Unlike his earlier interview with John he was now much more interested in ancient Soviet rainbows. Somehow they seemed to link to other more immediate issues that he was being confronted with. And like John he'd seen the report on the death in Munich of Vladimir Vladinsky. That had awakened several rather devious lines of thought in his mind. He wanted to explore these first.

'Got long memories, these guys,' he said. 'D'you suppose it's a set up? Kirovsky could have been planted in the West.'

'It's certainly a possibility. But until we get close to him we aren't going to know. And even then it'll take time to be sure he's doing a loner.'

That was a point that he had certainly discussed with the Colonel and Ross Metcalfe.

'The Colonel's going to do some research for us on Kirovsky and his contacts: where his friends, enemies and masters from the past have disappeared to, etc. He's going to let me know.'

'Well let's hope he doesn't end up like Vladinsky the moment he shows himself,' said the director.

'That's his risk. But he's been living with it for years now. If the old KGB were into score-settling they'd certainly wait for the dust to settle. However, it's over a decade since Kirovsky was booted out. That's a fairly long time even by their standards.'

John was aware that Vladinsky had been as powerful in his way as Kirovsky, but unless the Colonel was able to tell him otherwise, there was no evidence that he'd been active since he had moved to Germany. Kirovsky, on the other hand, was very active and he was a much more likely candidate for a revenge killing.

'Perhaps Vladinsky was a warning. Kirovsky would be bound to know about it; it was a very public killing and the media worried it to death,' he said.

The director was non-committal. Kirovsky wasn't his prime interest at the moment and he felt that he'd got all he needed out of the conversation. He'd just wanted to be briefed and to be aware of any links to his other problems. It was on these that he wanted John Harcourt to concentrate.

'Have you heard about this guy found dead in the States?'

'Frozen into a swimming pool in Detroit,' said John rather absently. The recollection of the conversation with Ross Metcalfe came flooding back into his mind. However, the images were not of faceless CIA agents but of that lively and stimulating young lady herself. John was surprised by his own adrenaline's reaction. He knew that he was to see her the next day, but he had a sudden desire for the next day to come quickly.

'Ah, so you know about that?'

'Oh, yes,' said John. The effort required to drag himself back to the business in hand was more than he had expected. It was a while since he had been sexually aroused by a woman and the feeling was still something of a novelty to him.

'The Colonel's partner,' he continued, deliberately trying to relegate the picture of her to the back of his mind, 'picked up the details on an information scan. She's researching it. Got a session with her tomorrow. I'll get updated then.'

The director nodded. He didn't know much more but he shared what he did. The most surprising bit of information to John was the fact that the director suspected the CIA themselves had killed their own man.

'Okay, John, this one's yours. Take all the time you need. We have to know what the CIA are up to, cousins or not, and what support, if any, they're getting from their political masters.' He had obviously then decided to say more. 'We know the dead bloke in Detroit was ex-KGB, a double presumably. We also know he was still active, despite the KGB being dead and gone for years. And he's unknown to the present Russian Security Service. You tell me this Kirovsky has been running agents ever since he was kicked out of the KGB. Okay, so what's missing here? Is there a link? And what's the CIA up to with this geriatric general, as you called him? My gut feeling says this is a bit more than just a bout of ritual CIA cleansing because a guy went astray.'

John wasn't so sure. This sort of thing had happened before. But the director signalled that the conversation was over with a nod.

'Okay, let me know how you get on. And remember, it's what the CIA is up to I'm interested in. If pursuing Kirovsky takes you away from that, forget him, stay with the CIA.'

'Right.'

Back in his office, John quickly reviewed the conversation. The key point for him was that the director had played back the information about the Detroit death with identical details to those he'd already had from Ross. That was the sort of verification he liked; he felt pleased. And this was also the sort of assignment he liked and he'd been recruited for. He had a free hand and his company gave him the cover to get about in Europe and even America to pursue things with reasonable ease. He wasn't quite sure what he'd got himself into yet but at least he'd get to be working with Ross Metcalfe. What more could he want?

Ross Metcalfe herself was looking forward to her meeting with John with every bit as much expectation as he was. The Colonel was far from convinced that she needed to go down to London to impart the information that she'd gathered, but he was a tolerant man as far as Ross was concerned, and he had sensed that she was attracted to this John Harcourt almost as quickly as she had recognised it herself.

John had gone rather unnecessarily to the St Pancras, Heathrow Terminus to meet her. He'd recognised her first by her walk as she strode boldly up the platform. She was wearing one of the long, ankle-length greatcoats that were the fashion at the moment and it billowed out as she marched up to him. He was glad that he'd been more careful with his own dressing than he was usually inclined to be. His suit and overcoat were definitely more recent than the comfortable if ancient apparel that he liked to travel in, and which he had worn when they had last met. His shoes, as Ross was quick to notice, were tasteful, discreet and very expensive.

With the crowds of people about, they didn't say much during their short wait for a taxi. Ross was quick to observe that John gave his instructions to the driver after she had entered the cab so she had no idea where they were heading. They were, in fact, heading for the offices of John Harcourt Associates, Commodity Traders. Halfway up what in the 1970s and 1980s had been the headquarters of British Petroleum, John Harcourt had a suite of offices and a mass of electronic gadgetry to match Ross's own, but about which he himself was largely ignorant. His staff of ten made the money and John, who showed his face rarely, took only a small portion of the profits. In his organisation profit-sharing was real and very rewarding for everybody, including the Treasury.

'There's more to you than I thought,' Ross said as she saw the company nameplate and was shown into John's spacious corner office.

He hadn't quite explained all about himself over dinner at the Colonel's farmhouse; people in his business didn't and people in the Colonel's didn't ask.

'Okay, so what have you got?' On his own ground John was more forceful. Ross liked that; it was what she would have expected.

'Vladinsky,' she said. 'He was dying of cancer. The people who paid the thugs to kill him hadn't done their homework. He'd barely three months to live. He skipped out of the KGB in return for treatment in a German sanatorium. He stayed alive about six or seven years longer than he would have done if he had been treated in Moscow according to the German doctors. But the information he brought had a sell-by date and the Germans kept him on a lead after his cancer was thought to be in remission. It wasn't.'

'Poor bastard,' muttered John. 'I reckon he might have been killed as a warning to Kirovsky.'

'Something like that.'

Ross got up and went over to the computer terminal that sat on John's desk. He watched as she did so. Somewhere inside him he was disappointed. She was no longer exotic. Her calf-length skirt was sensible for the weather and her cashmere jumper was loose fitting and not revealing. But even so, he felt that his Jermyn Street shirt and Church shoes had somehow still been upstaged by the plain ordinariness of her clothes.

'May I?' she asked.

'Help yourself.'

She did and the computer screen came alive as her fingers flitted across the keyboard and an array of screens flashed into and out of her vision. John was impressed all over again. He should have been; she had one of the best computer science degrees ever to hide behind a Cambridge BA. And her efforts on John's machine, as signified by the little grunts that she gave, were as successful as her academic career.

Christened Rosslyn, she had been orphaned in her early teens in circumstances known to the Colonel but never quite explained to her or her brother. Her parents had been killed in a car crash in Germany. The Colonel never referred to it as a car accident, which she found odd, but which she nonetheless never challenged. Her father had been a colleague of the Colonel's and he made it his business to see that the two of them were supported into adulthood. Ross and her brother were grateful and never questioned the assiduity with which the Colonel and his wife cared for them.

It didn't take Ross long to catch up with what her surveillance systems had been reporting during the short space of her journey to London. Even as she left college in 1995, with significant skills but no experience, had it then been possible, linking with her home computer would not have been much of a problem to her. With the sort of technology and experience that she now had, hooking into anybody else's computers anywhere in the world was not much trouble to her either, and that in simple terms, as John knew, was what she did for a living.

University had been a mixed feast for Ross. With only surrogate and rather remote 'parental' influences, her emotional immaturity had led her into an unsatisfactory relationship without the benefit of either guidance or hands-on support when disappointment came. It had started with all the fervour and intensity that two nineteen-year-olds could put into such a relationship and Ross was fully committed. But her boyfriend was not. He was happy to have Ross as his party-going companion, forever on his arm. She was pretty and vivacious, but he liked to play the field. It was when she discovered that he was dating another girl that she responded to the flirtations of another fellow student, although not to the extent of a one-to-one date. Her boyfriend was furious and when the supposed rival, who shared a tutor with Ross, arranged for his tutorials to align with hers, he attacked him with such ferocity that he ended up in hospital. Ross was confused and appalled at the violence and uncomprehending of the idea that she was tied exclusively to this man while he was free to indulge in whatever sexual adventures he liked. All she wanted to do was get away from Cambridge.

The experience left her wary of entanglements with men and undermined her growing confidence in herself. However, the Colonel was not wholly insensitive to her problems. Having gained her degree and after letting her find her way in London and then Edinburgh to prove her worth to herself, he offered her a job in his consultancy. What she had achieved for the Colonel was the development of one of the most sophisticated and complex computer-based surveillance systems in the world. Provided that it was linked to a telephone, satellite system or a computer network, there was virtually no electronic communication she couldn't access. It was just as the Colonel had said when he introduced her at the farmhouse; she was the organisation's eyes and ears.

Having updated herself from John's computer Ross reported her research into Yuri Kirovsky and his background, as far as she could discover it. It was not a lot.

Ross, but not the Colonel, was surprised by how successfully Kirovsky had faded into the landscape, while still apparently living openly in Paris. The French authorities were well aware of their visitor but since Kirovsky was very careful to never commit any crimes in France and to behave as a good citizen, there was nothing they could do beyond keeping a regular watch on him.

'They know the old fox is up to something,' said Ross, 'but the import/export company is legit, even if it won't declare its directors. This is one very clever and devious guy.'

There was a little more and John stored it in his memory banks without much analysis. He would get back to it later.

A picture of Kirovsky was emerging, but it added nothing to his knowledge of the CIA.

'Hell, Ross, it's three o'clock. We'd better break and get something to eat.'

With swift and effortless keystrokes she put John's computer into safe mode.

'I'm starving and so must you be,' he said by way of reinforcement.

12

2026

Back home in West Bexington John pondered his trip to Scotland. He felt a quiet glow when he thought about Ross but didn't dwell on the renewed relationship. He knew that it would have to mature at its own rate, and with the distance, and the difficulty of justifying face-to-face meetings, it was going to be a slow process for them. Ross, however, was nowhere in his thoughts as he pulled the pages of his favourite Sunday newspaper across his computer screen in the mild quiet of a slow Sunday morning. And then she was in his face.

As the Internet telephone link activated and the top right-hand corner of his screen became a cheerful and grinning Ross, his first reaction was irritation.

'Sorry if I interrupted your Sunday morning,' she said, the power of the grin quelling his annoyance at being forced from his perusal of the antics of a backbench MP who had managed to get caught both with his pants literally down and his hand in his constituency till.

'How are you?'

'Fine. It was wonderful to see you. I really missed you when you'd gone.'

It was a statement of fact offered in Ross's even and unemotional tones. John, however, was quick to detect the warmth that crept through the words into a faint sigh at the end.

'I thought you'd better see this, John.'

Almost instantly John's screen dissolved into a telephone conversation transcript.

'Good God, Ross. This is one of the US Ambassador to Europe's private telephone conversations.' Of course he knew that she was capable of accessing almost anything computer-based but when she actually did so he was always still surprised. 'So what's all this about?'

'Read,' she said.

He read. The conversation had taken over half an hour. It took John almost an hour to read over the words of the transcript and digest them.

'Wowee,' he said as the transcript came to an end. 'I'm amazed that they should be so arrogant as to talk like this on the phone. Surely they know phone hacking is easy and commonplace?'

'Arrogant sounds like a rather prissy word for a bastard like Fitzallan.'

'Well, okay. Yes.'

'Oh, come on, John. The guy's a shit. You know that; I know that; so let's call him one!'

'Yeah, okay.' He wasn't listening anymore; his brain was racing on. What he had just seen was a cameo of the SIE and what it was about, but it didn't actually tell him anything that would stand up in court.

'Fine,' he finally said, sounding a bit like the director. 'So the SIE has its own agenda. Not everybody in the organisation buys into it. So, not everybody in any organisation buys into every bit of corporate policy.'

'No, John, but no organisation that I'm aware of deals with the opponents of corporate policy by shooting them. Nor do agencies of the State like the SIE usually try to undermine the elected government of the day. Not in a supposed democracy they don't.'

'Fitzallan didn't quite say that.'

'He sure as hell meant that. It was plain incitement. The guy was urging the SIE to obey only the orders that fitted its game plan – whatever that is – until the likes of him could get into positions of more authority. Isn't that incitement?'

The debate lasted for nearly another hour as they ranged over what had been said and what had been meant. It was vigorous and at times intense but friendly. And John rediscovered that talking things over with Ross could be extremely challenging.

13

2004

The police knew from the frenetic way that the car was being driven that it was either being piloted by someone in deep stress or a foreigner.

'What's the matter with the guy? Doesn't he even know he's being followed?'

The casual half-Dutch, half-English language of the Amsterdam Police was a source of amusement to their countrymen, but it hid a professionalism that was well-respected by the law enforcement communities of Europe.

'Huh!' the passenger policeman responded to the rapid information message from headquarters. 'An American?'

The elderly Renault being driven by this American had started its journey in one of the more sleazy side-streets of the red-light district. He had rushed out of a bar dragging a young woman by the shoulders. The awkward and wooden way in which the girl had moved attracted the attention of an undercover policewoman who managed to get a quick message to her office. Two cars responded as the Renault squirmed its way out into the Damrak and took the tortuous route to the Rijksmuseum.

'Ahh!' the curse was pure Dutch as, taken by surprise, the helpless policemen watched the American suddenly swerve across the traffic and race into an instantly vacated parking space beside the Van Gogh Museum. By the time that they had extricated themselves from the seething mass of traffic and returned they only had the tattered Renault with which to console themselves. But their colleagues had had better luck.

'He's on foot heading off Willemsparkweg.'

The non-driving policeman in the second car was out and chasing the fleeing figures. Hampered by the woman's seeming inability to use her arms, the American was supporting her as they ran. Obscured by the side of the entrance porch the policeman didn't see what happened but he heard well enough. Panting from his run he poured the details of the action into his lapel microphone.

The door of the house was open, the American's keys still jingling in the lock. The American lay across the threshold, minus a large part of the back of his head. A mess of blood and bone trickled onto the doormat.

Futilely, the officer looked at the buildings opposite. They weren't going to tell him anything. If anybody could add to the sum of his knowledge it was going to be the woman crouched on the step beside him issuing strangled whimpers as she stared in mesmerised horror at the remains of her late companion.

* * *

'Another CIA mole killed.'

The news, wrapped up in various formats, rattled around the police and intelligence communities of Europe and America.

Ross Metcalfe's report to the Colonel was as blunt and to the point as ever. The details that were emerging were both gruesome and revealing.

'The CIA wanted to take over but the Dutch Police were having none of that.'

'Reckon this is another one of Kirovsky's, Ross?'

The atmosphere in the Colonel's study was companionable. The doleful tones of some obscure plainsong chant filled the background and the electronic gadgetry occasionally clicked and purred, the incongruity lost on Ross, if not the Colonel. The details of the new shooting were raw and unanalysed but in the warmth and peace of the surroundings both were already formulating their thoughts.

It was almost two weeks since Ross had met with John Harcourt in London and in those two weeks much more had been researched and the Colonel for one was much clearer on what was going on.

'This guy was a real charmer,' said Ross. 'Might even have been the source of Kirovsky's first dead body.'

'What?' Even the Colonel, cautious and analytical as he usually was, was not entirely immune to curiosity.

'Shot on the doorstep of a CIA safe house from the building opposite. Even the Amsterdam Police didn't know it was a safe house till the local CIA man told them. Bit of friction here, the local chap is a bit old school, not a favourite in Washington, but reliable.'

'So why was he heading for the safe house?'

'It seems our late and unlamented friend has, *had*,' she corrected, 'some pretty nasty habits. The local politzei seem to reckon the girl in the canal died when he was beating her up. She was a friend of the girl with him apparently, who incidentally was handcuffed for reasons not explained in the report. There was a lot of sex stuff in the house that maybe even the CIA wouldn't have approved of. Lives in Antwerp. Filthy wretch using the safe house in Amsterdam to avoid detection, I'd reckon?'

'There's no way the CIA wouldn't know about his propensities,' said the Colonel.

'Guess not, but who was using the leverage?'

'Both I'd say. Kirovsky wouldn't scruple if he had to.'

Ross wasn't inclined to disagree with the Colonel's minimal opinion of Kirovsky. The picture that she was building up of the Russian was not a very savoury one. She noted that both were assuming that the man was in fact one of Kirovsky's CIA moles.

'So,' she said, 'no reason why Kirovsky should kill him.'

'And plenty why the CIA might have. Guess we'll probably never know. Bit verminous, but ... horrible way to die.'

The Colonel hated loss of life. It was something that happened more frequently in his profession than in most but it was still a waste to him.

'Think there's any chance of the scent still being warm in Antwerp?' asked Ross.

'Maybe.'

The discovery of the CIA safe house in Amsterdam was not popular with the Dutch authorities. They knew well enough that the CIA were about (the head of station made sure of that), but there was a clear suspicion that even he hadn't known about this place until the killing had occurred. There were, however, plenty of reasons why the CIA would want a safe house in Amsterdam.

The Amsterdam Police Commissioner now had to explain two mysterious deaths, both with seeming intelligence overtones and in the case of the latter, evidence of CIA internal politics. Relations were never especially good with the CIA; aggravation he did not need. He called in the investigating officer to shed some light on the situation.

'So what the hell's going on?'

'Not sure. Looks like the CIA squabbling amongst themselves.'

It was an easy, glib answer. It was based on elements of truth, but was also a very convenient answer that didn't call for the inspector to make more investigative effort. That suited her, but she was not happy about the whole situation. Her discomfort, however, was for rather different reasons from the commissioner's. She knew rather more about the dead American than she had reported. Several prostitutes on her patch had alerted her to him but she had done nothing. Doing nothing had helped her bank balance, which was partly why she was uncomfortable, but it was the service yet to be called for that really bothered her.

'Better talk to the vice team, and try that Brit who just joined us; they must still know a lot about the Americans.'

The commissioner's irritation was going to make the inspector's life a misery for the foreseeable future and living with her conscience wasn't going to be that easy either. She headed back to her own office.

With a growing addiction to Internet gambling the inspector was always short of funds but with Amsterdam's red light district within her area of responsibility a variety of opportunities to enhance her income was inevitable. The offer of the hard-eyed Russian seemed innocuous enough. All he wanted was information, at least to start with. Experience told her it wouldn't stay like that. The death of his obnoxious friend was information.

'You'd better pass on what's happened,' she advised herself.

She left her office and made her phone call from a noisy canal bridge. Her contact's answering machine whined its impersonal message into her ear and she almost forgot what she was going to say. Back in her office again she tried to concentrate on the myriad of investigations that she had in hand.

'At least the old fool knows now,' she muttered.

* * *

'Anything to report?'

The director was positively living in John's office. For a man who declared himself a delegator, who trusted his subordinates to get the job done without undue interference or reporting back, he was manifestly not practising what he preached.

'For my money,' the director said, 'the cousins and Kirovsky are in this together; where one is we'll find the other.'

'So what the hell does that mean?'

John wasn't surprised not to get an answer.

14

2004

The street cafés hibernate in the winter. Great glass-panel shutters insulate customers from the sounds and smells of passing traffic and humanity. Marginal improvements to lung conditions are offset by comfort drinking and even less exercise to already out-of-condition bodies.

In Antwerp, as elsewhere, the café clientele concentrate on themselves and only the waiters and bar staff have any communication outside the individual table islands of beer consumption and garbled noise. It's every bit as intense as anywhere in France but the atmosphere is subtly detached and less neighbour-friendly in Belgium. Yuri Kirovsky liked it like that.

'Bier,' he said as he sat at a vacant table in the window.

He had time to spare; he always did have when he was out on the job. He never hurried, never took any course of action without thinking it through, testing the angles, the options, the possibilities.

'Stella? Amstel?' The waiter offered and Kirovsky chose.

Bier, beer – like the word – it was all the same to him. Compared to the hideous Russian brews of his youth, anything in the West was the nectar of the gods as far as he was concerned. Not that he had any gods.

'Thank you.'

He was so used to thinking in English that he often used it unconsciously. In Paris, where he lived, that would more often than not have been greeted with some gesture of contempt; in Belgium it barely attracted notice.

'Twenty minutes,' he told himself. He had a meeting with one of his agents from the Jewish quarter. Walking, with all the checks and rechecks to be sure that he had no company, it would take the man twenty minutes to reach the café. He had that time to wait, plus the ten minutes' contingency time.

Yuri Kirovsky was good at waiting. He had spent so much of his early service with the Russian military in places where time was on a different basis from that of the West. And one of the things that had distinguished him amongst his youthful peers was his adoption of this Western/American approach to time. If he was good at waiting he never wasted his time.

'Bier?'

The waiter offered a refill and Kirovsky consulted his Rolex. He also liked Western timepieces. How much he drank and his ready access to a suitable toilet were increasing considerations to him. Coy about how old he was, and seventy was beginning to become a memory, he knew he was too old for active service, but for some tasks who could he trust but himself?

'Thank you.'

He was halfway through his vigil and the toilet was easily accessible if he needed it.

'Bernsty, get your arse over here on time,' he muttered as be pushed his face into the foam of the broad, bowl glass of beer. It reminded him of Canberra. He'd enjoyed Canberra. Only an idiot wouldn't enjoy living in Australia. And Yuri Kirovsky was no idiot.

He was born in 1933. His parents had been collectivised on their own land. In 1951 he'd been forced into the army to ease the family living costs. He was a natural for the military. He was also, to the infinite disappointment of his father, a conviction Communist. He advanced rapidly and was soon recruited into the KGB as a potential highflyer. Focused only on his own wellbeing, the young Kirovsky had no problems with divided loyalties.

'Come on Bernsty, you got seven minutes.'

Lieutenant Colonel Kirovsky was trusted by his masters. He was also a good military attaché-cum-spy in Lagos, Hanoi and Canberra. Lagos wasn't a total waste of time. The British he discovered had given up on Nigeria many years back, but they had never really stamped out the graft before they left in 1960, and the locals had developed it into an art form. So his first Swiss bank account came into being and prospered from then on. Hanoi was too serious. It suited his austere Communist prejudices but not his growing taste for the ease and freedom of the Western lifestyle. Canberra, however, did and with it came the taste for beer; but not the stomach-crippling cold beer so beloved by the Australians.

If Kirovsky had been in any way sentimental he would have said, 'Those were the days!' at this point. But he was anything but sentimental. He was, however, something of a romantic. He was married; he had been young, she had been beautiful, but he hadn't seen or heard of her for thirty-odd years. And in those thirty-odd years he had had consolation aplenty. Except in Lagos that is; his racial prejudices were too great for that. In Paris he had Collette. She had lasted longer than most – another sign of age, he told himself – and she had become a part of his life and even on a small scale, a part of his business. Almost a kindred spirit, Collette was as hard, unfeeling and violent as her Russian. She only lacked his unconscious viciousness.

'Four minutes, you bastard!'

And now he needed to go. He had no Flemish so he couldn't understand the protests as he queue-jumped the toilet. He didn't like to bring attention to himself but the beer was working through quickly and his need was great. It was a sign of advancing age and although such an admission would never have escaped him, it was also a sign of nervousness. This Bernsty – 'Bernstein, damn Jew,' he usually said – was a nasty beast of a man who was rapidly getting past his sell-by date. And something had to be done.

The Swiss Bank Account grew. It spawned others, in Norfolk Island, in the Caymans and in Edinburgh. Only Collette knew about Edinburgh. There his money was not only in the bank, it was in real estate as well. A well-kept house in a quiet Borders village and an elderly couple to look after it; it was a part of a dream as well as a business reality.

'Why do you want property in Scotland for heaven's sake?' Collette had been incredulous. But then life for her was extinct more than 25 miles from Notre Dame. Rural Scotland seemed like another planet. Why spend your declining years there? But then if she had fully understood Kirovsky she would probably have left him way back; the unknown was what excited her about him.

Of course, by 1994, when the KGB eventually cut him off, Kirovsky was on the payroll in name only. From the slow beginnings of Lagos, he'd built himself a significant investment portfolio and a more than adequate secure income stream. His salary wasn't quite peanuts, but the pay of a Russian Colonel General of the KGB wasn't exactly in the big league. He didn't miss it that much.

Like John Harcourt, Yuri Kirovsky founded himself a business that gave him freedom and cover. His first serious freelancing efforts had been as early as 1986, with the said Jake Bernstein, doing a bit of illicit industrial espionage on the quiet. With very little persuasion Bernstein had been induced to switch his basic loyalty from the CIA to the KGB, and he had been one of the first of Kirovsky operatives.

'He's on borrowed time.'

The Russian had come alive. His brain was switched into active mode and he was all alertness. The third beer was beside his hand but his taste for it was gone.

To the CIA, Bernstein's moonlighting for a Bulgarian import/export business had proved very fruitful and Kirovsky got paid handsomely for intelligence that he knew full well was date limited. The insights into the collapse of the Soviet Union and the pseudo-demise of the KGB under Yeltsin were immensely and genuinely valuable to the Americans and the British at the time. Kirovsky, however, always quietly saw to it that the British were never upstaged by the cousins across the water.

'Contingency plan A,' muttered Kirovsky when his man was now five minutes overdue.

Contingency plans were one of his strong points. From 1990, he had concentrated entirely on salvaging something for himself out of the mess developing in his homeland. When the KGB establishment began to catch up with him he escaped first to Sofia and then to Paris. And he took his networks with him. As head of station for Western Europe, centred initially in East Berlin, he ran a close group of agents that was never penetrated. Towards the end of his officially active tenure he also took over in America when the CIA/FBI had taken out the top Russian echelons. He rebuilt the networks in the US but never got round to 'handing them back'. Now they were his own and a major source of income to him.

It hadn't been easy and still wasn't, and there had been and still were casualties. But he was beginning to know things about the CIA and their machinations. That got Kirovsky as close to excitement as he was ever likely to be. To be back in such a big game again was like the elixir of life to him. And the income generation potential was of course never far from his thoughts.

'Seven minutes.'

He was approaching his contingency margin and getting nervous; that worried him.

The Colonel and British Intelligence knew all about Kirovsky. But their perspective inevitably was different. He was not a favourite in the ageing and now recently revitalised minds of British Counter Intelligence.

A major general at forty-six and a ruthless, cunning commander, he had a reputation for the brutal treatment meted out to captured spies and for the personal interest he took in their executions. But there was nothing that anybody could put their hands on that could have put him behind bars. So, he was established legitimately in Paris as a fruit importer, as the Colonel suspected, and he ran his intelligence networks to the complete ignorance of the French intelligence services. Had they been challenged to take a closer look at him they would have very soon concluded that no court would ever convict him. And with time, much was forgotten if not forgiven, and apart from the elderly British veterans like the Colonel, nobody was much interested in him anymore.

'Nine minutes.'

He was beginning to form his next actions in his mind. He needed what Bernstein was supplying him with, even if his disgusting sexual habits were making him a liability. Without something to trade he knew that the Colonel would laugh in his face. That he did not want. He knew the man of old; he negotiated from a strength that needed to be matched. In the meantime he had to find out what was happening and why the foul Bernstein hadn't made the rendezvous. Then again maybe his failure to appear was the confirmation of CIA duplicity. If something had happened to him what did he care?

It was barely above freezing as Yuri Kirovsky left the café. He strode off along the De Keyserlei towards the Central Station. He scampered across the cobbled square in front of the station, more than once in peril of his life as the taxi drivers played some sort of schoolboy dare game with the pedestrians.

'Get moving,' he told himself. He was prone to giving himself orders when he was concentrating hard on what he was doing. In Belgium he had no reason whatsoever to suppose that he was being followed but only a fool would relax his vigilance.

He was heading for the Jewish quarter. That's where his man lived. Jews were another of his prejudices; he detested Bernstein for his origins as much as for his tendency to beat up his prostitutes before he used them.

Anybody who had wanted to follow the Russian would have found it hard going. All through his military and KGB service he had kept himself in good trim. And as much as Ross Metcalfe marvelled at the Colonel's superb fitness for his age, so Collette at a more basic level marvelled at Kirovsky's virility.

The route he took to the Jewish quarter was circuitous but the pace at which he took it was punishing. He didn't break sweat and he didn't wind his heartbeat up more than a few per cent.

'Okay, let's take it easy now,' he cautioned himself as he approached his target. The Jewish quarter was obvious enough when you got there but less obvious as you were getting to it. The streets often seemed narrower than the main thoroughfares and thronged with hurrying black-clad men and the occasional woman. Kirovsky, insensitive himself, barely noticed the lack of manners that the people around him displayed. Not once did he offer any apology when some head-down figure cannoned into him. Not once was he offered an apology until he was almost abreast of the apartment block where his agent lived.

'I do beg your pardon.'

Kirovsky was alert. He may not have noticed the lack of

apologies but he instantly recognised one when it was given. The man was not a Jew, he was not black-clad and his hair was brown.

'Police!'

Two police cars were blocking the pavement. The man who had walked into Yuri Kirovsky had just crept slowly past the cars, looking back over his shoulder. As the two disentangled, Kirovsky noticed the young woman in the stylish black leather suit and boots on the other side of the street. For a woman looking like that he'd probably have walked into the next man along the street as well.

He was still alert, so his admiration turned to a fleeting suspicion. Many prostitutes would have dressed like the woman. But she was strolling, obviously not going anywhere, right in front of the door to the apartments.

'So what the hell's going on here?'

There was a religious bookshop opposite the flats. Kirovsky dodged inside as two uniformed policemen and an angular, quick-walking woman came out of the street door of the flats. He knew the woman. There was definitely something wrong, of that he was now convinced. Retreat was necessary.

Getting out the shop was harder than getting in. His path was blocked by the Orthodox Jew who owned it, mutely demanding that he buy something. But his stare was enough in the end. The inattentive man who had barged into him and the young woman had left the scene by the time he'd made it back into the street. A little flicker of disappointment flared; he quite liked black leather and he didn't feel the need to draw blood before he enjoyed it.

As he later discovered, the whole sorry tale of his agent was sitting on his answering machine, put there by the Dutch police inspector he had just seen climbing into one of the police cars.

* * *

'I do beg your pardon.'

John Harcourt's February had been utterly frantic and it was only the fourth. Things had taken off with the CIA and there suddenly seemed to be bodies everywhere. The time since his meeting with Ross in London had been filled with all manner of research, and he was verging on being as knowledgeable as the Colonel on the famous Yuri Kirovsky, except that the former KGB general was a major claimant for the *Guinness Book of Records* as the least photographed human being on the planet. And now he was nursing a bruised ankle as a result of a collision with the very man.

'What the devil's she doing here?' John had muttered only seconds before the painful encounter.

He'd hopped over from Amsterdam on an unlikely expectation that there might be something to learn from the dead CIA man's flat. There probably would be from the police the next day but with time on his hands he'd gone to take a look for himself. The trip to Antwerp got him out of the way of complications in the CIA Amsterdam office and gave him time to think. At least that was the theory. His brain was near shutdown with all the data that had piled into in the last few days. And now there was Ross.

Why was she there? He was glad to see her, the surge of adrenaline told him that, but his built-in tradecraft prevented him from crossing the pavement to greet her. He would have loved to have just gone up to her, put his arms around her and pulled her to him. But all his fantasy had got him was the bruised shin from his contact with the nondescript old man who had vanished before he could look around. Whatever Ross was doing, he was going to have to talk to her about it; that was a business necessity, but one that he looked forward to pleasurably. There wasn't room for two spies in all of this.

'We'll have to work something out, then we can get the best of both worlds.'

With that conclusion he headed for his hotel.

* * *

'I'm going to have to do some chasing around here,' John had announced to the director on yet another of his visits to his office a few days before. This time he wasn't going to get away with bland, comforting words.

'Okay, if you think the Amsterdam bloke is going to help. But the CIA, or some part of it, is definitely up to something. How long will you be away?'

He didn't know and wasn't keen to tie himself down.

'Right, Thursday – report back today week. Then we go with this or drop it.'

John was happy. He knew the director wouldn't drop the investigation; he rarely ever did once he had allowed something to start. But just in case, he organised his trip before any second thoughts might emerge.

The Amsterdam CIA man was atypical; that made him both valuable and dangerous. John knew him of old and respected him. He wouldn't openly help John against his country but he would put things in his way. So John set off for Amsterdam not knowing where the journey would lead him, or who would cross his path in the few days he planned to be away.

15

2026

The extraordinary amalgam of Pro-Ab, the abortions-for-all group; Sisterlings, the disowned sibling of the Daughters of the Republic; a mark–2 Ku Klux Klan and the right-wing pressure group America Resugent, the more public face of the extreme religious right, was news – big news.

'My God, what's this?'

The speaker was addressing Senator Charles McGoldberg, ordinarily known as 'Chap' for reasons that no one in the US Senate can now remember. The senator was on his way back to the US from London via Stockholm after meeting with the itinerant American Ambassador to Europe, Melvin Fitzallan. He found such meetings wearing. His years of quiet diplomacy – or arm twisting and politico-moral blackmail, depending on your viewpoint – had made him a discreet man. Fitzallan's loud and bullying style irked him. He conceded that it was often successful in the hothouse conditions of American politics, but the Europeans, he had discovered, were generally disdainful of it. If Fitzallan was trying to anger the Europeans he wasn't succeeding. The Neoconservatives wanted their attention; being ignored was not helpful to their game plan.

'Looks like a riot to me.'

The senator had glanced at the mini-screen in front of his fellow passenger and then switched his own TV to the CNN World News 2 Channel. High above the Atlantic the reception was clear and the picture sharp. He had no need of the headphones to know what was happening.

'Sure, it's a riot,' the man responded, 'in Detroit, and there was another in New Orleans, and another in Cincinnati. It's like some goddamn South American arsehole republic we're living in. Who the hell are all these weirdo groups?'

'Funny I should have been thinking about Fitzallan,' the senator said to himself. 'Just the sort of comment he would have made.'

He wondered whether the overweight businessman next to him was a supporter of America Resurgent; he certainly didn't look as though solidarity with feminists or abortion was his thing. But he also looked too well-fed and self-satisfied to share views with the rather austere religious right.

As the military in New Orleans were seen on worldwide television getting a beating from the mob, the man spluttered his anger again.

'What does that arsehole in the White House think he's doing? Why doesn't he give the guys the money to sort this bloody lot out?'

Why indeed, thought the senator. Except that he knew full well that it was Congress and not the president who was holding up the money to re-equip the army and National Guard troops. Civil unrest was growing, promoted by the America Resurgent movement, although definitely not controlled by them, as the conflicting groups on the TV news demonstrated. Effective action was being prevented in Congress and the president was getting the blame.

'It was ever thus,' remarked the senator to his increasingly irate neighbour. That was American politics and it had been like that since 2024 when a Democrat was back again in the White House but with the Republicans entrenched in Congress. Stalemate between the president and Congress could arise so easily and the senator and his fellow thinkers knew how to create it. And worse, unlike the stand-offs of the past, the senator and his cronies like Fitzallan also knew how to exploit it quickly.

'Jesus, would you look at that. Twenty-seven riots and the police and National Guard guys beaten up in them all.'

The businessman's mental processes went into overload at the prospect. The senator went into a little internal chuckle. Things were definitely beginning to take shape, although the idea that they might not always be able to manage the riots once they snowballed was firmly suppressed. An anxiety that they were pushing too hard at the European Federation didn't even surface but the senator knew it was there.

The senator's conversations with Melvin Fitzallan had given him pause for thought. Fitzallan was all for exploiting the fact that many people, even in senior positions in the European Federation decision making processes, still hadn't made the leap from friend to adversary that now seemed necessary in dealing with America. And many had still not appreciated the position of weakness from which the US posturing stemmed. The mind-sets of several generations had to be changed and it was a difficult adjustment. Nonetheless, McGoldberg's concern that the massive exit of capital from the US and the breakdown of intelligence, cultural, commercial and sporting contacts had yet to be understood in the States was growing.

* * *

The young secretary flicked over the calendar on Dotty Wedgewood's desk. Adjusting the calendar was something that she did every day. That's how the colonel liked it, and what the colonel liked she generally got.

'Still want to see Rick Blackford at ten?'

Arranging the interview was the secretary's last action of the previous evening. It was a couple of weeks since the young agent had been through the traumas of seeing the second secretary, Spencer, gunned down and Dotty was worried about him, so much so that she had contacted the head of Amsterdam Station, Joe Longton, to ask if he could find a job for him for a few weeks.

'Sure could. There's a couple of things that I need followed up,' he told her.

Joe was well aware that he was not high on the popularity list with his masters in Washington. For a start, he had a nasty habit of keeping his European counterparts informed on what he was doing in the Benelux countries. This was entirely counter to the instructions that he had been given. All intelligence sharing and social communications was supposed have been closed down in 2024. But he was long in the tooth, had a Dutch wife and grandchildren, a fine house on the outskirts of Delft and not the slightest intention of ever returning to his homeland. He wasn't quite fireproof, to use his own expression, but his standing was just about high enough to prevent the new SIE moguls from calling him home. Whether it was enough to prevent them 'doing a Spencer' on him he doubted. And since he was close to retirement he was increasingly on his guard.

'Can always use a spare hand here,' he continued.

If they couldn't unseat him, headquarters could starve him of staff and money, and this was what they were doing. But Joe knew that Dotty's offer either had strings attached or was loaded in some other way.

After she had talked him through Rick Blackford he was blunt.

'This guy's hot I presume?'

'Yeah, he was with Spencer when he was killed and Fitzallan's real edgy about that. Why, I don't know. But Rick's a good guy and I wouldn't want anything to happen to him. As far as I can see he was just an innocent bystander.'

Needless to say Dotty knew more than she was telling but

this wasn't the moment. She rightly suspected that Rick knew that Spencer had been killed by his own side. That was dangerous knowledge for such small fry as him. But Dotty was a humane soldier in her way and that was why she felt that Rick ought to be somewhere else for a while, where he was easier to look out for and where the people around him weren't suspicious of him. Where better for him to be than with Joe Longton?

Her powers to transfer an SIE agent were vague to say the least, but the conversation was about a request from Amsterdam and they both knew it.

Joining the SIE had been the pinnacle of Rick Blackford's ambition. The selection process was so tough that around 75% of entrants fell by the wayside. And the selection process was the brainchild of one of the most extreme of the new SIE zealots. It was intended to produce an elite, loyal only to the SIE who would put the service before their duty to president and country. Drawn from this elite was a young Turk element who had now worked their way to the upper reaches of the decision-making process and who were calling the shots. Although at least two of the SIE's very top brass were still servants of the State rather than servants of the SIE, they were increasingly embattled and they struggled to keep what influence they had.

Rick didn't know anything about the aims and objectives of America Resurgent or any SIE hidden agenda, but he was young enough and naïve enough to still boast some patriotism and so had found the brainwashing on the training course worrying. Brought up to good Christian values, his wider education had been influenced more by an uncle than by his parents. The uncle, a prosperous businessman, led a double life. If it wasn't well known exactly where his income came from it was even less well known that he had other loyalties. Like many, his lack of political affiliation made him ideal as an active member of

Intercontinental Veterans Anonymous. That Rick was aware of his uncle's double life and shared many of his ideals was not something that he was inclined to discuss with his SIE colleagues.

Rick's London officemate had talked to him about the SIE factions and about the inner caucus that included the dangerous Mr Jordan, but Rick was not inclined to absorb his views. He didn't see his colleague as an agent provocateur but testing the loyalty of newcomers was an intelligence organisation's trick that was as old as time.

'Rick, you're a great guy, but you've got to wise up. If you want to get on in the SIE you've got to go with the flow.'

And the flow, Rick had already discovered, had a distinctly nasty side to it. So far he'd offended the American Ambassador to Europe, an unknown senator who the ambassador clearly listened to, and the said Mr Jordan. Not bad for one day's stroll to the office.

'Wonder what Colonel Wedgewood wants?' Rick had just got the message and his Jonah-companion was already postulating doom and gloom. 'You don't want to get mixed up with her; she's bad news; definitely not on the Christmas card list. This is the only embassy where the marines are in sole charge of security, and that's down to her. She's one tough lady, but she ain't a favourite with our lot.'

* * *

'Amsterdam, that'd be great. I'd be glad to get away from this place.'

'It's getting to you? You haven't been here five minutes.'

'Not really. It's just the politics. It's all politics; that isn't what I joined up for.'

Dotty resisted the temptation to ask him what he had joined up for. An SIE highflyer and he was disenchanted within days of his first posting. That was a novelty. Mostly his ilk had to be tied down before they could change the world too quickly.

'I've heard of Joe Longton. I thought he'd retired. Ex-CIA from way back I'm told; not so many of them left. Bit of a folk hero back home – well, away from the brass that is. It'll be great.'

This guy's in a time warp, thought Dotty. Hasn't he noticed he's just been trained as part of the new SIE super-race. If he isn't with them he's on a short life expectancy.

Rick had, in fact, noticed this somewhere in his subconscious but he wasn't keen to admit it to himself. At his age you don't dump your lifelong dreams that easily.

16

2026

'John, is it okay to talk?'

'Of course it is, Ross. I wouldn't have opened the connection if it wasn't.'

'Oh, you and modern technology! You seem to be into it rather more than you used to be.'

'Well, somewhere in the past I lost touch with my guru and had to make do for myself.'

'Yes, well. Maybe we'll go there some other day; we need to talk right now.'

'Okay. Sorry about that, Ross. The thought just popped out. What's the problem?'

'No problem; an opportunity more like.'

'Go on then; I like opportunities better than problems.'

'Ever heard of Dotty Wedgewood, John? US Marine Colonel, even now just about the only black woman ever to make it to that sort of rank and to manage to be respected by all sides.'

'Head of Security at the US Consulate in London? Not a universal favourite in some parts of Washington, I gather. Yep, I've heard of her, Ross.'

'She's one tough and loyal lady. The SIE have never been able to fault her because she's so well-tuned into what's going on around her. And she watches her back by reporting back to Marine Corps HQ both regularly and in detail.'

'And you're keeping tabs on her? Why's that?'

'Actually it's Alanda. You remember Alanda Ngozie? Of course you do! She concentrates on behaviour and communication patterns; that's why she's so good at mimicking communications when she needs to.'

'So what's she picked up?'

'In the first instance it's what she didn't pick up that got her attention. Somewhere in Washington Dotty Wedgewood and her Marine Corps chums have been building an archive on high-flying SIE recruits and what they're up to. Alanda thinks it's proxy counter-intelligence for some top notch SIE guy who's also protecting his back; but never mind that. Remember Rick Blackford? I told you about Rick Blackford didn't I?'

'Not that I can recall, Ross, but I'm sure you're going to now.'

'Ah! He's the London Embassy clerk-cum-SIE-high-flyer who was with our unlamented friend Spencer when the SIE hit-man took him out. Dotty has been watching out for him by the sound of her reports. Don't ask me why; the politics are far too obscure for me. The point is, she suddenly stopped talking about him and her reports to Washington suddenly halved in length and reverted to trivia.'

'I'm struggling with this, Ross.'

'God, you always were an impatient bastard. Anyway, Alanda's first thought was that Dotty was communicating some other way, mobile phone being the most likely. It took her a couple of days to track down Dotty's mobile, but she was right. During the time Alanda was searching, Dotty had made seven calls to Amsterdam. Seven calls to the SIE HQ in Amsterdam, in fact. I take it you're still in touch enough to know that Joe Longton is still the boss-man for the SIE in the Benelux area?'

'Yep, but just about on retirement, and if the stories are half right he's persona non grata to the high-priced SIE help in Washington.'

'That's the guy. You had any dealings with him recently?'

'No, not recently. I was in touch with him back in 2004 during our time gallivanting in Antwerp.'

Ross let the reference pass. It was still not the time to revisit that bit of the past.

'Rick Blackford's holed up in Amsterdam with Joe Longton and the SIE are not happy bunnies.'

'I'm still struggling, Ross.'

'Nice guy, Joe; I could have gone for him if he wasn't happily married. I know him too from 2004. He and the Colonel worked together on a couple of jobs after the Kirovsky thing died away. Okay, to cut it short I spoke to Joe. Dotty was right to worry. This Rick Blackford has attracted the attention of some pretty nasty suits in the SIE in no time at all and in all innocence. But he still has a foot in the door. We can use that.'

'We?'

'John, I agreed with Joe that Alanda might be able to help him with some problems he's having with Eastern European people trafficking that are getting in the way of the more usual work of undermining the Russian's attempts to turn the clock back. But never mind that either. Joe understands the code; we want to know what's going on in the US and he wants to stay alive until he retires, and long after. There's a deal if we need it but I can't deliver it.'

'But I can, eh?'

'Like old times, John.'

Once Ross had disappeared from John's monitor and he'd flogged his way through an increasing burden of text messages and emails about his new assignment, his mind reverted to the conversation that he'd just had with his old flame. The chemistry was still there somewhere he decided, but whether he wanted it to work again he wasn't yet sure. He had a sense that he was moving, being drawn, being pushed, towards something more intimate but he wanted to be sure he was ready for the full implications of the relationship if it did re-establish. He was retired, set in his ways and not immediately fired with the desire, let alone supplied with the energy, to make ever increasing trips to North East Scotland. At least so he told himself. Or at least so his self-delusionary mechanism told him.

'We're going to have to work much more together, that's very clear,' he told his flickering monitor in proxy of Ross. 'What the director has been telling me suggests that the Kirovsky thing didn't die away. It went on working in the background if not legitimately, at least effectively; and always with its eyes on the old foe, the extreme right-wing. How Yuri hated anything to do with the right wing, the old Colonel used to say.'

Another ping, another email and John's attention was back on his screen. A short digest of information purloined by Ross from the New York Intelligence Clearing House appeared. As he read and digested Ross's annotations, on cue and in support of John's musing at his monitor, Kirovsky's ghost showed itself through his proxy, Intercontinental Veterans Anonymous.

It was clear that Intercontinental Veterans Anonymous had survived, thrived and were still active in the information and intelligence supply market despite the efforts of the US authorities over the years to shut the organisation down. It was also clear that the SIE suspected that the veterans had a much broader political agenda. Since they were the heirs to Kirovsky's ways of thinking the SIE suspicions were largely justified.

* * *

'Rick, it's great to see you.'

Joe Longton was a genuine guy; he truly was pleased to see Rick.

'You've arrived on just the right day. Got a Brit coming to see me; someone I'm sure you'll want to meet.'

Rick missed the twinkle; his recent experiences had made him a little wary of bonhomie, false or otherwise, and he was concentrating too much on hearing what Joe was saying rather what he actually said. Looking out for the agenda was the product of his training and that was what he was doing. His response was positive but neutral.

'I'd be happy to get struck in straight away if that's what you need.'

Joe grinned and took Rick's response on its face value. But he was struck by what seemed to be a sense of relief showing through the cautiousness that was clearly also there.

Old Dotty hasn't told all, he grinned to himself. That means this guy really does know something he shouldn't.

And of course Rick did. He had been told it wilfully by the ambassador simply to feed that gentleman's crude desire to demonstrate his power.

The SIE Amsterdam Station was long established and fronted by an up-market office furniture import and supply business. It was an almost perfect cover. It gave Joe and his troops the opportunity to get into all sorts of office buildings and to poke around virtually at will. Overlooking the Herengracht, the head office was a classic canal-fronting, Dutch townhouse. In the money-no-object situation of the old CIA days Joe had invested wisely, so he not only had an impressive front for his activities but Uncle Sam also had a very nice piece of real estate that appreciated regularly in value. That said, the building had also seen its fair share of frontline action having been famously blown up in 2004.

'This is nice.' It was Rick's schoolboy best behaviour comment: a wary throwaway that also told Joe that he was beginning to relax. What he was relaxing from wasn't yet clear, but Joe guessed that it was something big for someone in his position, again confirming what he thought he'd understood from talking to Dotty Wedgewood.

Having been greeted, Rick was left very much to himself. He was given an office on the third floor above. He noted, the plushness of the office equipment business. The third and fourth floors were separated from the rest of the building by a complex double-door system that Rick was introduced to, beyond which the standard of décor dropped sharply. The furniture was plain, not to say spartan, and definitely not from stock.

'Could have managed a few sale-ends,' Rick muttered to himself.

Not much was seemingly expected of Rick for the present. He was given a file to read (not a very weighty one, but a file nonetheless) and the office routines he saw around him were anything but bureaucratic, unlike the monster organisation he had just left. He wasn't required to sign in triplicate every time he breathed and a trip to the toilet on the next floor was not a major undertaking.

He knew he was going to like it in Amsterdam. Certainly, by the time Joe Longton lumbered into his new office announcing the end of the day, Rick knew all there was to know from the contents of the file and about the Russian equivalent of the mafia.

'Okay, Rick, let's park your traps at your lodgings and get us a Chinese meal.'

Joe certainly had a relish for the latter endeavour, and they accomplished the former with the minimum of unnecessary time-wasting, talking as they walked.

'Never take to wheels in Amsterdam. Walk: you see more. Or use a waterbus.'

The walking bit Rick decided was why Joe, despite his advancing years, was so lean and tight-muscled. He'd pass the dark alleyway test, he thought, definitely glad to be on the same side as Joe.

The return journey from his nondescript lodgings took them through what Rick knew to be one of the more famous parts of Amsterdam, but Joe was beyond temptation. Despite the charms of rows of young women in windows possessed of jewellery and precious little else, Rick was also too preoccupied to raise even a minimum of curiosity and they headed across the Damrak, the city's more reputable main thoroughfare, and into the broad pedestrian-way that ran parallel to it. This was glitzy in a different way. Rows of expensive shops, still open for business since it was barely 7 o'clock, vied for Rick's attention. He was a small town boy and although the luxurious temptations of London had become almost commonplace to him, there was something much more seductive here.

'It's a great place,' remarked Joe. He'd been seduced by it years ago. 'And so's this,' he continued and steered Rick into the foyer of an opulent Chinese restaurant.

The Twin Dragons was vintage Chinese restaurant culture. It was a wonderful throwback to seventy or more years before when the Chinese were just beginning to take hold of the ethnic eating market in Europe. Regency-stripe, flock wallpaper abounded in bold burgundy patterns; ornate lantern decorations were everywhere and the central fish tank dominated the room. But it was the booths, high backed and private, that showed off the place's 1960s origins. And it was the booths that Joe liked most about it.

'Very private,' he said to Rick as they were guided to a reserved table in a corner booth at the back of the restaurant, almost totally enclosed and with a narrow entrance onto the main dining area.

Joe was treated as a valued customer, and so he was. Li Chiang Ji, the youthful owner, relished his small parts in Joe's intrigues as much as his accountant relished the modest but regular payments that came the restaurant's way. But tonight the restaurateur's role was watchdog and general panderer to the whims of his special guest. For Joe, his guests were always special and he was determined on this occasion to put on a good show.

Rick was directed to a chair at the circular table. His back was to the curtained window and he had a perfect view of the access to the booth. Since his role was expected to be minimal, it was a good security move.

'Whatever else he might be,' Rick said to himself, 'this guy's good.' And straight from the latest tradecraft course, he should know.

Joe took the seat opposite Rick, his back protected by a passage that Rick assumed led to the emergency exit.

Against the brighter light of the more central parts of the restaurant, Rick could only see the outline of the petite young woman who had just arrived. The dark dancing eyes and amiable grin emerged Cheshire-cat-like as she came forward. The silhouette emerged into a slender and perfectly proportioned black girl of around 5 feet 4 inches or so.

'Let me introduce Alanda Ngozie.'

Joe made a comic attempt to imitate an upper class English accent to match Alanda's. Not that he had much experience of such a manner of speaking, but he'd seen enough movies – the universal American academy of international learning – to have a vague notion of the sounds.

'That right?' he asked. 'Did I get that right?'

'Oh, yes,' Alanda said simply. 'It's only part of my name and the rest of it is a tongue twister even for me, let alone anybody else.'

'Good to see you,' Joe finished off the welcome before turning to his other guest.

'Rick Blackford.'

It was a great meal. The conversation was relaxed and fluid. Alanda, despite her youth – she was twenty-five, Rick guessed – was both a knowledgeable and entertaining talker. Rick looked and listened. This was another world to him.

European politics, arts and social habits were mysteries that he'd never been initiated into, yet here was the renowned Joe Longton talking on a range of such subjects with a confidence that Rick could only sit and admire. And the beautiful young woman who was beginning to dazzle him seemed to know as much if not more than Joe and to be equally knowledgeable about a vast range of things American. There was no technology, no science here, just cultured discussion. It was over all too soon but Rick knew that he was smitten. Being more rigorous in her mental processes, it took Alanda a night of contemplation to acknowledge that she too was definitely attracted to Rick.

* * *

With the spectre of Yuri Kirovsky raised and taking on a new importance in what he and Ross were beginning to get involved in, John couldn't get him out of his head. Even after all these years Kirovsky had that effect on people. John almost instantly resigned himself to the old Russian haunting his days to come as he sought to work his way back into the secret machinations of the former KGB man turned intelligence salesman par excellence and what they now meant.

Grudging admiration was never too far away in John's thoughts even in the past frenetic days of 2004. The tentacles of Kirovsky's twenty-two-year-old operations had not been cut off and had not even atrophied; they had thrived quietly, secretly and, by a mechanism that only Ross Metcalfe seemed to understand, they had reconnected. The timing was good; relations between the US and the European Federation were deteriorating fast and suddenly a valuable tool presented itself.

'Maybe old Yuri achieved something after all. He thought long and he was right to do so. A pity he didn't live to see the fruits of his foresight.'

A flashback was triggered. The thought of Kirovsky's demise threw John back through the twenty-two years to the final set-piece of the game in 2004. It wasn't hard to recall. The drama played out quickly and in public and he remembered it well; the horror, the shock, the pain, the hurt. The old sequence rehearsed itself through his brain one more time.

'So, John, that's it?'

His then-director was debriefing him in one of the rather more exclusive cult restaurants in Knightsbridge. It was dotting i's and crossing t's time, as the director put it. His report was all but complete and he was looking to John for something of the flavour of the hands-on events, rather than the boring detail, and at the same time saying his personal thank you in his own rather rarefied way.

'I think you've got it all, sir. My own report is on file if you need more.'

'Are there any loose ends?'

'Not many. We're meeting Kirovsky and his partner at Gatwick this evening. And we'll be seeing him on his way to retirement in Scotland.'

'Okay. Again, John, that's it?'

John could recall shrugging. Kirovsky's retirement was to be the end as far as he was concerned. What happened to his networks he didn't really care about. Having only a limited knowledge of their capabilities, he had assumed that they would be dismantled by the Americans and various European agencies. The deal with Kirovsky to retire to Scotland in exchange for the networks didn't include any deal about their fate or future. In fact, it was only in 2026 that John learned about a much more secret deal between the Colonel and Euan Fforde of the then-CIA that ensured their continued operation. If she knew, Ross never explained the rationale to the decision to let the networks survive.

John could also recall the careful way that his director

kept rehearsing what was to happen to Kirovsky. John sensed that he was far from happy that the deal had been done even if he had been privy to it and had agreed to it.

'And there's just getting Kirovsky off the plane and on the way to Edinburgh?'

For once, as John began to picture what had eventually happened in 2004, a vision of the youthful Ross didn't usurp all other thoughts. Having now reconnected with her again, looking into the past became much easier than it used to be.

The old director was still curious. 'Why doesn't he fly to Edinburgh directly? Why change to the train?'

'Kirovsky, sir, will do the unexpected, change the pattern, weave and dodge until he dies. He doesn't know any different.'

The director laughed; he acknowledged the ways of the old spies as much as he admired the music of the 1960s, intellectually rather than as a reality in his world.

John's thoughts remained twenty-two years in the past to the moment that he had met up with Ross at the Gatwick Hilton. Despite herself, she had dressed with special care.

The meeting with Kirovsky had been well thought out. John, like the Russian, did do the unexpected, but never the unplanned. And he was very careful how he exposed himself in public places always preferring to remain in the background. As he recalled Ross's teasing about what she called his professional shyness he gave a little self-deprecatory chuckle. Such tradecraft touches had been the story of his life for the succeeding years as well.

'Get a better lunch at the Hilton,' he had remarked by way of explanation of his choice of venue. Better or not, it was certainly more intimate and that was what John had wanted.

Ross was wearing a designer linen suit of a pale blue shade that miraculously matched his tie. In general her clothes were a greater concession to popular fashion than he had ever seen her make before. He was pleased. It passed through his mind that she was rising to the challenge of Kirovsky's partner Collette's well-known high fashion sense.

With the passage of time John found he could still recall the details of her outfit, a tribute to the indelible impact that the events had had on his mind.

'Why don't you take your jacket off? I'm sure they won't mind. It isn't that smart a joint,' she said with a laugh as they got seated. John remembered that as well.

He made no answer, nor any move to expose his shirtsleeves.

They both enjoyed the lunch, reflecting the general relaxation of the pressures they'd been exposed to and the fact that they were in the endgame. But they still had that endgame to play out. So, at the due time, John gently urged Ross to the airport terminal and to the disorganised and crowded area at the arrivals gates.

'I suppose we'll recognise Kirovsky. He won't come in disguise or something, will he?' Ross suddenly said a little anxiously, aware that they wanted the meeting and the transfer to go as smoothly as possible, but also of Kirovsky's unpredictability.

'We'll recognise him.'

Flight arrivals in 2004 weren't announced but John positioned himself so that he could see the television screens. Unlike the low-energy plasma giants of 2026 he had to stay fairly close to be able to see information emerging.

'Be any minute now,' he said.

As another spate of people poured out through the automatic doors from the customs hall Ross sensed John stiffen and move away from her.

He's nervous, she thought, but she never got to thinking why. And she never got to recognising Kirovsky either. Collette she saw before the explosion of noise and violent activity, but that was all. The later, endless replays in her mind saw John turn his back on Kirovsky as soon as he picked him out in the crowd. Again she never had time to wonder why he was searching faces behind them in the arrivals area.

The three crashing gunshots rattled around the vast cavern of the building and died quickly to be replaced by an instant silence and then a barrage of screams and cries of anger and fear.

Kirovsky lay on top of Collette, a trickle of blood spreading over the delicate pink leather of her jacket. Neither of them moved.

'John!' Ross shrieked the name. John was rising from one knee, the handgun seemingly weighing down his right arm. Five yards away, complete with a policeman quickly kneeling to test for life signs, lay another body.

'John,' said Ross again more quietly.

It was the last moment of contact. As the full impact of what had happened blasted into Ross's mind her brain shut down. Any memory of the next hours was expunged from her recollection; how she physically got through these hours and then days she could never have explained.

John said nothing. What could he say? And the policeman by the body, passport in hand, read the name of Pensky, replete with all of his forenames and wondered what the hell had just happened.

17

Ross had been utterly devastated by John's action to gun down Kirovsky and Collette's assassin. Nothing in her experience had told her that a public assassination could have taken place at Gatwick Airport or that the man who she was standing next to could have responded by shooting the killer. The aftermath of the deaths had been much more traumatic and longer lasting for her than they had been for John. But even for her, as the passage of time turned into decades, things eventually faded.

The days after the killings had been a blur of pain for Ross. All the feelings that she had had about the underlying violence in John flooded back. A sense of betrayal supplemented the hatred and anger and inhibited her from applying her usual powers of logic and analysis to the situation. If she could have she would have wiped John totally from her mind. But the vision of John, gun in hand, rising from his firing position, was indelibly imprinted in her memory banks.

Why did he have to kill the man? The question that John had also struggled with went through her mind many times but her focus was on John and not the man he had shot. Pensky was a hired killer; he was there to kill and he had done so.

During the ensuing months and then years a whole range of emotions came and went. Love turned to hatred. Hatred turned to anger and fear. Anger and fear turned to questioning. Ultimately, questioning turned to reasoning. As time and more experience gave Ross a broader insight into the harsh world that John and the Colonel inhabited, reasoning gave way to a process of rationalisation and she came to accept the reality of what had happened and John's unavoidable role in it.

'What else could he have done?'

It had been a painful experience for them both and had left them both scarred.

Twenty-two years on, rationalisation had turned to understanding. Reconnecting with John in 2026 after the long period of separation, understanding turned to acceptance and with it implicit forgiveness.

18

Even as his personal and business relations resumed with Ross the Gatwick moment remained in John's consciousness. Motivated by Ross's willingness to move on, the resolution of his own uncertainties was subconsciously beginning to happen. With so much from the past thrusting itself into the present, triggered by the re-emergence of Kirovsky's influence, it was inevitable that he was going to have to come to terms with his past rift with Ross.

The Colonel had understood the rift all too clearly. He could see the situation that had caused it from both sides; he'd killed a man or two in his time. Nonetheless, it was the feeling of helplessness in the face of Ross's anguish, as he saw her getting hurt yet again by a man, which caused him the most pain. His gentle efforts to warn his ward had failed. He blamed himself for that.

When she had been ready to hear the Colonel's words rather than his calming platitudes he rationalised the situation for Ross as he saw it. He justified John's response; it was what happened in his/their line of work. But Ross had not been able to free herself so easily from the horror of what she had seen. And for some time her hatred of John persisted.

Comparisons with her experiences with her Cambridge boyfriend and his fits of uncontrolled jealousy kept invading her mind. Violently abusing her for even talking to fellow students was something as incomprehensible to her as John's seemingly harsh and violent reactions to unforeseen situations. But in the end these images dissolved as John's more powerful and mature personality asserted itself in her mind.

However, even if she was unaware of it, healing was occurring and it started when information about John and one of his subsequent projects came within Ross's surveillance system.

'John's been busy,' she remarked to the Colonel.

The Colonel took the comment as a good sign. He understood the effort that Ross had had to put into even just making it.

Then came the period when the Colonel's health was failing and Ross had to accept the inevitable loss of her partner, mentor and friend.

Away in London and when his leave and period of recovery after the killing were over, John's career moved on again. His expertise was in demand and he was soon out of the country. He had planned to visit Scotland but the Colonel discouraged him. He was hurt by this rejection but something in his mind told him that maybe it was justified.

The years passed.

Neither John nor Ross forgot their relationship and as normality prevailed both recalled it as events, situations and other triggers brought it back into consciousness. Healing continued to a point where both knew that if they ever met again they ought to be able to deal with the contact maturely and without recrimination. But the relationship nonetheless remained frozen. Both recognised that their lack of serious effort to overcome the barriers that they had created or had been created by circumstances said something about the depth of their feelings for each other. But both had been bruised in other relationships and that also made reconnecting seem difficult. It never seemed impossible.

More years passed.

19

2004

Neither John nor Ross knew about the Chinese meal until Alanda fed back the details of her latter day trip to Amsterdam and Ross in turn fed them back to John. But Joe Longton and the Twin Dragons were very much a part of John's past. The restaurant may have prospered, gone up-market, been quietly co-opted into the fringes of the European intelligence scheme, but give or take a few changes of wallpaper it was much the same as it had been in 2004 when John was there last.

Then, the Chinese ambience faded somewhat as brandy and a large pot of coffee appeared and the reminiscences and gossip dried up. Whatever their reluctance, they had to talk business. Joe Longton had been supplied with all the information that John had about the infamous trail and the conversation immediately turned to its origin and meaning.

Joe and John had known each other since way back in their early days in the US, but Joe was now so embedded in the Benelux scene that he was almost seen as a part of the Dutch setup rather than the American. That suited Joe since he'd married a Dutch girl. And initially it suited the CIA because they knew that Amsterdam was a clearing house for almost every intelligence and terrorist activity in Western Europe, legitimate or otherwise, so Joe could keep his fingers in innumerable pies. The CIA's confidence in Joe, however, had faded as time went by. John, nonetheless, knew that he could rely on his American colleague; he could share his thoughts with him without the conversation being fed back to the CIA headquarters.

'There's no way this can be down to the present-day Russians,' Joe said.

'No,' John agreed. He had the benefit of the Colonel's considered view.

'And you reckon it can only be one guy?' Joe Longton's question was an invitation to name names.

'Yuri Kirovsky.'

It was clear that Joe also had a name in mind.

'Yep, Yuri Kirovsky.'

The fact that Joe Longton, with all of his independent knowledge and experience, instantly came up with the same name as the British had confirmed to John that his thinking was on the right track. There was a trail and it was one that the trail-layer was seriously keen to have discovered.

'The old bastard's leading us along. But where to?' said Joe.

'To credibility, Joe?'

The Russian's thinking was beginning to become clearer to Joe Longton too.

'But why would Kirovsky want credibility? Doesn't he have enough already?'

'Whatever he was in the past,' John said, 'Kirovsky's an information salesman now. Anything and everything, if it's worth a buck, he'll sell it. Most of what he's been trading, at least in the last three or four years, is technical stuff: commercial, business, patentable. He's supposed to be out of the political stuff.'

It was more from the Colonel's, or rather Ross's, briefing.

'Only now Kirovsky's got something different to trade. And it is political,' said John, 'and it's either very big or he wants something very special in return.'

Coffee fixes seemed appropriate, so the conversation lapsed for a while.

'You reckon, John?' Joe said as their thought processes resumed.

'That's how I see it,' said John, coming rather closer to giving an opinion than he generally cared to in such circumstances.

'But word on the street says that Kirovsky's networks have taken a couple of hits recently,' said Joe, shifting the focus of the conversation.

John knew what Joe was talking about.

'Guy in Detroit and now a guy in Miami, although I don't know too much about him,' Joe continued. 'Both have been working for Kirovsky for years I'd say. And there's many more like them in my book.'

'What d'you reckon we should be doing about this trail then?' John asked.

Both his director and the Colonel had views on what action they should take on Mr Kirovsky's skirmishing, although the views were far from being common between them.

'Get back to him?'

Cautious by nature, Joe's instinct was to gather more facts before they showed their hand. His experience said that things were never quite what they seemed. John noted Joe's hesitation.

'If it *is* Kirovsky he's going to want to know he's been heard and understood.'

'I'd agree with that, John, but maybe it's something we should leave until tomorrow. It's almost midnight. How about we sleep on it a bit?'

'Okay, Joe, but this guy Kirovsky's the best. If he's got something to sell that's important to him, we need to know. And we'll only know if we keep in contact. A million jokers will put messages in the paper; he'll have to spend days sussing them all out and if at the end the right one isn't there we'll never get to him. This is not just about meeting and talking to him; this is about his mind-set, his trusting us. He lives in Paris but it could be Beijing for all it matters; if he goes to ground in his head, he's dead to us. The games Kirovsky plays aren't kids' games, whatever you might think about what's been happening here.'

It was a long speech for John, but he knew that if the reply to Kirovsky didn't have a credible signature on it, and if the Colonel was right, he was looking for someone like himself from the old days, the trail would almost certainly become a blind alley. But John was not about to say this. He was on a recce visit. Amsterdam was the only place in Europe to get a finger-hold on what the CIA's latest strategies were since formal access in the cousins' home patch had become very difficult. Kirovsky's play-acting would only be relevant if it somehow linked to the new introverted CIA; if it didn't John's director would cut off all pursuit of the trail. John's only brief was to get an insight into the CIA and what their likely moves might be to re-establish their credibility in the world and what the impact of this would be on British and European activities. His director was still very clear which ball he had to keep his eye on; relations with the CIA were at an all-time low and life without CIA co-operation was very much the scenario for the future.

* * *

In the cosy warmth of the café, fogged with the pungency of a myriad of Camel cigarettes, past and present, Collette studied the old man in front of her. Yuri Kirovsky didn't see himself as old or even approaching old, and his body certainly wasn't showing much sign of wear and tear, but sometimes she'd noticed when his face was in repose, that he looked almost wizened. Not that his face was much in repose. His endless energy kept his mind and body in constant animation.

'Why do I stay with this man?' It was a question that she was asked by those who were close enough to her to take the risk but it was one that she asked herself mostly. And each time she made the enquiry she had a different answer.

Collette was grateful to Kirovsky. Half-French and half-Vietnamese, life around the docks at Marseilles had been tough. Escaping to Paris at fifteen she'd shut out her previous life and was now more Parisian than the Parisians; she had thrived on the streets and in the beds of a variety of men, but none like Kirovsky. He'd commandeered her late one night when the need came over him and being satisfied, simply ordered her to live with him. It turned out to be an inspired decision. It was only when the property in Scotland emerged, and she read all sorts of possible outcomes into the purchase, that she realised that she really couldn't face life without him.

'We're a great team, you know that, Yuri.'

He knew it. His face was out of repose but had a quiet look about it that she knew to be his version of affection.

They *were* a great team, and they knew and understood each other. She knew he was violent and vicious, but it was never directed at her, and it was never random. Right from their first encounter, when the protests of the man from whom he had commandeered her were met with efficient violence, she had been excited by this side of his character,

'But then I'm violent,' she'd told herself.

Her first pimp at fifteen had taught her the rudiments of self-defence and had then unwisely tried to take his payment in her grubby lodgings. Only Kirovsky knew that it was Collette who had broken the man's neck.

Kirovsky had had her taught to fight properly and loved her ruthless demolition of opponents in the boxing ring.

'A great team,' she muttered again, as she sipped her third Cognac.

Self-defence wasn't the only thing Kirovsky had taught

her. He taught her about her own country's cuisine and fine wines, something that delighted the Russian, although he would never have shared his pleasure with her. Showing feelings to him was losing control.

'Carson was drowned in Detroit,' he suddenly announced quietly.

Collette was increasingly privy to his business activities. For a prostitute she was unusually discreet and he had learned to trust her over the years. So, she knew who Carson was.

'Oh?' She didn't really want to know more and didn't expect to be told more. Carson was just a name, a valuable source of intelligence, a good earner for Kirovsky, but she knew well enough that Yuri would not show any regret. It wasn't a feeling he was capable of.

Carson's name was never mentioned again, nor was that of the man in Miami.

* * *

Leaving the Twin Dragons didn't turn out to be quite as unexciting as they might have expected. There was a group of Dutch louts outside. They jeered at the party when they heard the American accent; that wasn't particularly unusual. They hassled around them, following them along the street; that wasn't particularly unusual either. When a couple of policemen appeared the louts fell back into a rowdy chanting mob. The noise ricocheted back and forward across the street, killing conversation.

Neither of them heard the gunfire; there was too much pandemonium. The louts clearly heard or even felt the single shot then scattered and fled. A shop window crumpled into the street. The police weapons tracked the activity as John and Joe, both being intelligence operatives, adopted their own defensive postures.

Later, when Joe enquired of the Dutch Police, he learnt

that they'd had a tip-off from the Hungarians about a Russian hit-man. He was supposed to have got two contracts but that obviously couldn't be verified. The police were sceptical that this man was responsible for the late-night shooting; a hit-man would hardly have missed John or Joe if they had been the target. But they had no other explanation.

'One's a big one, they said,' Joe reported to John. 'The targets are non-Dutch; that's all the Hungarians know.'

20

2026

'Say no to confrontation!'

The placards had been freshly repaired and the Socialist Front retainers drummed up from all over London and the South East, but they still didn't make for a very convincing counter to the anger of the mob behind them.

'Oh, shit!' said Dolly Wedgewood to herself. 'Not again.'

'Looks like another hot day's work, Colonel.'

The colonel's exclamation was principally about the growing demonstration but could well have applied to the irritation of having the ambassador at her elbow once more.

'We'll cope, don't you worry.'

'So what's it about this time?'

'How the shit would I know?' But Dotty Wedgewood did know. She had picked out the slogans on the banners as they'd arrived and had been erected. Let the old fool read for himself, she thought. Why should I tell him?

The ambassador's PA was beside him. Like Dotty, she knew what the placards said and she found it hard to keep a straight face. Someone somewhere had picked up on Fitzallan's long philandering history and made the best of it. The obscenity of many of the slogans had attracted the attention of the police, but fearful of another boil-over, they had contented themselves with some over-enthusiastic photography. Without the hands that held the placards there wasn't a lot that they could do but the scrapbook enlivened many a weary night shift in the weeks to come.

'Issue rounds, Colonel. That's a direct order. And fire on my command.'

'But –'

'You heard me. If you want a future, do as I say.'

The ambassador had now seen the placards. Dotty Wedgewood shrugged. Ammunition had already been issued to the small band of marines. The new sergeant had his orders. But the new sergeant, along with the dozen additional marines he had brought with him had other orders too. The platoon had been forced on Colonel Wedgewood after the previous riot and she knew by whom and why. The ambassador might not be able to control the colonel herself but at least now he had the means to enforce his own writ.

'What a way to spend a Sunday,' muttered Colonel Wedgewood to the PA as she went off to check her deployments.

The Colonel's combat experience wasn't extensive; most of what she had learnt was from peacekeeping stints in Africa and the Middle East. But she knew about mobs and she knew about riots. And out there in front of the embassy there was a riot biding its time to erupt. The anger was tangible and Dotty Wedgewood for one, loyal as she was to her country, was inclined to share it.

'Fishing. Why is it always fishing that starts these things off?'

The marine she was with had no answer. He was a Midwestern boy; he'd never ever had any contact with the sea until he'd been dumped into it from a training helicopter.

The latest confrontation had been in the icy Atlantic a few miles into international waters and a few miles from the demarcation line with Canada. Protected by a flotilla of European destroyers, the Spanish fishing fleet had been straggled out by the gale-force winds that had been blowing for almost a week. Humiliated by their inability to scrape together a naval force large enough to match the Europeans, the American Navy had torpedoed the tail-end fishing vessel on the flimsy pretext of it violating territorial waters. Ordered not to return fire or pursue the Americans, a Danish destroyer had nonetheless managed to ram a coastguard cutter in circumstances that were going to be argued over for a lifetime.

'Stupid bastards,' Dotty had said at the time.

Living and working in Britain, she didn't have to be a genius to know that the incident would stoke the anti-American feelings that were building to boiling point.

'And we're on the arse-end of it.'

'Yes, Ma'am.'

'Okay, soldier, keep calm. Don't do anything until ordered.'

Dotty Wedgewood continued her round. Outside, the loudspeakers were in play, pounding out loud music that slowly built up in the brain until something snapped. Dotty prayed that it wasn't a marine who snapped.

'Those bastards in Washington ought to be over here with this. Wouldn't get half the crap we do if the brass had to sit it out with this shit rattling round their stupid skulls.'

The anger helped, Dotty knew that. Her real anger, however, was with the politicians at home. If Congress would only work with the president things wouldn't be falling apart. But somebody wanted things to fall apart. Stalemate was permanent; money was only voted after huge arguments and then was never enough. Everything the president did was opposed. The colonel was sufficiently close to what was happening (her brother was a congressman) to know that the power people who resisted the president's every move were elected by no one and known to very few.

'Bloody SIE,' she said to herself. 'Apart from the one or

two old-stagers, they seem to have appointed themselves. And how long will... What the shit was that?'

Dotty was about to bend her mind to the latest Washington gossip that the SIE was divided into two factions – one trying to reassert the traditional American values by argument and example, and the other, the so-called New SIE, trying to poke the tentacles of its power into every aspect of American life and rebuild the super-power image of the 1970s and 1980s by force – when the sharp rattle of gunfire propelled her back to the realities of the present.

'What the hell is going on?'

Back in the foyer of the embassy, and behind the temporary barricades, she confronted the newly arrived sergeant. Behind the sergeant, his eyes glinting with an almost demented pleasure, Dotty Wedgewood could see Ambassador Fitzallan.

'We thought we were being fired on, so we returned fire.' The sergeant had a precise and whining voice.

'Who ordered you to fire?'

'I did.'

Well, he'd said he'd order the marines to fire if he had to and she knew right from the first demonstration that Fitzallan was dying to cause a confrontation. He's one of the bastards that's doing all this, she thought furiously. Fitzallan's name had never been mentioned when she and her brother discussed the SIE's hidden agenda but he was a personal friend of every single one of the people whose names did come up.

21

2004

John's trip to Amsterdam had worked well.

Joe Longton was a good, solid field man. He was what espionage was all about. He got results even if it was hard to work out how. However, despite his respect for Joe and their good working relations, in the light of his director's priorities, John had to consider what the CIA's agenda over Kirovsky might be and whether Joe would be working to it. He was unclear. Joe might have been his own man but he was still a loyal American and still on the CIA payroll. What was his angle?

Since 'staying with the CIA' was his brief, John felt that the trail was now sufficiently interwoven with this brief that he could pursue Kirovsky as vigorously as he wanted in Amsterdam and elsewhere. If the CIA's interest was exposing old KGB/CIA double agents in the States that at least was one explanation for the CIA's current secretiveness in their dealings with the British. Post-9/11, washing their dirty linen in public was definitely a no-go area.

John didn't have much chance to pursue the topic on the Saturday evening. In a quiet bar in Delft with Joe and his wife they got to talk about many things but CIA/British relations was not one of them. Much of what Joe thought, John recognised, he wouldn't have said in public or even in front of his wife in private. It was a pleasant evening nonetheless and cemented the relationship between the two men.

And then another CIA mole had died on the Monday and Joe became politely unhelpful. John knew that Joe was not being deliberately obstructive. The bigger picture, unclear as it was to him, was bearing down on him. After 9/11, the CIA brass in Washington had been in violent motion but as it later transpired, in not too clear a direction. The blame game was still on and there were too many opportunities for score-settling for Joe to put a foot wrong. John sensed this. He still wasn't up in current CIA politics but he knew that Joe's face didn't fit for some reason and that was dangerous for him. Despite this, he did provide enough information to suggest that a trip to Antwerp might be worthwhile. It was to prove to be so.

Antwerp was another place John liked. It was also a place where he had an office through his company and access to resources. Maybe he could find out more about the dead man and if there was anything unusual behind why Joe had gone to ground. There wasn't much he could do on the day he arrived. By the time he had checked out the dead agent's home, been unknowingly trampled on by Yuri Kirovsky and had his hormones disturbed by the sight of Ross Metcalfe he was ready for a good Belgian dinner and a night's sleep.

'Let's see what tomorrow brings.' But the vision of the leather-clad Ross Metcalfe stayed with him into sleep.

* * *

Ross had tracked down Kirovsky's electronic mailbox and had invaded it. It was an easy piece of detection for one of Ross's skills, but the ease with which it was achieved and the tidy uncluttered nature of the mailbox aroused her suspicions.

She had also provided the Colonel with as much detail as she could find on the death of the suspected CIA double agent in Amsterdam before she headed off to Paris.

'Bloke called van Elders, Bernstein and several other names; American; linked with Kirovsky and the corpse in the Detroit swimming pool; shot on the doorstep of a CIA safe-house in Amsterdam around eight-thirty this morning.'

The Colonel didn't need much sleep and Ross made a point of briefing him early each day on the overnight events that her monitoring programmes had picked up. On this occasion the killing was fresh on the system and Ross hurriedly researched the background before she left. She filled in more detail for the Colonel from Paris. The electronic gadgetry in his study gave him voice communication if he wished, and Ross reported the information that she had found out.

'Carson, he was the guy in Detroit, and Bernstein/van Elders look like in-house jobs. Carson and Bernstein/van Elders were on Kirovsky's payroll. If the CIA knew about that, and we have to now assume that they did, they'd hit them.'

Ross wasn't planning to be long in Paris. It wasn't a place that she especially liked and from her reading of the Dutch Police reports on the dead man, Antwerp sounded much more interesting.

'Right now, let's see what our Mr Kirovsky is really made of.'

Ross had booked her Aberdeen-Paris flight through the most open and public route she could. She wanted Kirovsky to have the best possible chance of discovering that the Colonel was in action.

'Hotel Bon Fils.'

It wasn't really a hotel, just a block of flats. The Colonel had connections somewhere from the mists of time and a serviced apartment to use when in Paris. Not that the Colonel ever went to Paris.

'Crafty old what-name. I wonder how he got to having a pied-á-terre like this then.'

The apartment was modern, convenient and utterly devoid of character. But it was warm and well-stocked with food and drink.

Ross worked quickly. Kirovsky's electronic mailbox was easily found. The number of messages had grown. Her reply to the trail was amongst them – 'Should a military man worry about Hamburg and Amsterdam?' Kirovsky's response had taken a day or so. 'Forget what was underneath in Hamburg and Amsterdam. What's up front in Paris?'

Ross was pleased. Communication had been established.

'It looks like he had dozens of replies. Didn't take him long to suss out ours.'

The next minutes were full of furious typing, but it all seemed like a waste of time to Ross. As she rattled the agreed series of messages into her laptop she wondered again why the Colonel was so insistent that she come to Paris to do something that she could have done with a minimum of effort from her terminal at home.

'How am I supposed to give substance to the response?' she asked the room. 'Kirovsky isn't going to know what my role is in all of this.'

But she was wrong and the Colonel would have known that she was. Yuri Kirovsky hadn't survived all the years he had by taking risks. He'd done his homework long before he'd even contemplated starting his trail. He knew all about Ross and the Colonel's disability. He knew that the Colonel would send her to Paris once he had signalled his interest in a trade. That was how the Colonel worked; Kirovsky knew that and the Colonel knew that he knew. Kirovsky also knew that Ross was in the flat. At least Collette did and that was as good as the same thing.

'So who's in number six?'

Collette was in her best street uniform: a long, imitation fur coat pulled wide open and an orange PVC skirt that gleamed in the dim light of the hallway as she talked to the concierge. A sweater that revealed all and honey-coloured boots that reached up to her thighs completed the picture. Her question oozed out at the man as he wiped the growing beads of sweat from his brow, his fantasies running riot.

'A young English woman. Just arrived.'

The man described her, or at least her body. It was enough. The description fitted; Collette knew it was Ross. It was all she needed; she had the photographs taken at the airport and confirmation that Ross had access to the Colonel's apartment. Another piece in Yuri Kirovsky's jigsaw puzzle slotted into place.

Collette left and the concierge returned to the nagging of his wife.

Upstairs, Ross had laid more trail and returned her laptop to her capacious shoulder bag. The conversation with the Colonel that followed was short and to the point. The second CIA mole lived in Antwerp; she was going there to see what she could find out. The limited amount of information that she had garnered from the Amsterdam Police files was reported. The lack of detail was suspicious, she thought, but the Colonel wasn't really interested. Like Carson, van Elder or Bernstein, or whatever his name really was, was only of value when he was alive. It wasn't that the Colonel was callous; more that he only wanted to store information that would have future use for himself.

'Well,' said Ross, 'it's on file. If he needs it he can easily get it back.'

The trip to Antwerp didn't take Ross long. Absorbed by the uninhibited vulgarity of a French tabloid newspaper that she had picked up, she unconsciously appraised Collette in much the same way that she herself had been appraised by Collette at the airport. Standing over her prone opponent, her gloved hands held high, the sweat-streaked figure of

Collette Dubois grinned out of the back page of the paper. Ignorant of boxing, Ross read the brief recital in distaste, but the triumphant face was fixed in her mind.

On arrival, unencumbered by luggage, she set off for the Jewish quarter. It wasn't far from the hotel and the brisk walk livened her up. With an uncanny knack for navigation in dense, urban areas – surprising for one who dwelt in the country – the trip was soon accomplished.

'God, this is bad timing.'

The police were interviewing the concierge as she arrived. Intent on exercising her charms in the same way as Collette had done in Paris, she was disappointed. And she was having second thoughts about coming. Very much aware that she stood out rather obviously amongst the soberly dressed inhabitants of the district, she beat a hasty retreat.

'You're a back-room girl, Ross Metcalfe. Leave the clever stuff to the experts.'

And the only expert she knew was John Harcourt.

'So, what would you have done then, Mr Agent Harcourt?'

He wouldn't have walked up and down in the Jewish quarter in an outfit better suited to the red-light district, that was for sure. Ross didn't see her clothes in quite those terms but she would have readily admitted her tendency to flamboyance.

'He wears expensive clothes himself – better than anything I could afford – but I couldn't tell you a thing about what he was wearing when I last saw him.'

The steam-filled bathroom back at the hotel echoed gently with her announcement. Submerged in the warm water her thoughts drifted to her last meeting with John. It was in his office. She had enjoyed it. Feelings stirred, feelings long suppressed to avoid pain. There was something soft and companionable about John behind the tough, go-getting exterior.

'Another trip to London is called for, I think,' she told

the bathroom, 'if only for me to find out a bit more about the bloke.'

Ross would have found it hard to define what it was she wanted to find out about John. He'd already told her a lot about his life and work. There was something deeper. There was an anxiety about the roughness, the harshness of his reaction to situations that troubled her; something that reminded her of the violence that was often just below the surface with some men. After her experience with her relationship in Cambridge and the hidden capability for violence that her partner there had shown, pictures that disturbed her but also fascinated her were struggling to surface. But, ever-practical, what she couldn't deal with she relegated to her mental filing cabinet until she could. It was the here and now and her only uncertainty was about the wisdom of her being in Antwerp. And that was an uncertainty that she could readily deal with.

Ross ended the day feeling good. Not so far away, John Harcourt was feeling the same and he had the benefit of knowing that Ross was in Antwerp, whilst she had failed to see him. Yuri Kirovsky, in turn, also knew that Ross had been in Paris, but only after he had seen Collette's photographs.

22

2004

The hotel in the De Keyserlie was one of John Harcourt's favourites. And Antwerp, because of its concentration of diamond traders, was also one of his most successful business offices, which all added to his feeling of it also being one of his favourite cities. He liked everything about it: the food, the people, the ambience; even as the home of the objectionable Mr van Elders/Bernstein, it still attracted him.

He had slept well; that in itself said something about his relaxed relationship with the place. His first night away from his own bed was usually much less tranquil. But now it was time to get moving.

'Come on, you idle sod. Get yourself going.' Yuri Kirovsky wasn't the only one who gave himself orders.

As he wound himself up from half-sleep to full mental competence he was delighted at the first thoughts that surfaced in his head. It was the image of Ross Metcalfe in the half-light of the dingy street in the Jewish quarter, head-to-toe in black leather. Instinctively, he inspected the angry bruise on his ankle. The skin was tight over the swelling and it was painful if he kept his weight on it too long.

He took the lift to the restaurant. 'Spare the ankle,' he told himself.

It was rush hour. The line of would-be breakfasters stretched out of the restaurant door. Queue-jumping Germans were tactfully forced into their proper place by the head waiter, a lugubrious looking man with obvious colonial origins. There were no French people; the breakfast was too Anglo-American for the normal Gallic taste. The British chattered in pairs, or with their neighbours. John had no pair, only a neighbour immersed in the leading Flemish daily.

'John!'

The sing-song tone of voice displayed both surprise and delight. But the surprise and delight masked an instant concern. How would John react? Despite her good intentions to deal with him and his sharp reactions as she found them, she experienced a distinct moment of anxiety. She didn't like being shouted at and cringed at the thought as well as the act. But all of this took microseconds; John's response provided reassurance and Ross's normal ebullience overrode the anxiety.

'Ross. How nice to see you.'

There was cautious delight but no surprise in John's voice. He knew that Ross had been in Antwerp the previous day; before he went to sleep he had debated the possibility of her staying overnight and even of her being in the same hotel. But being good at computing probabilities he hadn't dwelt on the possibility.

'What are you doing here? I'd no idea you were here.'

'I'm waiting for my breakfast of course.'

'John, you idiot, you know I didn't mean that.'

They had reached the head of the queue. The head waiter, fluent in several languages and skilled at determining nationality, spoke before he had heard them speak.

'Two, sir?'

Ross was impressed.

'Please. Non-smoking.'

John knew the ritual. Ross glanced around as they were shown to their table and deduced it.

It was a vast dining room, seating a couple of hundred

people. As they threaded their way to their destination, a channel of quiet was created along their path. It was a businessman's hotel and businessmen were the norm. A black, leather skirt wider than it was long and an acre of fine, black, stocking-clad leg were seriously bad for any businessman's digestion, let alone his blood pressure.

'Wow, Ross!' said John to himself. 'You're back to the exotic again.'

If Ross knew the effect that she was having she wasn't bothered. She had all of John's attention; in that instant of time that was enough for her.

'John!' she had breathed to herself, a surge of excitement gripping her. After the meeting in John's London office she had come away with a whole raft of submerged feelings and long-latent thoughts struggling for expression. If she were to be honest with herself, the anxieties about John's roughness were not actually about him, they were about her. It was her baggage that kept surfacing. At least that was how she rationalised it to herself.

'In a word,' she had said then, 'I fancy him and it's time I had what I fancy.'

The Colonel had sensed the change and was both pleased and concerned. He was pleased because he wanted her to have a normal life and form lasting relationships, but he was concerned because she had been bruised by her youthful encounter at Cambridge and didn't want a repeat. And, all too aware of the sort of man John Harcourt had to be, the concern outweighed the pleasure.

As the head waiter seated her, Ross stretched out her left leg, whether to ease it or admire it John wasn't clear. It was an unconscious gesture that astonished him. His whole picture of the woman in front of him crumbled. The slick, efficient computer wizard playing concertos on the keyboard of his office PC was light years from a woman seeming to show such vanity.

Ross caught his puzzled look.

'What?'

John shook his head in bemused delight.

'I was in Paris yesterday; bought some new boots. They're killing me.'

The startled waitress slopped some coffee, as she poured it, onto the pristine tablecloth, as John erupted into delighted laughter at Ross's self-mocking comment.

* * *

Antwerp Central Station was only a few hundred yards from their hotel. John was returning to Amsterdam and Ross, on the spur of the moment, had decided to go with him. She was beginning to feel increasingly excited about being in his company and she noticed that his attitude to her had softened considerably. She was loath to part with him whilst she could scrape together even the flimsiest excuse for remaining with him. And pursuing the trail via the CIA in Amsterdam was excuse enough for her. It wasn't, however, for the Colonel, but since Ross could access her computers from almost anywhere, he was hard put to generate a sustainable argument for her to come home.

'Just take care. Kirovsky knows you're about. He'll be following you even now. You can count on it.'

'Don't worry; I've got a big strong man to protect me.'

The Colonel shrugged, mentally and physically. Ross, in great delight, scurried around to get herself organised.

'Okay,' she said when she re-joined John.

He was just as pleased as she was that they would be together but it was he who insisted that she check with the Colonel.

The walk was short, brisk and silent.

'I love the flower stalls. They're always out so early.'

John nodded to the arrays of flowers for sale marvelling as he usually did at the variety even in winter. It was a nod that had interesting consequences. It alerted a watcher, whose instinctive movement in turn confirmed her presence to John.

'Ross, by the refreshment stand, look for a woman your height, blonde. She was outside the hotel when I was waiting for you. She seems to be very interested in us.'

John had been watching the woman for some time. He recognised the style. She was well-trained, almost a professional. She had gone from her pitch by the time Ross could get a good look at her, but she had gained an adequate enough impression of her.

'Headed for the stairs on the platform. What's down there?'

'Loos, I'd say,' said Ross. 'Need to go myself.'

'Hey, hold on. What are you up to?'

'Nothing. Well, a bit of sleuthing.'

After her ineptitude in the Jewish quarter Ross was keen to recover her self-esteem in the matter of the James Bond stuff, so she set off before John could stop her. He was far from happy about this turn of events but he could hardly chase Ross down into the ladies' toilets.

Whether she knew she was being followed or not, the woman made no effort to hide when she entered the tiled mausoleum below the platform.

'Collette Dubois.'

The name leapt out of Ross as she almost collided with the French girl. Collette was seriously startled by such instant recognition. She shook her head but Ross knew it was her. She remembered the newspaper photograph. The face and hair told her. The boxing gear was gone but it was surely her.

'So, why are you following me?'

'Following you?'

'Oh come on, cut the innocent crap. I've got a train to catch. You were following me from the hotel, why?'

Ross advanced on Collette, forcing her to step back against the tiled wall of the toilet. Collette was uncomfortable. Backed up as she was there was no leverage for her to attack Ross if she needed to, but Ross had all the space in the world. It wasn't a situation that Collette had been expecting. She only wanted to let Ross know that she was being watched. Kirovsky's instructions to her were clear enough but neither of them had supposed that Ross, the shadowy computer freak, was going to confront Collette in quite such an aggressive manner. But then Collette had only just learned that Ross had a companion, and she neither knew who the man was nor was aware of Ross's desire to impress him at his own game.

'Okay, I was following you. It's good money. It's my job. So what?'

'Who's paying you?'

Ross knew from Collette's crooked grin that she wasn't going to get that information without something more drastic being attempted. So she shot her left hand forward as if she was going to land a punch on the French girl. Collette instinctively moved her own right hand away from her body to protect herself. She never quite knew how she got to be lying on her front with Ross kneeling painfully on her shoulder and neck. But she knew for a fact that Ross was well-versed in some combat sport or other.

'Now then. Who's paying you?'

'If she asks who's watching her, tell her.' It was Yuri Kirovsky's other instruction. It was Collette's own reluctance to be so craven in dealing with the threat from Ross that had got her onto the toilet floor with multiple bruises, not any wish to keep a secret.

'Yuri Kirovsky.'

Ross didn't react. She could see her watch; she needed to go. The train was due to leave and no doubt John would be anxious. She hoped that he would be; she wanted him to be; it would show his feelings much more than any words.

John certainly was anxious and it certainly wasn't about missing the train.

As she left the underground toilet Ross checked that Collette wasn't preparing to retaliate. She was sullenly rubbing her neck and avoiding eye contact.

Ross hurried down the platform to where John had located seats in an empty compartment for them.

'Guess what?' she said as they were comfortably installed.

'Come on, Ross. You know I can't know what went on down there.'

So she told him. She underplayed the attack on Collette but it was obvious to John what had happened.

'You stupid ... woman!'

There was a moment when it seemed to Ross that the word that John was searching for was 'cow'.

John's body tightened in frustration and anger. The roughness and violence of his reaction were there again. She was devastated. All her pragmatism and excitement at the growing relationship disappeared. The hard, tense face of the man that she was only moments before lusting after metamorphosed into an arrogant young student in Cambridge. Just as that young man, her partner of two years, suddenly erupted into an angry rage of jealousy and possessiveness, so John seemed to turn into a domineering ogre contemptuous of her actions and capabilities. At least in a railway carriage he was restricted on how he might take out his rage on her or, as her Cambridge boyfriend had done, on the fellow student who dared to flirt with her. And John had better control of himself. There were to be no broken bones and life-threatening injuries, just a deep fear generated in Ross's conscious as well as subconscious mind.

As she struggled to quell her sobs John struggled to control his breathing and his anger. The silence between them was hard and forbidding. But, as the minutes ticked by and they each struggled with their feelings, the silence softened. And as Ross willed him to bring his eyes back to make contact with hers the anguish in John's face reduced her to tears. The realisation of the pain that he had inflicted seemed to have momentarily destroyed him. Ross moved across the compartment to sit beside him and cradle his head into her breasts. Her anguish matched his.

'John.'

'Ross. I'm sorry.'

The words stood out in the silence, their inadequacy reinforcing John's horror at his unthinking and unfeeling outburst at Ross.

'But I *was* being stupid,' Ross said.

'But I didn't need to have said what I did. It was cruel and it was unnecessary. I could at least have tried to understand what you were trying to do.'

'John, she's a professional boxer,' Ross said simply. 'It was madness for me to have taken her on.'

The silence this time was different. Ross was trying to shift her fears about John's violent reaction back into the depths of her mind and John was struggling between his revulsion at his own lack of self-control and his admiration for what she had done. He knew that he had to express that admiration but this wasn't the moment.

The journey from Antwerp to Amsterdam isn't very long. Both John and Ross knew that they had to put this unexpected piece of conflict behind them. It took much of the remaining journey. Ross finally picked up the conversation from where they had left it. The spat was over but it wasn't forgotten; Ross would find it much harder than John to bury the hurt.

'So what d'you think is going on here, John? Kirovsky obviously wanted us to know he was following me. Collette surely wouldn't have run to earth in an underground loo like that if she was trying to avoid detection. She'd have legged it out of the station.'

'Oh, he wants us to know all right, Ross. Just part of the confidence-building process I'd guess. He'd know what the Colonel would be expected to do in the situation; an old fox like him would be bound to. He's just checking we're behaving as predicted.'

'Then what? Respond to our message? If he knew I was in Paris, he'd know we were thinking of a meeting.'

'It doesn't matter at this stage. It's patterns of behaviour he's into I imagine. When they feel right to him, he'll make another move.'

Ross shuffled on the seat next to John clawing hopelessly at her brief skirt. Any amount of pulling wasn't going to affect the area of leg it exposed whatever she did.

John noted the movement and the suggestiveness of it. He took it to signal that normal relations had resumed. They had. He was relieved.

This is one extraordinary woman, he thought. One minute she's macho and aggressive, the next she's in tears at my unforgivable behaviour. Then she's some super-brain computer wizard and now she's putting it on like the best of them.

'You're some woman, Ross Metcalfe. D'you know that?'

'Oh sure, I know that.'

There was only half the suggestion of a grin. She wasn't naturally modest, nor was she boastful for that matter. It was just how she felt at that moment. That's what the Colonel always preached to her: 'Be honest, admit your faults and don't be ashamed of your good points.' Judging by the way that John had moved away from her to take a long appraising look, she reckoned her good points here were her slim, tight figure, her firm breasts, her sleek leather-clad hips and her legs. But she was still wary. However, she returned the look, sweeping her eyes over his body in much the same way as he had done hers. His figure was just as tight but it was more muscle hard. There wasn't an ounce of spare fat on him; his stomach was flat and she could see the outline of his ribcage as he stripped off his jacket. She moved back beside him, jamming her hip against his and leaning back on his arm. He eased his position so that his left arm was around her shoulder. She rested her hand on his upper leg, feeling the material of his trousers stretched taut. He closed his right hand over hers as he felt the warmth of it on his leg.

'Must be some bloke, this Kirovsky, if he can keep a woman like Collette going.'

'I guess so, Ross. But she must be some girl too. He's stayed with her longer than any other of his women.'

Ross couldn't help being interested.

'It's a dangerous pastime being Kirovsky's girlfriend. At least three ended up dead. Garrotted. A method of execution he's known to favour.'

'You're joking!'

'I'm not. He never takes risks; all his girlfriends have been disposed of one way or another.'

'Charming.'

'Not quite the word I'd have used,' John said.

Ross didn't respond. In the warmth and comfort of his arms a brute like Kirovsky seemed unreal. She'd had enough of him for one day. When she got to Amsterdam she'd have to touch base with the Colonel; that was soon enough to think about the wretched Russian.

She relaxed back and curled her feet up on to the carriage seat. John watched her and felt her as she squirmed herself under his arm. The rhythmic clatter of the train lulled them into a semi-torpid state. They lapsed into a companionable silence and switched off time. Except that there wasn't much of the journey left and they soon had to resume normal living. Ross for one left the train without regret. Notwithstanding the intimacy of the last few minutes of the journey, she still heartily wished that she had never left Scotland. She needed to get her head around her relationship with John if it was going to be a bumpy as this.

John and Ross had checked into a small canal-side hotel overlooking the Singel. It wasn't far from the CIA office; John had used it for years. Ross's room was small, misshapen and more than a little noisy, but it was warm and next door to John's. Concentrating finally on living in the present she was happy enough, but first things first: she had to check in with the Colonel.

'So what's to report, Ross?' He was business-like and detached; that put Ross on the alert.

'John spoke to the Belgian Police. I think we know all we need to know about that shit van Elders.'

'Is Harcourt still with you?'

'He's gone to see his chum in the Amsterdam CIA. Bit worried that the Yanks will freelance it with Kirovsky and confuse things.'

'I wouldn't worry about that.'

Ross knew that the Colonel had something more to say and it was going to be personal. It was the way he drew in his breath before he spoke.

'You okay, Ross?'

'Of course I am.'

It ended the conversation before it even got started. Whether the Colonel was reassured she would have no way of knowing. But she was touched. She always was when the old man showed his concern. Their bond was tight and deep and he felt for her in a way that she was only just beginning to understand as she emerged from her years of self-denial and tried to build this new relationship. He was desperate that Harcourt shouldn't hurt her but knew that she really had to fight her battle for herself. John, however, had already hurt her and she had survived. It was a battle that she had already fought.

'I'm okay,' she said to the telephone as it went dead.

* * *

Yuri Kirovsky laughed and laughed when Collette told him her tale.

'Well my little firebrand, perhaps you should give up boxing and take up karate.'

'Next time!'

'No, no! Not next time. Next time it will be different. We will set it up properly. We will be more careful.'

'So when's this next time? It's weeks and still you play games. When will you trust them?'

'Not yet. The Colonel hasn't shown himself yet. The girl comes; she leaves me messages in my mailbox. She does the things the Colonel would do, but what does he think? How can I know he will deal with me? How can I know he will listen to what I have to say?'

Collette had no answers to his questions. Had she been better versed in the tortuous machinations of Kirovsky's mind she might have known there were no answers. He didn't have the feeling yet, and until he did he would hang back.

23

2026

Neither Ross nor John had been to Grasmere before. They chose the Lake District for their combined break and operational review because it was broadly halfway between Dorset and Aberdeenshire.

John had settled on West Bexington because he was able to have solitude and a sea view and still be within reasonable distance of a decent country town. Technology had long since removed the demarcation between home location and work location and the need to access large centres of population. Ross remained at the Buchan farmhouse because it was now hers and it held all she needed. Both set off for their rendezvous with mixed emotions and, conscious of the need to use the railways, with plenty of time to order these emotions. Except that at the moment of meeting all such order would disappear into the stirrings of long dead feelings. And of course they both knew that.

Anyone who knew Ross at all well might have detected a certain skittishness about her manner as she prepared herself for the trip. She dressed with more than her usual care and with very little effort transported herself back in time to belie the fifty-two years that she had now clocked up. It was a conscious action that surprised her and would have surprised John had he been aware of it. One of her stocks in trade of the past was a complete obliviousness to what anybody thought about her clothes, clothing style or turnout in general. Needless to say, John was not aware of her efforts; he was too focused on how he thought he would feel once in Ross's intimate company again.

'That's one ugly brute of a vehicle,' Ross said as they piled themselves and their luggage into their hire-car at the railway station. It was more like a golf buggy than a car.

'Half-electric, half-solar. Don't ask me how it works. I'm only the driver.'

The exchange lightened the atmosphere and combined with the business of driving and navigating, particularly since the brute was hardly a roadster, they arrived at the hotel in good spirits, feeling good about themselves and each other.

'There never was anyone else,' Ross said reflectively when they were alone after the processes of checking in. Ross couldn't explain the urge to offer this reassurance, it just seem right to do so in the circumstances.

Afternoon tea on the terrace followed unpacking in the adjacent rooms. Ross made no mention of this arrangement when she confirmed the booking with John; he in his turn was delighted when he realised what she had set up, but also said nothing.

Communication through the interconnecting door flowed easily and any tensions that might have arisen from the scene changing to the bedroom simply hadn't materialised.

John noted the suggestion of tears and moved himself closer to Ross on the couch that they had instinctively opted for.

'There never was for me either,' he said.

A strong sense of closing out the past came to John as he reciprocated Ross's sentiment. Even if he wasn't sure why she'd chosen that moment to offer her reassurance he was glad that she had.

The smile that flashed across Ross's face told John that his declaration was welcomed and appreciated, and removed a raft of half-hidden and unacknowledged uncertainties that had been milling around in her mind for many years. She tugged at her skirt to pull it over her knees, a gesture that again raised a lump in John's throat and stifled any words that might have been forming. It was a gesture so typical of her and induced visions of tight, black leather that were buried in his memory and which gleefully leapt out at him now. The gesture also focused John on Ross's clothes as she had wanted it to: expensive, fashionable but environmentally friendly, yet still playing to no audience but her own tastes. Her clothes pleased John. The fact that her style was subconsciously contrived to attract his attention passed him by.

Nothing man-made that you can see, he thought as he scanned the tartan skirt, cotton blouse and woollen waistcoat. And there was nothing plastic in the graceful ankle boots that she knew that John used to love. Not of course that there was anything man-made in John's fine worsted and cotton/silk clothing either.

He's greyed, Ross thought, lost a bit of hair, but... The surge of warmth told her that what she saw she still liked.

'Was it hard when the Colonel died?'

'Even though we were expecting it,' she said – unspoken, John knew that the 'we' was Ross and her brother – 'it came quite quickly in the end. He would have liked that.'

There was a silence of sadness which Ross eventually broke with a chuckle.

'For about the first time in his life his timing was bad: we were snowed under with work.'

'But you coped.'

Ross acknowledged his confidence with a half-smile, half-smirk that again stirred his insides as of old.

'Premonition or not, I don't know; the Colonel was having me update the files on Intercontinental Veterans Anonymous just before the end. Wanted to know where the sleepers were, those we knew about anyway. He never really stopped talking about Kirovsky. He knew he had left us a legacy of course but he was never sure when and how we might be able to use it.'

'So that was why you weren't surprised by Spencer's death?'

'Not surprised, John, no; miffed more like because it closed a door.'

'But as we discussed when I came to Scotland, Kirovsky's lot are still very much in place and capable of action.'

'Oh, yes. And after twenty-two years they're no longer superannuated KGB doubles; they've renewed themselves out of the disaffected young liberal element. Patriotic but ideologically opposed to the Neocons, the real power behind the America Resurgent movement.'

'America Resurgent and the religious right-wing want a powerful US again. That right? But with stalemate in government the Neoconservatives are creeping into power by default of any effective actions against them. No one is even arguing against their philosophy.'

'No. Some parts of the US media are beginning to confront their ideology but the SIE has its own media machine that so far has drowned out any voices in opposition to the Neocon view.'

'Alastair Browneton?'

'Sure, John.'

Ross moved on.

'In the real world people achieve their objectives not by theories, however highly placed their provenance is supposed to be, but by clear-cut actions with clear-cut outcomes.'

There was a pause. Ross changed tack.

'So why is your director friend so fixated on old missiles?'

'I'm not sure he knows why he thinks there's something important surrounding the old ICBMs. He implies a link to the SIE or the right-wing but then backs away.'

'What does imply a link mean for heaven's sake?'

'I'm certainly not privy to the thinking of the European intelligence community, Ross, but even back in 2004 you may recall there was concern about old missiles and those unaccounted for and presumed never destroyed. It's that knowledge and the potential consequences of it being true that seem to be bugging him, that and the common factor of Yuri Kirovsky.'

Ross's memory was less clear than John's.

'Okay, John, but all we knew then was that Kirovsky might – *might*, mind you – have found out that the missiles were still around and still within the US Air Force remit.'

'Jesus, Ross, they were old then and it's twenty-odd years later now.'

'Well, two things I know from the background noise, and so does your boss. One: an old rocket fuel installation has been mysteriously refurbished, and two: the SIE are looking for two IT specialists who went AWOL.'

Ross didn't explain the significance of this latter rather enigmatic statement but John's assumption that their expertise might be in rocket control system programming was pretty well on the mark.

The early evening television news was dominated by coverage of demonstrations in around thirty European cities. Most of the main regional bulletins concentrated on those in their own areas but John and Ross were able to get a reasonable picture by tracking the channels. In the more volatile parts of Europe the violence had been barely contained and many American-owned properties had been badly damaged. As the evening wore on, the reports became more dramatic and the devastation more apparent. A death toll emerged. But the exchange of fire at the American Consulate in London became the focus of attention because of the presence and implied involvement of the US Ambassador.

* * *

The centre of Amsterdam was packed with people. Anything American was attacked. The police had a hard time rescuing people from the mob. The crowd was not good-natured. Joe Longton was on his way home from work. Fortunately, he was away from his office and Rick Blackford was away in Antwerp with Alanda Ngozie. Joe's Dutch-speaking protected him but he was far from confident that Alanda, being British, would have been able to protect Rick the way that the crowds were working themselves up.

Joe was appalled at the speed with which the usual *laissez-faire* attitude of the Dutch had deteriorated into the rabid anti-Americanism that was sweeping Europe. And at one point even his ability to speak Dutch nearly didn't prove enough. He was sheltering a blood-stained and bewildered American schoolgirl until the police could spirit her away when he was recognised. The poor girl, knowing no Dutch herself, fortunately missed the nastiness of the taunts that were being hurled at her but Joe's cursing had dropped into its natural vernacular. It was enough for a café worker to be alerted and point him out.

The arrival of the police, one of whom was a senior officer who knew Joe by sight, allowed the situation to be defused. However, it left Joe with a jumble of feelings not least of which was an anxiety about his future retirement in an anti-American environment where mixed marriages might not be as appreciated or tolerated as they had been in the past.

* * *

'Thank God Alanda is in Antwerp.' Ross said to John. 'They seem to have been immune from the violence, well so far anyway.' She wasn't very confident that the mayhem wouldn't spread to Belgium.

'Except, Ross, she's gone there with Rick Blackford, an all-American boy, no doubt with an accent that would cleave the air at a hundred metres.'

'Hell, John, I was looking for reassurance not angst.'
'I'm sure she's a sensible girl. And this Blackford, if he's SIE, will know how to handle himself.'
'You're digging the hole bigger, John.'
'Well, maybe. But I can remember a young woman who was very keen to have a go at the James Bond stuff.'
'And who made a God Almighty pig's ear of it?'

* * *

'Jesus, what was that?'
The diners were on their feet, Alanda and Rick amongst them. A dull, crumping thud had rattled the windows as a pressure wave seemed to strike them. As the noise subsided so did the people. Then, as the seconds grew into minutes other more strident noises forced their attention onto the now nervous breakfasters. Antwerp seemed no longer to be isolated from the action.

Alanda and Rick had arrived the previous evening, intent on gathering information on the movements of several Belgium-based, Russian mafia-types with strong suspected links to people trafficking and fringe terror groups. Joe Longton had furnished introductions and sound advice to Rick to let Alanda take the lead as much as possible.

'An American accent isn't the flavour of the month, Rick. Let her do the talking.'

What Joe didn't say was that Alanda's amazing good looks would always be a focus and it ought to be easy for Rick to stay out of the limelight. Such had proved the case with the hotel staff but activities in the external world now seemed likely to put the advice to a much stronger test.

A haemorrhage of businessmen started from the restaurant as the silence resettled. By the time the shrilling of burglar and car alarms had started a quarter of the people had gone. As the sirens wailed and whined louder and closer another quarter had left.

'Bombs?' asked Alanda.

'Bombs,' said Rick quietly.

'Let's finish and go back to my room.'

Back at the hotel, after half an hour of watching the television, Alanda hooked up her laptop and demonstrated her technological prowess.

'Hell, Alanda, you're something else aren't you.'

The grin that lit up Alanda's face lit up her insides as well. Never one to duck the issue, she'd already decided that she liked this American, complicated as it might make her life, and so she was more than pleased with his praise.

After what seemed to Rick like a frenzy of typing, she turned the screen towards him and allowed him to read.

'Bombs,' he said. 'American-owned banks and other businesses; ten were attacked during the night and now a load more.'

'I logged into the police network,' Alanda said by way of explanation. 'A maximum damage campaign seemingly. Destroy as much American property as possible. This is only about Antwerp but I wouldn't be surprised if it wasn't elsewhere as well.'

'So, who the hell's bombing American businesses?'

'At a guess, Rick, I'd say your lot: the SIE.'

'What?'

Before the trip Alanda and Ross had discussed the possibilities surrounding Rick Blackford and the reasonable probability that he had been planted as a mole in the European camp. The assumption that they had made as a consequence was that that was exactly what he was and they had planned accordingly. Information and misinformation were now a part of Alanda's brief in dealing with Rick. Her growing attraction to him made her hope that he wasn't acting as a mole but until she had evidence one way or the other she decided that she could only be as straight as possible. And of course feed the European party line to him.

'It makes sense, Rick; the Europeans are getting up the noses of the US Administration by fishing along your territorial waters, your military is run down and doesn't have the stomach or the resources to do more than just shout back loudly. Congress and the president are going nowhere together, there's a vacuum in government and a chance for mischief making by special interest groups.'

'Hell, Alanda, that's a bit hard on us isn't it?'

'At least you didn't deny it.'

Alanda had a sudden picture of the waif-like researcher from British intelligence with whom she had been video conferencing.

'Bread and circuses,' the girl had said.

'What?'

'Bread and circuses.

And it was this conversation that she now fed to Rick.

'Bread and circuses, Rick,' she said. 'Ever since the beginning of time, governments have distracted their people by distributing largesse and putting on bellicose displays. They've threatened their weaker neighbours, moved troops about, that sort of thing. That's what's happening over the fishing.'

Rick didn't respond for a while. A series of fleeting expressions of distaste, disbelief and even anger passed across his face. Before he had left London his officemate had been bashing his ear about his future in the SIE and had given him an ill-informed and distorted view of the SIE, its future and therefore Rick's. The man also asked Rick if he knew anything about Intercontinental Veterans Anonymous but Rick denied any knowledge of such an organisation. That wasn't true but he had no wish to feed his colleague's speculation.

With an honesty that heartened Alanda he shared some of the office conversations.

There was growing evidence of a major split in the SIE hierarchy. What he had heard suggested that the SIE had a definite agenda of its own and that, as he saw it, it was megalomania. He wasn't sure where the power-crazed factions were headed but there was a whole load of score-settling and filling of policy vacuums created by the stalemate at the top.

'So why bomb Europe?' asked Rick.

'It's all part of the same thing I mentioned. Picking a fight with the European Federation distracts the populace.'

Rick knew his European history. 'Okay, history is littered with such adventures and they usually end badly. No, no, there's no sense in this. Destabilise US-European relations while your own country staggers into its own instability; that's insane. And it would be worse than insane if a revitalised US, in the wrong hands, tries to re-establish its dominance of the past.'

Rick's response was revealing and also showed that his loyalty was to a sound America rather than an America driven by fanatics.

'We'd be better impoverished and powerless with social justice than powerful, dominant and elitist,' he said.

It was an almost word perfect statement of the beliefs underpinning the new generation of thinking within Intercontinental Veterans Anonymous.

But Alanda wasn't listening. Her attention was attracted to her screen.

'The tally is fourteen incidents, twelve major. Seven banks, three airline offices, a press agency and a pizza bar. A pizza bar? Two dead and sixteen injured, and that's only Belgium.'

* * *

The hotel was fairly full with families taking the first quarter school break. The result for John and Ross was a long, slow dinner in the seclusion of a crowded restaurant. The conversation was about anything but the business in hand; they dropped easily into the old habit of shutting off their real world and reverting to the past. They walked around each other at first until John, with careful deliberation, returned to one of the key events of their former relationship that they'd bantered about earlier.

'I was in Antwerp last year waiting for a train to Amsterdam. The central station was almost unchanged. The ladies' toilet –'

'John, don't you dare!'

'Is that a blush I see, Ross?'

'It is now.'

Ross's foolhardy attack on Collette, what she called the 'James Bond stuff', had always been a difficult issue between them even when Ross's mortification had given way to self-mockery, although Collette's death had soured the joke. With the passage of the years John had reasoned, selfishly, that the events at Gatwick would have ceased to come between them. But he was unclear whether that was the way that Ross would feel. The reference to Collette and the Antwerp Station incident was still a little risky but Ross's reaction reassured him.

'Are you still into martial arts, Ross?'

John thought she might be; her figure was as tight and lean as ever.

'I still go to the gym but I take it more easily. I'm into Scottish country dancing, which keeps me fit enough.'

John had a silent mourn for the minimal satin shorts and sports bra that had held her firm, sweat-soaked and provocative figure. The calf-length tartan skirt that she had changed into was no substitute he decided.

'How about you? You look in pretty good shape.'

John's grin showed his appreciation of her assessment.

'Oh, I walk a lot now, along the beach mainly. I tried golf for a while but I didn't get on with the retired golfing types too well. They always seem to want to know how you'd spent your life and so much of the lives of people like me, us, we don't want to talk about.'

Ross looked at her watch. It was getting late, the banter was slowing down and the problem of the bedroom was looming. Suddenly they were both wary again. But they both also knew that the only way to lay any ghosts to rest in that department was to get back to their room and let things happen.

Things happened.

24

2004

The Dutch Police didn't have much joy in tracing the killer of the objectionable Mr van Elders/Bernstein.

'Why are we bothering?' the luckless sergeant-in-charge wanted to know of a colleague. There was enough crime against decent people to keep the police busy; wasting time on chasing the killer of a low life most people would have been glad to see dead wasn't to the sergeant's taste. Nor was it to his inspector's.

'If we don't get action by the end of the week we'll close the file.'

The sergeant was happy with his superior's decision but he still spent a further three days fruitlessly chasing rainbows.

'We heard anything about this Russian hit-man?'

It was a different conversation at police headquarters but the same senior detective. The question was to the colleague responsible for liaison with the intelligence services.

'Not a lot. He wasn't involved with the van Elders business. That was ex-mafia. And hired through a channel that usually leads back to the CIA themselves.'

'So they're out there killing their own. Van Elders, Bernstein, whatever his name was, was no loss.'

'Well, maybe not, but he was still killed on our patch. And if van Elders/Bernstein wasn't on his list, the Russian is still out there with two targets to go at. The Hungarians think he's a freelance, ex-KGB maybe. There's a few of these Russians still about, some went into their own mafia, and some still hawk themselves around the world.'

'And we really don't have a clue who he's after?'

'Not a clue. There are still a few defectors washing around Europe that the KGB lookalikes would be glad to see dead. It could be any of them. And if it's not score-settling, the possibilities are limitless.'

* * *

Yuri Kirovsky wasn't superstitious, so travelling on 1 April meant nothing to him. He knew why the aircraft from Paris to Amsterdam was half-empty but that was just a bonus to him; he wasn't a great lover of his fellow man sharing too much of his space. He didn't mind if it was Collette; in fact, he rather relished her physical contact, not that he would have recognised his feelings in quite such terms, and not that he would have ever told her so if he had.

It was getting on for a couple of months since a slightly battered Collette had limped back from Antwerp, her pride and her body damaged by Ross's excited attack on her.

'Poor little Collette,' he would sometimes say when he recalled the incident.

She hated him for reminding her but she knew that he had taken delight in her discomfiture. In fact, he took delight at anybody's discomfiture; that was the way he was.

'It's time, I think.'

Collette knew what he meant. He had been debating with himself and with her for some days now about the next moves in his trail. Time was moving on; the Colonel at least would be expecting some action from him.

'I have to go to Amsterdam.'

He didn't explain why and Collette didn't ask. That much she'd learnt about him. You don't ask unnecessary questions.

She saw him off at the airport. She always liked to see him go. He was so secretive and inclined to pop up so unexpectedly that she had a need for confirmation. It was as if she couldn't believe he'd gone unless she'd seen him board the aircraft. And he liked being seen off. To many eyes, the older man in the shabby and forgettable clothes and the younger woman in the flashy and easily noticeable ones were an incongruous couple but the obvious bond between them redeemed them.

'Take care.'

Kirovsky gave his nearest approximation to a grin. It took knowledge and experience to recognise the fleeting facial movements for what they were but Collette felt a warm glow inside.

'You too.'

She would. She always did. Survival was her greatest accomplishment.

Plane journeys, even short ones, were Kirovsky's preferred thinking times. He felt that since his body couldn't go anywhere or do anything, the only sensible way to use the inactive time was to think.

Unlike many Russians, he was not a chess player. Like the Colonel, however, he was addicted to jigsaw puzzles. They both saw life as a series of patterns, only hidden because they were divided into separate interlocking pieces. The strategies for constructing a jigsaw could be every bit as complex as those for playing chess. Except that since there was a pattern to everything in life, there was a finite solution to a jigsaw puzzle; given patience, everything would ultimately fit together. And Yuri Kirovsky had patience. He had demonstrated that time and time again.

'He won't be rushed,' the Colonel had said when Ross wanted to put messages galore in the newspaper to force the pace of the trail.

The Russian had got the attention of the European intelligence services, even that of the director in London, sceptical as he had been initially. That was his first objective.

He sat contemplating his successes, but one thing still eluded him: he had worked out who John was, but not his position in the puzzle. He could understand the Colonel working through his partner; after all, he was hardly up to the rigours of intelligence fieldwork anymore. But why involve the official guy?

'The Brits aren't that bureaucratic, so why's he in?'

He had options for an answer to his own question. John Harcourt's former contacts with the old CIA pointed him to some of them.

'What with Carson and Bernsty, I guess they're already thinking this has got something to do with the CIA.'

'Drink from the bar, sir?'

'Whisky,' he answered. He liked the Western luxuries, although decent whisky had been on tap throughout his KGB career.

The interruption from the stewardess broke up his thought processes momentarily. But the puzzle of why the British were getting interested in what was going on in the US soon attracted his thoughts again. After 9/11 the CIA had been badly damaged. He knew that, and he also knew that there were people in the CIA who didn't like the way things were going and who were far more supportive of the Neoconservative ethos than state employees ought to be. There were those in the CIA who held to the old values of US society and were determined to see a change. Yuri Kirovsky had been around long enough to understand where these guys were coming from. And he knew that even a twenty-year timescale was nothing to the CIA; thinking long was what all intelligence work was about. Kirovsky's quandary at the moment was what the Neoconservatives' long-term plans were and how they would use the power that they would inevitably be seeking. He knew all too well how uncontrolled power in a State could be manipulated. Hadn't he done lots of the manipulation in his time? It was this experience that made the information that was beginning to come his way all the more interesting. And he knew very well who else was going to be interested. Information was his business, and the inner workings of the CIA was information of incalculable value. And what was valuable to one party was usually saleable to another.

What Kirovsky also knew from hard experience was that very few politicians and very few governments truly knew what their intelligence services were up to, and worse still, how to effectively control them if they didn't want to be controlled.

He didn't understand nostalgia, he just had moments of regret that he was out of the old game and that Russia was no longer a world-class player. The sort of CIA politics he was hearing about reminded him so much of his old masters. Russia may have been out of his reach but he was still a Russian. Clashing with America would at least have meant that Russia was something in the world again.

Maybe he could have settled into a revitalised Russia; maybe his past infractions would have been forgiven? He didn't think so. That wasn't going happen. He had his place in Scotland; that was where retirement lay, even if he had to drag Collette there kicking and screaming. But not yet; when he retired he wanted to live in peace and not to have to watch his back every day. That needed working at.

* * *

John had had several interviews with his director since he had been given the go-ahead to stay with the action both on Kirovsky and the CIA.

'Well now, John, something's emerging here, don't you think?'

John did think so.

'The CIA are killing their own. Are they having a clear out of double agents? What do we make of that?'

John wasn't so sure that he wanted to answer. There was too much high-level political interest in what was going on. His information was too new and not yet checked out. And Kirovsky looked like the source of some of the information. That much he reported. What the CIA seemed to be doing was killing off Kirovsky's men as well as their own since they were one and the same. And why had Kirovsky suddenly let them have access to this information? John recognised that for the Russian things had moved on, but was suspicious of how he had signalled that. The director was in no doubt.

'Sprat to catch a mackerel, wouldn't you say? A taster of the goods for sale?'

John assumed that that was what it was but the ruthless way in which the Russian had put them in the way of the information wasn't exactly endearing.

* * *

Yuri Kirovsky's approach to his meeting in Amsterdam was even more circumspect than his usual habits. It was Friday and the crowds were out and about on a pleasant evening. The bars and cafés were surprisingly busy.

The aging American watched the Russian walk slowly off the Canal Bus at the Rijksmuseum landing stage.

'Jesus, he's a cautious old bugger.'

Rod Smith – Kirovsky assumed that it wasn't his real name – was at home in Amsterdam; like Joe Longton he'd lived there for years. Yuri Kirovsky was not. He knew his back was always under threat and he was alive because he didn't take risks. So he took his time and he took his precautions.

'Smith, how are you?'

It had taken Kirovsky nearly ten minutes to meander the few hundred yards from the bus stop to the side-street café. The Russian was known to be a racist. The American's choice of an Indonesian bar/restaurant was a deliberate piece of petty provocation.

'Bier, two,' said Smith to the hovering waitress, the daughter of the house and pretty enough to even attract Kirovsky's attention.

The beer arrived.

Kirovsky wasn't into small talk; his social graces weren't that well developed, but he knew that Westerners generally wouldn't come to the point without the usual forays into the inconsequential side of life. So he endured it.

'How's business, pretty good? Always a market for fruit I guess.'

'Suits me better than retirement, or even half retirement,' Kirovsky said.

Smith grinned; he'd never made any secret of his spare time activities. He wouldn't have been there if Kirovsky didn't also buy information.

'I hear your business is getting pretty big in the States.'

He was getting to the point much to the Russian's relief.

Smith knew that Kirovsky had something like thirty agents in America, mostly scattered around the big cities and each with an established network. It was hardly a secret in the fringe CIA world that he lived in. Kirovsky, however, chose to hear the question as being about his import/export business.

'Selling fruit into America is a tough job.'

'Are you looking for help?'

'Help?' The contempt in Kirovsky's voice almost ended the conversation but Smith needed funds and Kirovsky needed insider information on the CIA to verify what he was being told by his thirty agents in the US.

More beer, then food, and then coffee came. They sparred and got off the subject then they nudged closer again and backed off. Kirovsky's renowned patience was tested to the full. Smith knew that what he was slowly parcelling out in dribs and drabs of information was making him a traitor. The Russian had no interest in the American's heart searching, only the map of the inner CIA loyalties that was emerging.

The sticking point was always naming names. Harsh references to money usually overcame the problem but Smith became more and more surly as the evening wore on.

Eventually, Kirovsky realised that he was coming to the limit of Smith's knowledge rather than of his conscience.

'Okay,' said Kirovsky at midnight, 'I have to go.'

'So go, I'll follow you.'

As the huge bundle of euros passed, Smith's pretence at courtesy broke down.

Kirovsky left. He took two taxis, he walked and stopped at a couple of bars, and by two o'clock he was in his bed as confident as he could be that nobody had followed him.

Smith took a more direct route home.

From Kirovsky's point of view, the trip to Amsterdam had been very successful and in his humourless way he was very pleased. He now knew a lot more about the CIA's inner workings and about some of their most secret thinking. As far as he could tell, they knew no more about his activities than they did ten years ago.

The inspirational organisation that Ross was beginning to understand, and with her the Colonel and John, had entrenched Kirovsky's activities into the very fabric of American society by using Intercontinental Veterans Anonymous as a vehicle for his activities. Set up in the mid-1990s, the association had been nurtured by the KGB and then hijacked by Kirovsky. And the thing that delighted him most was that it was funded partly by government grants and partly by public subscription. In its official days, the association cost the Russian authorities next to nothing, and under Kirovsky's careful management it was entirely self-financing. And now, in 2004, it was totally in Kirovsky's control, with the seeds sown so that it could thrive almost indefinitely into the future. It was hardly surprising that it had now become of such interest to the CIA.

Kirovsky's only concern was that at seventy-one he hadn't

yet put in place a long-term, strategic plan for his asset. He knew what the eventualities that he wanted to guard against were, how they might arise and even the trigger to activate the secret side of his organisation. What was missing and needed to be established urgently was the trigger mechanism. The trail was gaining credibility; he had the next steps mapped out in his head; there was just this link to build into it. The Colonel was old and there was only the Colonel's partner, the delectable Ross, who represented the future. But Ross seemed to have a British Intelligence insider in tow. That was a problem.

* * *

'No meeting in Paris.'

'Hardly a surprise, Ross, wouldn't you say?'

'No. Kirovsky was never likely to choose his own backyard.'

Ross and the Colonel were taking a break from a period of intense activity; the Colonel had been indulging in what he called 'some direct action'. Ross made regular checks on the Kirovsky electronic mailbox. She had sensed correctly that the Russian would switch his communications from the very public trail to a very private correspondence as his confidence grew. The 'open' mailbox was simply an expendable link.

'Your persistence paid off, my dear.'

'No point in setting up the first mailbox if we weren't expected to use it. But he still needed a secure communications route.'

Ross knew she was right. She had always been bugged by the neatness of the 'open' mailbox and its messages. She knew it was contrived and she knew that Kirovsky had to have other electronic communications routes; how else could he conduct his clandestine activities? It was something that she was determined to get to the bottom of.

* * *

'Well?'

'These things take time, Comrade General.'

'Don't give me the Comrade General stuff Stalinsky! I'm not your comrade. I gave you a month. That was mid-January. It's the third of April. What happened?'

The hard faces of the four elderly men showed various signs of apprehension. They used to be middle-rankers in the KGB; they had fat pensions and comfort in a society where very little existed for the ex-servants of the old regime. The new elite were driven only by money, not by politics. And they were no longer a part of the elite. So they were keen to protect their situation. But they knew how difficult it was to track down people like General Kirovsky in the free-flowing world of the European Federation. There were no police checks, no internal security spies, there was none of the paraphernalia of state control that they had grown up with and which they still secretly yearned for.

'Our man's in Holland. One of the agents Kirovsky stole from us has been killed. Our man is still making enquiries. There has been contact with the mafia.'

'Mafia? Old men and old fools like you,' snapped the general.

One of the new breed of Russian military men, young for his rank and well versed in Western social philosophy, the general knew very well the problems a Russian assassin was going to have in Western Europe, but he didn't care. The old villains sitting uneasily in his office had to solve the problems not him.

'Okay, okay, never mind the life history. Find Kirovsky – that can't be that hard – and kill him. That's clear enough even for a bunch of slow-brainers like you lot, surely.'

Angry responses were bitten back. Four regulation KGB minds assessed the odds on successful rebellion and agreed that they understood their orders perfectly. And why this ambitious general wanted the dregs of the old KGB eliminated they never thought to question.

'So what's Pensky been doing?'

In the overheated, fug-ridden café opposite the army headquarters the three turned on Stalinsky. He was the oldest. He was almost certainly in his late seventies, but such things were lied about even in KGB central files, and with the files long destroyed he could be any age he liked.

'Pensky has traced Kirovsky to Amsterdam. He doesn't live there. Pensky's following up to find out where he does live.'

Actually Pensky was doing no such thing. He was keeping out of sight at the Golden Tulip guest house in Zandvoort. His fee for killing Kirovsky was modest to say the least, but he owed a favour, so he had taken the job on. It fitted well with his other 'contracts'. One of these he'd fulfilled, which was why he had taken the trip to the seaside to let the hue and cry die down, as he knew it quickly would.

25

2026

'John? John!'

Ross had always awoken slowly. John Harcourt, even in retirement, awoke almost instantly: the product of his trade and the regular need in the past to be alert even in sleep.

Ross moved her hand across the space in the bed beside her. It was still warm.

'John?' she said again, more dreamily as the gentle whirring of his cordless shaver told her that John was simply being John and was up and about, having had all the sleep he needed.

'He hasn't put the TV on,' she said to herself. 'He's not back in gear yet.'

Relaxed, happy and without regrets, despite the passage of the years, Ross allowed her mind to dwell on the last few waking hours. The dinner had been all that she could have wanted it to be, partly because they had had no difficulty in relating to each other, and partly because they had both clearly decided not to revisit their parting moments in 2004. Ross had chosen the hotel because it specialised in local and home-grown products on its restaurant menu. That not only meant that it cost fewer environmental credits but that the food was consequently much better. And she knew that John liked his food. He also liked his sex. Ross knew that too. The gurgling giggle that she desperately tried to suppress nonetheless erupted but was drowned in John's tuneless singing in the shower.

That much hasn't changed, she thought.

As they had lain naked beside each other the night before neither seemed willing to acknowledge the rather obvious fact that they were seriously out of practice in the lovemaking department. It just happened. Like an old married couple they had dealt with teeth, ablutions and careful stowage of discarded clothes. There was no hurry, no talk, no hesitation. They even fixed on Ross's bed without the need for negotiations – John's room had twin beds; there was no choice.

'It's been a long time, John,' Ross had said as he glided his hand further and further up her thigh.

He knew that. At forty-five his erection had always been in a hurry. Now at sixty-seven it was taking its time, even with encouragement from Ross.

'Tell me about it,' he replied, but as he rolled on top of her, he was forty-five again and she was thirty not fifty-two, and the fire rekindled. The action was slower, more measured and more cautious of causing pain to Ross, but as he rolled off her again they were both satisfied. But they were also back in the present.

'It's now, John,' Ross said as if trying to pre-empt his thoughts.

One thing that Ross had learnt from the Colonel was never to look back, never to regret the past; only to see it as an insight into the present and future. It was a mantra that John knew well. In her personal life it was a lesson that had been very hard to learn.

* * *

'Sixty-eight!'

Ross was picking up her overnight briefings. They'd had breakfast. The restaurant TV was switched to the children's channel as the graphic images of destroyed buildings and mangled bodies were not suitable for youngsters on school holidays.

'Sixty-eight bombings in the last three days. They've spread to Eastern Europe and now Turkey.' Ross was sharing the digest of reports as it came up on her screen. Since it covered all press, TV and Internet sources, she knew that she would have the gist of pretty well everything that was in the media overnight from the whole European Federation.

'The Federation Interior Minister has blamed the US directly.'

'How's that, Ross? I thought there was a view emerging that it was some sort of latter-day resurgence of Islamic terror groups?'

'Yep. There is, both in the Federation and from SIE insiders. But apart from the destruction of the oil flow-station in Kazakhstan, which looks like a copycat, the pattern is of the old al-Qaeda groups, as far as anyone can remember them, but the explosives are all American where there has been the chance to check.'

'Prehistoric Islamic terrorists are using American explosives to bomb American property in Europe. Is that what you're saying, Ross?'

'That's what I'm saying and that's what the SIE insiders are saying.'

'Hang on, Ross. Where did all of this about SIE insiders come from?'

'Well, two sources: Alanda challenged Rick Blackford on SIE involvement in the bombing campaign, and although he's only small beer in all of this, she says that he didn't deny it. Under pressure – I suspect of Alanda's body – he also suggested not too obliquely that he knows more about it via Intercontinental Veterans Anonymous than he does via the SIE. More on that no doubt when I see Alanda.'

'And the second source?'

'Much more dodgy. I checked my emails and there's one

from an American fruit and vegetable wholesale company – would you believe – with an attachment called 'The SIE Bombing Campaign'. I need to get back home to check this out before opening it but the title is interesting wouldn't you say?'

'And a bit too coincidental,' John said with appropriate emphasis.

'Oh yes, but...'

'Okay, Ross, don't keep me in suspense.'

'The email title also had one of the codes we used with our old friend Yuri Kirovsky.'

'What?'

'Do I have your attention?'

'Oh yes, Ross, you have my attention.'

Together, they trawled back through the media coverage and reviewed the reports of the bombings. As they did so they both gained the impression that there was an underlying PR-type campaign being conducted that was eroding some of the scepticism amongst the Europeans and allowing it to be replaced with a range of more bellicose attitudes. The riots in places like Amsterdam seemed to have fed off this changing attitude. It was a deliberate escalation of the tension again that seemed to point back to the SIE.

* * *

In the world of electronic communication it was always very difficult to know what was real and what was not, especially if there were those who didn't want you to know. Virtual reality was big business for entertainment, for education and training, and for many other aspects of life. Creating a virtual reality for politico-intelligence purposes, or at least abusing specific manifestations of it, was one of Ross Metcalfe's particular specialities. In much the same way as Alanda Ngozie was able to mimic almost any electronic communications ever created, Ross was able to create whole virtually real worlds within the media and within the media-scanning capabilities of intelligence and security agencies. Honed over the years with the CIA and now the SIE in mind, even in the days of supposed cooperation, the use of organisations like the Colonel's and Ross's allowed the formal organs of the State to do things that in an elective democracy would not be possible if subject to public scrutiny. And if Ross had a talent for manipulating the electronic media, Myra, one of her other young protégés had a talent for literary mimicry. Myra, through a pseudonym, had been a best-selling author online since she was sixteen and could, for example, write a short story in the style of virtually any English language author that nobody would know from the original, except for the fact that the author was long dead. What Ross now asked her to do was child's play for one of her skills.

'Time for another in-depth analysis of the bombing situation, don't you think?'

Following their brief trip to Grasmere, they were sitting in Ross's study. Being North East Scotland in early April, with global warming having passed the area by for the moment, it could still be a touch chilly. For Myra, it was still boots and anorak weather. For John, when he was introduced to Myra, it was nostalgia time. Another African like Alanda, Myra was every bit as statuesque and beautiful. Wondering where Ross found such gorgeous assistants was a constant preoccupation with John.

'Leon Salavis or Kenneth Bracken?' Ross asked Myra.

Both were political analysts. Salavis was noted for his acerbic comments on the vagaries and bureaucracies of the European Federation, but also for his insidious comparisons with the US. He ran a weekly column in the English language daily in Santiago, Chile, but more importantly he was an established stringer for the Nippon-Hispanic News Agency.

DISUNITED STATES

Kenneth Bracken was a freelance journalist who specialised in commentary on European affairs also. On the surface he was much more pro-American than Salavis but still by no means uncritical. He had a knack of illustrating his views with examples that on superficial consideration showed the US in a good light but which on deeper analysis had the opposite effect. Most of his work was sold to the Americas and Australasia but the Nippon-Hispanic Agency used him too. It said something for the global market in media services that two such people could become the leading gurus on transatlantic relations.

The pseudo-hysteria created by the outpourings of the US media, much of which was certainly manipulatedand some even controlled by the SIE, had begun to convince the general public in Europe that the supposed Islamic terrorists who had been bombing their way around the Federation were indeed sponsored by the Federation in an effort to sour relations with America. Undermining the anti-American clamour in Europe had been one of the SIE's early successes. But it was only that: an early success.

The articles and analyses submitted by Salavis and Bracken, and others as outside observers, first had the effect of calming the frayed nerves of the press and then of disingenuously countering the subliminal pro-American arguments. Ever anxious not to be the backmarker in the communications stakes, the rest of the media eagerly followed the Salavis/Bracken lead. Eventually, only modest and occasional interjections of comment from these original sources were necessary to build a huge momentum. By the middle of May, the European television current affairs programmes were beginning to challenge the prevailing wisdom that the instigators of the bombings were on their side of the Atlantic. After that, no one believed that the bombing campaign was anything but a deliberate American provocation. The fact that the Americans were using some sort of reincarnation of al-Qaeda as a surrogate was never mentioned directly but was nonetheless allowed to come into the public domain. Hypocrisy was added to the American transgressions.

Neither Salavis nor Bracken existed.

'Bracken I'd say,' said Myra, responding to Ross's offer of a choice, 'but I think we need to be more upfront now about the SIE.'

Ross grinned. She liked Bracken's style. Myra wrote him as a straight-down-the-line Aussie. 'More in sorrow than in anger at the spats between two old friends, but what the hell did the Yanks think they were up to?'

The Nippon-Hispanic News Agency did exist, in the electronic world of the international media, in the records of various official bodies, in the archives of innumerable publications worldwide, but nowhere in touchable reality. It was Ross's crowning success. She and Myra had created an entire business activity with meticulous care and attention to detail, but of no physical substance: a classic in the world of virtual reality. And apart from being a vehicle for her countermeasures against the SIE, it was a nice little earner for her in its own right.

'Better direct the piece at the meeting of the European Parliament on Friday I guess.'

'We could deride the SIE for the failure of their propaganda. That'd be a nice touch.'

'Careful now; we mustn't over-do it, Myra. You know me: gently, gently.'

Producing sufficient output to give credibility to Ross's inspirational creation, the Nippon-Hispanic News Agency was very demanding on Myra but she was young and keen. And Salavis and Bracken were not her only dramatis personae. Altogether she had a stable of eighteen reporters, analysts and columnists in play. Creating the whole campaign to counter the SIE-promoted misinformation had been one of the most demanding challenges of her career to-date. The fact that Ross had created the challenge for her added a special spice to the endeavour.

Ross in her turn was as much interested in the personalities as countering the SIE propaganda.

'Well now, let's see what these wretched SIE and Neocon. cohorts are up to.'

Ross dived into the pile of reports and cuttings that Myra had provided for her with relish.

'Melvin Fitzallan and Senator 'Chap' McGoldberg, let's start with them.'

Myra's information included a record of the comings and goings of these two worthy gentlemen.

'Likes his trips to Europe does our senator, considering how vigorously he's promoting the rift between us.'

Senator McGoldberg had visited Europe six times in three months, and the last entry in Myra's file showed that he was booked on Concorde II to Berlin on 18 May.

'Today,' remarked Ross.

* * *

At the moment that Myra was clattering away again on her word processor, the senator was fuming none too silently in a café-bar a hundred yards from the Brandenberg Gate.

'What the hell's keeping them?' he demanded for the hundredth time under his breath.

An hour after the scheduled meeting time with his Arab contacts, the senator left, not even protesting at the unbelievable price he was charged for the champagne he hadn't drunk. Elsewhere, the Arab gentlemen had had to make do with humbler fare, courtesy of the Amsterdam Police. Aided by several Middle-East governments anxious to avoid any risk of a return to the past, the European Federation intelligence services had swept up a significant number of the remaining geriatric al-Qaeda operatives and their present-day acolytes, hence the broken appointment with the irritated senator.

The bombing campaign was over.

* * *

'God, if the Yanks would only vote themselves half-decent presidents we wouldn't have all these problems.'

It was one of Ross's and Myra's, and hence Bracken's, hobbyhorses. The murky processes of American politics had made it increasingly difficult for individuals with integrity to get to the top of the US power heap. So often they were tainted with real or imagined sexual or financial scandals that left them as lame ducks before they even got a hand on the levers of government. Occasionally, as Ross readily conceded, a good man did get there but he was then so constrained by the hordes of party faithful that he was neutered almost immediately as well.

'Like the present incumbent,' Myra muttered as she put the finishing touches to her Bracken masterpiece.

The current US President was an honest and dedicated man, if of limited intellect, and the vice president was even a respected figure, but with a perversity that they had shown for many years the American people had denied themselves the effective services of the two men.

Myra reread the last sentences of her article aloud.

'Absolutely crazy! Why do they do it? Nothing gets done, politicians are held in ever-increasing contempt and powerful special-interest groups like the SIE, accountable only to themselves, take control of the country with the inevitable diminution of democracy, free speech and all the other tenets of the American Constitution.'

She liked the resonance of it. It was sufficiently accurate to attract the ordinary non-political reader but powerful enough to potentially cause offence in the corridors of power in Washington.

'The Yanks hate being preached at about their precious constitution,' muttered Myra.

The biased and closed-minded brigade of American politicians, of whom Melvin Fitzallan was an outstanding leader, certainly did hate being preached at about the imperfections of their system of government. With something bordering on a national inferiority complex, the US sensitivity about the gridlock on decision making currently in force was fertile ground for the extreme nationalism espoused by the likes of Fitzallan, fed as he was by the distorted views of the religious right and the more traditional Neoconservatives.

He was in Stockholm when the full-page analysis from Kenneth Bracken was published in several European, heavyweight newspapers. That this should have happened at the expense of other worthy news items was an astonishing tribute to Ross Metcalfe's ingenuity in establishing the Nippon-Hispanic Agency. This final piece, as Ross and Myra intended it to be, was remarkable for its accuracy and for the bold and unequivocal way that the points were made. Rebuttal and counter by the American media was going to be very hard.

'Bit too close to home,' the ambassador muttered, just out of earshot of his harassed PA.

There wasn't much he could do. He had little confidence in the security of his communication lines from Sweden, so calling up his contacts at SIE headquarters to try and 'discourage' Mr Bracken was not an option.

'How the hell did all this get started? The European Press were sold on the idea of a European conspiracy to destroy good relations with the US only a few weeks ago. Now they're accusing us of setting up the provocation ourselves.'

Of course Fitzallan knew that the SIE had set up the bombing campaign; it was largely his idea. But it had backfired. Worse, the bombers had been arrested in Holland and other parts of the EU. The speed with which this had happened made him uncomfortable.

He wasn't unschooled in the history of US-European intelligence relationships and somewhere in the back of his mind the exploits of one ex-KGB general were beginning to vie for his attention even if he had died nearly twenty years previously. And Fitzallan knew about Intercontinental Veterans Anonymous. He suspected treachery. However, what the exact links between the ghost figures of the past – the laundered, old KGB networks, etc. – and the slowly emerging resistance groups were now was something that was still hidden from his view. But the bombers were in custody and the bombings had abruptly stopped. What to do next was his most immediate problem.

'Well,' said Ross as the news of the arrests in Amsterdam came through, 'it was all worthwhile. We've got the initiative back from the SIE propaganda machine and we've proved that the media can still be manipulated.'

The last point did not make her very happy, both that it could be so easily done and that it was she and Myra who had done it. Using the SIE's own methods to undermine them didn't sit well with Ross.

Melvin Fitzallan would have had no such scruples, but nonetheless he still felt sufficiently uncomfortable for it to be necessary for him to head back to Washington for the inevitable 'consultations'.

* * *

'Absolutely brilliant!'

John had been in constant touch with Ross as the media campaign developed. His admiration soared to levels even greater than in the past. Ross had matured physically, mentally, in bed and in the innovation and subtlety of her responses to the changing situations that she was required to address. Ross's response to John's ecstatic praise was muted in his presence but in private her exaltation was unbounded. It was if the past had never happened.

26

2026

After a relatively short period of time the media campaign had a life of its own and as Ross predicted there was no longer any need for Myra to feed the views of Salavis or Bracken into the melee. The US media reacted in a range of ways, both depending on their political viewpoint and the extent to which they were themselves being manipulated by the SIE. The president publically deplored the muckraking that had almost inevitably grown out of the initial serious political debate, although privately he was more than happy for the various wayward politicians to be exposed as perverts, fraudsters or whatever. But at least the president felt that he had to maintain the proprieties of his office and remained silent. Not so the various members of Congress or the media, who piled into the action with ever-increasing venom and ever-increasing detachment from reality.

'Hell fire,' thought Ross after one particular foray into the private life of a leading light of the religious right. 'Free access to the house concubines of a Saudi prince and an Egyptian business oligarch, I hardly think so!'

The venerable gentleman's wayward love life, however, didn't seem to attract as much odium as his supposed intimate relations with the remnants of Middle-East terror groups. But with the bombing campaign stalled following vigorous European countermeasures, and the one-time fearsome reputation of al-Qaeda long since destroyed, it was now taken as read within the European Federation that the campaign was SIE inspired, but had failed. Bracken's original speculation that the organisation of the attacks would be readily recognised by the European intelligence services proved correct. The forensic evidence from at least three countries sourcing the explosives from the US base in Cuba, although carefully left hanging in the air, was soon the prevailing wisdom. That the evidence was to hand, and solid enough for any judge, was known only to John, his director, Ross and Myra.

* * *

'Hi, John.'

John's TV screen fractured to allow Ross's delighted grin to dominate his lounge room. With his Internet communication link permanently patched through to the TV sets throughout his house he was able to be contacted wherever he was and whatever he was doing.

'Ross, wonderful to see you.'

It was less than twenty-four hours since they had last spoken but every time they did John's sense of contentment and wellbeing increased. Ross, who needed very little incentive to contact him, was pleased with his reaction and as was now a matter of course with her, she felt an awakening longing that ramped up every time she saw his face. The traumas of 2004 and disappointments of the passing years now seemed to be part of a totally different and unconnected life to her. John, who had buried his feelings more effectively than Ross, had been slower to commit himself to the revival of the relationship. He was slower to make commitments, business or personal anyway, but now that he had, much of his former drive and intensity had also returned.

'I've sussed the message at last.'

The message, John knew well enough, was the email and attachment that Ross had received from a US company that imported fruit and vegetables. She had been very wary of the email and had spent some time, almost a week in fact, tracking its real origin before making any attempt to open the attachment. It was free of any virus or malicious software, but her caution and patience had been rewarded because of what it revealed and the links that it made.

'Ross! Come on, girlie, don't do this to me. I can see you're bursting to tell me, so tell me.'

'It's a message from the grave, John.'

'What? What do you mean a message from the grave? Whose grave?'

And as the question passed his lips John suddenly knew perfectly well whose grave.

'Yuri Kirovsky!'

Of course it was Kirovsky; who else would it have been? The sense of unreality that this revelation induced in John was firmly pushed aside.

'Okay, Ross, tell me more. I need the whole story.'

'I've sent you a copy.'

The TV screen divided again as John hit a few buttons on his remote and the email appeared underneath a now-Cheshire-cat-faced Ross.

'To Ross Metcalfe,' read John. 'What are the dots for?'

'Self-delete. If no account in the name of Ross Metcalfe with the appropriate submerged code existed the message would self-delete.'

'Clever.'

John read on quickly. 'If the Colonel is now dead, Miss Metcalfe, my condolences. He was a man I was proud to have known. If you are no longer carrying on his business in his name, I trust you to destroy this message. Otherwise, be aware that you will be receiving this message when the present-day leader of Intercontinental Veterans Anonymous deems the situation in the United States to be sufficiently perilous to require your intervention.'

'Our intervention?'

'Read on, John.'

'The Veterans are in place in every arm of the US Administration. A succession process is also in place to ensure that they remain there as a force. In the years between 2004 and now, whenever this turns out to be, they will be in the market to sell intelligence of all sorts if there is potential for a buyer for it. How do I know that this will be the case in an indeterminate length of time? Ask your friend John Harcourt. His company is a trust in which all his employees have an interest. Need I say more?'

'Crafty old bugger,' said John under his breath.

'There will be casualties, there will be gaps when the time comes, but the Veterans are all committed to a strong, fair and just United States of America, and when it is apparent that such is not the objective of the Administration or the bodies controlling the Administration, then the Veterans' leadership will contact you and offer you support and assistance to undermine the Administration in the interests of the US people.'

'Undermine the Administration? Who does he think you are?'

Ross had questions of her own. 'How could he have known that this would happen, John? How could he have assumed that we would have the capability?

'Jesus, Ross. Old Yuri, to quote the Colonel, was one hell of a perceptive guy.'

'When you are contacted, Miss Metcalfe, a route to a line of communication will be offered to you. The Veterans are patriots, even if they do make money out of selling certain of their country's non-essential secrets. They will spy on and they will sabotage the Administration that has become anathema to them, but they will not do anything to destroy the democracy that they believe in. Do not ask them to.'

'God, Ross, sanctimonious old bastard. He never believed a word of that himself.'

'Does that matter?'

'I guess not. The key thing is that there is a body of people in the US who are sufficiently worried about their democracy to want to overturn their democratically elected Administration. Bizarre; only in the US could that happen.'

'I have a link to these people. It's a name. And it had to have been added by the present day Veterans.'

John saw from the expression on Ross's face in the corner of his TV screen that this particular aspect of the unfolding situation had a special significance for her.

'And?'

'And, John, the name is Rick Blackford, SIE intern, out of favour with the SIE hierarchy and out circulation as far as they are concerned.'

'And?'

'Currently the biggest cause of distraction to one of my best people.'

'The delectable Alanda Ngozie.'

'Yes. Her concentration is being seriously threatened by her lust for this young American.'

'Hmm! Déjà-vu maybe?'

Ross gave a snorting giggle which she tried to make sound angry rather than amused, and failed. However, she was clearly worried about Alanda's involvement with the American.

John paged the email up on the screen to see the last paragraph. Rick's name wasn't mentioned but his SIE number and recruitment date were; Kirovsky's latter-day henchman clearly had no doubt that Ross would be able to put in the name for herself. As he finished reading the email Ross took it off the screen.

'I don't believe I just read that,' John said as much to himself as to Ross.

DISUNITED STATES

The feeling of unreality, of fantasy almost, was strong and difficult to relegate from his conscious mind. After twenty years or more how could such an organisation have survived, sustained and reproduced itself? It was a question that Ross hadn't bothered to consider; the email was the reality for her. But with a more practical bent John found it hard to get his head around the implications of the survival of the Veterans. His admiration for Yuri Kirovsky skyrocketed.

An automatic BBC World Newsflash divided John's TV again. His attention was recaptured.

'Jesus Christ!'

His exclamation was echoed from the other corner of the screen.

The newsflash was explicit. 'At sixteen hundred hours local time the US Vice President was gunned down at the St Johns fish market in Antigua. The assassin, who was using a high-powered rifle, shot the vice president as he was officially declaring the new market, funded by American commercial interests, open.'

The TV footage was disorganised as the cameraman was elbowed out of the way by the SIE guard team. The Antiguan police hurriedly tried to take control of the situation but the well-oiled security routines took over and the vice president, his wife and a small group of aids were spirited away in the ambulance that always formed a part of the worthy man's entourage.

The footage ended with a neat picture of the tail-lights of the last car in the cavalcade. After that it appeared that no more information was available.

'Well, well.' Ross's voice had become detached and the corner of the screen showed a perfect picture of the electronic kit that she was now so frantically working on.

'What? They didn't take him to the US embassy. Wow! What a lot of chatter; frantic telephone calls going from the ambassador and all and sundry to Washington. He got home to discover that the rest of the circus hadn't followed him.'

'Ross, what's going on? How d'you mean he didn't go home?'

'He's disappeared, John, gone; not at the embassy and not on the USS *John B. Smith* in the harbour. The vice president has vanished according to the ambassador. He's not best pleased.'

John turned the sound down on the TV, knowing that he would get much more information from Ross. But she'd disappeared from his view to take a turn or two around her computer room. John, who knew her well enough to know that this activity was a part of her thinking processes, waited.

'I don't know what you want to do, John. This'll take a while.'

'What will?'

Ross had moved into research mode; John recognised the signs. The best thing was for him to leave her to her investigations and get back to her later.

'Okay. I'm going to search all the Antiguan systems to see if I can get a clue as to where he is.'

As he had begun to realise that it was happening, the intimacy of the conversations with Ross and the ease with which they had re-established their old relationship was a matter of wonder and delight to John. It was all the more surprising to him when he reflected on the history of the intervening period. Working together again collapsed the years; the sense of excitement and optimism of 2004 and of Stockholm and the other trips that he had made with Ross, although mellowed, was very real to him as he tried to be patient while she worked her magic to get the information that she subsequently gave him. Of course deep down he knew that his mind was filtering the information from the past, putting a gloss on it. If he had allowed himself to be honest with himself he knew that he would have to resolve his buried uncertainties with or without Ross's involvement. There was too much guilt and too much regret to be disposed of.

As he waited for yet another contact with Ross he blamed himself all over again. Why had it taken him twenty-two years to unhook his self-blame from the reality of his desire for her? Why she had felt too hurt and constrained to approach him he could only speculate about but he still couldn't blame her for not trying to contact him. In her situation he wouldn't have wanted to court another rebuff on top of the rejection that she felt she had suffered from his actions.

Then, suddenly, it was as if the fateful events of twenty-two years ago had never happened. Except that there was Yuri Kirovsky and his legacy and that was definitely happening.

After two hours of feverish activity that would no doubt have mystified John even though he was now more versed in computers than he had ever been whilst a working man, Ross returned to his TV screen.

'He's gone to ground at an estate in the north-east of the island. It belongs to Alastair Browneton, the media tycoon. He's some relative or other of the vice president.'

John knew who Alastair Browneton was.

'There's something odd in all of this,' Ross continued. 'The SIE are furious, but not because they've lost him; it's more that they have lost control of the management of events.'

John wasn't sure what the significance of the vice president's death would be or that they would be able to get to the bottom of what had happened and who was responsible. The only thing that he was sure about was that it took them, in some way, a step closer to a climax between the US and Europe.

'I wouldn't doubt your instinct, John,' the director said

when John called him, 'but we will need something more tangible to link this to the situation between the US and Europe.'

'It's a step towards a right-wing takeover; that means more aggro with Europe,' was John's only response.

'Okay, we'll watch the space; you start working up contact with the Veterans or whatever they are called.'

Before he retired for the night, John scanned the worldwide TV news channels again; all were full of the death of the US Vice President and all were full of doom and gloom over the impact on the stability of the US Government; all, that is, except the religious right-wing channel. The commentators there were quietly confident that the world had moved one step closer to the endgame that they were seeking.

'Let's see what tomorrow brings, Ross. Goodnight.'

In his head there was an answer.

'Goodnight, John.'

27

2004

'Success.'

The Colonel was almost childishly pleased that he had been able to access Yuri Kirovsky's electronic mailbox. Ross had told him how to but he still saw it as an achievement.

'A meeting in Stockholm, eh?'

There were details.

* * *

'Igor Stalinsky, business or pleasure?'

'Pleasure.'

'I see you used to be a regular traveller to the Netherlands?'

'Before I retired.'

'Okay.'

The immigration officer stamped the elderly Russian's passport and checked that the photograph and details had been scanned into the central computer. Warning alarms triggered. Why was a retired, middle-ranking KGB bureaucrat taking such a circuitous route to Holland? Moscow to Sofia, Sofia to Berlin, Berlin to Copenhagen, Copenhagen to Amsterdam. At each place the man changed flights and was on his way within two hours, except in Berlin where he stayed overnight. The computer surveillance checklist flashed into motion and trawled the German police database. The cheap and rather seedy hotel at which Stalinsky had stayed was unexceptional.

'God knows!' said the Dutch immigration duty officer when the computer disgorged its analysis. Stalinsky probably wouldn't have known either. Such deviousness was more the product of his KGB upbringing than any need for security. It was instinctive. It simply would never have occurred to him to go anywhere directly.

* * *

A prostitute with scuffed boots and an ill-fitting PVC skirt was sitting in the ground floor window when Stalinsky arrived at the flat. His route this time had been devious too, but not through any intent, merely ignorance. Speaking no Dutch and unable to overcome his inbred reluctance to signal his Russian-ness unnecessarily, he had floundered up and down the canals in the red-light district until he finally hit upon the right street.

The girl wasn't smiling but she beckoned to him as he stared at her. Her bare upper body had no effect on him. The slight nod told her that he was there on business which she took to be her business. She gestured him up the stairs and forced him to brush past her breasts as he entered the flat.

He wasn't very good at what he was supposed to do. The ready availability of young KGB operatives and women prisoners in his past hadn't taught him very much subtlety. As he pulled the handcuffs out of his pocket the woman held out her right hand and signalled five twice with her left. Surprised by him paying up without argument, she stuffed the ten €100 notes into a drawer and held out her hands together. Gesturing her to turn around he handcuffed her hands behind her.

'Hey!'

Stalinsky ripped the skirt from her bottom, shattering the fragile zip and ripping the fabric, and tossed the lump of red plastic into the corner. The woman was angry at the vandalism and then frightened at the violence. He fetched a chair and sat her astride it facing backwards, the stretchers pressing into her exposed breasts. She never saw where he produced the rope from but he bound her to the chair-back before she could so much as wriggle. Her scream was hardly formed before it was taped over. Stalinsky sat down behind her for a while watching her stare at her own terrified reflection in a greasy and cracked mirror. He was panting slightly; his seventy-five years might have been obscured from KGB records but they were real enough to him.

'So you've been busy. I wouldn't have thought you still had it in you.'

'Pensky! You were supposed to have been here.'

Stalinsky had just recovered his thousand euros when Pensky materialised in the room behind him. The newcomer ripped the tape from the woman's mouth but the coldness of his stare, totally devoid of pity, killed off her renewed scream.

'Now then,' he said in slow, precise Dutch. 'I want you to tell me where General Kirovsky lives. I know you know, just as I know he visits you here when he's in Amsterdam.'

When the police found the woman the next day the chair was toppled sideways. She was alive but paralysed from fear rather than from any of the blows that she had received. During the weeks, as she slowly recovered, she was unable to tell the police anything, and by the time she could form images of the two men in her mind the information was no longer of any value.

Igor Stalinsky, having met with his man, Pensky, and renewed his instructions with some distinct urgency, headed for home. He was detained by immigration and despite his protests was put on to a direct flight to Moscow. Back home, a minor motoring offence assumed the proportions of a major infraction and it was several months before he was able to resume his coffee and vodka sessions with his three henchmen. Although he was well aware of the old man's difficulties, the young general recognised that his political masters would see it as desirable to stay sweet with the Europeans; Stalinsky's illegalities were too trivial to be of concern. As a consequence, he accepted that his man had to be taken out of circulation and failed to secure his release.

* * *

When they arrived in Stockholm, John wondered why they were staying at the Regal Hotel. It was the sort of steel and glass monster that was rare in Stockholm, and which he would have expected the Colonel to avoid. He, however, was not wheelchair-bound.

'Okay, you two, I've got a load of thinking to do. I'll eat in my room.'

They didn't need any second telling. It was six o'clock.

'The Swedes eat fairly early,' remarked John as Ross rejoined him in the hotel foyer.

It was mild for the time of year and John was trailing his lightweight coat over his arm.

'Oh, we're exotic tonight,' Ross said in mocking imitation of his comments on previous occasions.

He was wearing an Armani suit; it was smart, light in colour as well as weight, but had all the signs of having been worn and loved. His silk tie was bright, bold and definitely exotic. The grin she received made her tingle down the spine.

'Right. Where to then?'

'You lead on, John. You've been here before. I haven't.'

They walked to the Old Town and John headed into the mass of narrow and confusing streets. Ross scampered along with him, exhilarated by the excitement of being by his side and reluctant to call for him to slow down, at least that was until they came to the cobbled and uneven streets.

Progress to the fish restaurant that he was heading for was more measured after that.

There was a mixture of small tables and long benches where people sat in parties or as couples. The atmosphere was warm and friendly. John questioned Ross about whether the restaurant suited her with a raised eyebrow.

'Okay with me.' Nodding, she headed for the long table in the window. The good-humoured shuffling on benches and window seats to accommodate them delighted her. And in the middle of the mass of people it was very private.

'John, isn't this wonderful.'

He grinned his agreement at her enjoyment of the ambience and reached across the table to hold her hand. Her straightforward pleasure at every new experience was one of the things that so attracted him to her. It was so unexpected in such a seemingly worldly wise thirty-year-old woman.

They ate only fish. Peeling prawns messily, they wallowed in the rarity of being able to eat with their fingers in public.

'Don't eat too many; there's a main course as well,' said John.

They toasted the Colonel for releasing them for such enjoyment, laughed at each other when they were decked out in bibs for the lobster course, and John revelled again in Ross's delight when, giving her no choice of sweet, she tucked so enthusiastically into the huge dish of cloudberries, raspberries and wild strawberries that was presented to her.

'Famous delicacy, I presume,' she said savouring a spoonful of the puce/orange-coloured and slightly tart cloudberries.

Ross dawdled over the coffee, not wanting to let go of the closeness that they were developing.

'I'm really enjoying this,' she said. 'Wonderful how a place and a moment in time can be so special when you don't know why, or whether you can ever make it happen again.'

'Oh, we can make it happen again,' John said.

He'd been married as a young man; he had memories of the euphoria of the first weeks of that relationship, the lack of responsibility and the feeling of a world out there waiting for them to take hold of. They had made it happen again and again, right up to the altar. Then reality had cut in and he had to go off to some unremembered place for several weeks. The spell had been quickly broken. His wife had been impatient and easily promiscuous in his absence. When her wilful behaviour had threatened his job John had summarily divorced her. It was the sort of harsh and violent act that Ross had been so distressed about when he reacted as roughly to her.

'What you thinking?'

'I'm not sure you'd want to know, Ross.'

'I want to know everything about you.'

'I was married once, when I left university. There were similar feelings...'

She knew he had been married.

'Come on, let's get back to the hotel. I'll tell you another day.'

Ross felt deflated. She had wanted him to talk about his wife; there was obviously a story there. And she wondered why he had even alluded to his ex-wife; he could so easily have not made the comment. There was something compelling about the relatively short relationship and the quick divorce. Whether it was the sense of guilt that John occasionally felt, or the insincerity of his selfish actions once he found that his wife's behaviour was a threat to his career, he could never make up his mind. He knew his own behaviour had hardly been exemplary but he always rationalised that by telling himself that she didn't have to leap into the bed of anyone who made her an offer once he was out of the country. One thing he was sure of; he wasn't going to expose himself to Ross over his ex-wife, and he never did.

'And I'll tell you about me one day,' she said with a gaiety that she didn't feel.

It was still only ten-thirty when they got back to the hotel and Ross went to see the Colonel, as she did every night that they were away together. Nothing had been said – no goodnights, no lingering partings – so despite the vague chill that he had felt as they returned to the hotel, John knew that she intended to come back to him. He was showered and in bed when she tapped gently on the door. She slipped into his room on exaggerated tiptoe and disappeared into the bathroom. Her singing was off key, but jubilant; the issue of his ex-wife was obviously forgotten.

'Hey, Ross, hurry up.' There was something urgent about his tone. She accelerated her towelling and powdering.

He had been flicking through the TV channels as he waited for her. Unexpectedly, he caught the full-screen face of Collette Dubois, sweating with wet hair rats-tailing around her face. In another cameo a black girl was hurriedly wiping the beads of perspiration away and pouring water down her throat. Behind, there were rows of spectators waiting expectantly for the renewal of battle.

'What? Oh, wow, Collette! It's proper boxing.'

'Yep, Marquis of Queensberry stuff.'

Despite herself and her previous feelings of distaste, Ross's attention was immediately fixed on Collette and the action in the ring. The bout didn't last long. With destructive ruthlessness Collette dumped her opponent onto her backside and the referee called the fight off. The impact on Ross of the few brief moments of theatrically violent action was electric. John could feel her body beside him quivering with some inbuilt energy that was bursting to give itself expression. He was amazed and bemused. Ross herself didn't think to wonder why remote violence was so stimulating when violence addressed at her personally was so devastating.

She was naked as she had scrambled into the bed beside him, and she made her warm, soap-scented body touch his wherever she could. Her breasts were crushed against his chest as she kissed him. Her right hand was down around his genitals encouraging his erection as she allowed her lips and tongue to explore his face. The roughness of his chin against her delicate softness further stimulated her as much as his hands massaging their way down her back and around to grasp her full breasts.

The clanging of bells, the thudding and thumping, and grunts and squeals of the next contestants in the television boxing ring filled the background. The following sounds were lost as Ross was submerged in the power of John's final arousal. John was amazed all over again.

* * *

'I guess you had a good evening,' said the Colonel.

'We certainly did,' Ross responded. Her delight and enthusiasm made the Colonel take a closer look at her. He was long enough in the tooth to know what had happened, but that was yesterday; today they had the tricky job of meeting up with Yuri Kirovsky.

'The taxi's here. We should go,' announced Ross, now back into her brisk business-partner mode.

The taxi crawled through the traffic, past the old, red-brick Olympic stadium and onwards to the docks. The meeting had been arranged on a ferry.

Ross sat close to John, but beyond that and the shared glow, the events of the previous evening were not much in evidence. However, an inner excitement consumed both of them.

The Colonel had already briefed them about the day's events; they knew what was going to happen and what their roles were. Not even thinking about the immediate tasks, John worked his mind over the peripheral activities to his and Ross's evening. Something was niggling him deep in his brain. It was about Kirovsky.

'Got it!'

'Got what?' said both Ross and the Colonel.

'Kirovsky; he was on television last night.'

'I beg your pardon?'

'I know, Colonel, that's extraordinary isn't it, but he was there, watching his girlfriend beat hell out of some poor black girl.'

'I'm lost, John.'

'Kirovsky's live-in partner, Colonel, Collette Dubois. She's a professional boxer. He was there live in Paris on television last night watching her do her stuff. At the ringside, two rows back in the full view of everybody who wanted to see him. Amazing! No security at all.'

'He won't come here like that,' said the Colonel with the hint of a smile. 'The Swedes are going to sweep behind as he arrives, see if he's got any company; just a favour being returned.'

'He's definitely got a soft spot for our Collette,' said Ross, almost with approval.

Identical trains of thought took off in John's and the Colonel's minds. Was this a situation to be exploited?

* * *

Pensky was not a fan of female pugilism, so he was unaware of both Collette's prowess and Yuri Kirovsky's dedicated support for her activities. He was, however, aware of Collette's existence and of Kirovsky's whereabouts in Paris.

28

2004

By virtue of his disability, the Colonel had been accorded a large two-roomed cabin on the ferry. It was readily accessible and close to the main leisure facilities on the vessel. Ross and John's cabins adjoined and a small contribution secured the unlocking of the interconnecting doors.

'Pity we won't have much chance to use the beds,' said Ross with an arch look at John that was met with a grin of mischievous intensity. It was one of the last of the light-hearted moments before the serious business of the trip began.

The modest increase in noise and the sense of motion announced that the ferry was underway. The Colonel nodded approvingly. The departure was on time; the weather was expected to be fair. Things augured well for a successful day.

'Come in!'

'You are expecting to be joined by a gentleman?' the steward enquired in careful English once invited into the cabin.

The Colonel acknowledged that he was.

'He will be here in five minutes.'

The departing steward was succeeded a few moments later by a stewardess of such classic beauty that only Ross had time to notice that the coffee serving was for five before a quiet but firm knock on the door steeled them for the arrival of their visitor.

There were sharp discharges of adrenaline. Ross and John moved away from where the Colonel was sitting, leaving him an open area to manage his wheelchair if he needed to. Ross nervously smoothed down her skirt, passing uncertain glances at John. John made space between himself and Ross and tucked his right hand across his body and inside his jacket. It was a movement that attracted one of Ross's glances but she hadn't time to wonder what it meant before the door opened in response to the Colonel's clear, resonant and uncharacteristically loud invitation. It was a call that could have been heard in the adjoining cabins.

We're all here, thought Ross. Why the need to be so loud?

They all knew it was Kirovsky. They had all seen the one and only photograph. The recognition of the face in the background of Collette's flailing fists on last night's television brought renewed surges of excitement to John that he hurriedly suppressed. Ross, checking John and the Colonel's faces could read absolutely nothing in them.

A softening around the eyes, visible momentarily to the Colonel, was the only sign of recognition from Yuri Kirovsky. His face was otherwise impassive.

'Colonel,' he said, his English perfect, his accent negligible, 'a pleasure and an honour.'

John managed to get his sneer under control; only Ross had seen it. His school of espionage didn't include the honourable foe amongst its characters. Kirovsky had been the death of too many people for him to see him in the quaint and chivalrous light that the Colonel might have done. But then the Colonel had been the death of quite a score-list of Russians himself and holding their activities almost at the level of a grown-up game was the only way to stay detached and objective.

'Yuri, how are you?'

The parody of the manners of a world to which he didn't

belong gave Kirovsky silent and undetectable amusement. He'd set the tone by his own greeting; the Colonel's ready response told him that immobile as he might now be, his old enemy was as sharp as ever.

'You will record our conversation?' the Russian asked.

'Of course. As will you?'

The responding nod was almost imperceptible. Afterwards, John pointed out to Ross the likely places that Kirovsky would be hiding a micro-camera. She knew all about such things. Their own kit was already in place and her computer at the Buchan farmhouse was printing out the speech as it occurred.

Introductions were made. Ross found the Russian's handshake firm but impersonal. However, Kirovsky looked her over with unashamed interest.

'You have met my friend Collette,' he said with a flicker of a smile of chilling innocence that made Ross's flesh creep.

'In Antwerp.'

'John Harcourt. Ex-CIA as well as British Intelligence. Strange bedfellows as it has turned out.'

'John's knowledge of the CIA will be useful I think,' said the Colonel smoothly.

It was a slightly ill-natured remark from Kirovsky but for the Colonel it was a way into the conversation that they wanted to have. The Russian understood.

'Yes, the trail doesn't lead to the CIA, but it might have eventually.'

'The trail?' prompted the Colonel.

'You are aware of it,' Kirovsky said dismissively. 'Amsterdam was easy. That animal Bernsty, Bernstein if you prefer, beat up one prostitute too many. The child had a weak heart. But it was a ready-made body. Hamburg was harder but chance again.' There wasn't the slightest sign of feeling. The bodies grabbed the attention, the underwear attracted the security service and the security service contacted the Colonel.

'Most Russian women would have killed for such knickers. Always kept a stock; they didn't sandpaper your arse like the State-made ones.'

Kirovsky looked at Ross. She was sitting opposite him. He supposed that she would wear classy knickers like Collette. In modern times, most Russian women would have killed for the designer label, denim miniskirt that she was wearing.

The cold-blooded way that Kirovsky made his comments was not well received.

'Okay,' said the Colonel sensing that John's fuse was lit, 'we know about the trail. That's over. What's next?'

It was the sort of direct approach that Kirovsky was unused to and didn't like. The Colonel knew that. He knew that the Russian liked the challenge of the devious and the obscure. They were his stock in trade. The Colonel was also conceding that the trail was devious and obscure, that it established Kirovsky's bona fides for whatever he wanted to sell. Now he was signalling they had better get on to whatever that was.

'What's next I would reckon is a conspiracy.'

As he heard the voice behind him Kirovsky was on his feet with a speed that more than denied his advancing years. Ross was startled by his sudden movement but relaxed as she saw that the Colonel was unfazed by the new arrival. John had his hand back in his jacket, but she didn't have time to feel the strength of the horror that she felt about John being armed.

'Euan, come and sit over here with Ross,' said the Colonel.

The newcomer was tall, slightly stooping and dressed John Harcourt-style in entirely forgettable clothes. The dayroom of the Colonel's suite boasted two settees, one of which had been occupied by Yuri Kirovsky and the other, the larger, by Ross. The furniture was modern, functional and not in the least bit comfortable. John, with more experience of commercial living and a desire to retain mobility, had remained standing. The Colonel, as if wishing to reduce the intimidating impact of three people facing the Russian, moved his wheelchair a few inches towards him.

Both Ross and John had seen the man step into the room from the adjoining bedroom but the suddenness of it and the immediate entry into the conversation had taken them off guard.

'Euan Fforde,' said Kirovsky. It was a statement; he knew who the new arrival was. Only Ross was unfamiliar with the lanky American, which he proved to be from his accent, as he greeted the Colonel with something like affection.

What the hell's going on here? thought John. This guy's a high-ranking CIA insider even if he is only my age. I hope the Colonel knows what he's up to.

Needless to say, the Colonel did.

'Yuri, we're taking a risk inviting Euan here. It's a sign of good faith. Only we five know he is here. You understand what I'm saying?'

Kirovsky understood perfectly. If any suggestion at all of Fforde's presence got back to Washington, he knew all too well that his plans for the future would die. And recognising the sort of people that the Colonel was still likely to know, he had a good chance of dying himself with his plans into the bargain. It was not an outcome that he had in mind.

'I wish to retire to my property in Scotland,' he said.

That's it? thought Ross. All this is about one elderly Russian with a lousy record with the authorities retiring in peace in Scotland. There must be more.

John and the Colonel knew that there wasn't more from Kirovsky's point of view. The British knew enough, with a bit of imagination and creative evidence, to put him in jail. It didn't have to be for long, but it would certainly be long enough for him to be too old to enjoy his ill-gotten inheritance, and long enough to ensure that the property in Scotland was never occupied. Kirovsky knew how these things could be done. The purchase of his peace and security had a high price on it for him; resisting the temptation to sell the titbits of knowledge about the whereabouts of one Euan Fforde on this particular day was not so hard.

'So how many plants have you still got inside the CIA?' The American, like the Colonel, knew that such direct questions put Kirovsky off his stroke. There was no immediate answer. 'Yuri, this isn't about exposing your agents. If we're right, and you want to sell us something real big, the guess is we're going to need them where they are.'

'We only want to be able to assess what you tell us,' said the Colonel, trying to reinforce the American's reassurance.

Kirovsky's answer took nearly half an hour. At the end of that time they had a complete picture of his penetration of the organs of US government and were familiar with the real world of Intercontinental Veterans Anonymous. The complexity of this organisation and its powers of sustainability were beyond anything that John, let alone Ross, had ever come across. If Euan Fforde or the Colonel were surprised by the extent of the Russian's operations, John and Ross would never have known.

Coffee was served; there were enough cups to go around. They all took the exactitude for granted. Ross, however, felt vaguely miffed that she didn't know that Fforde was to be there. How had the Colonel arranged it?

'Post–9/11, the CIA is split into two factions. You knew that, Fforde. Some want to force the old values onto the people, revitalise America against its will, be a dominant world power answerable to no one, least of all the UN. Others have moved on; they want the same things, but only if the people can be persuaded.' The contempt in Kirovsky's voice made it abundantly clear which faction he might have supported.

Nobody spoke for a while. Kirovsky was drawing a picture that Fforde recognised and which the Colonel was well aware was secretly being turned into a battle for hearts and minds for the future of the USA. The Neoconservatives were in the ascendant in many parts of Washington and the religious right was beginning to coalesce into something far more powerful than even the Neoconservatives had imagined. What nobody knew was how all of this would play out in the near future, let alone the longer term. Kirovsky didn't know either of course, but he did know that he was fashioning a tool that would be valuable to those with more democratic and more realistic views and would therefore be well able to fund his retirement. It was the sheer incongruity of this practical and democratic realism against his totalitarian background that was so difficult for John to accept. The Colonel and Euan Fforde found it easier but they still needed more tangible evidence.

Kirovsky resumed.

'You've heard of the America Resurgent movement. They're fascists intent on building an unstoppable military power but with a strong nationalist agenda. They're small, badly organised, more intellectual than practical at the moment, but with increasing numbers of supporters in all walks of life. They believe the people should be told what's good for them and let the government get on with it.'

Again, it was obviously a philosophy that struck a chord with the Russian; it was one that he'd been brought up with.

The Colonel looked at Ross. He could imagine what she was thinking; how could Kirovsky be so sure about all of this? He couldn't, but his lifelong instincts honed in an endless world of intrigue told him that there was both a serious political movement emerging and that there was undoubtedly something in it for him if he kept in touch with the action.

'It wasn't always the case,' said Fforde in a vague tone of regret. 'The America Resurgent movement started with a bunch of Midwestern academics. It grew through the universities and colleges. It's only in the last year or so, as the Neoconservatives have grown more out of touch with world realities that it has been hijacked by the faceless bureaucrats and apparatchiks in Washington and been given an increasingly extreme political edge. America Resurgent, the Neocons and the religious right have exploited the situation, hidden in the bureaucracy. They've thrived and are now almost indistinguishable as separate groups. They may not be many in numbers but they are beginning to exert a disproportionate influence.'

'Aided and abetted by your chums in the CIA, it would seem,' remarked the Colonel.

'I fear so; but they too are still small in numbers,' said Fforde.

'But what substance has this lot got?' asked Ross. She was getting frustrated. She couldn't see anything tangible, anything that she might put her hand on, as she saw it. It was all talk. If there was such a group trying to undermine the US State, who was out there doing something about it?

Kirovsky looked at Ross with renewed interest. This was not only the first woman ever to put Collette on her back, but she spoke up among the men-folk as well, and she sounded as if she had brains.

Ross had got up. The settee had a limited comfort index and she needed to move about. For once, Kirovsky ignored the tight breasts in the designer T-shirt and the long legs that took up half her height. He wanted to hear what the response to her common-sense question was. He knew the substance, of course; that was what he was there to sell. But would they have any idea? Fforde ought to and the Colonel would soon start to guess; there were pointers enough in the American media.

'The substance, my dear, is what friend Yuri here is going to try to sell us. He only knows so much, but he has the organisation to learn more if we want him to. But we aren't in the same hurry to buy as he is to sell,' the Colonel said in response to Ross's plea.

'Lunch,' said John, recognising that a break would help concentrate minds. 'St Petersburg is a long way off. We've got plenty of time.'

The party broke into three. Kirovsky, after some careful telephoning, left first. Ross and John followed him into the corridor. Fforde and the Colonel opted to be served in the suite. The steward who had announced Kirovsky and the lissom stewardess did the honours.

'Think I'll apply for a transfer to the Swedish branch,' remarked John as they passed the classic blonde propelling the lunch trolley.

'What? Damn you, John!'

As it dawned on Ross that the stewarding staff were Swedish Security Service she cuffed John gently about the ears before retreating into confused blushes. She was suddenly embarrassed that their relationship hadn't advanced to the level of such horseplay.

Along the corridor in front of them the Russian was joined by a woman.

'Collette,' said John. 'I imagine they'll be having a quiet tête-à-tête lunch in their cabin. Seems our Yuri is not popular in Sweden and it's only the good offices of my illustrious director that has allowed this to happen.'

Ross was taking a better look at the French woman. John noticed the little shudder but put it down to the rather fierce air conditioning in the ship. It was not that, although she was cold. Having seen Collette in action, she was now all too aware of the force of John's remonstration with her in Antwerp.

Smorgasbord always makes for a quick lunch, so Ross and

John were back in their cabins with ample time to spare. It was what John had planned and Ross had hoped for.

Without her T-shirt Ross shivered. Without her bra she shivered again.

'John!'

His hands explored her bare skin. The shivers multiplied as she giggled about the cold, but it was no longer the over-enthusiastic air conditioning that was the prime cause of the shivers. He released her skirt and pants. Kirovsky was right; she did wear classy knickers. He was ready as she unzipped his trousers. It was quick and intense as they leant against the cabin wall.

'Oh no, John; I've got to check the monitoring programmes.'

He kept hold of her as she tried to get her modem set up.

'John, I can't do this. Make yourself useful; find me some warmer clothes.'

They were serious for the next ten minutes. John didn't want to be, but the expression on her face as she scanned the media digest told him that the fun time was over.

* * *

'That was one hell of a day.'

John was sitting next to Ross on the flight back to London. They were at ease and relaxed. The trip had been amazingly successful from Ross's viewpoint and her delight and excitement kept bubbling up inside her. The Colonel had noticed the change but his analytical processes hadn't yet worked through the implications.

Yuri Kirovsky had spent an hour going through the intelligence that he was getting from his agents in America, something he did every day wherever he was. He was pleased with the day too, although he would perhaps not have expressed himself in such terms. He had given up something in the interests of progress.

Intercontinental Veterans Anonymous was news to Fforde. He'd heard of it in its cover guise but not in its true purpose. That established the Russian's credibility. He knew his agents were safe in the US. Some in the CIA might have rushed to sweep up the networks, but Fforde, Kirovsky was confident, would play a long game and keep his peace. He was entirely correct in his judgement but even Kirovsky would have been amazed that the information remained stored in Euan Fforde's brain for twenty-two years.

Overall, Kirovsky was gratified by the success of his trip but disappointed that he wasn't given any firmer guarantees about his eventual move to Scotland.

On the train back to Paris, Kirovsky and Collette's lovemaking was every bit as intense as John and Ross's with the added impetus of an unacknowledged slowing of his impulses.

29

2026

'The whole worldwide media is in a frenzy of rumours that the vice president isn't dead, only wounded,' said Ross. She had linked up her surveillance system report section to John's computer so he was able to share the unfolding events in real time whenever he wanted to. Thanks to Ross's routine wizardry he was spending a lot more of his time in front of a computer, or TV screen, than he would have wanted to. Increasingly, he was feeling that he would rather be sitting companionably next to her while they studied events. Except of course when Ross was in business mode in her computer room; John was well aware that she was inclined to go about her activities with only scant awareness of his presence. He recognised that he rather slipped in her priorities list when she was engaged in her analysis work.

'John, I've had another voice from the past on an SIE scrambled satellite telephone.'

'Okay, Ross, surprise me.'

'Euan Fforde. Old CIA. You remember? Stockholm 2004 and thereafter, and then silent for all these years. You would hardly have forgotten Stockholm.'

'Euan?'

John was so surprised at the announcement that he didn't react to the back reference until much later.

'Yes, Euan. He's still with the SIE. I've kept track of him

for obvious reasons over the years. He's increasingly embattled with the extremists and the religious right. The SIE Board have never been able to oust him – too close to too many key people – but with the vice president dead the list is shortening. I asked him if the VP was actually dead, or was alive somewhere. It's an offline recording since I don't have the latest update of the SIE online unscrambling software yet for you to hear directly as the conversation was taking place. Alanda's working on that.'

'Okay, Ross, let's hear it.'

'He never was dead, Ross. But he damn well soon will be.'

Euan Fforde's voice was monotone and dead but recognisable enough to John whose memory for voices was exceptional.

'How d'you mean?'

'He was hurt pretty bad. He obviously wasn't supposed to survive. The local guys had to improvise to get him safe. In his condition that was pretty rough on him.'

'But why rush him off into the countryside?' asked Ross.

'The embassy head of security is a known supporter of Fitzallan. Left with him... Well, I reckon he'd have been dead in no time.'

'And the local police?'

'The local police and security services are more than a little miffed, Ross, about what happened. There'll be an enquiry but our lot won't cooperate.' Fforde sounded a shade angrier about that than the rest of his report.

There was a recording pause.

'Okay,' he continued, 'while I've got your attention, there are a few other things I can fill you in on.'

I'll bet there are, thought John.

'First, the SIE are split down the middle, as you already know. The director is also a friend of Melvin Fitzallan. Need I say more? Those of us who want to see America return to its former position in the world by reform of our political system probably make up less than half of the top two or three levels in the SIE. We have no organisation. We have support amongst the population at large, amongst the military and in Congress, but this is minimal and dwindling. What we need is a focus; the build-up of animosity with Europe has proved a winner for Fitzallan, especially as until recently the European media seemed to be lending a helping hand.

'The US media are with us, but they keep getting deflected into contentious issues, like Medicare and the Welfare Bill. There's a group on Capitol Hill who are manipulating the traffic between the White House and Congress. Misinformation and late night votes, you know – the classic tactics. The public only gets to know what's going on when things are out of hand. The president is too weak to throw out the second tier officials who are pulling the strings. The VP was doing his best; that's partly why they wanted to take him out.'

'And what better way than on a foreign trip. Blame somebody else.' Ross had interjected because she didn't want to get bogged down in detail now that Fforde was opening up.

'It's our analysis,' he continued, 'that if the VP is killed off, and the House Chairman takes over, they will have moved their man into the White House. Stopping the VP interfering is a negative; much better to have your own man calling the shots. In our political system, the president has no chance if Congress and the vice president are against him.'

'So, Euan, if you had the resources, what would you do?'

John winced slightly at Ross's rather strident question but the SIE man didn't seem to notice. John sensed that he was trying to get a lot off his chest in a very short time.

'Get intelligence. We need intelligence, we need to get

in front, we need to know what's going on and more importantly what's likely to happen, and we need to be able to use it to start changing opinions and the balance of power.'

'Kirovsky's Veterans?' Ross's question hung in the air for a minute before the American made any attempt to reply.

Both John and Ross knew that only Fforde knew of the real purpose of the Veterans and of the power they could wield if needed; they also knew that Fforde's patriotism and integrity were at stake if he went down that road.

Ross decided that her question was maybe best left hanging in the air. 'So is this Melvin Fitzallan the brains behind all of this?' she asked.

Having invaded his electronic mailbox more than once, Ross had conceived a distinct dislike for the ambassador.

'Hard to be sure,' said Fforde. 'He's in the right sort of place, but there's a great mass of senators and the like who would give limbs and more to get the seat in the Oval Office.'

'I guess we should take a bit more interest in our Mr Fitzallan. At least he's usually on our side of the Atlantic.'

'Whatever you can find out, Ross. We've got a few trusties left in Europe, past and present, and a few secure communications routes too. But if the idiots in Congress whip up more anti-European feeling things might get harder.'

'I think, Euan, you'd find that it's next to impossible to cut off electronic communications, even if we were at war.'

'Joe Longton and Rick Blackford?' John said to himself.

Ross clearly agreed when John fed the thought back to her later but in much the way the Colonel had twenty-two years ago, she worried about the relationship of Alanda and Rick Blackford. The parallels weren't lost on her; however, she had long since decided that this was perhaps not a topic to debate with John.

30

2004

Since they arrived back from Stockholm late on the Friday afternoon the Colonel had opted to spend the night at his club in London and make his way home the next day. Needless to say, Ross wasn't keen to rush back by herself.

'Well, at least we'll have the evening together,' she said.

The relationship was beginning to mature. Ross was lively and active, with an immense sense of fun that John found a delight. The intriguing combination of a highly sexually attractive young woman and an intellect second to none was beyond his experience. Yet for all that she was somehow vulnerable. She let herself go and then she pulled back as if afraid to release her true feelings. He had to feel his way with her. But he was learning. He found that if he reacted positively to her and she knew where she stood, she would respond. It was all about safety. For all her knowledge and intellectual capability, within personal relationships she needed to be reassured, to feel safe. From the things that she had let slip she'd been hurt somewhere back in time and didn't want to be hurt again. That seemed to be the clue to her behaviour.

What John hadn't detected was Ross's fear and hatred of violence, both physical and verbal. His tendency to react roughly, even violently, to the unforeseen, and Ross's fear of that, was something that ebbed and flowed in her feelings for him depending how tense things were in the work they were doing.

'John, not tonight. This is going too fast,' Ross said.

They were settled in the warmth of John's bed in his flat and he began to move his hands over the silky skin of her thighs. Whereas she had got into the bed willingly enough, she now tightened her body at his touch and then relaxed it as if fearing to offend him.

'It was good in Stockholm, John, especially on the boat, but this is different. We aren't walking away afterwards. It seems like we're making commitments.'

'Don't you want a commitment?'

'I want to be ready for a commitment. This is too fast. I don't even know whether I would mean it at this moment, let alone know what you really feel. It happened before; I don't want it like that again.'

'Want to talk about it?'

'Not really. It was at college. I loved him and shared his bed thinking there was a future. There wasn't. He didn't want to make the effort at a proper relationship.'

This wasn't entirely true but Ross was fearful of raising the issue of the man's violent jealousy in case John made linkages to his harsh responses to her and forced the topic into the open. However much Ross feared violence she didn't want it to be put into personal terms. She had no fear of physical violence to herself from John, but couldn't be sure that John wouldn't interpret her response as if she had.

'Okay, no problem. I'll sleep on the couch.'

'I didn't mean that. I don't want that, John. I don't mind you beside me. I just don't want you to...'

He kissed her gently on the mouth, cupping her head in his hands as he leant over her.

'When you're ready,' he said quietly.

* * *

Despite his nondescript and often scruffy appearance, Yuri Kirovsky lived comfortably in modest luxury. He had always recognised the inconsistency between his Communist convictions and his inability to resist the routine benefits of good food and decent whisky offered by the West. He was not alone in his former times in enjoying such benefits, nor was he alone in becoming addicted to them. His efforts to convince Collette of the purity of his doctrine and the austerity of his lifestyle when they first met were greeted with derision. However, such fantasies were more about his conscience, deeply submerged as it was, than anything else and soon faded when he needed to make no more defences of his extravagance.

'Yuri, why don't you come and eat? You've been sat at that computer for hours.'

'Yes, yes. In a minute.'

He'd been sifting through the reports from his organisations in America. The questions that John Harcourt had wanted answered were already dealt with.

'So,' he said to himself as he read, 'the CIA's objectives are pretty ambitious. Go for the top.'

The report he was reading was from a White House press secretary. Harcourt's surmise that some of the CIA infiltrators were in fact Kirovsky's men was correct in this particular case.

Mindful that Collette could get very irritable if the food that she had prepared wasn't consumed when it was at its best, he eventually scanned the list of messages yet to be read and hurried to the dining area.

'What's so interesting then?'

'Interesting, Collette? We're in a commanding position. We have access to the very thought processes of the US Administration. The foresight in putting all those sleepers into the CIA was a coup that is unequalled in the history of espionage.'

'Magnificent! Bravo, Yuri!'

He was always one to wax eloquent about the achievements of the KGB, especially if he had some claim to responsibility. And in this case he was right to be pleased with himself. He had given the Colonel, John Harcourt and Euan Fforde a flavour of the scale of things on the ferry, but being who he was, it was only half the tale.

'You laugh, but I will know what is going to happen at the heart of American politics almost before the key players know themselves.'

'US military takeover paralyses government. Something like that?' said Collette, continuing the banter.

'It's worse than that. At least it is if you're a caring American,' replied Kirovsky.

'And if you're an information peddler?'

Kirovsky laughed his cold laugh.

'It's money in the bank, and plenty.'

'So what's really going to happen, Yuri? War?' asked Collette.

Kirovsky wondered why she'd said that. In his heart he had always known that the US and Europe would eventually fall out and then war would be possible. Not now but in the future. He also knew that the pendulum of US politics would swing and could swing far enough to allow the rundown of what at that time was the most powerful military machine ever. And it wouldn't take long for decay to set in. He should know; the fastest ever decay of a military machine was the Soviet one and from the inside he knew just how dramatic that had been.

'Maybe.'

Later, back at his computer, he continued his electronic debrief of his agents. The elements of the CIA game plan began to emerge. Uniquely in the position to see the whole picture, he was impressed with the thinking. And he was particularly impressed by just how far into the future they were thinking.

'They're being much more long-term than they ever were before.'

He noted a number of aspects that he felt required more detail and he puzzled for a while over a number of references to missiles. But never one to dwell on something when he lacked sufficient information, he closed down his machine and wandered into the bedroom that Collette used as a home gymnasium. Pounding the punch-bag she had already worked up a considerable sweat by the time he arrived.

'Who the hell is that?'

Kirovsky had hardly settled to enjoy the sight of Collette's tightly muscled body working in overdrive when the doorbell rang. He didn't recognise the two men he could see through the spy hole. He did recognise the tools for battering his door down.

'Yes?'

The question hung around the empty hall as three men surged past him into the flat. A fourth, older and perhaps the most senior, shepherded him into the spare bedroom where the other three were grouped around Collette. She had stopped her punching and was wiping the sweat from her face with the back of her forearm.

'Like to get some proper clothes on?' said the man with Kirovsky.

'Like to give us an explanation?' demanded Kirovsky, dropping automatically into French.

'Collette Dubois? We need to talk to you.'

Yuri Kirovsky's question was ignored. Ignoring him was something you didn't do.

'A moment,' he said coldly. 'This is my flat. What authority have you got to burst in here like this?'

'We have all the authority we need.'

It was a difficult situation for Kirovsky. He recognised the code. This was security service business. But he knew that he had to make some attempt at a defence of Collette.

However, since his position in France was only tolerated because he was careful not to commit any transgressions, he was inhibited from being his usual forceful self.

'So what's she done?' he asked.

Collette had returned with a tracksuit over her boxing strip.

'Yes?' she demanded, in no way inhibited. 'So what have I done?'

'That will be explained.'

'Yuri, they can't do this to me. They have to have a warrant; I have to have done something!'

'Not this lot,' he said sourly.

She understood. She was being arrested because of him. No explanations were offered but they both knew it to be so. For someone with the Colonel's contacts it was an easy enough trick to pull.

Collette didn't protest any more. She was afraid to say something that would make it worse for her partner.

'Bastard!'

Kirovsky saved the brunt of his anger until they had gone. He had helped Collette pack. He had tried to reassure her but it wasn't easy.

'Bastard!' he said again.

He didn't need telling who had arranged the arrest. It was the sort of easy pressure that he might have used himself in former times. The irony of that was not lost on him. He knew it was his own fault. The habit of holding something back, of never telling it all, was so ingrained that he doubted if he'd ever overcome it. On the ferry they knew he was holding back, but counteraction in America, particularly by Euan Fforde, wasn't possible without the sort of detail that he had and which they knew he was wanting to trade.

'We won't mess about,' the Colonel had said. 'Twist his arm straight away: something reasonably subtle. He won't react to brute force.'

DISUNITED STATES

That was how the plan to arrest Collette emerged. The Colonel knew the message would be easily read by Kirovsky. His only worry was that the Russian wouldn't react. Notoriously insensitive and unfeeling with a long history of the callous treatment of women, there was always a chance that he would just abandon Collette and pursue his own agenda at his own speed. But it was a gamble that paid off. Kirovsky's desire for a peaceful retirement with all the trimmings was strong, and although no force on earth could have made him admit it openly, he desperately wanted Collette to be there to share his latter-day ease with him.

In the end, the Colonel knew his Russian.

* * *

Pensky (even those who had known him for years didn't know his first name) watched the commotion at Kirovsky's flat with interest. No effort was made at secrecy. Used to the tortuous lengths that the old KGB would go to keep even the delivery of its laundry secret, he was surprised. He recognised the group accompanying Collette for what they were and couldn't get his head around such open behaviour.

He was in a small café right opposite the block of flats where Kirovsky lived and he was on his second coffee. That his old master lived in an apartment so openly exposed to surveillance he put down to the superior cunning of the colonel general.

He had a filled half-baguette with his third coffee and stayed long enough to enjoy it, allowing him to confirm that Kirovsky's flat was now under very strict surveillance.

'Change of plan,' he told himself. 'Better do the Amsterdam job and come back to Paris later.'

31

2026

Keeps some interesting company, thought Joe Longton. He was wandering around the Military Museum at Delft. He found the reminders of past conflicts salutary and wondered at the endurance of people in past years.

It was his teenaged daughter who remarked on some oddity on a passing canal tour-boat that drew his eye to the passengers. Chap McGoldberg he recognised at once. It took him a minute or two to put a name to the man that he was talking to so earnestly.

'Jordan,' he muttered. 'Alex Jordan!' It was then that he marvelled at McGoldberg's choice of company and worried. The word on the street, as Joe had heard it, was that McGoldberg was a leading Neoconservative. Jordan's views weren't known beyond his supposedly being motivated by self-interest and possessing a purchasable loyalty. Joe didn't automatically assume that being with McGoldberg meant that Jordan was a part of the rising, self-seeking faction in the SIE. For the Neoconservatives, Jordan would be a formidable opponent; against them, a powerful ally.

'Why Delft?'

Jordan was the SIE's fixer, a thug and a bully. Rick Blackford's brush with him was still in Joe's mind and he wondered whether that had anything to do with Jordan's visit.

Rick wasn't on Jordan's mind, but the planning of Melvin

Fitzallan's public protection was. Notoriously contemptuous of 'mollycoddling', getting close to the ambassador was easy enough. Knowing where he would be in the weeks ahead was the reason for Jordan's canal trip with Senator McGoldberg.

* * *

'Hell, Ross, I'm getting even more square-eyed than you.'

It was one of an increasing number of occasions when John ventured into humour with Ross. Of old he knew she had had a lively sense of humour. Slowly as the old barriers began to come down and Ross's vague sense of betrayal lost its force, they dropped back into the more relaxed and happy-go-lucky relationship of twenty-two years ago.

'Concentrate. It's important. The vice president is definitely alive. At least that's what the SIE think, and that's what their director is saying on TV. 'Being well cared for' is the message. But the SIE traffic in the Caribbean is frantic. The volume is extraordinary. You could hardly miss it. Every intelligence service in the world must be listening in by now.'

'So what are they hearing?'

'I'll get back to you. There's so much it needs editing and analysing. Myra's on it right now. In the meantime, I'll patch a British Airways incident report to you. You might find it interesting.'

One of the outcomes of the building tension between Europe and the US was the blocking of all foreign transmissions into America. Even with the massive array of communications satellites it was only partially successful; but the retaliatory action from Europe meant that airline pilots over the Atlantic could only transmit to their European bases when they were well on the way back. The replay of the voice recorder that Ross played back to John told its own tale.

'Ladies and gentlemen, this is the captain. Our route today will take us on a southerly sweep towards the South Atlantic and then we will fly due west to St Lucia. This will take us around nine hundred kilometres further than we would normally go and lengthen our journey by nearly two hours. You should not be alarmed; the United States Navy has moved an aircraft carrier to an area east of Bermuda and has announced flying exercises across our original flight path.'

Both John and Ross had been aware of this piece of provocation. The European Federation had lodged a formal complaint with both the US and the UN without the least expectation that any notice would be taken of it. The American aircraft carrier was old and its armaments limited and no threat to the civilian aircraft was anticipated. There was no fishing in the area. More troubling to John, however, was the despatch of a French aircraft carrier of substantially greater capability and the rerouting of two British Trident–2 submarines.

'This is getting stupid,' John said to himself. 'It's all very well the British saying that the US capability is impaired. So they're underfunded, their systems are rundown and old-fashioned, but they can still do major damage. And they can still push Europe to the point of no return in this phoney war.'

The atmosphere in Europe was becoming oppressive; anger and a desire to settle the issue with the US were the pervading feelings. Some sort of conflict was thought inevitable by many people. Some it seemed even desired it. And some on the other side of the Atlantic were actively courting it.

'John, I'll switch you to the CNN South-East Asia transmission. It's not blocked by Europe.'

As the CNN picture came into focus the unmistakable face of Melvin Fitzallan and his arch henchman Senator McGoldberg filled the screen. The ambassador was angry.

'The European action,' he was saying, 'is offensive, provocative and unjustifiable by any criteria of international relations.'

Having missed the opening sequence of the transmission it was not clear to John where the interview was taking place. It was certainly a press conference, and it seemed most likely that it was in the US as the majority of the questions were not hostile and seemed designed to give Fitzallan a platform. The gist of the message was clear. The decision to send European warships to the area of the US Navy exercises was a challenge that they could not ignore; the responsibility for the outcome must rest squarely with the Europeans.

'But Mr Ambassador, with the whole of the Atlantic to exercise in, would you not say the choice of an area directly under the main air routes from Europe to the Caribbean and South America was less than fortuitous?'

A snarl of contempt escaped Fitzallan. The questioner was from *The Washington Echo*, not a strong supporter of the Fitzallan faction and about the only major US newspaper to challenge the nationalistic and isolationist pitch of the opposition to the president.

Chap McGoldberg nodded into the audience. He was not a fan of press conferences; he preferred podcasts and online blogs; there was a much better chance of the message being received unadulterated by challenges like the one that Fitzallan had just failed to answer.

'Could you tell us something about the condition of the vice president?' The planted, toady reporter, responding to McGoldberg's nod, rushed his question into the silence developing as the ambassador sought a suitably crushing response to the *Echo*.

'His condition remains critical but stable,' said McGoldberg, relieving Fitzallan of the necessity of giving a reply.

'Which,' said John, beginning to understand something of Ross's interest in the electronic traffic in the Caribbean, 'means he hasn't got a clue because he doesn't know where the VP is.'

It was an accurate summary. To the amazement of the world community, a grievously injured man had disappeared from the face of the earth, or at least from the face of a relatively small island in the Caribbean.

Wonder how long they can keep this up? thought John. It was something that everybody from the president downwards was wondering. Paralysis at the top of the political heap was complete. All the machinations of Fitzallan and the SIE and their supporters were on hold until the fate of the vice president was known.

CNN lost interest in the press conference pretty quickly. They had a feature on the breakdown of law and order to transmit and the violence and destitution running through the country that was much more viewer-riveting than the mock histrionics of the cynical ambassador.

John switched the TV off. Ross was about her business and the catalogue of horrors was not something that he wanted to burden himself with unnecessarily. But the statistics were awesome. There were riots in no less than 240 US towns and cities, not against Europe, or the ever-increasing risk of conflagration, but against hunger and hopelessness. The impact of the collapse of commercial and financial relations with Europe was coming home to roost. In line with the Neoconservatives and their narrow-minded view of the world, Americans were being urged to work hard, be self-reliant and take responsibility for their own destinies. In a computer-based, banker-dominated and import-driven consumer economy this was a message that was meaningless to the average American.

The Neoconservatives' self-righteous, self-delusionary view that they knew best was a recipe for disaster. US businesses closed down in ever-increasing numbers and unemployment sky-rocketed. With a welfare system unable to cope and the necessary changes mired in Congress, violent protest seemed to be the only option. Many black areas had been surrendered by the police. Many police personnel had refused to undertake the massive use of force prescribed by the authorities to put the riots down.

'They've lost control,' John said to himself as he settled to his meal. 'How the hell does Fitzallan think he's going to get it back?'

But of course John already thought he knew the answer to his own question.

'Killing the vice president abroad gives one of the nationalist thugs a chance to get into the White House courtesy of the US Constitution, which was designed by honest men behaving honourably. Nationalist? Nationalist, religious right winger? What's the difference?' Except that at that time nobody was sure that the vice president was dead.

Despite the obvious logic of the situation, the idea of ousting the US President took some energy to get lodged in John's brain. He conceded that the American constitutional process wasn't as robust as many would have liked to believe but still it did seem far-fetched.

'Taking over the vice president's office was possible,' John mused, 'according to such loyalists as Euan Fforde. And he's both a patriot and pro-European, and in a better position to know other than those trying to engineer the supposed takeover.'

In the absence of the opportunity to talk through his thoughts with Ross, who was committed to monitoring the Caribbean and mainland American electronic transmissions, John found himself increasingly talking out his thoughts aloud. It was a way of achieving clarity that had served him well over the years.

How Fforde's views became known John didn't bother to consider. John was well aware of the view that two thirds of Congress were for sale or had been at one time or another. The ever-friendly SIE had a dirt file on 14 million Americans, John had also been reliably told; that was a power position if ever there was one, and with twenty-seven of the key White House staff SIE plants, only a very few immediate members of the president's personal staff could be trusted. Fforde was one of these and his credibility and integrity, despite many efforts to undermine it, had never been doubted.

A day later, John's director called him in to see how things were going.

'So, you think this old Russian Kirovsky's buried networks in the US are being offered to us to help counter the anti-European feeling. And you think that this Euan Fforde, a known SIE insider, is behind the offer.'

'Not so much behind it, sir,' said John carefully, 'as letting it happen without interference. The present trends in US politics are challenging the loyalties and fundamental beliefs of a whole range of thinking Americans who are wondering which world they are living in: the liberal world of Europe or the rigid, almost pseudo-fascist one of the Neocons and the religious right.'

'And they're prepared to betray their country, like this long-running Russian network has been doing for years?'

'Betray is too harsh a word in the days of mass communication and porous national boundaries. The network is basically a business that evolved from a spy ring when spying was no longer appropriate; Fforde is letting it drift back into being a spy ring and protecting it from his less liberal colleagues.'

'John, that sounds like a rationalisation that's flawed but I'm not sure it will do much good to debate it. More to the point is the analysis that they've been doing here on the bombings.'

The message of the analytical report was fairly straightforward. There were definite patterns in the American provocations. The targets were always high profile, always where internal European frictions were the most prevalent, and never where there was a real risk of European retaliation.

'A bit like some half-brave, half-frightened five-year-old challenging his harassed father,' remarked the director.

John laughed at the description. He understood exactly what he meant, but he also knew that just as with the five-year-old, there would come a day when the bravado went too far.

'Winding up Europe is only distracting some amongst the home audience,' the director continued. 'The latest data suggests that foreign adventures aren't on the agenda of most Americans.'

'You mean the bread and circuses may not be working?' John said. 'But stirring up the home front while they consolidate their hold on the government machine seems to be what this is also all about. D'you reckon a serious confrontation with Europe is possible?'

'Yes, John,' the director said, 'I do. It might be a rogue action but it's more likely to be momentum driven.'

'Starting something they can't stop.'

They debated this possibility for a while. It was an important matter for the director. The Joint Security Commission was meeting in Brussels the next day and his views were likely to carry considerable weight. He was also interested in the latest on the vice president situation.

John fed back to the director the contents of brief that Ross had obtained from the Antiguan authorities.

The refurbishment of the St Johns fish market was an American-funded project. An upsurge in the taste for exotic fish as a result of overfishing the common species had induced the US importers to invest in more sophisticated facilities and to pander to the images of modern food hygiene. The net result was a sterile semi-enclosed market hated by the local traders but welcomed by the impoverished government who were hit by the ever-fickle tourist trade moving on to pastures new.

With rare generosity, the vice president had offered to open the new market. Driven perhaps by a desire to get a brief respite from the horrors of internal politics and spend a day or so in friendly surroundings, the arrangements were made in great secrecy and in last minute haste. Leakage of information had been minimal as far as his most trusted staff could tell. The presence of a US warship in harbour was coincidental, and more to do with a lack of money for serious maintenance than any ceremonial purpose.

Unknown to John of course, the response in Washington to the VP's planned trip had verged on panic. The hurriedly arranged planeload of SIE men was a frantic response from Melvin Fitzallan's henchmen when they realised that they had almost been outwitted.

'That bastard Browneton's got a place in Antigua, ain't he?' Fitzallan had demanded when he heard the news.

'Estate. Owns a small promontory of land in the east of the main island; own jetty, big ocean-going yacht. He's very popular locally.'

'Better keep a watch on the place, Euan.'

Euan Fforde promised to do so. But no effective watch was kept.

Euan Fforde was an enigma to Fitzallan. Of the whole of the SIE top brass, he was virtually the only one that the ambassador hadn't been able to subvert openly to the cause of revitalising the American way of life, yet he was loud and prominent in such a cause. But his colleagues didn't trust him. They suspected him of undermining their efforts to force a consensus on the Administration in favour of their right-wing agenda and its pretty draconian solutions to current problems whilst paying lip service to them. But they never caught him at it.

The vice president's arrival had been chaotic. His entourage of cars, control vehicles, support trucks and his ambulance was really too large for the market area and some of them were so dispersed as to be useless. The Antiguan authorities, having taken serious umbrage at the aggressive and high-handed way that the SIE men were trying to take over the whole day, swamped the inside of the market with armed police, a few soldiers and a mass of invited guests whose credentials were not apparently being checked.

The single shot rang out. The force of the bullet hitting him in the middle of the chest threw the vice president's body back into the arms of the train of local worthies and Antiguan Government Ministers.

In the mêlée that followed, more shots were fired but into the air. Trapped inside the ranks of fish stalls, the dignitaries and watching populace began an agitated surge to the exits. Despite firing over the crowd, the enraged SIE men were swept away from the scene of the shooting and only a trusted three or four of the vice president's personal bodyguard were with him.

The Antiguan report suggested a high-velocity target rifle fired at around 150 to 200 yards distance. It was a good clean shot, of no great difficulty for an experienced marksman, and within the car park surrounding the market there were ample vantage points to access the open-sided building. It was merely a question of awaiting the opportunity.

'It was very efficient and professional,' was the opinion of the head of the Antiguan Security organisation.

'Like the removal of the body?'

The Antiguan Security Service had followed the trail to the villa of Alastair Browneton, noted the absence of the ocean-going yacht and retreated to make enquiries further afield.

'Relations between the US and Antigua are at an all-time

low,' remarked John as he finished retailing the details of the exploit to his director. 'And the vice president is safe in Texas, you say. All our transmission analysis suggests that the SIE don't know that and are putting on a huge front to hide their ignorance.'

'Safe isn't the word I'd use, John,' remarked the director. 'After the pounding he took getting away, his life expectancy isn't so high.'

'Okay,' said John, 'he's safe for the present and while he's still alive, or not known to be dead, the government is largely paralysed.'

'I guess the US Government's paralysed through its own incompetence, venality and the weakness of its leaders rather than the non-availability of the vice president.'

'I won't debate the point, sir. It's where this takes us not where we've come from that's important.'

'I think it takes us to your old Russian and his – what did you say they're called?'

'Intercontinental Veterans Anonymous.'

'It's how the power struggle's unfolding, is it not? What will happen if the VP isn't there to bolster the president, etc. The SIE power base is developing quickly, but if the distraction of the people isn't working, they'll have to go for an even bigger distraction, clampdown or meet the popular demands.'

'They aren't going to do that, are they? Meet demands.'

'No, John, they aren't. My money's on a bigger distraction, with a clampdown to follow if it doesn't work.'

Clampdown with what? John wondered.

It was a fair point: the American military were not really in a position to undertake a major role in managing civil disruption. Their weaponry was outdated and geared to an offensive war not crowd control, their numbers were depleted and their morale was so low as to be almost non-existent.

When his conversation with the director had ended John

allowed his mind to wonder and ponder. At times, when he could no longer process all the information coming at him, this is what he would do: relax, switch off conscious control of the analysis machine and let his brain take its own path. Perhaps not surprisingly, his thoughts first reverted to Ross. A brief sense of yearning flashed out of his subconscious before recognition of her great common sense told him that the key to his musings was the old Russian Yuri Kirovsky. Ross had always seen him as a remarkable man whose influence was far greater than it appeared to be on first acquaintance, so to speak. As the brilliance of what the ex-KGB General had done began to dawn on him, with the level of perception and forward thinking that he had been capable of, John began to understand why the Colonel was able to excuse the Russian many of his brutalities and excesses.

The last time that John had seen Kirovsky, setting aside that fateful day at Gatwick, was at the restaurant in Antwerp when the final briefing by Kirovsky took place. At the time of the meeting, of course John and Ross had no idea that there was a KGB contract out on Kirovsky for the settlement of old scores, or that there was a CIA one out on Joe Longton. These were things that emerged later, just as he was later to learn that it wasn't exactly a KGB contract out on Kirovsky. The KGB had been replaced but some of its pensioners had been recruited for some score-settling of a private and personal nature by an aggrieved son now in a position of power in Moscow.

Memories flooded into the mental void that John had deliberately created. A meeting had been arranged with Yuri Kirovsky that in their various ways, John, Ross and the Colonel had all been looking forward to. Across twenty-two years, smells and sounds re-invaded John's senses.

The atmosphere at the Red Shoe restaurant in Antwerp had been warm and steamy, reflecting the open-sided kitchen from which the tantalising smells of cooking fish wafted, reinforcing anticipation and building expectation. It had been one of the Colonel's favourite eating houses and one where his patronage, offered only occasionally and erratically, was always nonetheless well appreciated.

Opening straight from the street (a plus point for the wheelchair-bound Colonel), the Red Shoe was divided into old wooden booths of ancient and primitive construction but of an intimacy that suited the purposes of the evening. The restaurant was one of Antwerp's cult places to eat and one that the Colonel felt sure would appeal to Yuri Kirovsky's barely suppressed bourgeois sensibilities.

'Thought we'd get here a bit early,' the Colonel had said. 'We need to sort out a few ground rules.'

Ross grinned at seeing John's surprised expression. She was used to the Colonel and his way of doing things.

'Old Yuri has done a good job so far. We have to make him feel welcome and valued. At least we have to try. It's debatable whether he'd recognise such finer feelings, but there you go – we try. We have to make him feel that he's going to get his retirement. I can't deliver that, John; that's one for your lot, but he'll believe I can. And we mustn't get irritated if we think he's holding something back. He will be; that's how he thinks.'

They had been halfway through a carafe of house red – the Colonel liked unpretentious country wines – when the Russian appeared in the restaurant. John and the Colonel shared a quiet grin at the way that Kirovsky materialised at their table.

'Dear old Yuri; ever the spy. He'll never change.' John read the Colonel's thought instantly: a rare feat. John was just delighted at the way the former KGB man still seemed to enjoy the mechanics of their mutual business.

'Yuri, it's good to see you again. You know everybody.'

Kirovsky had acknowledged the greetings. Whether he

sensed the atmosphere that the Colonel was trying to create, none of them could be sure. A quick glass of wine from the carafe seemed to settle him and a slower second glass brought him to the point of reasonable communication. The other three watched the process with interest but without reaction.

'Found yourself a home?'

Kirovsky nodded to John.

The recent destruction of Kirovsky's Paris flat was known to the Colonel and his party. The French authorities had been very accommodating after the intervention of John's boss. Anxious not to distract the Russian unnecessarily, John had seen to it that the French, far from taking the opportunity of the destruction of his flat to shift Kirovsky from their bailiwick, had found him some serviceable accommodation that he would be comfortable in. Their cooperation was grudging. The French authorities were seriously miffed at Kirovsky's success at conducting his business under their noses.

'Any idea who bombed the flat?' asked the Colonel.

Kirovsky shrugged. He had a fair idea, but saw no point in sharing his thoughts.

'So, my friend, what's all this really about?' The Colonel had no need to explain what he meant by 'this'. The Russian had come intending to unburden himself and draw a line under the current period of his life; he knew very well what 'this' was.

'It's about power and a new Puritanism, Colonel.'

'Really?' The Colonel thought the choice of a religious reference point curious but merely offered the Russian a prompt.

Kirovsky knew that he was expected to expand on his statement.

'Stop the decline in all-American values by whatever means. The Neoconservative religious right reckon democracy has gone too far. The average American is too self-interested to recognise the greater good of an all-powerful, world-leading America. The Neocons don't see the messes being made in Iraq and Afghanistan; all they see is the need for democracy to be subordinated to the requirements of the State as defined by the ruling elite.'

John winced as he thought back to those words, not because they there wrong in some way, more because of how accurately they represented the situation as it eventually developed. With his life's experience as proof, he knew all too well how difficult it had been to reconcile the parties to the various conflicts in the Middle East. And even now in 2026 the solutions were still untried and fragile. In 2004 they were not even in the dreams of most politicians.

'But old Yuri had an inkling,' muttered John as his mind drifted back to the Antwerp meal.

'Fascism?'

'Fascism, Colonel.'

'Okay, take that as read,' John had said. 'Where's it going?'

'The text book agenda,' said the Russian, 'is taking over through the constitutional process, repression of opposition, some sort of answer to the question of ethnic minorities. Isn't that the fascist way?'

John remembered that Ross had challenged the notion on the basis that the role of the president was still central to the American political model and there was a powerful president in place. The American Constitution was supposed to be coup-proof since the president had immediate executive power.

Kirovsky's shrug at the time said that he didn't believe that that amounted to too much. Was he inspirationally perceptive or just an old cynic? In 2026, John was inclined to the former with the benefit of hindsight and history.

'I don't think Fitzallan and his SIE friends see that as a

problem at the present time,' John muttered. 'They've sussed the way to neutralise the president.'

The Colonel hadn't wanted to let the Russian get away with generalisations. 'Want to say some more about that, Yuri?'

Since the next ten to fifteen minutes had been devoted to mussels and generous helpings of the house white, Kirovsky didn't get to saying any more, despite the Colonel's prompt. Mellowed by the communal nature of their hors d'oeuvre and pausing while digestion absorbed their energies, the conversation resumed. The Colonel let things flow.

'We certainly got to understand about Intercontinental Veterans Anonymous,' John recalled. 'In detail and in glorious Technicolor, you might say.'

Once again, as his mind wandered to and fro, John marvelled anew at just how far-sighted the old KGB man had been. The brilliance of the concept of a sleeping spy ring feeding itself on industrial espionage on an industrial scale, confident that one day it would have to return to its spying activities to defend US democracy against an American internal threat, still left John gasping. Yet in 2026 it was so and Ross had received the trigger message from the Veterans just as Kirovsky had planned it.

Swordfish and salmon, halibut and turbot then intervened. The men ate desserts. Ross didn't. Coffee allowed a switch of topic.

'I guess we'd talked ourselves out by the time we got to coffee,' John remembered.

The Colonel knew when a meeting was at an end and that allowing it to drag on was often destructive to the confidence and ambience that the meeting had created.

'So, Yuri, how are your plans for the future?'

The Colonel of course knew that the Russian's plans depended on him as much as on Kirovsky himself.

'My business is up for sale.'

'What business?'

'Colonel, I import fruit, exotic vegetables, many other things. You know that. It is all proper and allowed by the French.'

'But you still want to retire to Scotland?'

'Of course I do... With Collette, damn you!' It had been a rare show of feeling from Kirovsky. The Colonel hadn't responded as he sensed that there was more to be said.

'What more do you want from me now? I've given you all I have. I've proved myself. I've given you my organisation, done things for you that your precious intelligence service could never do. What more?'

'John here has already started action within the British bureaucracy. Narrowed it down the 'unsolved mysteries', you might say. There's not a lot left on the books.'

Kirovsky knew that it was all he was going to get. He'd taken a risk by advertising his services in the first place; his services had been taken up. It was a gamble that he still thought would pay off. He knew that he was in the hands of the British establishment and distasteful as that was, his reading of them was that they wouldn't be bothered in the end to chase down enough dirt against him to get him into court. He had, of course, done his best to see that as much of the evidence as possible was no longer available to the authorities to chase down.

The tension that had grown up over Kirovsky's retirement had ebbed away as quickly as it had arisen. The conversation became more general and Ross for one was amazed at the rapport that seemed to exist between the two old adversaries, bearing in mind that they had only met once before the present meeting.

'What an amazing old bloke,' Ross had said to John later. 'All the spy thrillers would have you believe that people like Kirovsky were single-minded monsters without conscience, compassion or any other finer feeling. At times he seemed more like your favourite granddad.'

'Seemed?' said John. 'Well, maybe.' Having studied the old Russian in great depth Ross's first description still made more sense to him than her grandfather theory. About his only redeeming feature, John thought, even after the years since he had seen Kirovsky violently gunned down, was his obvious love for Collette.

The baleful effect that Kirovsky, alive and dead, had had on John and his relationship with Ross was something that never seemed to quite go away. Much as he believed that they had both come through that dark period and were ready for a new and hopefully more lasting relationship, if they couldn't now after twenty-two years lay the ghost of Kirovsky to rest he doubted that they ever would.

32

2026

When John had enquired whether she still used the gym in Aberdeen Ross had been rather coy. John had noticed that her figure was as trim as ever and didn't put it down entirely to country dancing. There remained a faint mortification at her antics with the redoubtable Collette in Antwerp that coloured Ross's willingness to admit to still keeping up her interest in karate. Alanda, who usually accompanied Ross to the gym, would have been well able to vouch for her lasting capabilities in this area and although her youth would have allowed her to prevail in any serious competition, she readily conceded that Ross was a tough opponent on whom to hone her skills.

The bus journey to the gym in Aberdeen was one of Ross's minor pleasures. One of the more welcome spin-offs of the responses to global warming she always felt was the reversion to older forms of transport and the consequential slowing of the pace of life. The more youthful Alanda would normally have found such journeys tedious but they also offered the opportunity to discuss their work and now for her, also the opportunity to share her feelings over her burgeoning relationship with Rick Blackford. The sense of déjà-vu that this gave Ross was almost palpable as her own resurgent relationship with John increasingly preoccupied her mind. But although the wasted twenty-two years were a part of the preoccupation, it manifested itself more in challenging her caution over the problems of a relationship with an intelligence service insider. Ross, however, wasn't yet ready to take a more relaxed view of Alanda's growing attraction to Rick.

'So who's this Alastair Browneton then?' asked Alanda as they settled and the bus pulled out onto the main Huntly to Aberdeen road.

Ross had spent the hour before she needed to leave for Aberdeen researching Alastair Browneton; she was planning to build a more comprehensive database on Intercontinental Veterans Anonymous and on all of Yuri Kirovsky's organisations, past and present, but Browneton, whose role she was unclear about, had taken her attention.

'Browneton's the vice president's cousin. He's a media mogul.'

'Is the vice president really still thought to be alive, Ross? If he is the poor sod must be on his last legs. God, isn't that a terrible way to have to end your life.'

Ross agreed but rather than dwell on the sadness of the situation she started on a biography of the obviously redoubtable Mr Browneton.

'Combative, shrewd, austere in his lifestyle, very much wedded to the concepts of the end justifying the means, not particularly scrupulous when his interests are at stake, slow to anger, but unforgiving as an opponent.'

'Some guy I reckon, Ross. So where does he fit into this?'

'That's what we're going to have to figure out. John reckons that he's a valuable ally, since he's not exactly the blue-eyed boy of the SIE and their ilk. His papers, digital media and podcasts are very traditionalist, you might say, which again is not to the SIE's taste.'

Ross let Alanda's quick smirk at the mention of John pass.

Ross knew that the description fitted Browneton very well. Cynical as she was, she also knew that it could just as well have applied to any first-quarter, twenty-first-century, US presidential candidate, incumbent or deputy. With the odd notable exception, the system didn't seem to allow for first-rate brains, unimpeachable integrity or inherent honesty to survive too readily in the holders of high office. That said, the dead or dying vice president was probably one of these exceptions.

Following a somewhat circuitous train of thought Ross drew the comparison for Alanda. 'How about this, then? Hardworking, straightforward, driven by a clear uncomplicated view of the world, devoid of the usual vices of the rich and he has never been known to stray from the marital bed. You'd hardly credit that as the stuff of contemporary political aspirants would you?'

'The vice president, Ross? Is he for real?'

In the picture that Ross was building for Alanda, Alastair Browneton clearly overshadowed and outshone his vice-presidential cousin. Both were staunch in resisting the new corporatism of the SIE and both were very outspoken about the disintegration of the American federal state under the multiple pressures of the nationalism of individual states, isolationism and the overweening aspirations of an increasing number of powerful individuals. Democracy, the rights of the weak and the good of the nation were phrases often on their lips but they hadn't put enough space between themselves and the likes of Melvin Fitzallan. The ambassador used the same words but certainly not with the same meaning, or with the same conviction.

'I'd still like to know where this guy fits in, Ross.'

'Well, he's the guy with the newspapers and TV stations and the Internet clout; what he's got to do is get out there and start campaigning. We know what can be done if you try.'

And of course, spurred on by the death of his cousin, because by now he must have known that the vice president was certainly dead, Alastair Browneton was formulating plans to do just that, and to try and redress the balance of power. Ross's prowess and example in the business of media manipulation weren't lost on him either. Inevitably, he'd heard of it.

Essentially selfish, when it came down to it, he deeply resented the challenge to his way of life posed by the America Resurgent movement and their desire to resurrect the power of the USA based on the paranoid but rose-tinted periods of the 1970s and 1980s. He believed that the average American had the right to seek whatever lifestyle they wanted according to his or her needs and wishes and according to his or her means, and a new state-controlled puritanism that was founded on an elite, all-powerful, all-knowing and exclusive group was to be resisted at all costs. Strong on the history of the middle to late twentieth century, he saw the lives of countless Americans wasted if Fitzallan's view of the world was allowed to succeed.

'This is powerful stuff, Ross,' Alanda said once Ross had shared the results of her research.

'Yes it is, and we're going to have to do something as well. We've been called into the action by Intercontinental Veterans Anonymous just as that old Russian reprobate intended us to be. And we need to do something before Europe and the US drift into open conflict. Only today a Spanish destroyer exchanged fire with an American patrol vessel, harassing French fishing boats well out into international waters off the US eastern seaboard. The inability to be able to stop what's been started, as John and the European intelligence community recognises, is a serious and real risk.'

'True enough. I checked the surveillance before we left. Now we're in the loop there was a huge amount of traffic. The Veterans have been very active.'

'Doing what?'

'I'm not sure where to begin. They've got a finger in

everywhere. The vice president is definitely dead; the president's known it for at least two days. The Washington Grand Jury has thrown out corruption charges against Rick Uhlemann, the Chairman of the House of Representatives, the new vice president. The Vets were trying to get Uhlemann debarred, but a joint meeting of Congress railroaded the president.'

'So, they've got their man in as vice president. That didn't take long. The squeeze is on with a vengeance.'

'There's a lot of stuff about the military. One of the Vets has got a bee in his bonnet about START weaponry, whatever that is.'

'START weaponry is, are, intercontinental ballistic missiles, Alanda,' Ross said, pronouncing the words with more than a hint of curiosity in her voice. 'John said something about them ages ago when he first got drawn back into this lot.'

* * *

The US Air Force base at Lost Springs, Arizona was a hell hole by common consent. It didn't exist in the records of the Pentagon, at least those normally available to the Senate Armed Services Committee, but it was real enough to those stationed there.

The complement at Lost Springs was sixteen intercontinental ballistic missiles, ICBMs to those in the know, eight officers and forty-six enlisted men, more than half of whom were women. It didn't exist as far as the US Treasury and public at large were concerned because its weapons were supposed to have been destroyed as a part of the US quota in the 1990s. Except that the more far-sighted of the CIA senior brass of the period induced the Air Force to forget this little package of death and destruction and substitute a satellite tracking station that tracked nothing and which was staffed with the requisite number of personnel with little or nothing to occupy them.

DISUNITED STATES

Even when the various attempts to revitalise the old 'Star Wars' projects were in their periods of success, nobody thought to included Lost Springs in the study programme. Equally, when the 'Star Wars' projects were finally starved of funds and died, the base in the Arizona desert continued its unheralded existence even as the US missiles in Europe were withdrawn.

The base was commanded by an Air Force colonel of advancing years and as far as anyone could find out, of totally undistinguished record. But he was also the only person around who had even the faintest knowledge about the missiles stored deep in the desert sand in silos positioned around the 3 mile perimeter of the restricted area.

'Have a good trip to Washington, sir?'

The young captain, who performed the duties of base adjutant and the colonel's sexual partner with equal facility, greeted her lover formally for form's sake before retreating with him to his quarters to catch up on his fantasies. If he had been required to answer the question he would have said that his visit to Washington had been a disaster. It was the day after the vice president had been shot and his meeting with a group of nameless SIE management types, but no Air Force officers, was uncomfortable and he suspected, life threatening.

'For God's sake! It's Saturday,' the captain whined.

'We have work to do. Get dressed in fatigues.'

It was a long hot day. The captain had no idea what the colonel was doing as he worked at the computers in the underground control room. The equipment seemed to be old but was clearly serviceable, and the atmosphere stuffy but surprisingly cool. Had she the least technical knowledge she would have recognised that some sort of reprogramming was going on.

'Shit! These things actually work,' she said as lights flashed on the console.

'They work.'

The captain began to look vaguely anxious. Her time in bed with the colonel had told her that there were missiles around the site but she had never thought that they might ever be used. They had joked about the finger on the trigger but here he was doing things that turned the joke into something real.

As the colonel waited, the lights flashed again. He looked relieved.

'Don't ask,' he snapped. He needed her as a witness, as insurance, but he didn't need her to know more than that he had reprogrammed the missiles. Under expert questioning she would have to give just enough information. And he was sure that there would be expert questioning if the SIE plans went wrong.

'Okay, let's get back. See you in the mess at six.'

They were entertaining a group from Intercontinental Veterans Anonymous. The social life on the base was so inbred, the atmosphere so fetid with an ever-changing matrix of bed partners, that any external intrusion was welcome.

But the captain wasn't in the mess at six. The colonel, doing his host duties, didn't notice her absence for nearly an hour. Nobody had seen her. And when the guests had gone and the whole base was searched, nobody could find her.

The local Intercontinental Veterans Anonymous leader never saw the captain either but he still knew most of what the colonel was up to. Spirited away from her quarters the captain had been subject to questioning that was most certainly expert and she had found it very hard to resist providing the information that the Veterans were seeking.

* * *

Both Ross and Alanda relished their gym session and returned to the farmhouse refreshed in body and mind. Having resisted retail therapy beyond a few agreed necessities and a visit to Costa, they were ready for action again.

The return bus trip gave Alanda a chance to share some of the feedback she had obtained from various conversations with Rick Blackford.

'He knows about us, Ross, I'm sure he does, and it's not just because you and Joe Longton go back to the ice age. It's almost as if he's been set up to talk to me, or rather to communicate with us.'

'But he has, Alanda. That's exactly what he's been set to do, but not by the SIE.'

'Pardon me?'

'You said he's SIE; that we know to be true. You also said he's *persona non grata* as far as the London SIE unit is concerned?'

'Yes, Ross, that is true. But you're right, the more he thinks about how he was treated in London, the more he reckons that he was set up in some way. Not over the death of Spencer, or whatever his name was, but after the ambassador had a go at him. And after that man Jordan had interviewed him.'

'Okay, but what d'you reckon the situation is, Alanda? You're close to him.'

'But not too close, I hope,' Ross said to herself as an afterthought. She was far from confident that the relationship hadn't already developed too far for the wellbeing of Alanda and the business. She pushed the thought away.

'Well, frankly, I reckon he's a Vet, and I reckon that someone on high in the SIE is protecting him so that he can build bridges with people like us.'

'But no one could have known that you and he would meet up, unless Joe Longton was a party to the deal, and he's so out of it as far as the SIE brass are concerned I don't believe that.'

'No, Ross, I don't think it was as contrived as that. I think he was got out of London by some SIE good guy, and then because he's a Veteran they exploited my presence in Amsterdam.'

Ross gave her companion a wry smile. Alanda was absolutely right; the messages she had got from the latter-day fruit importer as much as confirmed that. Not that that did anything to allay her concerns over Alanda. Exploiting the relationship as it had formed naturally would have been old Kirovsky's style.

As the bus dawdled through the back streets of Inverurie and picked up and dropped off passengers the situation that had developed worried Ross. Alanda may have been right but it did raise questions about the loyalties of Jordan, the SIE Head of Internal Security, something that Ross was already aware of from Alanda's previous reports. Jordan had satisfied himself of Rick Blackford's knowledge about the killing of Spencer in London but had seemingly been uninterested in his posting to Amsterdam. Why? There were too many unanswered questions about Mr Jordan in all of this for Ross, although she didn't rule out the possibility that he was a good guy.

'Well, okay, Alanda, d'you know what Rick thinks about what's going on?'

There didn't seem to be much point in speculating about why Rick had been sent to Holland; he was there.

'As far as he's concerned the SIE are definitely into distractions abroad. The old Roman bread and circuses ploy, Ross. With their own agents taking over at local level and the opposition being dealt with also at local level, despite appearances, the SIE and its front organisations are taking a creeping stranglehold within the individual states. It seems to be their intention to consolidate their power out of sight of the federal system.'

'And then at the right moment move at national level while the population is hyped up over Europe,' said Ross.

'That's about it.'

'Okay, Alanda, what if Europe turns nasty? Does Rick think that the US military would be a match for us?'

Alanda was an African, daughter of a minor politician in Port Harcourt in Nigeria; her perceptions of power politics were drawn from a much lower level than Ross's and any other European. It always took her time to get her head around the sort of bigger picture that her boss was drawing. Her ability to think in small boxes, which stemmed from her small town background, was useful in her normal work but in the present debate she found herself having to take time to grasp what she was being asked. Ross in turn liked Alanda's confidence to take time and reason things out.

'I can't answer that. But doesn't history suggest that in such a situation you make a pre-emptive strike?'

'Maybe, but that doesn't answer my question.' Ross changed tack. 'Okay, do you have any idea whether Rick understands why Fitzallan and his cronies aren't too worried about the president getting in their way?'

'They didn't allow the vice president to, did they, Ross?'

'Maybe so but the president is something else.'

'Is he?'

It was a fair point.

'As a Veteran,' said Alanda, 'Rick would be expecting Fitzallan to be planning some further action to negate what little influence the president still has left. Otherwise, why take the vice president out and put his own man in his place?'

'And if the president is ineffective, it's what the vice president is up to that we should be concentrating on. Uhlemann's just a political thug as far as I can see, set up to bludgeon Congress into submission and see to it that the SIE get the best chance to infiltrate the whole government structure.' Ross continued with her colleague's line of thought.

'Seems to be where the Veterans are coming from,' suggested Alanda. 'And, according to Rick, the SIE have got a placement in every individual state and every federal department. Some states are quietening down, people are disappearing from the political scene; there have been a lot of road accident victims suddenly in Texas.'

'And how does Rick suppose that Fitzallan and the faceless America Resurgent, or whoever, plan to get final control of the Federal Government?'

'Hell, Ross, I don't suppose he knows all of the answers!'

'No, of course not.' Ross moved the conversation on again. 'The feedback from the line that Kirovsky opened up for us from the grave, you might say, suggests that it's getting tougher for the Veterans to get information. The SIE have started harassing them in their public guise, which suggests that they're somehow aware of their secret guise even if they can't penetrate it.'

'Also, Ross, despite what we were saying earlier, there's evidence that the SIE are linking some of their failures, and there are some, with Alastair Browneton and Shirley Addamms, so he must be doing something and getting it right.'

Ross knew who Shirley Addamms was.

'And the SIE are likely to be sore losers.'

Alanda knew what Ross meant. They had shared a gruesome news report concerning a suspected member of Intercontinental Veterans Anonymous named Adelle K. She had been met off the flight from Paris by a man and a woman who the New York Police had been unable to trace. Her naked body, bound to a plank, had been picked out of the East River only the day before. Injected with a massive dose of pure heroin, with her head tied up in a plastic bag from an up-market boutique, the horror of her death shocked the two women.

'A message to the Veterans, I guess,' said Alanda.

What Alanda and Ross didn't know, since it wasn't reported, was that the dark-haired woman who had featured in a beating incident shown on a Shirley Addamms's TV show and who answered the description of the woman the New York Police say met Adelle, was also found dead. Those who needed to know understood the riposte that Intercontinental Veterans Anonymous were making.

At a more public level, as John and Ross had discussed only the previous day, there was more that could be done in America to raise the awareness of the usually silent masses. The media in America and wide sections of the population of the American middle classes were still not intimidated by the SIE and their supporters. It was still possible to mobilise public opinion. The evidence that the Veterans were amassing against Fitzallan and his cohorts, the religious right, America Resurgent and their SIE collaborators, was credible and overwhelming. Despite threats, people like Alastair Browneton still had powerful voices.

33

2026

Joe Longton really liked Rick Blackford, but it didn't take him long to realise that there was a lot more to him than was immediately obvious. The boyish charm that had so captivated Alanda was always there, and the initial vulnerability of one so new to so complex a world, but underneath there was a steeliness that was easy to recognise when you had seen as much of life in the intelligence world as Joe had. And slowly, as relations cemented themselves, Rick began to carefully let slip something of his more secret Veterans side, and something of the more dangerous world that was developing in and around the SIE. Joe of course was not unaware of the dangers; he'd had his life on the line more than once and nearly lost it more than once. But it was a combination of Rick's enthusiasm and his growing interest in the black British girl that focused Joe and tugged out hidden memories of another vivacious young spy, and an all too narrow escape with his life.

At the height of the Kirovsky action in 2004, Joe had agreed to another meeting with John at his Amsterdam office. John was in Antwerp; it was a short trip to Amsterdam; there were CIA issues that John wanted to clarify.

'Whatever the guy's up to I really think I don't need to know,' Joe had told himself. His CIA masters were suspicious enough about his relationship with Harcourt.

Notwithstanding a shared background in the CIA, Joe

knew that John was a loyal and conscientious servant of Britain and as a consequence an uncertain friend of the US. While Joe trusted him, he knew very well that he shouldn't be seen to be too close to him. It was a memory that now came back to him even after the years that had passed. As the events that unfolded on the day of that fateful meeting flashed through his mind Joe was struck by another thought. The similarities with the situation he still found himself in in 2026 weren't lost on him; he was still at odds with his superiors and still closer to his European counterparts than his own. In fact, Joe's relations with his masters in Washington were now so bad that he was seriously concerned about his future. And it wasn't only his pension that bothered him; the messages coming out of the SIE headquarters about the new men at the top clearly suggested that they had a habit of solving their problems more finally than the US Constitution might allow. Not, as it turned out, that the new SIE brass in general showed much interest in living within the confines of what they tended to see as a rather antiquated and anachronistic document.

There was not a lot that Joe could do to improve his situation. His last reliable contact in Washington was the aging and isolated Euan Fforde, and Fforde's own position seemed to be becoming more and more precarious every day. But that too had always been the case. Fforde had passed his retirement date and was only holding on by sheer force of personality.

More memories from 2004 surfaced. After a supposedly clandestine visit to British Intelligence, which Joe chose to believe hadn't happened, Fforde had stopped off in Holland and called his Head of Station to a meeting in the airport transit area. After the death of a CIA agent in Amsterdam the Dutch authorities weren't keen to allow Fforde into the country but Joe had just about enough credit left for the get-together to be allowed.

If we had that conversation again today, twenty-two years on, thought Joe, it would be word for word.

'You're isolated, Joe, you and me both, in fact. There's really not a lot more I can do to protect you.'

'It's that bad?'

'It's that bad.'

It wasn't a message that Joe particularly wanted to hear in 2004 and it wasn't one that he would have wanted to hear in 2026 either, except that now what he wanted from Fforde had changed. In the earlier time he'd decided to meet with Fforde in the hope of some practical support. That would be nice now but all he wanted at the present time was the freedom to retire and take his well-earned pension.

As he pondered the events of twenty-two years ago something still niggled at him about his recent sighting of Senator McGoldberg in Delft. Joe decided to do some careful checking. He wasn't in Ross's or Alanda's league when it came to invading people's computer systems but he had little difficulty in prying into the senator's electronic mailbox. What he found was appalling to one of Joe's basic loyalty and patriotism.

'Looks like Melvin Fitzallan's making a lot of the running here, and McGoldberg's his leg-man, dirty dealer and wannabe chief of staff. What a charming lot. Pity they don't do something about improving the economy and getting people back to work. Half the population are so taken up with the struggles of just staying alive they simply aren't noticing what the SIE are up to. When they wake up to it it'll be too late.'

It was a long speech; Joe was another one not given to long speeches. It spoke eloquently for his anxieties. But anxious or not, the one bright spot on his horizon was another meeting with the delectable Alanda and Rick Blackford, this time on more relevant things than people smuggling, important as that was.

DISUNITED STATES

As Joe's musings moved back and forward between events in 2004 and the present he recalled John's description of what had happened back then with something like cold terror. It was still vivid in his memory and it replayed now as clearly as the actual events.

Joe had been pleased to find that John had brought Ross Metcalfe with him. The meeting hadn't challenged Joe's loyalties too much and hadn't lasted that long. Joe hadn't joined John and Ross for lunch but they had promised to return after their canal-side meal.

He could almost hear John's voice telling him what had happened and the distress that it had caused Ross. But John was a thoughtful and caring man and Joe knew that he would deal with Ross's anguish sensitively.

'What the blazes was that?'

John knew what it was. Ross, sitting with her back partially towards the canal and away from the central area of the city, was startled into the exclamation by the dull thudding sound that broke the silence of their shared coffee.

'Sounded like an explosion,' said John scanning the skyline in the direction of the sound for any signs. But the buildings were too high and the separation between them too small for anything other than an immediate view to be possible. John waited. The air was filled with the clamour of emergency vehicles within a few brief minutes. As the sound intensity increased John saw what he was looking for: a slow, lazy trail of brown smoke drifted up over the rooftops opposite. He didn't mention that the smoke trail was very much in the direction of Joe's up-market office furniture premises.

'Maybe we should go,' he said to Ross.

As they left, John let the assumption stand that they were heading back to their hotel. Their route took them close to Joe's office, where a check could readily be made. As they strolled over the bridges and then turned along the Singel, the commotion soon focused Ross's attention on the area of the CIA office. She was far too bright for her companion's thoughts not to have also occurred to her.

'John!'

'Yes, I know.'

Ross had seen the police barriers and the stacked emergency vehicles. The gaping hole where the office furniture showroom had been was painfully obvious.

'You can't go down there.'

The policewoman had hurriedly translated her sanction when John responded in English.

'What happened?'

'Looks like a bomb, somewhere in the middle of the building. Most of the blast came out of the front.' The dishevelled cars and smashed windows on the other side of the canal seemed to confirm her statement.

'Anybody –' Ross started to ask.

'Two bodies, so far.'

'John.' Ross clung to John in sudden shock.

'I know, Ross. I know.'

It had quickly dawned on John, and now on Ross, that they could have been victims rather than bystanders. But since so few people knew that they were coming John had given no credence to the likelihood that they were the targets. It had to have been Joe Longton. Whether Joe was one of the dead was something that they had yet to find out.

'We could have been in there.' Ross shuddered. As she rapidly analysed the possible scenarios her thoughts were more concentrated on what might have happened rather than on what had happened.

'It's okay, Ross. We escaped. That's all there is. We escaped.'

'John, how can you be so...? Yes, we escaped. We were lucky. Who didn't, I wonder?'

'Let's get away from here. There's nothing we can do.'

'Shouldn't we tell the police we were there?'

'Not now. Better to let them deal with the mess first. Get a better idea of what happened. We'll talk to them later.' The last thing John wanted was to be held in the police station for the rest of the day while the local constabulary put a story together. Everybody who had visited the building that day was bound to be suspect.

'Okay,' said Ross, something of the shock beginning to catch up with her as she followed John towards their hotel.

It wasn't far. The people at the hotel were in a ferment. Such incidents were not common in Amsterdam.

People handle shock in different ways and John was concerned by Ross's silence. She needs to talk it out, he thought. That's what *he* did; that's what he wanted her to do. But after her first mechanical reaction when she was grasping what had happened, she had lapsed into a quietness that John found worrying.

'Ross,' he said gently, 'it's okay to cry or scream and shout if you want to. If you want to let it go, do what's best for you.'

'I can't,' she said simply.

But she did eventually. John turned the television on and as the pictures flooded the screen on the twenty-four hour news channel he felt his own tension draining away. Ross watched it as if it were a film, something totally outside herself, until the policewoman who had turned them back appeared briefly before her. The reality that this presented released her pent-up angst.

The names of the dead were not announced on the television but John was too concerned with coping with Ross's suffering to have noticed.

'Oh, John,' she sobbed, 'it could have been you. You could have been killed. If I hadn't come you wouldn't have gone to lunch. You would have sat there and –'

John took her into his arms. As he felt her against him,

the sticky wetness of her tears staining the shoulder of his shirt, he realised that he really didn't know Ross at all. Somewhere in the relationship her feelings had become committed to him and he hadn't even registered the fact. Her distress at the prospect of his death was the first time that such a depth of feeling had impinged on him.

He ran his fingers gently through her hair. It was something that had calmed his sister when they were children. Whatever half-buried instinct made him do it now, the effect was the same. Slowly, as he moved his hand in and out of her silky hair, her sobs subsided, the wracking shudders that went with them faded and she began to shift her position to one of more comfort for both of them.

He hadn't hugged her like this before. She had made love on the ferry with all the vigour and urgency of a whore against a lamppost; she had also slept beside him having no desire to do more than sleep. As she settled herself more companionable against him on the couch in his hotel room, John wondered almost anxiously what it was to be this night. He was desperate not to get it wrong. He wanted the closeness that events had forced on them; he wanted the depth of feelings that she had shown to be real and reliable. As he waited for her to compose herself and show a lead, he knew that he was as hooked on her as she was on him.

'John?' It was a quiet whisper of a question. 'John, I'm sorry. I'm being silly. I have to get used to such things. The Colonel keeps telling me it's a nasty business we're in. Somehow I haven't been able to believe him until now.'

The rest of the evening was very special. It was only the next day when the chaos of the bedroom and the scattered remains of a meal eaten in joy and abandon confronted them that they acknowledged the depths of passion that had overtaken them.

This was a John that Ross had never experienced before. The barriers that she had erected around herself to protect her from the roughness that John sometimes displayed were still there but not needed in the present euphoric situation. But John was still the same John.

'John.' Ross's sleepy voice barely made it through to John's comatose brain.

'Umm?'

'Why is it always me having to break it up?'

'Don't then.'

'It's nine o'clock. Don't we have things to do?'

'Oh, God! Why does it always have to be nine o'clock?'

John leapt out of bed and into the shower. Ross scurried in after him and another new experience grew. As they soaped each other down all the desires of the small hours re-emerged. It was the ferry all over again. The grinding bodies pinked and puckered in the heat of the pouring water and the surging vigour of their lovemaking. Bedraggled, the bathroom awash, they escaped to dress and start a new day in a state of high intoxication. Even long hours on the telephone and at the police headquarters didn't abate the intensity of their excitement.

* * *

Joe had deeply regretted the death of his furniture store manager and the young female customer caught up in the horror of the bomb blast. And now in the long re-furbished office equipment showroom, as he went down to meet Alanda Ngozie, the events of 2004 remained as real to him as they were on the day.

Joe had been searching for files in the bomb-proof basement at the time of the blast. He had escaped with only temporary damage to his eardrums, after a two-hour wait in the plaster dust-filled darkness. His escape was something that his wife cherished rather more than he did. Death was a hazard of his job.

Of course Joe had no way of knowing that in another

part of Amsterdam on that day there was another person who, ignorant of his failure, was celebrating Joe Longton's death.

'That's the fee-paying stuff!'

Pensky was enjoying a leisurely ride on an Amsterdam Canal Bus, spending a tiny fraction of the dollars that had poured into his Swiss bank account from the CIA. He liked the water; it reminded him of a childhood long gone and innocent of the carnage that he had created in his adult life.

He was fastidious as killers go. The impersonal nature of bombs offended his sensibilities. He felt no achievement in blowing his targets to pieces any more than he felt regret. He liked to see the consequences of his actions directly. And he liked to exercise his skills. A long-range rifle shot gave him most satisfaction, but he had been up against another professional here; the windows of Joe Longton's offices at the back of the building had been overlooked by a brick wall at 3 yards distance; there was no way that he could have got a shot at any of them.

'Now let's work off the favours.'

Stalinsky was still lost in the Moscow criminal justice system but the messages that Pensky was getting from certain high-military quarters told him that the favour was still required, and urgently.

'The colonel general must still be a powerful figure,' he said to himself, 'if they want his funeral this badly.' But it wasn't a job he relished; he had rather liked Yuri Kirovsky.

34

2026

Alanda Ngozie's latest trip to Amsterdam by train and ferry had once again given her time to think as well as work. She wasn't really sure why Ross had wanted her to meet up with Joe Longton again, although the intended presence of Rick Blackford at the meeting gave her a surge of excitement that settled into quiet satisfaction. And even as she caught up with the unfolding events in both the US and Europe via her laptop, she couldn't relate anything that she was reading or hearing to any need for her to make such a trip. As always, Alanda couldn't understand what the significance of Joe Longton was in Ross and John's thinking.

'I know they go back a long way, but…'

What Alanda didn't know was that it was Joe's still-existing links to the SIE that was his importance. Joe had a private line to Euan Fforde through SIE channels that Ross had penetrated but which she didn't dare exploit for fear of compromising Fforde and Joe.

'Still, there's Rick,' Alanda said to herself, smiling. She was undoubtedly attracted to Rick Blackford; that much Ross had readily discerned from their conversations on the way to the gym and back. Ross had also discerned in herself a latent feeling of concern that she recognised in the things that the Colonel had said to her in the early days of her relationship with John. Knowing the nature of Rick's work from her dealings with John – and John had been much more in control of his life than Rick – Ross slowly came to a decision. She would counsel Alanda on what Rick was involved in but she would not seek to influence the choices she wanted to make. She was not going to be as protective as the Colonel had been of her.

'He was only trying to prevent me from getting hurt again,' she told herself, 'but I did get hurt again.'

The brutal end to the involvement with Yuri Kirovsky had scarred Ross. She well knew that her reaction to John's killing of the assassin had closed off her feelings for him for so long that he had moved on. His shock had passed away so much more quickly than hers. They now both knew that in their innermost souls they hadn't wanted that but with distance and other pressures they had never been able to re-join their feelings. Ross didn't want that to happen with Alanda. Rick was trained in the arts of his trade; Ross doubted that he was a killer because of his youth. Whether he could be one, she decided, was something that in the end Alanda would have to deal with herself.

I can't stop her getting hurt if that's the way things turn out. She's not me; she's her own person, she mused, and contrived an opportunity for Alanda to meet up with Rick again, resolving not to interfere. At the same time it kept Joe Longton in the loop of their most secret communications.

* * *

As Joe Longton remembered it, the trauma of the bombing of his offices soon passed. The original Hungarian-based story about an ex-KGB hit-man freelancing in Western Europe resurfaced and everybody was happy to believe it, especially as Kirovsky was subsequently killed and Pensky was exposed. Much of what was also subsequently learnt about Pensky came from a distraught Amsterdam prostitute with whom it seemed the Russian had struck up an unlikely relationship.

* * *

Since the SIE cover business was within the prescribed taxi ban distance from Amsterdam Central Station, Alanda had no choice but to walk. She had plenty of time and being a young woman with normal appetites she set off up the Damrak and browsed her way through the fashion and luxury goods shops that plied their trade along her route. With Aberdeen as her more regular shopping arena, if you discounted the fact that most of what she bought was via the Internet, Alanda was delighted and excited by the range of clothing, shoes and the like that were for sale. With sustainable development now the norm and trade barriers largely eliminated, much of what she was admiring was imported from all the corners of the world. Ethnic had lost its rather patronising connotations and much of what was so described was now high-class and expensive, notwithstanding its origins in parts of the world never associated with haute couture in the past.

'You like that?'

The soft, coffee-coloured boots that Alanda was looking at with impossibly high heels had been made in Nigeria. It was a surprise since she hadn't yet taken on board that her homeland was so prominent in such manufactures. It was also a surprise that the tall, casually dressed man who was now addressing her displayed such a familiarity as to suggest some foreknowledge of her.

'Hardly suitable for this time of year,' she said coldly.

The man looked her up and down, his dead eyes peering from a dead face, then finally resting on her white, patent shoes. It was an elegant comment on her response to his question.

Alanda made to move on. The man stepped aside but

fell in beside her. In the Damrak she didn't feel threatened but she was soon going to have cut through the side-streets to access Joe Longton's office furniture showroom.

'We're going the same way Miss Ngozie,' the man said.

Alanda stopped dead in her tracks, her exquisite features puckered into a frown of anger and concern. 'Who the hell are you?' she demanded, her tone sounding rather fiercer than the man had been expecting.

Having done his homework via Euan Fforde, Mr Jordan was well acquainted with Alanda Ngozie on paper and by reputation. Although he would never have let his features show it, his sight of her well-proportioned figure and stunningly beautiful face raised a surge of excitement in his rather austere mind and body. He knew that he wouldn't rate a second look from someone like Alanda but nonetheless was ready to admit that the actuality of the woman was infinitely better than the description and the secretly taken photographs that he had seen. That Rick had got himself a rare catch Jordan was more than ready to admit.

'Alanda!'

The quick kiss that she gave him took Rick by surprise. He wasn't aware that their relationship had advanced that far despite at least two spirited episodes in bed. It was only later that Alanda admitted that the kiss was almost as much for Jordan as it was for him.

Wandering around the office furniture showroom, introductions were made and Alanda began to pick up some of the vibrations surrounding Mr Jordan. Being escorted by the Head of SIE Internal Security wasn't something that she would have sought and it was very clear that neither Rick nor Joe Longton were best pleased by the arrival of this gloomy and undemonstrative man. Apart from anything else, Alanda supposed that it would completely block off any sort of conversation around the developing resistance to the increasing stranglehold of the Neoconservatives and religious right on American society, and the activities of Intercontinental Veterans Anonymous. But she was wrong.

'Euan Fforde asked me to give you this.' Jordan handed Joe a flash-drive. It wasn't the most up-to-date means of transferring information but it was still amongst the most secure. 'You should only open it using a laptop not physically connected to any Internet or telephone connection and which is wireless disabled.'

'We'll use mine,' said Alanda quickly. 'It's protected and I can disable it.'

Joe and Mr Jordan looked on in admiration as Alanda slickly readied her laptop and worked her way through the security procedures. As the computer fired up a talking head appeared set against a background that clearly was not a government office.

'Euan Fforde!' The only photos that Alanda had seen of Fforde were from 2004. He had aged considerably in the past twenty-two years.

Fforde's brief opening explanation was followed by a detailed plan of action which Jordan apparently had stored in his head as he took no interest in the details of the presentation.

'We are aware that the emerging SIE game plan and the inability of the US President to take any firm action are causing serious concern in the corridors of European power. We are also aware that the Federation Government recognises that its processes are too cumbersome for any prompt and effective action to be taken in the intelligence and counter-intelligence fields. John Harcourt we know has been asked to freelance and finesse this area of activity to avoid any provocations being offered when the usual suspects are involved. We are equally aware that Intercontinental Veterans Anonymous has opened a line of communication with Ross Metcalfe based on the frozen relationship with the organisation of Yuri Kirovsky.

'We, in case you are wondering, are a select group from the SIE and US commerce and social areas committed to resisting the activities of the religious right and the Neoconservatives who are set upon destroying American life as we would want to know it.

'The situation in the US has now reached a point where direct action to stem the tide of what is essentially a fascist takeover is required and it will be taken.'

As the screen of Alanda's laptop turned from Euan Fforde's talking head to a series of diagrams and script documents Mr Jordan halted the presentation.

'The rest is for Rick and myself. Neither of you have any part in the action plan.'

It was coldly said. Joe, versed in the need-to-know concepts of his trade, shrugged and headed for his office shepherding Alanda in front of him. Less versed, Alanda's first reaction was to linger but when Joe urged her she followed him glowering at the slight that she thought that she had been offered.

Later at their hotel as Rick climbed into bed beside her, he sensed that Alanda was wound up and ready to go. In the time that she had spent with Joe while the rest of the presentation was being digested, her anger had turned to longing and a desire for sex with Rick that was undimmed by dinner, a walk around the red-light district of Amsterdam and several glasses of cold, Dutch beer. She pulled Rick to her, aware that his excitement was also rising, and began kissing him hungrily. It was much later when they lapsed into an exhausted sleep.

At no time that evening or the next day did Alanda ask, nor Rick offer, any clue to what the direct action proposed by Euan Fforde was. And back in Scotland at no time did Ross, or John when he arrived, enquire either. That Jordan was Fforde's man came as a surprise, that he was actively involved in the countermeasures against the deteriorating situation was welcomed but caution with respect to the SIE Head of Internal Security seemed to be the best policy.

35

2026

The Buchan farmhouse had always been the ideal setting for the meetings that no one was supposed to know about. Ross, at the prompting of John and him by proxy of the European intelligence community, had arranged one such meeting in late June 2026. John travelled up by the overnight train to give himself a full day with Ross before the visitor arrived. It had been a clear, bright day and the daylight was still lingering at eleven o'clock in the evening. Sat out in the enclosed terrace of the farmhouse with wine and single malt whisky on tap, the atmosphere was relaxed and mildly expectant as the visitor was shown out to where Ross and John were sitting. Myra, who delivered the guest, looked from Ross to John in an arch manner that showed both approval and encouragement. Ross being happy was one of her staff's greatest ambitions. At that moment in time she was happy.

'Alastair Browneton. Hi, this is John Harcourt. John used to work for a leading financial services house. He's retired now.'

Mr Browneton was clearly aware of the nature of the named company's business and that John's retirement was largely in suspension.

Ross introduced herself although it was hardly necessary. Again Browneton clearly knew about Ross's particular skills. The easy way that he encompassed his knowledge in his conversation defined him to both Ross and John as a very personable man, despite the rather harsher descriptions of him that they had received.

'The late vice president,' John said, 'I'm sorry.'

Browneton acknowledged John's sympathy. In such company there was no need for any charades. He was sure that they knew that his cousin was dead and like him were concerned only with the future actions of the US establishment.

'Dreadful way to go,' said Ross quietly. The death wasn't something that touched her personally but she was sensitive to Browneton's anger both at the killing and the situation that had brought it about.

'Okay, well, best move on. We've got to get back at these goddamn SIE bastards.'

'Yes.' John was happy to do so. 'We've got some thoughts on that. But... care to share with us where you think they're headed?'

'They're headed for a right-wing takeover. Just that.' Browneton was emphatic.

John grunted. Ross noted it as a 'you talk, we'll listen' grunt.

'Some years ago a bunch of academics got together to see what could be done to revitalise US moral fibre. It had been degrading for years in their eyes. My papers had been warning about it for years too. I guess you could say we gave the America Resurgent movement its first platform.' It was Alastair Browneton's role in giving birth to the movement that made him so bitter now that it had been hijacked.

'After the academics, a few public servants crept in and a few of the alumni went into government; either way, steadily, the movement took on a more right-wing, isolationist and then fascist tone. And submerged in all of this were the right-wing religious fanatics and their baleful view of the world. This was too much for some of the earlier and more idealistic members. They left. The rump rapidly coalesced around the likes of Melvin Fitzallan and some of his less-public cronies.'

Melvin Fitzallan, as John and Ross knew, was an archetypal, successful American. He had started life as a small-town university professor who had made good in the management consultancy business and then as an advisor to both Democrat and Republican Presidents. The pay-off for services rendered was his current post. Fitzallan had been careful to ensure that those who had any idea what the services that he had rendered were had been tainted in some way, or were seriously beholden to him.

'So how d'you reckon the SIE are going to move this thing forward?' asked John as Browneton relapsed into a rather moody silence.

'Fill my cousin's slot with one of their men; that's the first thing.'

'Uhlemann?'

'Yeah, they've got him in, legit; nothing the president could do about it. He's totally hamstrung in Congress.'

'Okay, the president's already powerless,' said John, 'but he's a barrier, and you're years away from an election, and with your system the results of such elections can be a bit of a lottery anyway. Don't you reckon they'll try and take him out as well?'

Browneton nodded. 'Has to be in the game plan, otherwise how do they exercise the ultimate power?'

'Any evidence?' asked Ross.

Like John she was sufficiently surprised by the emphatic nature of Browneton's statement to also give up her listen-only stance.

'Nothing you could hang your hat on.'

'Enough to take countermeasures?' asked John. It had already occurred to him that some judicious feedback to

Intercontinental Veterans Anonymous might promote a campaign to stiffen the president's will and increase his support. It was a long shot but one he planned to talk to Ross about at a suitable moment. He glanced at her, staring at the American in bemused interest, and wondered what was going through her mind.

Two thoughts were going through Ross's mind. One was simple: what could this one man do to resist the move to the right in America? She knew the power of the US media, but she also knew that Browneton was swimming against the stream. Most of the American press and TV had, to varying degrees, been seduced by the right-wing movement, and the jingoistic nonsense whipped up against Europe. How could he turn the tide? The scale of activity necessary was colossal. Her second thought was equally simple but was being firmly suppressed. How could she get John alone with her? Sitting with him so close gave her an aching need that had resonance with her feelings in the past. It was the ambience of the warm summer evening she supposed.

John's attention was prised away from Ross by Alastair Browneton's reply to his question.

'The countermeasures have started. We've set up a nationwide campaign. The SIE bad guys have to be exposed. We're pulling them into the glare of publicity at every opportunity: a hundred and one subtle – and not so subtle – ways to point the finger at a secret government official. Get the public used to hearing about the faceless ones then make the faces appear.'

'A little risky,' remarked John.

Browneton shrugged. Of course it was, but the risk was worth taking in his view.

'We might be able to help here,' John continued. 'We've still got some contacts in the US from former times, you might say. Perhaps Ross and I could start a few hares of our own once we've heard what you're planning.'

John wasn't entirely clear whether Browneton would have known about the Veterans. He thought possibly not. The man was a patriot; he might not favour help from such a source.

Later, when they were in Ross's computer room, a surge of memories overtook them both. The jungle of kit, screens with lazy drifting patterns, printers that rattled into life apparently without instruction, and the occasional faint whir of disc drives were familiar to Ross. To John it was still a little awe-inspiring; he had always seen it as naked power and now, years later and several generations more sophisticated, that was still how it struck him.

Ross was looking at him. The expression on her face was unfathomable to him.

'What?'

'It's a long time since we were in here together,' Ross said.

The grin that spread across her face turned the clock back twenty-two years. Suddenly, he realised that she was thinking what she had been thinking in 2004.

Naked body not naked power was what had suggested itself to Ross then and it was clear that that was what was prompting her lascivious grin now. As John had been registering the technology then, Ross had been stepping out of her almost non-existent skirt and underwear, her hands searching for John's trouser belt. But this time Ross didn't back herself against the only bit of spare wall in the room, nor did she pull John onto her and urge him with gyrations of her body.

'Don't worry we'll do the computer tricks in a moment.'

She led the way to her bedroom in the farmhouse. It wasn't as quick and as intense as it had been but it was far more charged than their previous return to lovemaking.

John's amazement at her swift changes of mood was renewed. It was nothing like it had been on the ferry or the computer room before; she wasn't like an overcharged alley cat any more, and in a moment he knew she would be the disembodied computer brain working wizardry way beyond his comprehension.

Back in the sterile world of Ross's computer banks she was more smug than he had ever known her. And somewhere in his nether regions things were still going on that he hadn't felt for many years.

'The Veterans have been dumping stuff into our mailbox again, sharing their plans. I guess they're beginning to trust us. They're winding up their activities.'

John read over Ross's shoulder. The Veterans were deploying their networks to undermine the SIE's efforts to psyche up the American people against Europe. It was exactly the sort of thing that John himself had had in mind.

'What a man that Kirovsky was,' Ross said, thinking rather sadly that even the Colonel might have been impressed with the way that the old Russian's long-laid plans were coming to fruition.

'This is incredible,' John said as he began to digest what the Veterans were up to. 'They're doing precisely what I would have asked them to do in this situation.'

'John, you're becoming a real fan of these people. They've got thirty networks out there. It's the first time they've ever actually confirmed the number. That means that after twenty-two years all of Kirovsky's networks are still intact. That's what's amazing. Incredible!'

They both knew that they were putting aside some issues of morality and patriotism but the bigger threat had to be their focus.

'They got a nationwide campaign running in only a few days. None of our foreign correspondent stuff; this is real grassroots protests about the way that Congress is obstructing the president. Sweat and blood, but it's getting results.'

'Masons and trades unions,' Ross continued with a laugh.

'Remember they've been working those particular groups for years and they've run campaigns before. I trawled the US Press Association records. Intercontinental Veterans Anonymous have won a few votes in Congress I can tell you. They even got the pensions of retired CIA/SIE agents increased a couple of years back.'

'What?'

'Yep, I didn't tell you that before. I thought you might rupture yourself laughing. Isn't it delicious? The heirs to a bunch of old Soviet double agents and they jack up their own pensions. They must own half the banks in Switzerland between them; they've creamed off so much from both sides.'

'Wonderful,' said John. He couldn't stop the chuckle. Ross paused from her labours to share his giggles. But of course it was serious.

John watched as Ross's busy fingers played more concertos on the keyboard and a seemingly endless succession of screens flashed up reporting the activities of Intercontinental Veterans Anonymous across the whole of the US. The media in small towns seemed to be the starting point. An endless variety of incidents and local-issue problems were highlighted, illustrating the effects of the absence of federal legislation for nearly two years. Hardship stories from low-paid federal employees were the most effective. Careful seeding of the inter-state and national media was beginning and John and Ross were able to see how the manipulation and strategically placed letters from the 'public' were leading the big TV networks to perceive conspiracies and to extrapolate non-existent trends. And it had all happened in a couple of weeks.

'Give it a month and the roll will be irresistible,' said Ross.

'Astonishing, a head of steam is building that Fitzallan and the SIE must know is synthetic but they can't do anything about.'

'Oh yes they can.'

'How so?'

'Look,' Ross rapidly scrolled back to a press digest from Minnesota. 'Small town newspaper office firebombed. That would be the SIE or their local chums for sure.'

'So, is there anything left for us to do?'

'Bit of encouragement and appreciation to the Veterans I guess,' said Ross.

* * *

The body of the adjutant of the Lost Springs Airbase showed up in an alley in a small town, 200 miles from the base. The pristine state of her expensive leatherwear signalled that she had been dumped there, a point so obvious that the local police chief started looking for signs of the transportation before he even bothered to start identification. Underneath the studded dog collar, a tell-tale needle mark immediately put the cause of death as a lethal injection. There were other needle marks in her arms.

'A hooker?'

'Don't reckon so.' The detective had seen many hookers, most of them dead, and was sure that her chief was wrong.

'That's expensive leatherwear. And that was one fit lady. Who ever saw a hooker with muscle tone like that? Oh, shit! You think that's her?'

'It's that Air Force captain missing from the satellite station at Lost Springs. Shit indeed,' responded the police chief.

The young officer's face was on the top of the heap of missing persons' dossiers, the detective's usual first port of call. A dead female service officer hardly dressed for a mess dinner was all that the civil police needed. Wearily, he made his telephone calls and cooked up his story for the media. The military police arrived with the base commander in tow and demanded the body. The civilian resistance to the military intervention was only nominal. The police chief was more than happy to let somebody else handle the problem and himself sink back into the more relaxed pace of life in his town. If he'd wanted action he would hardly have stood for election in such a backwater.

The base commander of course knew exactly when his adjutant and sex partner had disappeared. That she was in the leather gear meant that she had at least been in his quarters long enough to get changed and was planning a little relaxation before the mess reception. That her body was unblemished but full of a cocktail of unusual and highly sophisticated drugs said that she had been interrogated by a specialist of some knowledge and skill. Notwithstanding the requirements of the federal/state relations and etiquette, the moment that the post-mortem revealed the horrors of the captain's last hours, the SIE commandeered the body, the evidence and the conduct of the investigation. The SIE soon revealed that the drugs had origins in Eastern Europe where they had been in use for over sixty years.

'The KGB, or at least their successors,' remarked Euan Fforde when the matter was reported to him. 'No violence, only needle marks, the body deposited with some finesse; no clues to culprits; typical of the old KGB style.'

The younger whizz-kids of the SIE believed him; the KGB was a fairy-tale to them. But they did at least question how such an historic approach to dealing death had suddenly emerged in their midst decades after the demise of the KGB. Fforde thought he knew the answer but nonetheless allowed his minions to waste their energies trying to find their own answer to the question.

'No violence,' was also the base commander's comment, although the poor colonel's feelings were first of relief and then of horror when something of the nature of the captain's death was explained to him.

There was, however, violence in his own death, which

followed shortly after. His failure to return from a trip into the local town sparked a routine alert. The discovery of his battered body in the back of an empty rail wagon sparked another spate of activity by the military police. The failure of the SIE to take even a token interest in the second death attracted the attention of a couple of the members of the local Intercontinental Veterans Anonymous.

The appointment of a new base commander the day after the demise of the old one provoked even more interest. When the news was reported to the local Veterans' network leader he was pleased. The information yielded by the drugged captain had already told him why such a prompt appointment was likely to occur.

'Once again,' he said to himself, 'the SIE have killed off their own.'

36

2026

'Tuesday 14th July, 2026'

The date flicked up on the wall-mounted video screen as the clock clicked silently to midnight. Melvin Fitzallan mouthed the new date as he tried to keep his mind on the presentation that was going on in front of him. It was a presentation to him but the earnest young man enthusing a few feet away from him had no skills in interpreting body language. Melvin Fitzallan was plainly bored.

'Okay, let's call it a day at that.'

Ten minutes later and the presentation at an end, Senator McGoldberg intervened. He had been chairing the meeting and knew well enough that even the SIE professionals present couldn't absorb much more of the minutiae being hurled at them. A 'big picture' man like Fitzallan had no chance.

'Hell, Chap, I can't get my head around all this crap. The old brain ain't digital like these shits. Can't you get someone to give it to me in a couple of one-liners?'

The senator laughed. Fitzallan was always making out that he was not up to the briefings that he was given but usually tossed in a comment or two later that proved that he had grasped every relevant detail.

'Okay,' said McGoldberg, 'three levels of activity. One, we crank up the action with Europe.'

'More bread and circuses,' muttered Fitzallan.

McGoldberg ignored the ambassador's comment. 'Two, we take over the Administration, and three, we eliminate the opposition as fast as we can.'

'Can't see why that pompous little creep couldn't have said just that. Three hours of clap-trap and bullshit. Why should I care which small town newspapers we need to firebomb? All I want is this trend in support for the president stopped.'

It was barely three weeks since the meeting between Alastair Browneton and Ross and John. The campaign that they had agreed on had been started. The president had reacted. And the SIE were reacting too.

'And, I want to know what the hell's going on in the gossip and scandal columns. Every story rocketing around the country is about some SIE guy with his hand in the till, or his cock up some other bloke's wife. There's too much of it to be coincidence.'

'Mel, we're working on it.'

'Maybe you are, Chap, but every time it happens it puts the whole damn local SIE unit out of action. They always seem to manage to get something in about how many agents the guy has under his control or what his secret budget is. Where the hell is all of this shit coming from?' Fitzallan wasn't as angry as he made out to be; it was just his way of bullying the action that he wanted into happening.

* * *

The reception at the SIE headquarters, somewhere in Kentucky, as the media were want to say, was intended for SIE senior staff and a few privileged outsiders like Melvin Fitzallan, Chap McGoldberg and the new vice-president. The presence of Euan Fforde was an embarrassment but his seniority meant that he couldn't be entirely ignored.

'Euan, sorry you weren't able to make it to the presentation last night.' McGoldberg wasn't of course; the whole thing had been arranged with the specific purpose of Euan Fforde not being present. Not that his presence was essential, one of his own earnest young men having purloined a copy of the presentation before it was even made.

'Mr Uhlemann, good to see you, sir.'

McGoldberg's second greeting was much more cordial. Both the senator and Fitzallan were delighted by the easy way in which the new vice president had taken over the ropes and how quickly he had started hassling the beleaguered president, considering he really didn't have any proper role in the Administration.

Melvin Fitzallan was convinced that the SIE second-in-command was actively opposing their plans and he was determined to have an end to the interference. Fforde, having made the token appearance that was expected of him, and sensing the underlying hostility, quickly removed himself from the gathering.

Fitzallan's well-laid plans were about to come to fruition. Except that Euan Fforde wasn't minded to get himself killed, and so was, as Fitzallan was welcoming Rick Uhlemann, being flown off the roof in his own helicopter. The explosion of his car when his chauffeur went to move it later was, in the way of these things, left unexplained.

Circulation amongst the fifty or sixty guests at the reception was easy enough and the ambassador found little trouble in first getting alongside and then extricating a tall, fresh-faced man with gingery hair and a profusion of freckles. The greetings were cautious but mutual respect was instantly apparent as they began to talk. This was Wilbur Egbert, the Head of the SIE, and a man who until a few days previous was totally unknown to the American public.

'Melvin, I think we know how *The Washington Echo* got its information.'

'Really? Great!'

The Washington Echo was Alastair Browneton's flagship newspaper. In an uncharacteristic dip into the dirt that seemed to surround almost all public and many private figures in American society, the *Echo* had published a centre spread of photographs of Wilbur Egbert in a position of naked subservience to a young woman of substantial charms that brutally caricatured the SIE man's domination of all around him.

'They got to the girl,' said Egbert. 'It seems it was another aged ex-KGB double we didn't know about still active. He worked in the department of trade. He worked with your man Spencer in the past and he was a crony of Joe Longton. It was real goddamn spy-thriller stuff. Screwed the girl, set her up with me, fiddled the vetting so we wouldn't suspect her and got into some classy camera work.'

'So, where's the bastard now?'

'Oh, he's disappeared. Went to an Intercontinental Veterans' rally and just disappeared. We took the whole place apart. You heard the outcry... Nothing.'

'What the girl tell you?'

'Not a lot. She met two guys. Our ex-KGB friend and somebody she thought was either an aide to some government high-up or a journalist.'

'Well now,' said Fitzallan, 'suppose the high-up was linked to the old VP; suppose the journalist worked for Browneton?'

'It has to be something like that.'

It had been, but the girl was now beyond even a minimum of coherent thought, and in a soundproof room literally 30 yards below their feet. The amiable but ruthlessly efficient SIE specialist in these matters was coming to the conclusion that he had got all the information he was going to get.

She was naked and strapped to a solid, wooden-armed chair. Her head was wrapped in a towel. Her wrists, ankles and heart pattern were wired up to an electro-cardiogram. Both her forearms were equipped for drug injection.

Slumped forward and held from falling only by the leather straps, she was silent and still.

When they found the girl later she too had suffocated in a plastic bag from an up-market boutique that had been tied over her head. To the infinite benefit of numerous column centimetres, Wilbur Egbert attended the funeral.

In the ebb and flow of the reception Fitzallan and Egbert were joined by a sour-faced, squat, Afro-American with the physique of a wrestler and a suit that even Fitzallan couldn't have afforded. A man of serious private means, he was one of Egbert's most trusted henchmen, always known simply as George.

'Nice work with the Air Force colonel,' said Egbert.

'Yeah, great,' said Fitzallan. 'Now we got our own man in we're all ready. The missiles are fully operative they tell me.'

But the Afro-American had other things on his mind. 'We haven't worked out what happened to the adjutant. Wasn't at the Intercontinental Veterans Anonymous reception, ended up dead in high-class leather gear. And then there was Sergeant Ryan.'

'Who, for Christ's sake, is Sergeant Ryan, George?' asked Egbert sensing something of the ambassador's mystification and concern. The sour black face was looking even more sour.

'He's another Air Force guy, but we're not sure otherwise. He organised the Intercontinental Veterans Anonymous do. We found part of the missile code insertion procedure in his locker in a routine search. He wouldn't give an explanation.'

'What happened to him?' asked Melvin Fitzallan.

'Had an accident,' said George laconically.

'Hmm, the Intercontinental Veterans Anonymous is an impeccable organisation, noted for good works, for looking after its own and for the obscurity of its leaders. They keep cropping up, don't they?'

'They sure do, and they're perfect cover for a subversive opposition, Wilbur.'

'And when you think about it, for many other things, Melvin,' said the SIE chief.

'Like,' said George, 'undermining our efforts to promote a Wall Street crash.'

'What?' said Fitzallan, surprised.

'Little sideshow,' responded Egbert. 'Destabilise the money markets, bankrupt a few worthy citizens who we'll never convert to our cause, do a bit of damage to European markets, you know.'

'But the Intercontinental Veterans lot put money in as a counter. Not very much but well placed. It taught the market not to panic. They were getting very good advice and they made a few dollars into the bargain.'

George, who had started life as a bond dealer was impressed by the way that the counter had been played, especially when they'd achieved what they had wanted to and still walked away with millions of dollars. George also had suspicions about where the outside help was coming from.

'Couple of interesting things came out of Joe Longton's office logs. He must be getting help there too; took us days to break in. He met up with a couple of British agents, one of whom could very easily have been able to plan the market moves that the Intercontinental Veterans Anonymous made and the other is a known computer surveillance wizard.'

'So, what are you saying, George?' demanded Fitzallan who had no idea who Joe Longton was.

'Oh, the game's hotting up. The Europeans are taking us seriously. The quality of the opposition is high and in depth.' The dusky face turned grim but there was a hint of respect. He wasn't one of those who discounted the European cyber-war capability. There was ample evidence that they were now well ahead of the US; and unlike their US counterparts there was no shortage of funds.

'Nothing we can't handle,' said Egbert dismissively. 'We worked with the Brits in the past; not much they can teach us.'

George didn't think it appropriate to voice his disagreement to this statement; not only was the past a long time ago, but some of the key players from the past were still in the game, according to his information.

'A combination of old Russian doubles and the Brits would certainly be interesting though,' Egbert said after rather more thought than had gone into his previous remark.

Fitzallan wondered who the old Russian doubles might be and how they had got into the conversation. Egbert didn't enlighten him.

* * *

There was no doubt that much of George and Egbert's information was speculative. It was just after the death of Sergeant Ryan, another faceless casualty of the war that they were waging, when John and Ross indulged in another of their online conferences.

'Ross, any updates on the rioting in America?'

'Yep, it's widespread and heavily racially oriented. Looting seems to be a prime purpose; more than a little equalisation of wealth going on, you might say. The police and troops have refused to intervene in ten or so states. The president has declared martial law in most of the areas of the disturbances but Congress has refused to vote emergency aid. There's heaps more but that's the general picture.'

'It's like we said, Ross. It's gone too far for the religious right and their hangers-on to pull back now. Whoever gets control in the end won't be able to handle the ethnic minorities; they've nothing to deliver.'

'I know. It increasingly looks as if starting a war with Europe is supposed to solve the problem.'

'But how, Ross? How can a war solve the problem? You

can't fight a war from a destroyed social and cultural base. How will you keep discipline in your troops? Worse, what will you do with them when the fighting's over?'

'No idea. The whole thing's mad. It's a kind of chaos theory on such a grand scale that it's impossible to see how the madmen behind all of this can possibly win out.'

'Well, it'll still be here in the morning. What was the other thing you wanted to talk about?'

'There are two things, John, actually. I've got a new bit of kit to pick up from the airport but more to the point I've been doing a bit of research on old US missiles: your director's nightmare scenario.'

Ross's skills were legendary amongst the intelligence community, although many things attributed to her were overstated. Some weeks earlier, as a part of an exploratory search of the US Defense Department computers she had come across an old missile control system and some other command links that she didn't initially understand. She was intrigued; apart from the absurdly easy way in which she was able to penetrate even their supposedly most secure systems, the logic of what she was seeing took some figuring out. The hook-ups between the Pentagon and places like the air force computer centre were easily detected. It was only when attention was drawn to the Lost Springs complex and its non-existent satellite tracking station role that Ross began to grasp what the command links might be for. Introducing such a vulnerability in such a vital system seemed incomprehensible to her.

Her reading of mid to late twentieth century history told her that all but a controlled number of these missile systems should have been destroyed. But there was evidence that the US had been cheating on the Russians almost from the start of the treaty negotiations. The second thing that she had found was much more interesting. Certain of the protocols for the firing codes of the missiles had been modified. A two-out-of-three voting system had been introduced to initiate the firing.

'And,' she told John, 'an ultra-modern, high-speed programmed switch has been installed to allow targeting programmes to be installed more easily.'

'From the SIE headquarters, I don't doubt,' remarked John. 'To do what?'

'Programme or re-programme the flight computers from Washington.'

'The only time the rocket's computers are linked to any other system would be at the point of remote programming,' Ross continued, 'which doesn't make sense and which is why what I've found is so hard to credit.'

'And one hell of a weak point?'

'Absolutely. Has to be, John.'

John was not convinced. All his knowledge and experience of military command structures told him that such an unnecessarily complicated way of programming the missiles would have been unlikely.

It was a weak point that Ross planned to exploit. The data transmission would only have to be for a miniscule fraction of time. To hijack the transmission, which was what Ross had in mind, would require both a pre-programmed access but also a split second deletion and insertion sequence. At least that was how she explained it to John. As John well knew, it was a rather more complicated and sophisticated operation than that requiring some pretty detailed and highly classified information from the US Air Force. If it hadn't been Ross attempting it John would have said it was impossible.

'The point is,' said Ross, 'the individual missile control systems must have been modified as well and updated several generations. Because the missiles themselves are old they can't do too much about physical management of the trajectory but what they seem to have done is add the very latest guidance technology to ensure the best accuracy possible. And because the modern stuff is miniaturised compared with the original, the missiles now have much more sophisticated systems than they were ever designed for.'

'Okay, Ross, but they can't know whether this technology will work. There's no way they could be tested in secret.'

'True, but in reality they now have much greater control over the missiles. It may not matter about pinpoint accuracy so long as they fly and hit the target area.'

John didn't respond to this. From his puckered face on the screen in front of her, Ross could see that he was pondering some new thought.

'It's probably more important to know where these updated missiles are,' he said.

'Ah, well, I think we do. Lost Springs the base where this Sergeant Ryan worked.'

'Said to be a satellite tracking station as I recall, Ross.'

'With a colonel who was a missile expert, now deceased, and adjutant prepared to do a few unusual things for her commanding officer, now also deceased.'

It was when a scrap of procedure found in Sergeant Ryan's locker, which Ross had received via the Veterans, had been matched with the output of her defense department search that answers to the many questions in her mind began to form. It was also then that orders were placed in Japan for some state-of-the-art software and hardware. Ross was looking forward to working with such high-speed kit.

Her trip to the Aberdeen Airport customs shed to collect her parcel from Japan was something of an extravagance, but she wanted to get her hands on the new equipment as soon as possible rather than wait for it to be couriered to her.

37

2026

'So, who the shit is Yuri Kirovsky?'

General Shepilov, the head of the Joint US Chiefs of Staff was renowned for his foul language and impregnable integrity. In the world of high US politics he was almost alone in being seen as being beyond the greasy reach of the SIE and the backroom fixers of the likes of Melvin Fitzallan and his henchmen.

'*Was*, General, *was*. He was an ex-KGB general who died twenty-two years ago.'

'So what the shit are we interested in a long-dead commie secret policeman for?'

'You're not going to like this, General, but in the old Soviet days he set up and ran a network of KGB double agents, straight agents, CIA moles and general information grubbers. The network, or networks – there are thirty – outlived him and are now run under the cover of Intercontinental Veterans Anonymous. And they are now Egbert's public enemy number one.'

'What? Are you telling me this shit – dead shit, ex-shit, whatever – is on the side of the American people? And he's no longer a double-dealing commie Russian bastard? Been undermining our society for as long as anyone can remember, and now he's a good guy?' Shepilov was apoplectic.

Euan Fforde, via a complex of telephone links manufactured by Ross Metcalfe, was calling the general from his office, although the SIE listeners who detected the call assumed that it was from Vermont. By a careful routing and a synthetic message that initiated when the SIE monitor switched in, the conversation appeared to be between the irascible army man and his equally querulous sister. It was a protection system that Ross had perfected over a number of months and its elegance was a matter of pride to her. Subsequent debriefing caused immense amusement to the general and his sister when the conversation heard by the SIE was exposed.

'Yep, that's exactly what I'm telling you. He's a good guy now, albeit a dead one, since he bequeathed his networks to the Veterans and to the Brits. And they are using the networks to undermine the SIE and to expose their dirty tricks,'

'Hell, Euan, what am I supposed to do with this?'

'Shep, you don't have to do anything with it if you don't want to. You're a professional soldier. This is politics; it isn't your fight. Just watch. Or just follow your conscience. If you reckon the legacy of an aged Russian KGB colonel general is a better bet for saving America from itself than Egbert and his mob of right-wing fascist maniacs, then just let the Vets and the Brits get on with it. If you don't, we have a problem.'

Euan Fforde was suddenly depressed.

'What Kirovsky set up all those years ago is being used because we don't have many choices left; it's almost all there is. And if you want evidence that the Veterans are a power in the country, well... Well, you know they are, don't you?'

'Are you serious?'

'Yeah, I'm serious; never more so. All this started with Kirovsky approaching the Brits to come in from the cold. And hard as it is to believe, a peaceful retirement was all he wanted in exchange for his networks and a chance to use them for good in America and Europe when the right situation arose. After years of deceit and counter-deceit, violence and mayhem, the old guy had had enough; he wanted out of the foul world he inhabited and he wanted a bit of peace and dignity in his old age, however little many might say he deserved it.'

Fforde paused; Kirovsky was beginning to sound too saintly.

'Intercontinental Veterans Anonymous were the heirs to his spy networks, charged with reactivating them when the sort of situation that we are now in arose. Kirovsky's foresight was amazing; almost beyond believe. He anticipated the way relations between the US and Europe would go and implanted the trigger to bring the networks back into use when a breakdown of relations was imminent. And twenty-two years on, a breakdown is imminent in the opinion of the Vets and the networks are back in the intelligence business. How did he achieve this? He used all his credit with the Brits in his last years to get his networks accepted as bona fide and reliable. Now it's show time.'

'Bloody hell, Euan! The mad games you crazy sodding spies play!'

'Mad they may be, but they're deadly enough when they need to be.'

General Shepilov agreed with him. His own military intelligence, an organisation regarded with infinite contempt by the SIE, was telling him on an almost daily basis about the casualties in the hidden warfare. And as he hung up on both Euan Fforde and 'his sister', another casualty was being lined up on TV before his very eyes.

* * *

'Okay, Dirk, you tell me you work in the Department of the Interior, sorting out inter-state tax evasions.'

The late-night TV chat-show hosts were a law unto themselves and Shirley Addamms was amongst the most acerbic and the most persistent in her probing. She was also the most popular. The general liked her and watched her whenever he could. She stood no nonsense and took no prisoners. She wrecked reputations, she made fools of the most pretentious of the political classes and for an aspiring politician she was hard to avoid if you wanted to get all the right markings on your CV.

Shirley Addamms was also Alastair Browneton's star performer and as committed to resisting the SIE encroachments and the right-wing shift in the political consensus as her boss was. Not that General Shepilov knew this positively; his instincts simply aligned him with such thinking.

Dirk Westwood was a lawyer: the slick, Greek-god, good-looking type that chat-show hosts love and, Shirley Addamms in particular, ate regularly for supper.

'That's it Shirley. Always on the move. See the wife and kids weekends only, but have the greatest time when I do.'

'So, you were in Mississippi last week with the Justice Department; a nasty little bit of trucker fraud across the state line.'

'That was it, Shirley.'

Was it hell, she thought as she chose her words carefully.

'At least, Dirk, that was what your office told us.'

The fixed grin didn't waver.

'But, we followed you, Dirk. Had a little surveillance going to see exactly what you did do in Mississippi.'

The fixed grin erupted into a too-eager laugh. Dirk Westwood knew all about Ms Addamms and her ambushes. That's why he was there. Years as a criminal lawyer, and a few none-too-savoury clients had taught him a thing or two; his SIE bosses thought him fireproof against even the dreaded Addamms.

'Guess you found it rather boring, Shirley.'

'Guess we did... until the last evening.' There was a commercial break coming and she had to get the punch lines in fast now. 'Guess we did until the motel at Tupelo.

Led us a merry dance there you did, Dirk. What would you call the joint at the back of the motel; plenty of girls in and out of there weren't there? Brothel? Bordello? What would the wife and kids say about that then? At least most of the girls went in and came out didn't they? There was one – wasn't there, Dirk? – who went in and didn't come out, at least alive.'

'Come on now, Shirley. You never saw me go into any joint at the back of any motel, now did you? And what am I supposed to know about some dead hooker?'

The television screen wall behind Westwood stopped its soothing patterns and showed a rapid-fire sequence of film clips. First Westwood was seen dancing wrapped around a dark-haired woman. Then the dark-haired woman was seen beating a naked and bound blonde girl as Westwood watched. Two superimposed photographs of an attractive airline stewardess and a motionless figure in the boot of a car persisted on the screen.

'So what's all that supposed to prove, Shirley?'

'Doesn't prove anything does it, Dirk. Just shows you as a pretty nasty guy, with a lot of questions to answer about the death of a young woman. She was the daughter of the local president of Intercontinental Veterans Anonymous wasn't she? So what is it with you SIE guys and the Veterans?'

'Oh, come on! You accusing me of being in the SIE?'

Westwood had just seen a couple of shadowy figures in the wings of the stage set. They were not his men. The tension was getting to him.

'Okay, folks, we must leave it there. Tonight my guest was Dirk Westwood, area chief for the SIE in Mississippi and, as you saw, an accessory at least to the murder of Charlene Choi. Goodnight.'

The beating of the blonde girl remained on the screen behind the credits briefly as Westwood and Addamms faded from viewers' sight.

'Jesus! Another one! Every night the bitch picks one. How many of the SIE are there left?' The general was all too accurate in his comment but it was a part of Browneton's campaign. Shirley Addamms had identified over twenty-five top SIE operatives in the last few weeks. It was not always by such direct means as the Westwood exposé; it was rare that she had been able to get such immediate evidence. But through his TV channels and newspapers Alastair Browneton was not only steadily unmasking the SIE organisation, he was also providing analysis, often now furnished by the Veterans, on whole areas of the SIE plans. And the SIE weren't supposed to operate within the US mainland, only overseas.

'God, what a sodding mess!'

General Shepilov continued watching the TV. The chat show was followed by a nationwide news bulletin. It was a long saga of riots, looting and general destruction among the poorest sections of the community. Although, he noted that one of his army units had responded rather slowly when a mob in California had burst into one of the new, defended housing areas.

'Bloody hell! What's the guy think he's up to?' The general stormed at the television and his local commander as the screen filled with mobs of black and white youths rampaging through the pristine and secluded housing areas of the exclusive development. The action seemed to be right in his living room.

'Let's go! Here we go!'

The cries of the youths egging each other on were clearly audible from the TV. The battered pick-up truck that had demolished the condominium entrance barrier was aimed at the plate glass windows of a large house deep inside the defended area. Gunfire from the house did not deter the hyped-up youths. And as they beat up and disarmed the terrified occupants, a truck-load of soldiers appeared and with rather less enthusiasm than the general would have approved of, began to round up the youths. They didn't capture many. Most of the youngsters made off through the extensive grounds of the house and the park that surrounded it with as much portable property as they could carry.

'Bastards!' exclaimed the general. Then, with a rapid change of tone, added, 'Who can blame them, I guess.'

There was more: another hour of televised mayhem, unavoidable evidence that his troops were increasingly reluctant to take action, and mouthed anger from the politicians at this failing.

'Karl, what the shit's going on here? Why are we letting the media into our action?'

With the TV still pouring out horror and destruction the general was calling his office. The PR colonel was embarrassed. He had strict orders to keep the military off the television; he had failed. And he had failed because all over the country the troops were making it clear that they didn't want to be seen as siding with the government in suppressing the protests of the poor and impoverished. The colonel had no choice but tell it as it was.

Shepilov listened to the extent of disaffection in the ranks of the armed forces with rather less surprise and anger than the colonel would have expected. However colourful his superior's remarks were, condemnation was not a part of the conversation.

'Okay, Karl, I guess I've been expecting this. The guys out there aren't stupid; they know what's going on just as well as we do.'

Thanks to Alastair Browneton and his persistent reporting, and the almost nightly evidence of the president's inability to rule Congress and achieve any sort of viable government, the US population now had a very clear idea that a small group of faceless and powerful people were trying to undermine their society. The poor and disadvantaged were increasingly prone to taking their grievances to the streets and the SIE and its less scrupulous hangers-on were increasingly inclined to take the law into their own hands. Firebombing any centre of opposition was the latest of many tactics to force the right-wing views onto the public and to try to mould the population to the views of the America Resurgent movement, now the vocal front for the whole right-wing ménage.

On the other hand, the efforts of the SIE and its tame Congress to whip up the fury of the American people against Europe had almost totally failed.

'Too much like the 1930s,' said General Shepilov to himself as he finally made it to his bed. Too much like many attempts to create chaos in countries around the world over time, he thought. No one had ever tried it in a country as large and as sophisticated as the US, but the weight of its own decadence had provided an ideal opportunity.

'Thank God there's still a free press.'

It was a common enough reaction, if barely true. The public had become aware of the plan to destabilise the dollar, for example, only through the Browneton press. Through careful and measured, rather than hysterical, reporting, the public had also been made aware of the impact on their pensions, savings and house values. The exposé was cleverly done. It was a perfect cameo of the way that Ross and John thought that the SIE, Fitzallan and their rising pretensions should be combated.

It was also the SIE's first major setback. Melvin Fitzallan was furious, because of the failure, but also because the whole currency destabilisation thing was a freelance effort not included in his overall plans.

* * *

'So,' muttered Ross as her media surveillance report disgorged its hourly burden, 'why should a cousin of the new vice president be the only possible candidate to command a satellite-tracking station in the middle of nowhere that tracks no satellites? The late adjutant of the base,' she recalled, 'seemed to think that there were live missiles on the site. Well, we know all that. They control two of the firing codes now. Just the president's left.'

The report that Ross read next was rather more structured. The Veterans' report-writer was in fact a very senior state department insider with a talent for succinct presentation and economy of words. The key points were obvious. The Fitzallan clique had got effective control of the whole administrative machine. Vice president Uhlemann's obvious contribution was to obstruct not to govern. The report writer was unclear in his mind whose resolve would give way first: the president's or that of the people.

On the ground it seemed that it wasn't to be the people's. Simultaneous rioting was again taking place in over a hundred towns and cities but the action seemed a bit too well organised for a show of spontaneous anger. However, since the Veterans had organised such riots in the past, spontaneity was perhaps not to be expected.

'Now this is more interesting.' Ross was beginning to read a report from a mole that the Veterans had implanted in the justice department. The man was gay, of particularly nasty habits, but had as shrewd a brain as had ever been put to prying and double-dealing. To the Veterans' disappointment he was found dead – strangled with an obscure part of his leather gear – only hours after the transmission that Ross was reading. The death was put down to a jealous lover but an SIE report that Ross later got access to told a more accurate story.

It seemed that the SIE had been purging its files of all known 'dissidents'. At least that is all of those who didn't agree with their right-wing views as usually expressed by America Resurgent.

'Looks like the SIE only want purity in their ranks,' Ross mused as she finally broke the encryption of what turned out to be a list of names apparently removed from the records. However, try as she might, she couldn't construct a logic for the removal of the names; these were the very people that she would have expected them to want to keep track of.

'Rick Blackford?' Ross read aloud. 'Jordan. There are some high-powered names here. What does all of this mean? Better warn Alanda in case there's a plan to remove these people for real. Maybe that's what this means?'

The idea that the SIE had relegated the 'dissidents' names to their hit-list was hardly earth-shattering.

38

2026

'Good morning on the day that Europe has erupted into a wave of anger and frustration against the United States and its anti-European provocations.' The *Breakfast News* anchor-man was his usual cheerful and ebullient self in the face of an ever-increasing volume of news reports about demonstrations, riots and violent confrontations on both sides of the Atlantic.

'Our first report comes from Paris where police have sealed off the area surrounding the Place de la Concorde following an attack on a US embassy car and an exchange of fire between gendarmes and American marines.'

* * *

Rick Blackford had never been to Paris before so Joe Longton had decided that the meeting place set up for Rick with one of his key contacts from Washington would have to be easy to find. With his clean-cut appearance and his southern drawl Rick screamed American at a hundred yards. The Place de la Concorde was the obvious place, but ill-chosen as a consequence of the shooting incident.

After his meeting with the sardonic Mr Jordan, much to Alanda's bemusement, a different Rick had been activated. Joe Longton, longer in the tooth than the young Nigerian girl, understood the metamorphosis only too well. He had always suspected that Rick might be a sleeper, if a rather young one; now he knew he must be.

'I need to go to Paris,' Rick had said.

When it emerged that he had never been to the French capital Joe set about setting up the rendezvous to minimise the need for Rick to open his mouth. The panicked reaction of the marines rather undermined Joe's arrangements.

'If she speaks good French and English with no accent let her do the talking. She'll be okay, but in this sort of mayhem strangers get noticed.'

It was sound advice that Rick was happy to take. He had only referred to his contact as 'she' and Joe hadn't asked for a name.

'Can't be helped,' he muttered as he skirted around the police cordon and headed for the Rue de Rivoli and the new meeting point at the entrance to the Louvre.

'Can't be helped,' was also what his contact was saying as she arrived at the rendezvous by an unnecessarily complicated route.

As Rick matched the pictured stored on his mobile phone with the woman in front of him he was appreciative. He noted his companion's quality footwear, the matching suede suit, suntanned face and neatly sculptured hair. He knew she was forty-six, but such a perfectly preserved specimen of womanhood was a little out of Rick's experience. No names were exchanged, none needed to be.

They drifted out of the Louvre pyramid together and headed for the more intimate surroundings of one of the few remaining cafés of the area.

'Not the Paris I was brought up to,' remarked the woman whose university days had been spent in Paris, Rome and London.

Rick grunted. He'd seen all of the Paris of his experience within the last hour or so.

'So,' she said, realising that she would have to make the

conversational running. 'The president's dead in the water. He's trying to rule the country by edict as the only way to bypass Congress. But half the public service are in hock to the SIE and the other half are scared witless, so nothing gets done anyway.'

'But you're getting things done?'

'Oh yes. I'm shitting on the vice president whenever I can. Feed titbits to the press, lose important papers. Obstruction, you know the sort of thing. You've no idea what marvels of SIE bullshit my cat gets to crap on via the office shredder.'

Rick laughed although they both knew that the situation really wasn't funny. He already knew that there was no effective government in Washington. The president was at odds with Congress on almost every issue of policy; the public servants, for example, were only paid because Melvin Fitzallan and his cohorts knew that they would need an Administration in the future. All other money bills were stalled in Congress. The military barely had enough cash to pay the troops, and were extended beyond any reasonable point of operational efficiency by the pointless re-introduction of conscription.

'How the hell do these idiots think they'll confront the Europeans if they start to reach for their guns?'

'You tell me. The talk around the Hill is they've got other plans. When Joe Smits, he's just about the last guy in Congress to support the president, asked the same question he ended up in a fist fight. It's bullyboys all the way there. Forget the constitution; if you don't agree with Uhlemann and his cronies, and are fool enough to say so, you're likely to get punched out, or worse. Women as well.'

Rick's small-town background had left him with just about enough naivety to be shocked by this last statement.

'And nowhere is safe,' she went on. 'General Shepilov's car was stoned the other day. What sort of country is it when the joint chief isn't safe?'

Rick knew all about the violence in Congress, the death of anything like free speech, and the street violence. But at that moment he was more interested in, and vaguely worried about, what it was that this nameless contact from Washington was going to instruct him to do. She seemed in no hurry to get to the point.

Vast sections of America were no-go areas after dark; the police were so starved of resources that they had no chance of stemming the rising tide of violence and disorder. Individual states did what they could but their own funds were constantly being held up in Congress. Increasing local taxation wasn't a solution favoured by anybody except the Neoconservatives who were largely oblivious to the likely impact of such an action. Mayhem was what they wanted to create anyway. And there were those who wondered whether the police even had the will to take action in most states; their sympathies were too much with their fellow citizens.

Drugs were so readily available that the price had dropped to almost below cost. Private fiefdoms were springing up where even the army in its tanks and armoured cars were reluctant to go. The right to bear arms once again was coming back to haunt the ordinary people of America. And it was not only in the exclusive middle-class, defended-property areas; in the poorer suburbs and the rural expanses, anarchy and local control were the order of the day. The federal writ was barely recognised in much of the US.

'Shirley Addamms... You've heard of Shirley Addamms?' The woman dragged Rick back from his thoughts.

Of course Rick had. He wasn't quite the fan that General Shepilov was, but he'd certainly heard of her.

'You know how many people the SIE are said to employ, according to Addamms?'

'How many?'

'According to her, three hundred and eighty thousand;

of these only fifteen thousand are engaged on intelligence activities.'

Rick was incredulous but had no way of knowing if the figure was accurate.

'So what do the rest do? Does the great Shirley Addamms know that?'

The woman patted a few stray hairs into place and repaired her make-up, something Rick noted that Alanda would never have done at a meal table. When she had finished she reached into her shoulder bag and passed a copy of *Intercontinental Time* magazine to Rick.

Later, as he digested the magazine, Rick discovered the existence of a modest but well-armed 'private' army. Shirley Addamms had failed to get the SIE headman from Kansas to admit this on her programme a couple of days earlier but the watching American public, made more conscious by Ms Addamms's revelations, gave a corporate shudder as they began to understand what a monster was growing up inside their poor, battered country. And it seemed that they were paying for the privilege of suffering the chaos and the lurch into right-wing politics that was developing. For all the disruption, disorganisation and plain disorder, the SIE had seen to it that the Internal Revenue Service still functioned with its usual efficiency in raising money, if not in verifying where it was being spent.

Suddenly they were at the point of communication. The slender, white envelope that obscured something of the magazine's centrefold contained, as Rick knew, the route to a website that would give him his next instructions. Mr Jordan had already told him his basic role; the details were now being passed to him. The woman moved the conversation smoothly on.

'The navy's been ordered to stage a confrontation, sink a Spanish fishing boat or something.'

'Why?'

'Why d'you think? Provocation. Stir the shit. Turn up the heat. Force the Europeans to retaliate. They need a confrontation to get the plebs back on their side. For Christ's sakes, this is about a bloody coup, isn't it?'

'But why?' repeated Rick. 'It makes no sense.'

'Well, they think it does obviously. And they're cooking up something that doesn't rely on the military. I'm not in the right place to find out what unfortunately, but I'm working on it.'

The goings-on at the Lost Springs Airbase were something that neither Rick nor the woman knew about, but since she was in touch with the Veterans regularly Rick didn't bother to pursue her rather enigmatic statement. 'Need to know' was okay by him and what he needed to know was what the envelope and the hidden website contained.

* * *

The *Breakfast News* anchor-man was coming to the end of his tale of woe. Unrest and turmoil were rife in Europe and across most of America. The Europeans were striving to keep the temperature down; the SIE and their supporters were seeking the opposite.

'Finally, news is just coming in of a naval clash off the coast of Bermuda. Two deep-water, Spanish tuna vessels are reported to have been sunk by gun-fire from the USS *John B. Smith*, an American destroyer of the politician class. There is no word of the eighteen crew members. The British destroyer HMS *Moray* has been ordered to the scene but is instructed to avoid confrontation.'

'Fat chance,' remarked John Harcourt as he switched the television off.

* * *

'I've got to get back. The big shit at the State Department wants an explanation.'

'Okay, Mr Ambassador. Your diplomatic immunity is still in place. I'll call the protection squad for an escort.'

'Bullshit, Colonel. I'll take the marines. That's what they're for.'

'Not after Paris you won't. No marines allowed on escort duty.'

'Colonel Wedgewood, you heard me. I will be escorted to the airport by a squad of US marines, not a mob of shitty British police.'

Dotty Wedgewood had been expecting this. She produced a Presidential Order.

'For God's sake! Is that all? Who takes any notice of that old fart?'

'I do, Mr Ambassador. That old fart, as you call him, is my commander-in-chief and I take notice of his orders. No marines.'

There were no marines. The ambassador was bundled onto a US military jet at Heathrow with a bare minimum of diplomatic courtesy. Seen as the origin of much of the ill feeling that was developing, the ambassador was not welcome in Europe but the Federation Government was not yet ready to provoke further problems by demanding his withdrawal.

The secretary of state, the ambassador's titular boss, was not so reticent. At least at first he wasn't.

'Fitzallan, I'm relieving you of your responsibilities. The president is anxious to calm our relations with Europe and you're seen as deliberately stirring up bad feeling. Your association with some of the more right-wing elements of the SIE, who the president has demanded resign, is also seen as a provocation in Europe.'

'Stuff the president, Edwards. You can't sack me and you know it.'

'I can and I have. You're out of a job.'

Fitzallan had come prepared. He knew that one day the

secretary of state was going to get his courage up and try to throw him out. But that was not in Fitzallan's plans. The post of ambassador was a stepping stone for things to come and he was not going to forego anything for a deadbeat president and a deadbeat secretary of state. He carefully laid a couple of photographs on the desk in front of both of them.

Secretary of State Edwards blanched. For a moment Fitzallan thought he was having a heart attack.

'You're clearly a very virile gentleman, Mr Edwards.'

'You...' Whatever he was going to threaten he thought better of it. The young woman, recognisable in full detail in her nakedness, had been traced by the SIE. Her description of Mr Edwards's extramarital activities had been explicit and comprehensive. The rather portly figure was so easily recognisable as the secretary of state that any denial or justification would only have brought Fitzallan's derision down on his head. For a Bible-belt Christian this sort of exposure was enough.

The ambassador retained his post in Europe. His boss succumbed to a real heart attack a few days later.

* * *

Rick took some time to think through what his Washington contact had been telling him but he easily recognised that his thought processes were actually procrastination.

'Some woman,' he told himself.

She had been one of the Veterans' longest-standing agents and her information was of the highest quality. If it was happening in Washington she knew about it. That made her just about the most reliable courier possible.

Rick and the Veterans, now with some help from Ross, protected their computer systems by interspersing electronic information with verbal and hard-copy communications. The risks and costs of even overseas trips were well justified in their eyes. But word of mouth still wasn't 100% secure, as the Washington woman's subsequent death confirmed. Rick was shocked by the news, not just about the cruel and vicious nature of it but also at the loss of human life, yet he knew that they were in effect at war and in war there are casualties.

39

2026

Ross woke up on the Friday morning with a feeling of impending doom. John was at home in Dorset and she was in Scotland; her yearning for him had intensified recently and was almost painful again, much as it had been in the past. Every separation was now harder than the last. Twenty-two years of her life seemed to evaporate.

'When this is over...' John had said. What was unsaid exercised Ross more than she would at first admit. It was not so much that the relationship might stall again; it was more that she still wasn't confident that she was clear about John's own feelings.

It wasn't just her separation from John that was the cause of her gloom; it was more the sense she had that the situation in America was going to spill over into Europe very soon and the world that she had grown up in was going to change and be replaced with something nastier, more bigoted and more self-seeking. Her feeling was not diminished by the early-morning reports that her media-monitoring programme poured out onto her computer screen.

'Oh my God!' she exclaimed. 'Now what?'

The US President was on national television condemning the overnight destruction of the offices of *The Washington Echo*, Alastair Browneton's flagship publication, and over twenty other of his printing plants. It was a concerted effort to quieten the opposition to the creeping takeover that was steadily eroding the freedoms of the American people.

The reaction to the president's condemnation was hostile amongst the general mass of Congress, now almost all committed to the cause of creating a new America. The reaction among the population at large was one of dismay that such action could be taken by a public body like the SIE, seemingly in open contravention of the constitution. But the response was not coherent; protests were uncoordinated and largely ineffective, despite the efforts of Intercontinental Veterans Anonymous to focus the blame firmly on the SIE and leading figures like Melvin Fitzallan.

'It's open warfare,' muttered Ross as it became apparent that the SIE and the Veterans were no longer pulling their punches. 'Hell fire!'

Two video clips flashed up onto Ross's screen. The first was a section of *The Shirley Addamms Show*: late-night television that was now watched by a phenomenal 90 to 100 million Americans. The interviewee was Rick Uhlemann, the vice president.

'So, Mr Vice President, how do you feel about the way things are going in the country at present?'

'Things are going great; couldn't be better.'

'So, you're happy with the suppression of the media, with the country's external security service intimidating large sections of the public service and the Government disenfranchising huge sections of the population?'

'I'm happy Ms Addamms with the suppression of a rabble-rousing media intent on undermining the government's efforts to introduce integrity and standards of decency and honesty into public life. Far too many people have been bleeding the country of its resources for personal gain; we're living in a country driven by plain greed. Things have got to change. America has got to be made great again. People have got to accept that the government is in a better position than they are as individuals to decide what is best for country overall. And they have to learn that opposing this...' the pause was full of menace, 'will not be tolerated.'

'Mr Vice President, the only sense that I can make of the garbage you're dumping on us is that you're advocating fascism. Is it true that you and your colleagues, both in and out of the government, are set on abandoning the democratic processes of the US Constitution and establishing a one-party state?'

Addamms had no expectation that the vice president would actually give a straight, let alone honest, answer to her question. In front of the millions, she did not anticipate his reaction.

'You're a filthy bitch, Addamms. There's no place in the new America for the likes of you. Every fucking loser, scrounger and deadbeat thinks he's a right to a free living thanks to people like you. You're a bloody cancer on the body of the country. You've got to be cut out, burned, wiped from the face of the earth.'

He ranted on for several more minutes; Ross skipped the ravings and cut to Ms Addamms's response. It was easy to see why she had a reputation for coolness under pressure.

'Ladies and gentleman, the Vice President of the United States: a fascist advocating fascism and slavery for anybody who is not white, middle class and brainwashed to his pernicious view of the world.'

Somebody in the background pulled the plug; the screen went blank.

'Wow!' said Ross. 'Powerful stuff.'

The second video followed. The monitoring programme provided no editing or comments. The Washington Police found Shirley Addamms in her apartment. How the police video got to be available Ross could only guess at, but she assumed that it was a deliberate attempt by the SIE to get a message to any other opponents of their drive for the new fascism.

Addamms' naked body was on her bed. A liberal use of packaging tape had bound her ankles, knees and thighs together, her arms to her sides, and sealed her mouth. The post-mortem again showed massive doses of pure heroin in her bloodstream.

Ross felt sick. So too did Alastair Browneton, but it didn't stop him publishing a photograph, along with an unequivocal accusation, on the front page of his remaining newspapers. The shockwaves rattled around America but with martial law declared as a precaution in over thirty states, the final reaction was muted. The websites, blogs and podcasts of the underground media, however, had a field day in focusing dissent where the published and public media could not.

'And,' Ross said to herself as she ploughed through the rest of the computers' outpourings, 'Fitzallan has let it be known that he'll stand for president next time. There's a surprise!'

* * *

'Mr President, as the US Ambassador my place is in Europe at my post. How else can US interests be protected?'

It was an ingenuous statement carried to the point of absurdity. The president knew perfectly well what was meant by the statement, just as he knew that a direct order to Fitzallan to stay in the US would be ignored. If he didn't seemingly have the power to sack Fitzallan how could he expect to contain him?

'The official US policy towards Europe is conciliatory; I do not want any confrontation! You will make it your business to see to it that there isn't any. Is that clear?'

Fitzallan didn't bother with an answer. His trip to Europe was hardly intended to achieve the president's objectives.

* * *

John Harcourt was not best pleased to be asked, or rather to be instructed, to attend the US Ambassador's press conference. But the director had insisted. John knew himself to be too unfit for any serious action and with every man and boy threatening to demonstrate inside and outside of the conference hall he was not expecting it to be a peaceful event.

Neither was he expecting to see young Rick Blackford in the audience, close and accessible to Fitzallan. Clearly Fitzallan, whose initial brush with Rick had ensured his exile to Amsterdam, had no recognition of Rick and seeing him in the position that he had taken up, like John, he would have assumed that he was on bodyguard duty.

'That's Jordan,' said John in rather more puzzlement. He had Jordan's photo stored on his mobile and he quickly checked before putting it on vibrate.

Jordan was an SIE insider. Fitzallan would hardly have been surprised to see him there in view of the state of relations with the British and in the light of his protests about the lack of a proper security function at the consulate.

Whatever John might have thought about either of these two presences, Fitzallan, with his usual contempt for the media, kicked off the press conference in his normal provocative way.

'Gentlemen.' Fitzallan never acknowledged any women in the media corps. 'The United States is committed to retaining exclusive use of the resources within the two hundred mile limit from its coastlines.' Like the old trouper that he fancied himself to be, he attempted to stun his audience with an opening statement that he was neither authorised to make, nor in any position to deliver or enforce. Everybody present understood this very well. There was certainly silence at his pronouncement but it was more bemusement than consternation or any other stronger feeling.

'The man's mad,' John muttered. He had just made it

into the press conference in the Astoria-Majestic Hotel in London's Mayfair and had had his brief look about him, taking in Rick Blackford and Mr Jordan, when the ambassador opened the proceedings.

'Europe should be very clear that the United States will not tolerate any further incursions by European fishing vessels, nor any other commercial or threatening activities.'

'Is that an ultimatum, Mr Ambassador?' demanded the *European Times* correspondent.

'Take it any way you like. It's a statement of fact.'

'We understand the President of the United States is in favour of conciliation. How does that sit with your statement, Mr Ambassador?' The correspondent for the BBC 24-hour news was well respected and noted for asking direct questions.

'The president's position is no different from what I have just said. He may state it differently but then I'm the diplomat.'

The laugh that followed the ambassador's attempt at European humour was confined to the few American reporters not employed by Alastair Browneton.

'Mr Ambassador, is it true that you are planning to stand against the president at the next election?' It was *Times* man again.

'You must wait and see. At the moment the American people are more concerned about the provocations occurring on their doorstep. The United States is not happy with the threats to the livelihoods of the peoples of its coastal areas posed by the continual exploitation of the fish stocks by the mass-fishing of European fleets. During the last two years there have been one hundred and seventy-seven reported incursions by European vessels. There have been eight exchanges of fire between US and European warships and twelve American servicemen have been killed.'

The rumbles of protest began to drown the ambassador out.

'How is it that the two hundred mile limit is not recognised by any other country in the world?'

'What about the seven fishing boats sunk in unprovoked attacks?'

'No US vessel has fired unless fired upon,' snapped Fitzallan.

'He's getting irritated,' John said to himself.

'Mr Ambassador, this press conference is going nowhere,' said the BBC man. 'Your version of the situation is complete and utter nonsense. You know that and we know that. The United States is weak. It's tearing itself apart internally and has no possible military capability to enforce anything against Europe. You know that too, and we know that.'

'Our military capability is hardly a topic of conversation for a press conference,' said Fitzallan angrily.

'But it would be if the United States had anything like the military strength it had even five years ago. You'd be jamming it down our throats at every opportunity. The fact that you're not says it all.'

There was a distinct jeer as the ambassador started, stopped and restarted to refute the BBC correspondent's claim. His sudden passage into incoherence only encouraged the jeers and challenges.

'If you want to know what the US's military capability is,' the ambassador finally said, his composure partially restored after a few gulps of water and a consultation with his aides, 'you'll find out if you persist in violating US territorial waters.'

'Is that a threat, Mr Ambassador?'

Fitzallan didn't see where the question came from.

'Gentlemen,' he said. 'The present situation is of your making, not ours. We will not tolerate your interference. That's what I came to say. I've said it. You've heard it. So too will your government hear it. If you want to be fools enough to ignore the warning, so be it.'

Melvin Fitzallan mustered what dignity one such as he could and made it clear by his body language that the conference was over. As he prepared to leave, his message, signed by the ubiquitous vice president was indeed being delivered as an ultimatum in Brussels.

'God almighty!' said John to himself. 'What the hell's going on here?'

John wasn't the only one unhappy with the content of the press conference. The atmosphere as Fitzallan stepped off the platform and headed down the aisle between the rows of angry and disappointed reporters and TV camera crews, was so different from the triumphal progress he made to the stage only a few brief minutes earlier. Then the audience, while not particularly respectful of Fitzallan, had at least been nominally courteous. They had kept to their seats, their questions as yet unasked and his answers as yet unheard. Now, with anger, frustration and the closest to Nationalism that the media scions ever got to, the mob was on its feet and milling around the ambassador and his harassed and uncertain bodyguards.

'Bloody hell! What a scrum,' John said to his neighbour and somewhere in his mind he stored the image of Mr Jordan close by the ambassador on the one side and Rick Blackford on the other.

The ambassador forged his way down the room and towards the double doors at the end. The SIE men around him looked worried and muttered urgently into their label microphones. Why hadn't the fool listened to them and used the door at the back of the stage? The ambassador's arrogant disregard for the milling crowd around him was a nightmare come true for his bodyguards.

John stood at the edge of the crowd bombarding the ambassador with questions.

'Mr Ambassador are you going to...?'

'Is there any chance that...?'

'Say again, Mr Ambassador, you are standing...?'

He had no questions to ask; he was an interested observer, he told himself, not quite clear why he had been asked to come in the first place.

The press of bodies was soon at the hall doors. They were a constriction. Reluctant to miss their chance of a question, few of the media people were keen to be first through the doors and the seething mass stalled until the pressure of bodies extruded some of their number out into the foyer of the hotel. Again John had an image of Jordan and Rick Blackford now with arms linked behind Fitzallan.

Finally, Fitzallan responded to the question that they had all been desperately asking. 'Yes, I'm standing.'

John immediately understood, just as Ross had, that Fitzallan was moving himself into place for the final push to the White House and the new right-wing America he hankered after. But something distracted him momentarily from the chaos. It was a glimpse of the expression on Jordan's face. As the kaleidoscope of bodies and equipment swirled around him John had a vision of another crowded room flash in and out of his mind. Years back, he'd been in another situation like this. It had ended in tragedy.

He was uncharacteristically agitated. A sense of impending doom overcame him. The vision persisted. Frightened faces had predominated, people had been trying to get away, bodies had been falling and then there had been a slow-motion silence and just that angry, vengeful face. The face came into brief focus; it was the one that he had just glimpsed in the scrum in front of him – Jordan. He had seen Jordan before and someone had died.

'Oh my God!'

Was the outcome going to be the same as before?

The cork came out of the bottle. The shoulder and elbow pressure of the SIE minders had forced a critical mass of people through the double doors and the main body then surged out as the resistance eased.

'Jesus Christ!'

As the bodies almost tumbled out into the foyer, the group around Fitzallan lurched and toppled. An SIE man at Fitzallan's right shoulder elbowing Rick Blackford away let out the anguished cry that alerted the rest of his fellows. As the crush cleared the ambassador didn't get carried forward with it; he sagged against Jordan and the SIE bodyguards and then, unsupported, he slipped to the floor.

* * *

'Poison?'

'Yep! It was obscure, quick and very effective.'

John's director had got him into the mortuary against the better judgement of both John himself and Special Branch, but then what are contacts for if not for favours for the old boys of the intelligence service? The pathologist, by an invaluable coincidence, was a bit of an expert on the death-dealing antics of the 1970s and 1980s East European Security Services, and the 'old Bulgarian umbrella trick' as he called it was almost the first thing that had occurred to him.

The vision of Rick Blackford, and Jordan in particular, being so close and in physical contact with Fitzallan refused to fade from John's mind.

* * *

'The death of the US Ambassador to Europe at this time is a tragedy that must not be allowed to sour further the relations between our two peoples. We will naturally do everything in our power to bring the perpetrator of this hideous crime to justice.'

The formal words from Brussels to the US President were received with very little emotion. The president didn't expect to miss the late ambassador, nor did he expect his own situation to improve by the loss of the principal architect of the creeping coup that was occurring around him. The president now also had no expectation that a sensible accommodation could be made with Europe. He read about the ultimatum in the truncated edition of *The Washington Echo* that Alastair Browneton was now bringing out clandestinely. How a copy made it to his breakfast table every day he didn't ask.

'The Government of the United States of America requires that no vessel of commercial intent, no vessel of war and no aerial activity beyond the agreed number of over-flights enter United States sea or air space within two hundred miles of the coastline for whatever purpose. All vessels currently within the limits should be withdrawn immediately and the European Federation will give an undertaking that the limits will not be violated. Such undertaking should be given by midnight Washington time, Sunday, 2 August 2026. If no such undertaking is given, the United States will consider itself free to take whatever action it sees as necessary to protect its interests.'

The row that erupted between the president and his deputy over the ultimatum was audible within the bulk of the White House. It was a futile and overly stressful encounter. The president was in the impossible position of either making a craven withdrawal, or being carried along by the new American fascists of the America Resurgent movement. It was not much of a choice. It was the dilemma that the faceless planners intended him to be in. The president's proposal that no action be taken if the Europeans failed to comply was treated with derision by Vice President Uhlemann.

'Shit! Even Shepilov couldn't back off now,' said Uhlemann, aware that not only the president but the military as well were over a barrel.

* * *

Ross was at the gym again in Aberdeen with Alanda when John telephoned. It was Myra who took the call. He told her about the death of Melvin Fitzallan.

'Not sure that it will make that much difference. In fact it may be better that Uhlemann takes over the leadership; he's somewhat devoid of brains compared to Fitzallan and a much more predictable, if inept, opponent,' was Ross's remark when told later.

'Maybe,' said Myra. 'But I can't help thinking it's almost too convenient that he gets killed just at this time.'

'What d'you mean?'

'Destabilise the SIE and their fascist mob, give us more time to react; isn't that how you would have dealt with the situation if you were the Veterans?'

'Of course it is. You're right. Any action to destabilise the Neocons is exactly the sort of thing I would propose in this situation,' said Ross, 'I wonder what's next?'

What was next was the ultimatum. There was no chance that the Europeans would agree to the demands made on them.

40

2026

The death of the United States' President was on nationwide television and was networked around the world.

Within seconds of the usual camera fade from the national emblems to the close-up of the president, life was extinguished. The bland face, the stress lines belying the amiable expression, contorted. The bulging eyes took on a look of disbelief as, clutching at his chest and emitting a harrowing gurgling sound, the president's head crashed down onto the desk in front of him. The camera dwelled on the scene rather longer than good taste would have demanded.

There was a worldwide stunned silence.

* * *

There were times, as John well knew deep in his brain, when all the schoolboy games and the dancing around reality that make up espionage have to give way to common sense. The death of the US President and the urgent information that was pouring out of his computer directly or patched onto him by Ross told him that such a situation had now arisen.

'Thank you for calling *The Washington Echo*. Who may I connect you to?'

'Mr Alastair Browneton.'

'Mr Browneton is not taking calls,' said the operator.

'Now you listen to me; you get through to his office and tell him that John Harcourt is on the line. You don't have a job or a future if you don't connect this call.'

The sheer nastiness of John's delivery frightened the girl almost witless and promoted a sense of self-loathing in John that went deep. He was glad that Ross would not be aware of this little passage, which he recognised as an unwelcome throwback from the past. Like everybody in Browneton's media organisation the poor girl was living way beyond the normal limits of her nerves; this sort of intimidation she did not need.

'I'll try, sir.'

'You do that!'

The ensuing buzzes and clicks rather bothered John but he knew he was too far down the road now.

'John, I'm sorry to have kept you waiting. I had to set the scrambler up.'

The measured tones of Alastair Browneton rather surprised him. Possessed of a largely desensitised nervous system himself he was nonetheless used to the sounds of stress in the voices of others, and what he knew of this American's current lifestyle, stress would have been something of an understated description.

'I'll be quick. You know the Veterans have got sources in high places in the US Government and around. The message I'm getting is that the president didn't just die, he was killed. Obscure synthetic drug. It was supposed to get him in the bathroom. A public death was not in the SIE plan.'

John and Ross had long since given up worrying over Browneton's patriotic sensitivities about dealing with the Veterans.

'Okay, it's recording. Just keep going.' Browneton didn't want a conversation; his newsman's nose told him this was a big one; all he wanted was to have the basic facts on tape.

John spelt out the name of the drug that the Veterans' source had been told had been used.

'Talk to Professor George Niacardes-Smith, Harvard; he's the expert. And he's anti-SIE.' The professor would give the information the media needed; he was beholden to the local branch of Intercontinental Veterans Anonymous for protecting him from the more extreme consequences of his rather uninhibited approach to high-stakes poker.

'The drug was administered by the president's valet. Being a diabetic, it was easy enough to pump stuff into him. The Veterans' source doesn't think the valet knew what he was doing. Ross is putting out rumours but it'd be a good idea if you can work up the story.'

'President killed by SIE,' mused Alastair Browneton. 'How the hell do we run that? Every man, boy and a dog around the guy is on the SIE payroll; and protected. Uhlemann's being sworn in as we speak. Shit, this is a tough one. We'll only get one shot at it.'

'Yeah,' agreed John, 'and it has to be good.'

John had a few more titbits from Ross to share but he soon rang off and left Browneton to call in his senior staff and discuss what he felt was to be their last and assuredly suicidal campaign.

'Go for broke' was the feeling amongst Browneton's workforce; it was the message that came back to him within minutes of his meeting ending.

'There's still a mass of people out there who simply don't like what's going on around them. SIE thuggery has paralysed many good folk but traditional loyalties will be tested once Uhlemann gets into the Oval Office. And, the bastards have played too much on ordinary people's respect for the constitution. We have to shock the whole damn country rigid and take the consequences.'

Alastair Browneton knew his editor-in-chief was right. What was happening was a classic coup in many ways, the masses being intimidated or distracted; minor officialdom deluded into supporting the oversimplified ideals presented to them, and pushing the hidden agenda away as so unthinkable that it would never happen. Even, that is, as it was happening and as they dug their heads into the sand.

The headlines were banner and the news item hardly a challenge to the skills of the journalists. Never could Browneton remember putting out a message so brutally and so briefly. At both local and national level the population at large in the US were told that their president had been done to death in a most foul way simply to serve the interests of a bunch of faceless fanatics.

'... And your new president is one of them. The leader of the world's greatest nation is a thug, a killer and now a dictator. With the death in London of Ambassador Fitzallan the last restraining influence on the SIE and their fascist allies has been removed. America is back into the sort of dark ages that we thought only European countries had had.'

The response was swift, equally brutal and equally brief. Who fired the rockets that destroyed the last remaining shreds of *The Washington Echo*'s offices nobody admitted to knowing. Despite General Shepilov's rapid action on behalf of the military to consolidate his command of the armed forces, the new president, as commander-in-chief, still attracted blind obedience from some quarters. Who ordered the firing of the rockets everybody knew.

* * *

Ross started her own rumour campaign from the Buchan farmhouse. What she was planning carried the risk of exposure for many of the Veterans' agents and would provide the SIE with their best chance yet to cripple the organisation. The stakes were now too high to worry about such risks; the Veterans knew that full well and acknowledged and accepted the potential peril they were putting themselves in.

'It's like John said,' Ross remarked to Alanda and Myra, 'we only have one shot at this now.'

The two girls both wondered who they thought Ross was trying to convince – them or herself. But they both sensed, as Ross did, that the end of the playacting was somehow very close.

'When's John due?' asked Alanda.

'Tomorrow. Early.'

It was one of those still, hot days that occasionally occurred in North East Scotland. By common consent the population strips off on the principle of 'grab the sun while you can'. Ross, Alanda and Myra were in the garden of the farmhouse. Facing south-east, and framed by the buildings on two sides, the garden was secluded and sheltered and allowed them to enjoy the warmth of the sunshine in privacy and comfort.

Ross had already briefed the two girls with the news of the president's death and on the reaction so far, both to this and to the campaign to convince the US public that the assassination was part of an evil plot by the SIE.

John's impending arrival gave Ross heart and the two young women comfort. Worried by the intensity at which Ross had been working they were glad that his support and common sense was now going to be permanently available until the US/Europe situation was resolved. With Ross a prime mover in the final countermeasures planned, John's director had suggested that he decamp to Scotland. John, needless to say, didn't have any objections.

The deadline for the ultimatum was approaching and Ross was in a state of permanent readiness for any response from the Americans after rejection. At least her new Japanese kit was in a state of permanent readiness.

'I guess they're bound to reject the ultimatum; what else

could they do?' Ross said, voicing a thought that had been with her for some time.

The absurdity of the situation was hard for the average European person-in-the-street to get their head around. With the well-advertised state of American military preparedness nobody supposed that an effective response would be possible if the fishing fleets didn't withdraw. Rejecting the ultimatum and risking the worst that the Americans could do was, by common consent, the only action open to Europe.

Those like Ross and John who had a rather better idea of what the US could actually do faced a few anxious days until the situation clarified.

'There's a message from the Veterans saying the commander of the Lost Springs Airbase has been called to Washington. They say this one's not screwing his adjutant and tends to keep his mind on his job. Half the base complement has been sent on leave.'

'Cousin of Uhlemann, didn't you say?' said Myra.

'Yes. Vice presidents always seem to have useful cousins.'

'Was there anything else from the Veterans?'

Ross, who had been stretched out on a lounger, got up and poured herself a drink from the thermos flask.

Wonder what's agitating her? It was a thought that went through both Alanda's and Myra's minds.

Ross walked around, cradling her drink in her two hands. She was wearing a rather shorter skirt than the two girls had seen her in recently and there was a new girlishness about her that they were pleased to see, but they were equally puzzled now by the sudden solemnity.

For Ross, the situation had stopped being a theoretical exercise. Something new had crept into what she was doing. The action was no longer being driven by the computer screens and the electronic gobbledegook; what was happening would have a real impact on real people's lives.

This had just struck home with her. She was desperate for John to come and for him to take command of the situation.

With the confidence of youth and little of the experience of the world that Ross had grown up in, the two girls affectionately watched their boss work with her angst; they were sympathetic if uncomprehending.

Ross's mobile screen activated.

'They've answered the ultimatum. John's on his way. He'll be here later this afternoon, not tomorrow.'

Ross's mood lightened. John was coming and everything was going to be fine and dandy. Alanda and Myra read Ross's mood exactly. They were pleased. They were back in the computer room, each settled at their particular workstation. Ross had another briefing from her monitoring system on her screen.

'So what's happening, Ross?'

'Brussels has advised the American Government that it considers the two hundred mile territorial limit as having no force and has declined to order any fishing vessels there to move outside the limit.'

'Predictable,' said Myra. 'And?'

'And Europe will take all necessary steps to protect its fishing vessels from molestation.'

'Usual diplomatic nonsense. I wonder if there's anybody still left who understands such rubbish. We all know what it really means.'

'Yep,' said Ross, 'the European naval presence has been reinforced but the warships are ordered to stay out of the two hundred mile limit unless any fishing vessels are directly threatened.'

'Just window dressing. We know there won't be any serious action at sea,' said Alanda. 'The Americans aren't up to it. Been any reaction?'

'Uhlemann has called a meeting of his inner group of henchmen for seven o'clock our time. General Shepilov has cancelled all leave and ordered all military personnel to their bases. But it doesn't look as if he's going to do anything; there's no increase in coded military traffic, at least not of the sort you would expect if they were dusting off their mobilisation plans for example.'

But it was early days yet and interpreting what the US military was thinking had so far proved to be very difficult.

'John once met Shepilov. He's a straight-up guy in a very difficult situation. He probably wants to keep his troops under control and out of reach of the SIE and Uhlemann's flunkies.'

'There's another message from the Veterans, in the open,' said Myra. 'I guess they feel it doesn't matter anymore. Uhlemann's famous cousin has high-tailed it back to Lost Springs. Helicopter from the White House lawn, would you believe?'

'Has he now?'

'And,' said Myra, enjoying the process of slow revelation, 'and, the air force computer centre in Virginia has brought on its backup systems in parallel with the normal operating mode. There's frantic action going on there. It's been reprogrammed to block communication with the Pentagon but not the White House.'

Whatever Ross thought of this piece of news she never got to sharing it with the other two. The appearance of the housekeeper was all Ross needed to recognise the arrival of John.

'We've got an hour before the Americans are due to respond to the European rejection.' Ross led John away to her room exaggeratedly setting her alarm clock as she made this statement.

In the computer room Alanda was emailing Rick back in Amsterdam and Myra was on watch duty, well aware that she might need to interrupt what she hoped would be a period of joyful bonding if not basic sex.

Their naked bodies soon intertwined, their passion as fiery as years past. They both knew that the stresses of the situation were driving them but they both equally knew that they wanted to give themselves again to each other unreservedly.

Maybe we can't be sure what the Americans are going to do, John thought as he did his best to follow the basic sex route, but I sure as hell know what I'm going to do.

And at sixty-seven both he and Ross were over the moon that he could still do it.

41

2026

Ross's hour of passion turned out to be forty minutes. Determined both to extract the maximum out of John's presence in her bed, but also to be ready and focused for the tasks ahead, she had set the alarm short. But she was not disappointed.

'Hell, John! Who'd have thought you'd still got that in you,' she said as she lay back in his arms in the now hopelessly disorganised bed.

Soaked with sweat, the sheets clinging to them, neither spoke after this initial exclamation. Ross lay on her left side feeling the dribbles of perspiration running down the small of her back and down her thighs. John, his heart pounding and his breath coming more in short pants than in an even rhythm, lay on his back, his hand still idling its way around her breasts and stomach.

Their relationship had been through some dramatic periods in the past before the twenty-two-year gap had solidified. They had each hidden behind the pressures of the work and the lifestyles that they had adopted but somehow in this one passage of almost youthfully, raw sex they had well and truly relegated the gap in their relationship to the past. The weeks of game playing and growing mayhem in the US had thrown them into each other's company again and once Ross had been able to let down her guard and put the hurt of their previous experiences behind her, the relationship had matured and grown deep again almost without their realising it until it had happened. Anxious that no blame game should start, they had both re-committed themselves in the most fundamental way possible.

'Jesus, Ross! What the hell is that?'

The alarm shattered the silence and their comfortable companionability.

'Come on, you idle what-name. There's work to be done.'

They showered together. It was cramped, boisterous and invigorating. Ross's adrenaline production went into overdrive again, not just at the suggestions of horseplay but also at the prospect of the actions that she knew she would have to take if the analysis of the American reaction that she and her staff had undertaken proved correct.

The housekeeper had laid out a tray of sandwiches and stocked the refrigerator in Ross's computer room with beer and soft drinks. It was eight o'clock in the evening; they were expecting a long night.

Both Ross and John had returned to the computer room more casually dressed than the other two girls had ever seen them before.

John hovered in the background as Ross, Alanda and Myra opened up a series of information websites and cleared one of the larger screens of the surveillance information it was automatically scrolling. Ross adjusted the screen's position so that John would be able to see it over her shoulder without having to lean over her. It was not that she wouldn't have welcomed such contact but concentration was the name of the game and however delicious it might have been to feel John close to her, Ross knew that she needed to keep focused.

Alanda's role was to manage the information flows from the world reaction. Much of what she was calling up to her screen was anticipatory. The whole world was watching and waiting. Myra's role was less clear to John but she was essentially acting as a cross between Ross's chief-of-staff and forward planner.

* * *

'Alanda, what's bugging you?'

'The SIE Internal Digest claims that Jordan and Rick killed Melvin Fitzallan. They claim they injected him with a synthetic poison.'

'Do you believe that?'

'I don't know, Ross. I don't know if I could live with the idea of Rick as a killer.'

'That wasn't quite what I asked, Alanda. Do you believe Rick killed Fitzallan? You have to make up your mind about that before all else.'

'Ross, I don't know. I don't know! I don't know if I know anything about him.'

'Why would it surprise you if he had had to kill someone? It's a sad but often necessary part of what the likes of Rick – and John – do, Alanda. That's their job. It's their chosen life.'

Alanda was too focused on her own sense of shock and hurt to hear the undertone in Ross's voice. Myra, who was as anxious as her boss about this sudden interjection into the already tense situation, nonetheless, had. What Ross had said seemed reasonable to Myra; there must have been something else. In the way of people under stress, Alanda picked up on a detail in what Ross had said rather than what lay behind her comment.

'John, Ross? John? How did John get into this?'

'Alanda, twenty-two years ago at Gatwick Airport, two people that John and I were there to meet were shot dead in front of us. They weren't nice people but that wasn't the point; they'd been gunned down. And before I could take in what had happened John had shot and killed their assassin. It was his job. It was an instinctive reaction from his training. He was confronting a paid killer who wouldn't have hesitated to kill again. To kill John. To kill me. It was the most horrendously heart-breaking, agonising thing that I had ever had to confront in my life, even including the breakup of a previous relationship. There's nowhere to hide in that sort of situation. You have to deal with it.'

Ross paused. Alanda stared at her as she fought for control of her emotions. Myra was almost in tears. Then Ross continued.

'I recoiled from John. I hated that he could be a killer, that he could do such a thing. I just didn't want him to be in my life, or so I thought. But by the time I had rationalised my feelings against the reality of the world he lived in and realised that I desperately did want him in my life he'd gone. He had done his job and moved onto the next one. My coming to terms with this reality was a process that took me many years. And then it was too late.'

'Oh, Ross!'

'Worse, Alanda, I didn't know how he felt. I didn't know if he was equally tormented by the breakdown of the relationship. And even worse than that, I didn't know how to reach out to him and neither, it turns out, did he to me. The gulf widened yet we both in our innermost hearts still really cared. Now twenty-two years later and purely by chance we've been thrown together again and the chemistry is still there.

'Maybe we should have tried harder. Maybe we could have tried harder. Maybe many things. Hindsight is a wonderful thing, of course it is. But it's only when you don't have it that you know what it is you've lost and it's only when you can't see how to get it back that you see the value of what you've lost. And in the end life moves you on at such a pace you just can't keep pulling yourself back into the past.

'Now I have a second chance. You've no idea how rare that is. I won't let him go again, old and older as we are.'

Ross paused again, struggling to get hold of her emotions and express the feeling that was dominant in her mind.

'Alanda, if you really love Rick above all else and despite what you now think he might have done, you shouldn't make the same mistake.'

* * *

'So how long before you reckon it'll start?' asked John.

They were together again. John had a clearer idea what had been set up in Europe and they were a couple of coffees a piece down the road. Ross, Alanda and Myra were completing a scan of their monitoring equipment. Something had developed.

'It already has,' said Ross with tinges of both excitement and anxiety creeping into her voice.

'What?'

Only Ross noticed the slight sharpness that indicated that John too, despite appearances, was not immune to the rising tensions around him. Unlike in the past, she took this sharpness for what it was and no longer reacted to it. Her fingers flashed across the keyboard of the new Japanese computer that she had so recently installed. With a virtuosity that once again reminded John of a concert pianist, she called up a rapid array of data screens and images.

'The air force computer in Virginia has gone super-active,' she said in an urgent whisper.

John exchanged looks with Alanda and Myra. Super-active? The significance of the air force computer was totally lost on him. But the girls knew only too well what was going on and gestured to John not to say anything to distract Ross.

From the look of deep concentration on Ross's face it was debatable whether a bomb in the next room would have distracted her attention. She was completely focused on the screen in front of her, absorbed right into it. Only she knew what she was looking for among the rapid succession of computer gobbledygook that she called up. Finally, she found what she was seeking.

'Yes!' she exclaimed in total exultation.

The young girls beside Ross relaxed a fraction and smiled. Ross herself, sweat pouring down her face, looked relieved and then anxious again.

'You can't do any more,' Myra said cryptically.

'Someone like to tell me what's going on here?' said John.

They told him. As he understood Ross looked into his eyes; she found his expression unfathomable. Was it love, admiration or just plain amazement?

* * *

'... and the US Government has rejected all compromise.'

Despite the universal contempt for the once-mighty American military machine, and the general expectation of some sort of climb-down, tens of millions of European citizens were tuned into the BBC 24-hour news programme and were listening with more anxiety than most would have admitted to, as the Federation President relayed the response from Washington.

'As a consequence, all military units have been put onto a high state of readiness. All Federation fishing vessels are ordered to withdraw from the US self-proclaimed two hundred mile limit to avoid provocation.'

There were plenty in Europe, tired of US posturing, who would not have minded a bit of provocation or even a bit of a brawl with their former ally. Only the inner circle of the military hierarchy in the European Continental Defence Command noted the absence of evidence of any activity by the US military and began to look at options and scenarios to try to understand what this meant.

* * *

'Yes, this is Buchan One.' Ross was talking on the secure satellite radio link to the European Air Force command post at Southwood near London. 'Acknowledged, we're in the highest state of readiness,' she said to the unseen co-ordinating officer.

'Someone in the US Air Force has initiated their coded message sequence which means that Operation Resolve has started,' she then reported to the others.

'Operation Resolve,' muttered John.

Now knowing what Ross and the European military thought this was, the name seemed rather ill-chosen. The fact that the US Air Force computer system had been activated on the authority of the president without the involvement of the air force command structure sent shockwaves through the US military hierarchy.

The air-commodore at Southwood and Ross had become good friends over the past few days as a series of countermeasures were put in place. Since the Veterans' intelligence had been shared with the European military the monitoring and tracking units had been on maximum readiness. The web of units, many of which no one had ever admitted even existed, came to life. Suddenly, there was no need for staff officers to invent complex and barely credible attack and defence exercise situations. A barely credible situation was about to be thrust upon them. The European military was as ready as it was ever going to be.

'The TV'll switch to whichever channel is broadcasting a news bulletin,' Ross said somewhat unnecessarily as the BBC 24-hour news programme flashed onto the wall-mounted TV and the sound automatically activated. Alanda activated various media surveillance programmes to begin recording and analysing the world's reaction. No one expected anybody to support the US but it was necessary to safeguard against such a possibility.

'We interrupt the bulletin to advise that the US President has rejected the European response to his ultimatum and has said that Europe must now bear any consequences.'

The US President must have 'pressed the button' almost as he stopped talking to the European Ambassador. The first of the Lost Springs missiles were in the air in an instant.

The voice log of the European Continental Defence Command monitoring control room flashed up on Ross's big screen monitor. The four of them watched, fascinated, aware that they were among only a very small privileged few who were watching the action unfold blow by blow.

'They sure as hell didn't waste any time,' said John.

42

2026

The history of the next few hours was never going to be written down. In the gathering gloom of a late European evening, computers on both sides of the Atlantic played out their sophisticated and unfathomable functions.

For those intimately involved, events moved so fast that it was hardly possible to grasp what had happened before the next sequence in the action was forcing itself on their attention. John was not alone in being confused, bemused and not a little unnerved by the deluge of information.

'Ross, what the hell's happening?' he asked once the communications traffic began to exceed his digestion capability.

'The Yanks have fired eight rockets in sequence from Lost Springs. They're ICBMs. That means they travel up through to the upper atmosphere before they level out and position themselves. The satellite tracking stations have picked up seven of them; the overload at the moment is because they don't know where the eighth one is.'

'Not the best time to lose a missile,' remarked John dryly.

'No,' said Ross with a gravity that alarmed her three colleagues.

There was an unspoken question. Years of intimate association rendered speech unnecessary between the three women, except that John, being an outsider to this professional intimacy, was there and looking distinctly uncomfortable.

'Five of the missiles have high-explosive warheads designed to cause maximum civilian damage,' said Ross.

'Fire storms,' remarked Myra sourly.

'The other three have nuclear warheads.'

'And we don't know which each rogue missile is armed with?'

'That's about it, John.'

For the moment all that they could do was worry.

'It's the first two missiles, ETA,' Ross said to John as another spate of activity flashed across her screens.

'Jesus, minutes! We've only got minutes!'

John was more incredulous than anxious. At the speed at which the missiles travelled the flight time was bound to be calculated in minutes.

Ross was on the satellite link again.

'Hello, Buchan One here. Yes, sir, we'll know very quickly if our countermeasures have been successful; but if we can we should take some precautions I agree.' The rest of the conversation was a high-speed listening brief for Ross. She didn't need telling that European civil defence systems, with the Cold War a distant memory, had long since been dismantled, or that the European strategic anti-nuclear response capability was long overdue an update. Long-term reliance on a friendly USA was potentially about to come home to roost. The whole of Europe was horribly exposed to a treacherous attack of the sort underway. But there wasn't a lot of point in the Federation President ranting on about the US's duplicity in not destroying all of its rockets.

If there was no currently credible capability for a second strike from Europe – both the French and British nuclear armaments had been dismantled – the Russians and Chinese had the reach to mount a missile attack on mainland America. Neither of these countries, however, had shown any interest in the growing controversy between Europe and the US and intelligence suggested that neither wanted to have any part of it. The situation could very well change quickly if the US missiles proved effective.

The European military had long since contracted out its defence strategic analysis to people like Ross and had become increasingly dependent on this outsourced service. Both more flexible and more nimble in understanding and developing the countermeasures to unforeseen threats, the present situation was just the sort of eventuality that Ross had been retained to advise about and to respond to.

Having analysed a whole range of scenarios, Ross, with the input from Intercontinental Veterans Anonymous had built a picture of possible US actions. Paid to assume the worst, she had done just that and had planned accordingly. Making assumptions on the US military capability based on European satellite and the Veterans' information, she had assessed that any sort of conventional attack was unlikely. The mysterious goings on at Lost Springs, once Ross had been made aware of them, defined the potential threat more clearly. She had done what she could; her assumptions had proved to be devastatingly correct and the missile attack was rapidly approaching fruition. The first rockets had positioned themselves and were headed directly for their programmed targets. At least that was what the SIE hierarchy wanted them to do.

The TV on the wall kicked into life. The face of the man that Ross had just been talking to appeared in front of them. His briefing was short, largely fact-less but of sufficient gravity to secure the attention of the mass audience now tuned into almost every form of media. It took him no more than forty seconds to convey the nature of the threat. The viewing public in Europe were now aware that something was desperately wrong. The simultaneous translation and on-screen subtitles then initiated as the Federation President was announced. Being a politician, his speech was longer, repetitive of what the air-commodore had said, but added nothing to the sum of knowledge to the worried citizens of Europe.

'Ladies and gentlemen, the United States has unleashed an unprovoked missile attack on Europe using ICBMs that should have been destroyed many years ago under the US-Russian disarmament treaties. As I speak, eight rockets are speeding towards targets in Europe. The Euro-Defence Commission is tracking the missiles to try and determine the target areas. Countermeasures have been undertaken, but in the time available to us, these will necessarily be limited. Please stay calm.'

'Stay calm after that!' John exclaimed.

'So what the hell else could he have said?' Alanda's angry retort showed just how much pressure they were all under.

John looked at her in surprise. Ross, who was well aware of the extra stress Alanda was under, gave her a flashing grin of encouragement and tried to concentrate on a new surge of messages flooding her monitor screens.

'First two missiles ETA update,' said Ross, her voice rather more under control than her brain.

'But where? Where?' snapped John.

The trajectory of the two rockets was well established. The computers at Southwood and at the astrophysics laboratories in Oxford and Manchester Universities were overheating in their efforts to project target envelopes. The seconds were ticking away as they worked their feverish magic.

'Southern Sweden, Denmark and the Baltic Coast around Gdansk,' said Ross slowly as the emerging data formed into a map simulation in front of her eyes.

The information was frantically relayed to the regional governments in these areas. Local emergency plans were initiated. In Stockholm the alert system from former times clicked into place and the authorities in the affected areas went into action, praying that at least some of the older people would remember what to do. In the post-World-War-II era, Sweden was the most thoroughly prepared nation in the world when it came to nuclear defences. How much was now serviceable? Or did it matter when nobody would be able to get to safety in time?

'They've changed course,' whispered Ross in a tone of awe, and then of relief.

Against the background noise of the computer room only John at first heard what she had said. Ross's intervention and corruption of the rocket's control systems was beginning to work; how successfully they were soon going to find out. In the US, the Veterans noted the frantic communications activity between Lost Springs and Washington. What was happening was not in the SIE's plans.

The two rockets veered off onto a tangential course that carried them away from the earth into the outer atmosphere. They accelerated towards space. Then with their fuel exhausted by the sudden surge of power, they were caught up again in the earth's gravity and pulled back. They plunged back into the atmosphere over the Canadian Arctic. Not on a re-entry trajectory and not designed for re-entry heat of the intensity that they were encountering, the two rockets disintegrated.

'It worked,' breathed Ross in wonder. 'It worked.'

In the light of their age, Ross and the air force experts had had no idea whether it really was possible to remotely re-fire the engines of the rockets to make major course changes so late on. Details of the technology were buried in the archives. Equally, if physical modifications had been made to the rockets as well as the control and guidance systems, they would have had no way of knowing. There was nothing in the Veterans' reports to say so. But then the missiles changed course. This provided the confirmation that the countermeasures had been successful.

John gave her a quick hug but Ross was still concentrated on the information deluging her monitor screens.

'The second two missiles, they're only seconds behind,' she whispered, her voiced quietened by the mounting stress levels.

Again the target envelopes enfolded in front of them.

'Holy shit!' said John.

It was almost as if one of the rockets was targeted at them personally. The other was scheduled to make a serious mess of Paris.

'That's the new ETA,' muttered Ross.

It was the critical time again. And then the tracking systems picked up that only one missile had changed course. There was instant consternation. Paris was saved as the debris sprayed down onto a vast uninhabited area on the edge of the Russian Arctic; Northeast Scotland was still in the firing line. Alarm bells rang in Moscow but no one was interested.

Four brains went into overload in the computer room of the Buchan farmhouse. All that could have been done had been done. All they could do now was await the missile strike.

Your whole life flashes before your eyes before death, thought Ross, at least it's supposed to. But it was the immediate past that confronted her.

'John?' breathed Ross.

The years of separation returned as an ache. The waste of those years was the common thought between Ross and John. No words were necessary; they both knew what the other was thinking. They both knew that at that moment they were as close as they were ever going to be.

'Be safe! Be safe!'

As she grasped that the missile was heading their way, Alanda had only one thought. She wanted to be with Rick. Ross was right. If he had to kill as a part of his job that was something that she would have to get used to. In the clarity of vision that was induced by the apparent danger that they were in, Rick being a killer seemed to be the least important thing. The thought that perhaps it was Jordan who had done the killing formed itself in her mind but Alanda didn't want to go there; it deflected her from Rick and Rick was all she wanted to think about.

Myra wept quietly. More emotional than any of them, tears were her normal release. But an awareness of the sort of privileged life that she had had as a Lagos shanty town kid was never far from her mind, along with the gratitude to Ross that she always felt when this thought surfaced for her.

But the action was moving forward whatever their innermost feelings might be.

The Scottish First Minister appeared briefly before them on the television screen. They never found out what he had to say. An unsteady image of a rocket vapour trail took over the transmission. As the tracked missile was almost lost from view the screen was filled with a distant blinding flash and the camera cut to a group of excited British sailors.

'So what was all that about?' asked a bemused John.

'The third two missiles...' said Ross.

'What was that?' demanded John again. But there wasn't time to follow up on what had occurred. The jumbled sequence of events unfolded in front of them and then things moved on again.

It transpired that a German television crew was on board HMS *Tewkesbury*, an antiquated, guided-missile destroyer of almost museum rather than fighting status. They were filming background material for a series on modern electronic warfare when an unlooked for opportunity was offered to them. Following a battle plan from the past, the *Tewkesbury*'s captain fired a pair of anti-missile missiles in what was seen as a vain and despairing attempt to halt the incoming

American rocket. Not only was the outdated technology better than the captain's wildest dreams but the destroyer was just about in the right place for optimum launch as the attacking missile's trajectory turned down.

'Amazing!'

Both Alanda and Myra had been distracted from screen-watching by the latest small drama; it was a reaction shared in high places all over Europe.

'That was a close call,' remarked Ross. 'Fortunate some naval type thought to chance his arm. If it had carried on it would have landed neatly in Peterhead fish market.' It was Ross's only concession to her relief at the outcome. She was back studying the computer monitors.

'Hell fire!' Myra interjected into Ross's thoughts. One of the monitoring screens had come alive and seemed to be reporting a level of almost frenetic activity in a number of US states.

'All the Neocon State Governors have called out the National Guard – thirty-seven. In more than half they have refused to muster. The president has declared martial law and asked Congress for extra funds for law and order purposes.'

'Myra,' said Ross in some exasperation, 'we don't have time for this.'

'The military communications traffic has sky-rocketed,' Alanda put in.

'Both of you, shut it!' John had never seen Ross so irritated. Nonetheless, he moved to read over Alanda's shoulder. The National Guard had been called again to deal with widespread rioting in a long list of states. In many of these states the governor's writ seemed not to run. The police were increasingly refusing to deal with the rioters and the National Guard were increasingly supporting their refusal. President Uhlemann was furious but his authority over the National Guard seemed to be non-existent.

Alanda was busy accessing the Pentagon's command computers. The security had been changed since she had last done so but in anticipation of the night's events she had bypassed the new barriers and was now checking on what the activity was all about.

'Oh, wow!' she muttered.

What she was looking at was too much data for John but Alanda interpreted it for herself. The US Army had put itself on the highest level of alert and kicked off the first stages of its mobilisation plan. The most intense of the traffic was around the president's order to stand down and the SIE's more specific threats against the generals and anyone who disobeyed the president. The SIE were also launching a campaign against Intercontinental Veterans Anonymous but the last traffic erupting before Alanda and John's eyes was specific to ordering the military to take action against the Veterans. There was nothing in the traffic that suggested the military had any intention of doing as they were ordered.

All of this was going on within a couple of minutes and before the next phase of the action unfolded.

'The third pair has exploded at the top of their trajectory. Don't know why.'

'So who cares,' said John.

There were some mutterings in the background. The two girls knew that Ross cared. What was going on was one of the most daring and sophisticated pieces of computer hacking of all time and Alanda and Myra were well aware that Ross needed to know what the mechanism was that had destroyed the latest two rockets. With two more to come, one of which had still not been tracked, Ross needed all the information that she could get.

Six rockets had been destroyed and two remained: one winging its way towards Europe and the other still apparently lost from the tracking station's view. With the final ETA imminent, the missing missile was beginning to cause Ross and several high-ranking air force officers some serious anxiety. Being Ross, she spent no time speculating why the missile was missing or why it hadn't or couldn't be detected.

'Well,' said Ross, 'at least we know that only one of the last two has a nuclear warhead.'

'Comforting,' said John.

It had also transpired that a Norwegian environmental protection aircraft, collecting air samples, had flown through the fallout from HMS *Tewkesbury*'s sea-launched missile-to-missile destruction success. And fallout was just what it turned out to be. Hurriedly scurrying from the area, the pilot reported his findings. It helped the final arithmetic, but it seriously added to the environmental worries as most of the debris landed in the sea not too far from the northwest coastline of Iceland.

'Buchan One here. No, sir, we have no idea where the eighth missile is or why it hasn't been picked up by the tracking systems.'

Elsewhere the Federation President was beginning to relax. Europe was barely seconds away from defeat of the US attack. The only anxiety was the missing rocket, but the damage that that could cause, horrific as it would be, would now inevitably be restricted. John would have understood the president's calculation, but his contempt for politicians would have grown by an order of magnitude in consequence. What the next steps after the missile attack were to be were the subject of a massive amount of activity on both sides of the Atlantic. However, the focus of the activity was rather different.

The seventh missile only partially burned up when it headed back from space after following Ross's spurious instructions. But as it crashed into the sea, exactly on the International Date Line in the Bering Sea, a few hundred miles south of the Aleutian Islands, the Russian military increased its declared state of readiness and redeployed a number of its own tracking stations. Alerted to the activity surrounding the American missiles, they were fully aware that the eighth missile was still unaccounted for.

The American military, however, were much less interested in what had happened to the eighth ICBM than in the increasing activities of the SIE and in particular their unreported auxiliary organisation. Having received clear approval from President Uhlemann to operate within the boundaries of the US, the SIE was flexing its muscles or at least those of its private army.

43

2026

General Shepilov wasn't a household name in the US, unlike the heroes of the twentieth-century wars in Iraq and the ones of the earlier decades of the century in Afghanistan and North Africa. To be a military hero you needed to fight and win wars. General Shepilov had had opportunities as a young man but at such a junior rank that it was hard for him to distinguish himself amongst the crowd. His career, nonetheless, had been steady and measured and he had benefited from the inbred distrust that US presidents seemed to have of installing the better known and more charismatic fighting generals to the highest military appointments.

Shepilov was articulate, often foul mouthed, but always open and honest at all levels of his communications. Anyone who had dealings with him knew where they stood with him. In the generally debased upper reaches of US politics he was known as a man of unshakable integrity and had a reputation for acting firmly and decisively on his principles. In the complex situation developing in the US, for those who knew of and valued his worth, Shepilov was a beacon of hope and stability. Although adverse to publicity, as the new president began to rule by decree, the general knew that he was going to have to take both a more active role and one that was likely to be unconstitutional. However, such niceties were clearly of no concern to President Uhlemann and his cronies. In their turn, the general's cronies, fellow officers, opposition representatives and senators, urged him to similarly pay less regard to the traditional role of the military. If that violated the constitution the consensus was that the American people and history would in the end come to understand the need that the military were fulfilling.

'Someone has to act. Someone with the muscle has to stand up to the SIE. The media tried and have slowly been worn down. Only the military is left.'

The leader of the remaining Democrats was desperate. The SIE and their increasingly less-hidden, private army were rampant in many parts of the Union as the federal authorities grew more and more impotent. With the Neoconservatives largely ousting the traditional Republicans, both in Congress and more importantly as State Governors, power had shifted away from Washington and to the largely unelected coterie of SIE officials and their hangers-on. There was very little now that the Democrats and displaced loyalist Republicans could do to halt the move to the inflexible right. The Supreme Court was hamstrung by the simple expedient of forcing three Justices out and Uhlemann appointing his own supporters to the bench. Only issues requiring unanimity were allowed to the court, so it was in effect powerless.

'Feedback says that most of the troops are on our side,' remarked Shepilov's PR colonel, a man of wide experience and a fighting record that spoke for his integrity and determination. 'The guys that got shipped back from Europe and tossed out of Japan are more than pissed off at their treatment.'

Since isolation was the kernel of the Neoconservatives' theory of government, large numbers of US troops had been withdrawn from around the world over the years but for reasons that made no sense to the generals, the size of the army and other forces had not been reduced commensurately, quite the opposite. The disgruntled rank and file were the backbone of the resistance, since not only were the bulk of them without meaningful duties to perform but they were also mostly from the class of people worst affected by the Neoconservatives' actions. As one of Shepilov's more widely read colleagues pointed out, when the 'bread and circuses' didn't work out the mob in Rome usually got violent and the legions usually supported them.

The large body of enlisted men and now conscripts in all three services was ripe for action and unconcerned with their constitutional position, unlike their seniors. They were more than ready to get out there and take on the SIE and its private army. They only needed the signal.

Deeply religious, Shepliov's faith was based on his valuation of his fellow men and was light years away from the fire and brimstone Bible-thumping of the religious right who held him in contempt for the shallowness of his beliefs. The general was equally contemptuous of the religious right but he in no way underestimated them.

'Shit!' he was prone to say. 'Why can't their new Jerusalem be a fun place?'

He respected people with real faith irrespective of what it was and was opposed to extremism in any form. What he supposed the faith of Intercontinental Veterans Anonymous to be he had never ever indicated, but as he got to know them and the way that they worked, and the ethos that had sustained them for nearly thirty years, he found it very easy to discount their origins as traitors to their country. The only thing left from their KGB origins, as far as the general could see, was their single-mindedness and their commitment to the long term. That they had turned into right-thinking patriots over the years he had no doubt.

'They ain't sold any military secrets that I can identify,' he told his inner group of confidants, 'not that we've had that many secrets in the last few years. Who the hell wants last year's technology?'

The day before the missile launch, General Shepilov was advised by a senior member of the Veterans, whom he had come to trust, that the air force control systems for the rockets had been activated. Shepilov already knew that this was without the agreement or support of the air force top brass. Equally, neither he nor the Veterans knew about Ross's countermeasures.

'Okay,' he ordered his team, 'let's get the Star Wars stuff dusted off.'

It was Shepilov's initiation of these countermeasures that later was to so anger the president.

Military communications traffic increased.

'Make sure that the SIE are listening in to what we want them to hear.'

Since the general had no doubt about the loyalty of his officers and troops he was happy, in fact keen, for the SIE to be aware that the military were stirring themselves to oppose what the right-wing elite were trying to do.

The military were determined that there would be no coup.

The outbreak of rioting in so many states had clearly been coordinated. The counteraction was confused and not coordinated but it did serve to tell the military which of the governors they needed to concentrate on.

'Okay, you guys. Let's get plan B going and stop these shitty bastards from buggering up our country anymore.'

The officers being addressed by the commander all knew what plan B was. Troop movements began, nosily and publicly. Warships limped to sea but hugged the coast to avoid provoking the more powerful European fleet. The number of air force sorties flown was minimal; serviceable aircraft were being conserved against the theoretical possibility of actual conflict with Europe.

Alastair Browneton's newspapers, hard copy and digital, were given a boost by allowing them to be produced in various army warehouses across the country. The SIE's mastery of the Internet and its use as a propaganda tool was suddenly turned against them. A shadowy body of hackers, who suddenly found patriotism and exemption from prosecution, moved in at the behest of the Veterans to bring order into the growing online movement to resist the creeping takeover of the country. With a steady stream of facts and figures about the SIE and their activities made available to ordinary citizens, the hackers picked up where the TV talk shows had left off.

Since the pace of events now took on an urgency driven by the pace of electronic communications, General Shepilov found himself the servant of events rather than their master. And as the news fed back of the Europeans' successful countermeasures against the successive waves of missiles he was quick to realise that the time had come for the decisive and final action.

Equally suddenly, Intercontinental Veterans Anonymous became the good guys. All their resources were put at the disposal of the military once they recognised both that they were of common purpose and that no action for past sins would be undertaken.

The news ricocheting around the world that the last of the missiles had gone rogue and the Europeans couldn't track it brought consternation and not a little anxiety to General Shepilov; it was the failed Stars Wars attempt to down this rocket that had sent it off into the atmosphere with no understanding of where or even whether it would re-emerge.

It was only later that the US Air Force learnt that the Chinese had developed a serious anti-missile capability and that it had been in place for many years.

44

2026

'General Shepilov, what the hell d'you think you're doing?'

President Uhlemann was furious. He had soon learnt that the chief of staff had ordered the attempted destruction of the missiles. But the elderly, Star Wars, anti-missile missiles were no longer reliable and their control systems outdated. The short-sightedness of the US Congress in trying to choke off past presidents' finances had meant that no funds had been spent on such defences for some significant time, even when it was known that the Europeans, let alone the Russians and Chinese, were beginning to actively develop a new generation of missile weapons. Much of the Star Wars research had been developed and proved but at the point of implementation the political expediency of crippling the sitting president, following on from years of Democratic stringency, seems to have been preferred to the more sensible course of putting such defences in place.

'It seems, sir, that some of the high-level defence control systems have been corrupted and a number of old rockets inadvertently fired. In view of the tense situation with Europe I thought it better to try and intervene.'

Both Shepilov and Uhlemann knew that this statement was a load of total nonsense and that the military had intervened to attempt to prevent an unprovoked attack on the Europeans. Since such an attack was exactly what

Uhlemann thought he had initiated his reaction was at first uncomprehending.

'Pardon me,' said the president; he wasn't sure that he had truly heard what had just been said to him.

'Unfortunately, the anti-missile missiles weren't up to it. They didn't lock on to seven of the ICBMs. The missiles were still headed for Europe but got dealt with in the upper atmosphere somehow, presumably by the Europeans. The eighth was blown off course by a Star Wars missile that got close, but not close enough, when it exploded. God knows where it's headed.'

The general had chosen to ignore the president's interruption. He knew perfectly well of course what was going on and what the SIE were attempting to do, but encouraged by the handful of remaining dissident Congressmen and the bulk of his senior colleagues, the military had decided to intervene. It had been a difficult and unprecedented decision to make. So deeply ingrained was respect for the constitution and obedience to the commander-in-chief that it took many hours of hard argument to sway particularly the middle-ranking officers. Known SIE plants and sympathisers were consigned to an enlarged garrison in Alaska against a spurious fear of embroilment in a series of Russian-Chinese border disputes that had suddenly erupted.

'General, the missiles were fired by my direct order. The Europeans have ignored our ultimatum.'

There was a pause. The general heaved a silent sigh of relief. Condemned out of his own mouth, the president had given him the legitimacy he needed. Congress had given no approval for the attack on Europe even if many had urged it. The president's action was completely unconstitutional and therefore illegal. A command issued into his lapel microphone prompted immediate action. The General had come prepared.

'Bastard, you'll... What the hell now?'

The Oval Office was suddenly filled with a mass of brawling, angry men. Two presidential aides and a number of bleeding SIE security guards were thrust against his desk. A group of military policemen, led by a lieutenant colonel of massive proportions dressed in battle fatigues, was herding the milling mass in front of them. Resistance was quelled with rifle butts.

'You're impeached, Mr President,' said the colonel.

In theory, only after a vote in Congress could the president be impeached but General Shepilov was happy to ignore this bit of the constitution.

Through the wall-mounted TV screen the president watched himself, via the White House internal security system, being bundled from the Oval Office and his immediate supporters led away.

* * *

In the short timescale of the drama, the attention of most people in America and the world at large was focused on the antics of the missing missile, and they had barely begun to notice the beginning of an extraordinary period in American history. Over the next few days, however, total mayhem broke out in the higher reaches of US society. The ruling classes and the military clashed in a way unknown since Independence. But it was the military leadership who had the action plan and who prevailed in the end. Europe was to look on in amazement and some amusement, aware that to look on was all that they could do or needed to do.

* * *

'The Chinese have got it.'

'What?' said John, the sharpness of his tone portraying both his amazement and his anxiety.

DISUNITED STATES

'A Chinese tracking station near the Mongolian border has picked up what they believe to be the rogue missile.'

'Where is it?'

Ross giggled at John and Myra's simultaneous question, her own disbelief also clearly showing.

'It's in orbit. The simultaneous translation is very slow for Chinese but it seems that the missile is in orbit around the earth.'

Later analysis by academic experts at Oxford and Manchester Universities concluded that the missile had been deflected by the US Star Wars anti-missile missile's explosion and had headed, having lost power, into the upper atmosphere. But it didn't have enough momentum to escape earth's gravity.

'Amazing,' Ross said. 'It's amazing that such an ancient piece of engineering could have withstood both the explosion that seems to have pushed it off course, and out of range of the European tracking systems, and the forces it's exposed to in accelerating into the upper atmosphere.'

'Ross, for Christ's sake, a rocket with a nuclear warhead is charging around the earth's upper atmosphere headed God knows where and you're admiring its workmanship?'

'A lot of lives might depend on the quality of that workmanship, John,' Ross said quietly.

'We'd still like to know where it's headed,' Alanda remarked equally quietly.

'That's the problem. If it's in orbit its exit angle and speed must have prevented it from immediately heading back to earth and being burned up. But we have to assume that its control systems are unusable.'

The telephone rang.

'Buchan One.' Ross went into listening mode as the air-commodore briefed her.

'No, sir, none of the missiles had working self-destruct functions. I can only assume that they had been disabled.'

Ross did more listening. The conversation ended.

'The Chinese say that the missile appears inert; just a great lump of metal. It's in a low-level orbit having, they believe, fallen back or been pulled back by the earth's gravity, which confirms what we thought. It's not a safe orbit. Each circuit of the earth it falls back closer to a dangerous re-entry. The orbit is skewed. It's currently passing over Central Asia, Indonesia, the edge of Australia, the southern ocean, the Pacific and Canada.'

The science was now beyond Ross. The European experts were in contact with their Chinese colleagues; such contacts always seem to survive whatever the politics. Having clearer information, the Canadian tracking stations began to identify the missile's passage, at least confirming that unless it precessed significantly, probable re-entry would not be over any major population areas.

'Not much of a comfort!'

The Federation President made another brief announcement to the watching and listening public of Europe; it was not very informative.

* * *

The world went into slow motion. Although there was more time than when the missiles were powering in from the US, now there was uncertainty on a much greater scale. All over Europe, and now much of the rest of the world, the section of the population with immediate access to radio and television knew that some dreadful catastrophe was pending. But few of these had a clear idea of what was really happening, nor if or when disaster would strike. A dead lump of metal hurtling around the earth on the edge of space was easy enough to visualise but hard to understand in terms of where it might crash down. In the few populated areas where the missile might come down, communications were more primitive and awareness very limited. Rather more prayers than were customary winged their way upwards to the offending rocket.

* * *

'Something's happened,' said Ross.
Ross's exclamation focused the three of them.
'What? What's happened?'
Neither John nor the two girls could at first see what was exciting her. She pointed. Where previously the screen she was looking at, although full of Chinese text, showed a trace of light, now there was none.
'What's happened?' demanded John again, unsure that what he thought had happened had done so.
'The missile's gone,' said Alanda. 'How can it have gone?'
The satellite radio sprang into life and the wall TV screen switched to the excited face of the Federation President who was tearfully trying to disseminate the news of the missile's destruction. Over Ross's conversation John and the others found it hard to hear what was being said.
The telephone rang again.
'The Chinese brought it down, destroyed it, sir?' The explanation was short. The detailed account emerged later.
'The Chinese destroyed the rocket with an anti-missile missile. The rocket was apparently teetering on re-entry and the precession of the orbit had taken it closer to over-flying Beijing.'
The missile crisis was over, but for John, others in his profession and the military leaders of Europe, the destruction of the rogue missile by the Chinese raised more questions than it answered. Memories stirred. The Chinese had destroyed one of their own communications satellites by rocket fire in the early years of the century. Alarm bells had rung then and then fallen quiet.
If the crisis was over in terms of the missile attack there was still action needed but that, as Ross well knew, was in

the political sphere and was John's domain not hers. That didn't bother her unless it took John away from her. What happened, or was happening, next (for the action in the US was initially fast and furious) was, however, of interest to Alanda as she set about trying to make contact with Rick to tell him how much she loved him and how much she wanted to be with him.

* * *

General Shepilov's intervention was quick, brief and effective, although the ramifications took weeks if not months to work through. US officialdom – like officialdom the world over – both resisted change and abhorred a vacuum. But the Administration of the country remained largely in place and the States made little effort to retain the powers that they had usurped from the Federal government. Despite an inclination to contest the infantry unit that surrounded their Langley headquarters, the SIE hierarchy were quickly arrested within the first few hours after the rockets were launched. The countercoup was carried through in the small hours. By the time that lunch made it onto European tables, all the east-coast military and civilian prisons were full and the Houses of Congress were urgently voting themselves leaders who were more acceptable to the military and to the population. As the hours moved on military action across the time zones ensured that the rest of the country was also released from the increasing grip of the SIE and its supporters. With a manifesto for change defined by the leading Washington daily newspaper, or more specifically Alastair Browneton, the military and the remaining loyal politicians had a template for the country that they wanted.

'I think we've got the measure of it,' Browneton was reporting to John Harcourt around nine o'clock the next morning.

'Euan Fforde?'

'He'll be okay. And most of the absentee politicians and place seekers are scurrying home. We'll need Euan to sort the corrupt from the no-hopers, and the closet dissidents who fancy trying again. If we're having a clear out, best do it properly. Going to take a few weeks to get things settled; be a hell of lot longer, years probably, before normal service is resumed, and a lifetime before all of this gets forgotten.'

'A new America,' said John thoughtfully.

'A new America.'